THE
AMAZON
WAS
THEIR
WHITE-HOT
WORLD . . .

Raul—He could carve a new fortune from the jungle, but his love for two women tore him apart.

Chica—With flawless skin the color of burnt sugar, she was a legend even in a city of sinners for the ways she could pleasure a man— as long as he paid her price.

Carlos—He knew the primitive savagery of the jungle intimately, but he was easy prey to the charms of a foreign beauty.

Peggy—A young American reporter whose fearless independence plunged her into the dark heart of the woman-starved jungle.

Eduardo—He betrayed his family and ravaged his body in the wild pursuit of Rio's choicest drugs and sex.

Viviane—Amidst decaying plantation splendor she pursued the most desperate love of her life.

De Onis—Raging with a blood-lust for money and power, he was lord of an empire of secret vice and corruption.

Odete—A beautiful innocent set free by the fevered rhythms of *Carnival* that exposed her shameless appetites for loving.

ROY SPARKIA

BANTAM BOOKS
Toronto · New York · London · Sydney

AMAZON

*A Bantam Book / published by arrangement with
Book Creations, Inc.*

PRINTING HISTORY
Bantam edition / December 1981

*Produced by Book Creations, Inc.
Executive Producer Lyle Kenyon Engel*

ISBN 0-553-13808-1

Published simultaneously in the United States and Canada

Bantam Books are published by Bantam Books, Inc. Its trademark, consisting of the words "Bantam Books" and the por-
trayal of a rooster, is Registered in U.S. Patent and Trademark
Office and in other countries. Marca Registrada. Bantam
Books, Inc., 666 Fifth Avenue, New York, New York 10103.

PRINTED IN THE UNITED STATES OF AMERICA

0 9 8 7 6 5 4 3 2 1

For Lyle,
the maestro of drama and dreams

PROLOGUE

The Amazonian jungle rises lofty, silent, deadly, guarding its secrets passionately behind its sprawling riot of green life. Enormous enough to swallow all of England, France, Spain, Portugal, Germany, Italy, and half of the United States within its wild boundaries, this last of the world's great primal forests has been virtually unknown by man, untouched, unchanged over millions of years.

Then came the road builders . . .

First they came with axes and machetes to hack an opening through the tangled density for the survey stakes; at their heels came the chain saws, the dynamiters, the bulldozers, and the great monsters whose steel arms can clamp around a tree fifty feet high and pull it up by its roots. Next came the caravan of gigantic power shovels and crawler tractors—mechanized dinosaurs that gobbled away terrestrial obstacles within minutes. Then the bottom dump trucks, road graders, and finally the fifty-ton vibratory rollers to smooth and compact the road surface for automotive traffic. All growling, roaring, thundering, spouting plumes of poisonous smoke. Shaking the earth, frightening the wildlife, and driving the Indians from their ancestral homelands, pressing them ever deeper into the jungle.

The roadworkers labor in sweltering heat in twelve-hour shifts, around the clock, seven days a week. The drudgery lames their muscles, knots their stomachs, dries the saliva in their mouths while the sweat runs from their pores, draining bodily reserves of sodium and phosphorus that are never fully replenished by the wide-spaced meals of rice and beans with mandioca—and sometimes meat. The laborers are

ix

chronically exhausted, their minds closed inward in a gray blur as they mechanically perform the required motions of the job. Foot by foot they advance, never stopping. Slowly, but with the ineluctable certainty of another sunrise—or sunset.

But the jungle fights back . . .

Jaime Blasco stared in quiet fury at the body in the water. A torrid morning sun poured its white brilliance through an opening in the verdant jungle canopy, slanting rays blindingly across the yellowish stream.

Brought into hideous clarity, the glistening white row of human ribs thrust a few inches above water.

Barely twenty minutes ago the ribs had been part of a live and healthy peon, one of Blasco's road crew who had rashly tried to wade the stream. Now, virtually every scrap of his clothing, along with the flesh, had been stripped away by the razor-toothed piranhas still swarming around their victim.

A grappling hook attached to a long line had been flung far out into the stream, snagging the cadaver around the middle, and two of the road crew were hauling it toward shore. The piranhas, an agitated mass of greenish black fish, each one averaging about ten inches long, followed.

Splashing, churning the water to a bloody foam, they battled against the sheer weight of their own numbers in their frenzy to get at their prey. Greedily they tore at the residual fragments of flesh that clung to the bone, at the bone itself, and at the trailing shreds of cloth. Some even attacked the rope and had eaten it half through. A few still clung by their teeth to the skeletal remains that were dragged ashore.

Blasco looked down at what had once been a man. Remnants of a leather sandal clung to the bony metatarsals of one foot. Only a few bits of tendon and gristle were left on the skeleton. Big white teeth grinned up at him from the grisly skull.

One of the piranhas fell away, flopping on the ground. Its oversized mouth, all scoop-shovel jaw and rows of pointed teeth, was open. Ugliness spawned in hell. The icy, unblinking eyes, glazed with bloodlust, watched balefully as Blasco crushed it under the heel of his boot until the backbone snapped.

Turning, he rapped out an order. "Felipe—bring the *cotia. Apresse-se!* Hurry!"

"*Sim, chefe.*" Felipe, a barefoot *mulato*, trotted away to fetch the tethered goat, which was part of a small herd brought along for food and just such emergencies as this.

Waiting, Blasco swatted absently at one of the *borrachudos*, the "biting flies." Most common were the *piums*, little black flies that quickly covered exposed skin with hard red pimples that itched furiously; the *motuca*, a voracious type of bluebottle fly whose bites drew blood; and the *carrapatos*, ticks whose heads, buried in flesh, could swell limbs to twice their size from blood poisoning. The flies plagued the men by day; swarms of mosquitoes were a harassment at night.

Blasco's slap caught a *motuca*. With a tiny sense of satisfaction he crushed the insect against his arm, leaving a scarlet smear. Blood for blood.

The goat arrived and was led about a hundred yards downstream, where its squeals were quickly stilled with a knife wielded by Felipe. With long poles, the kicking animal was shoved out into the stream as gouting blood ran rich and dark over its spotted hide, staining the water.

As if by magic the piranhas materialized in darting dark swarms. They could smell blood for miles, were irresistibly drawn to it, crazed by it, and some of the first arrivals were frantically leaping out of the water to champ their razor teeth into the warm goat's belly.

Upstream at the crossing site, Blasco turned to the twenty or so men who composed the advance party. They were the chain saw operators, the dynamiters, and those skilled only with ax or machete. They were hunkered on the stream bank, a mixture of Negro, Indian, Italian, and Portuguese ancestries, smoking and talking in somber voices of their comrade's death and the monsters that plagued the jungle. Above all they feared the piranhas, the curse of the river. The piranhas were worse than the deadly but sluggish crocodile, more fearsome than the sinister thirty-foot anaconda.

"It is safe now," Blasco called. "Take your equipment and cross the river."

The men stirred uneasily, making no move to rise from their squatting positions.

Blasco understood their fear and their apathy. They were *caboclos*, ignorant peasants recruited from the *sertão*, the drought-plagued northeast bulge of Brazil. For their grueling labor they were paid a miserable thirty dollars a month, with a good chunk of it deducted to pay the commission to the recruiting contractor and the inflated costs of food and lodging charged to them while awaiting transportation to the job site. Rarely did they get a chance even to buy warm beer at a dollar a bottle, or to visit one of the plump whores in the nearest *agrovilas* to pay fifty *cruzeiros*, about three dollars, for three minutes of her intimacy. It was a hard life, but better than starving.

But even starving was better than being dead.

Jaime Blasco knew all this, but his own urgent motivations overrode any transient sympathies. For Blasco himself was a *moreno*, a "brown person," and in Brazil's multilayered social and racial class system, the old ways still persisted of judging a man primarily by his degree of color. It had been a long struggle for Blasco to forge his way upward into the privileged ranks of the *brancos*, the whites who controlled the power structure. His civil engineering degree, achieved with honors, had opened the door to a good job with the Superintendency for the Development of Amazonia, the prestigious government agency known as SUDAM. Its prime goal was the construction of the world's greatest highway, which was to extend an eventual nine thousand miles and fuel a whole new economic momentum calculated to propel Brazil to the forefront of the richest nations on earth.

Top engineers being at a premium, Blasco had been put in full charge of nearly one hundred construction workers. A coveted position indeed for a *moreno*.

"*Covardes!*" he spat at his workers, then floundered into the stream and waded out until he was hip-deep. There were safer ways to cross the stream, but they would take considerably more time, and Blasco was in a hurry. He was determined to ram his leg of highway through in record time. Midstream, he turned.

"Follow me you worthless dogs! *Vá-se embora!* Get moving!"

Raimundo, chief powderman and foreman of the advance party, rose with a sheepish grin. He was a big likable *chulo* with crisp rolled hair and skin the color of tobacco. He shrugged.

"*Pois não?* Why not?" Hoisting his load of fuse cord, primacord, explosive metal caps, and dynamite to his back, he wallowed into the stream. One by one the others shouldered their own loads of paraphernalia and followed.

On the opposite shore Blasco scanned the treescape ahead as a general would study enemy terrain. This was the region of the *cão-apoam*, the "great woods" of the Indians. The tallest trees, trunks smooth and bare until somewhere near 90 feet above the ground, branched out into umbrella-shaped crowns at about 135 feet, lording it over the green tumult of lesser trees that filled the spaces in between, all battling for a share of the light, all entangled in a crisscrossing of looping lianas and other vine crawlers. The ground itself was concealed beneath an exuberance of giant ferns, herbs, saplings, and numerous flowering shrubs.

Blasco shuddered slightly. The jungle was an intrusive presence, like the shadow of death peering over his shoulder morning, noon, and night. The cloying scents of its flowers and rich dark soil, its thick humidity, its rankness of growth and overabundance of life were part of every breath he took. Sometimes it seemed voiceless; mostly it throbbed with the hum of insects, vague rustlings, slitherings, the glissading whispers of threat, odd croaks, whistlings, and the hushed chokings of death that were necessary to make room for its teeming, enlarging assortment of greedy, competing life-forms.

The jungle was not merely a collection of trees and shrubs. It was not solid, familiar land. It was another element entirely. Its inhabitants were arboreal—creatures fashioned for living in their dense leafy medium just as birds were for the air, fish for water.

Man was never meant to live within its murky, steamy depths, any more than nature had prepared him to walk in the twilight of the ocean floor.

Blasco's own parents had tried to battle the jungle by clearing a few acres to plant in crops, and both had lost their lives in the fruitless effort. His mother by sickness and poverty; his father by Indian arrows. Jaime Blasco hated the jungle bitterly.

Yet he was drawn to the awesome majesty by a hypnotic attraction fully as strong as the hatred that fueled his fury to conquer it.

His gaze swept over the mosaic of vivid and somber greens, singling out the largest tree ahead, a giant jacaranda several feet in diameter that towered directly in the path of the projected roadway. Jabbing a finger at it, he savagely turned toward Raimundo.

"Blast the hell out of that one!"

"*Sim*." Followed by his assistant powderman, Raimundo trotted forward.

He stopped abruptly, his mouth sagging open in astonishment.

A frail arrow protruded from his chest.

"Hit the ground!"

Even as Blasco was shouting, his men were throwing themselves on their bellies, scrabbling into hollows, behind trees. Raimundo was falling as in slow motion, his first feeble grip on the arrow frozen in place by the paralyzing action of its poisoned point.

In a rage, Blasco jerked out the 7.65-mm Pistola Savage he carried for killing poisonous snakes. Pointing in the direction from which the arrow had come, he triggered off three shots, aiming high enough to go well over a man's head. He wanted only to frighten, not to kill.

He would have preferred to kill, but the laws were too tough. Once numbered in the millions, Brazilian Indians had been ruthlessly slaughtered or enslaved by early settlers until now only a few thousand were left. Belatedly, the government had gone all out to protect them, and strict laws decreed that Indians were not to be harmed or provoked, under penalty of heavy fine or imprisonment. Every effort was to be made to win their friendship.

In the event of Indian hostility, the laws mandated that FUNAI—the *Fundacão Nacional do Indio*—must be notified promptly. They would send in a trained team to pacify the Indians.

But to wait for the FUNAI team would cause further delays that Blasco could not tolerate.

Rising to his feet, he called out to the men who still lay flattened on the ground. "I need two men to bury Raimundo."

None of the men moved to volunteer.

Blasco's eyes swept over them contemptuously. "*Que diabo, idiotas!* The Indians are gone. The shots scared them. If any of you *covardes* who fear to stand up like men should get killed, I promise you won't even get a burial. I'll throw you to the piranhas!"

One man rose. He was squat, ugly, muscular. A coal-black *preto*. A new man. His heavy lips twisted into what could have been either a smile or a sneer.

"I'll bury him."

"What's your name?"

"Tomaz."

"Tomaz, I'm making you the new advance crew foreman."

The man's eyes widened. "Me? They no take orders from me."

"They damned well better." Blasco unbuckled his ammunition belt with the holstered gun and handed it to Tomaz, who took it eagerly and began buckling it on. Though the construction outfit carried an assortment of rifles and side arms, they were kept locked in the supply wagon and issued only for brief periods for such purposes as hunting and killing snakes. Only bosses and men of importance were allowed to wear side arms, symbols of power.

"Now, Tomaz, get those men up there cutting right away. Knock their heads together all you want. And don't worry about the Indians. They're afraid of guns. If they come again, just shoot at the sky. But if you miss the clouds and happen to nick one of them in the ass, don't you worry about it. I'll take full responsibility."

"Sim, senhor."

Tomaz began bellowing out orders, and Blasco stood back and watched, pleased to see how the men jumped to obey. Color didn't matter when a man was invested with enough power and authority. Tomaz would make a good, tough foreman—for as long as he managed to stay alive.

The deaths today were but two of the dozen or more men lost in the past two months to disease, snakebites, accidents. Some of the tragedy could have been avoided were it not for the urgencies of haste.

At times he felt so futile, as if they were all the tiniest of ants crawling somewhat noisily and clumsily through an immense labyrinth that extended into eternity.

Yet the arrogance of man, the arrogance of Jaime

Blasco himself, was as limitless as the green hell that he was determined to conquer.

"Move faster, you lazy monkeys!" he shouted at the men. "We've got to make up for lost time!"

ONE

Against billowing white clouds, the blue Learjet appeared to be but a misplaced speck of sky as it jetted an arrow-straight line above the forest.

In its sumptuous interior was a single passenger, a young man who was plainly a *branco*, one of the whites, and just as obviously of the moneyed class. Garbed in a suit of unbleached silk shantung, he was tall and rather roughhewn, with heavy dark brows, somewhat unruly dark hair, and blue eyes that could turn dark and stormy in anger; his face was both aristocratic and sensual. He sat close to a window surveying the vista below.

Viewed from five thousand feet, the world seemed to be an endless green ocean stretching in every direction. Beyond imagination, beyond human comprehension. The only tangible evidence of solid ground was a tenuous clay-red scratch bisecting the impenetrable density.

The red scratch vanished suddenly, engulfed by the forest, and the young man turned and called to the pilot.

"Pio, the highway seems to have ended. How much farther will it have to go to reach my land?"

The pilot shrugged. "I would guess about a hundred more kilometers."

"Then it should be only a few more weeks before it gets there."

"It could be many more weeks. Maybe many months. The jungle is not friendly to *civilizados*."

Raul de Carvalho laughed. "You're a pessimist, Pio, like my old man. Maybe that's why he keeps you around."

Pio, a lean young *moreno*, half Indian and half

1

Portuguese, worked for Raul's father, who owned the Learjet. Though Pio had virtually grown up with Raul as a childhood playmate on the de Carvalho cattle *fazenda*, never for a moment did he forget that subtle barrier between them: Raul was son of the master, and he was but an employee.

"Let me know when we reach the boundary of my land."

Minutes later, Pio called out, "Just ahead—at the bend of the stream—that is roughly the northeast corner of your property."

Excitement welled in Raul's chest as he stared down. It looked no different from the rest of the immense green panorama they had flown over, but it was—enormously different.

The huge chunk of jungle below, over a million acres, belonged to him!

Or soon would. On his thirtieth birthday, less than a week away, the deed to the property would become his, in accordance with the terms of his late grandfather's will.

Soon they were passing over the squared cleared area and an assortment of tiny oblongs that were the decaying old plantation house, the outbuildings, and the slave cabins. During the rubber boom, when Brazil had a total monopoly on the wild hevea rubber trees that were so plentiful, the plantation had earned huge profits, making his grandfather very rich before the boom ended—sliced off by competition from plantations in the Far East that had been grown from stolen hevea seeds smuggled out of Brazil. With his wealth, Raul's grandfather had moved to the Mato Grosso and become a cattle rancher, leaving the plantation to fall into disrepair, maintained only by a minimal crew who worked a few acres of the land for barely enough profit to pay their wages.

But that would soon end. Raul de Carvalho had big dreams for turning all those remote acres into a profitable kingdom. Very profitable indeed.

2

All thanks to the new highway that would soon be cutting across his land.

"I've seen enough, Pio. Better swing around now and head for Rio. It's important that I get there promptly at one o'clock."

"No problem, *Senhor* Raul."

Arriving in Rio by air, though he had done so countless times, was always a thrill for Raul. First came the gentle rocking of the plane from the powerful drafts that swept up from the fantastically peaked mountains near the coast; then came the fast slipping downward through layers of silvery mist before the rich fantasyland of the city came into view. On one side, satiny waterfalls, verdured mountainsides, cliffs serried with elegant houses. Gardens, terraces, volcanic eruptions of color, surrealistic effusions of crimson, blue, purple, and yellow flowers. On the other side, miles of pancake-gold beach, a ruffle of white froth separating it from the azure ocean, stately palms, gay-roofed villas, hotels, casinos, and finally the heart of the great city itself.

Unlike the average tourist, expectant of exotic sights, samba rhythms, beautiful girls in string bikinis, and a citizenry with a superheated zest for living, Raul was more attuned to the geographic beauty and the architectural splendor of this dream city. He drank in as a tonic the soaring grace of tall steel-framed buildings, the glistening walls of glass rising above tiled and gilded cathedral domes, the shadowed gash of the broad Avenida Rio Branco, the Monroe Palace, the copper-domed Municipal Theater, and the National Art Gallery. Wondrous buildings everywhere. In the bay were miles of moored steamers, freighters, and battleships; basins were crowded with barges brimming to the gunwales with colorful fruit.

The crawling trams, buses, sports cars, and people thronging the streets lifted his spirits.

This was vitality! This was the heart of Brazil, a beautiful present and the promise of an even more glorious future.

And he was a part of the surging forces that were helping to create it.

Four minutes late! Raul hurried past the luxuriant shrubbery shielding the entry to the Ouro Verde Hotel, past the curved wall of glass tiles, across the elegant lobby.

Cosme Almeida Branco da Silva had already arrived at the restaurant. Even without the solicitous maître d', Raul would have had little trouble in finding him. In the rarified atmosphere of the Ouro Verde, where the impressively rich were no novelty, da Silva was unquestionably the most impressive personage in the crowded room. He was a large man with a craggy face, olive skin, a mass of silvery hair, and a hawklike nose that indicated a trace of Indian blood from several generations back. His large hands were gnarled with veins, tendons, and thickened skin from early years of toil, impervious to the pamperings and manicures that wealth had brought. He gave the impression of the ageless strength of solid rock.

He was seated at a select table in a corner, next to a window overlooking Copacabana Beach. One of the suave, multilingual waiters was bending to light da Silva's cigar as Raul came up.

"*Boa tarde, Senhor* da Silva," said Raul. "My apologies for being late."

"A few minutes? *Não, e nada.*" Flashing his white teeth in a smile, da Silva rose ponderously to shake hands—a good indication of his character, Raul decided. Many men of equal wealth might have remained seated when greeting other men inferior in age and money. The bigger the man, it seemed, the greater his courtesy. "*Como está,* young man?"

"Very well, thank you. And you?"

"*Estou bem.* Fine." Da Silva indicated the chair held out by the waiter. "Please sit down. Do you wish

4

to order your lunch now, or would you rather discuss your proposition first?"

"Whichever is your preference, *senhor*."

"With me, business is always first. There is ample time afterward for the pleasures. Would you care for a drink while we talk?"

"If you do, *senhor*."

Da Silva turned to the waiter. "Bring my friend whatever he desires. For me, a *batida*." It was a drink made from *cachaça*, a clear, powerful alcohol distilled from fermented cane and known as the poor man's whiskey because it was so cheap. To the uninitiated, it had a foul smell and taste, but mixed with lemon or the orangish fruit *maracujá*, it became a *batida*, a popular aperitif.

Raul ordered the same.

Da Silva puffed gently on his cigar and regarded Raul. "So your visit to the Banco da Amazonia yesterday in Brasilia was not successful?" he prompted.

The Banco da Amazonia SA, known as BASA, had been created by the Brazilian government to aid in the development of the Amazonian region by granting big loans at low interest rates, special tax dispensations for several years, long grace periods, and years to pay back.

"It was not completely discouraging. It was explained to me that the government development funds are presently quite low. There is a long backlog of projects awaiting approval. It could take several months before my application can even be approved, then perhaps another long wait before funds are available."

"Ah, yes. Too much public overspending, too much inflation, and now tightened credit policies."

"I was assured that eventually the loan will be granted, but I am anxious to get started as soon as possible."

"As an old friend of your father, I am curious. Why do you not go to him for the financial backing you need?"

"Aside from the fact that my father's capital is tied up in his own business, he is not in favor of my plan. In any case, I wish to do this on my own without family help."

The older man smiled benignly. "So you come to me as a last resort. But you must realize that I and my colleagues do not give long-term loans—only for a year or two—and our interest rate is high."

Very high indeed, as Raul well knew. Da Silva headed a consortium of rich investors who had no trouble keeping their money at work in Brazil's sky-rocketing economy, where for years the inflation rate had hovered close to 50 percent and interest rates on small installment loans for such things as refrigerators or cars sometimes soared as high as 70 percent.

"Of course I would expect to repay as soon as the government loan is released, and I offer all of my property as security."

"Yes, of course. We would not lend without sufficient collateral. But tell me more about this great plan of yours. All I know is that you wish to manufacture commercial alcohol from the jungle trees, *simi*?"

"Yes. Alcohol for fuel, for both automobiles and industry."

Da Silva shrugged. "It is nothing new. Our Brazilian gasoline is already mixed with 20 percent alcohol to conserve petroleum."

"That's only scratching the surface of the market potential. Brazilian gasoline is now over two dollars a gallon, and with oil imports getting costlier all the time, the price of gasoline will keep climbing. At the same time, our need for such fuel is mushrooming. We will have no choice but to mix more and more alcohol with our gas to stretch out the supply, and eventually all our automobiles, farm machinery, and most factories will be forced to convert completely to alcohol fuel. It is the same the world over. The world oil reserves are dwindling. Oil is rapidly becoming too scarce and too expensive to waste as fuel; it is far more valuable for other uses, such as manufacture into plastics."

Raul paused to catch his breath, his eyes glowing with the enthusiasm that had seized him. "Fortunately, the time has come when we can produce alcohol at less cost than we can buy and refine oil into gasoline. By the grace of God and a favorable climate, Brazil is blessed with an inexhaustible supply of such fuel, and it can be produced cheaper in the Amazonian jungle than anywhere else in the world."

"Inexhaustible? You make alcohol from the trees, I understand. If you cut them down, they are not inexhaustible. Some of them are hundreds of years old. If you destroy the forest, we will be worse off than before."

Raul laughed. "There is no need to destroy the forest. I will clear but a few hundred acres of jungle trees, and on the cleared land plant close-packed stands of fast-growing 'weed trees' that mature in from one to three years. The entire aboveground portion of the trees can be chopped up for making alcohol, and in the case of sycamore, poplar, ash, and others, new trees sprout rapidly from the cut stump. There are many varieties of such trees suitable for our purpose that replenish themselves quickly and can be harvested in seasonal cycles, as any other crops."

"I have heard that jungle soil is almost worthless when cleared of trees. All the nutrients that haven't gone into the trees have been washed deep into the ground by millions of years of tropical rains. If the trees are cut, two or three years under our tropical sun burns away the rest of the chemicals and finishes the death of the ground. How can you expect to make money from worthless soil?"

"No soil is worthless, *senhor*. Knowing that someday I would become a big landowner, I went to study at Michigan State University in the United States, which has the finest agricultural college in the world. I learned much about soil management, how to do soil

7

tests, how to fertilize properly, how to return chemicals to the ground by certain plantings. Even the residual wood pulp left after the alcohol fermentation process contains many valuable nutrients that can be used to enrich the ground."

"Ah, yes. I know about your educational background. But you are not an engineer. It would take highly specialized knowledge, expensive machinery and equipment to turn your run-down property into an energy plantation."

"I intend, of course, to hire a chemical engineer to help me."

Da Silva expelled a plume of blue smoke. "You will also have the problem of transportation. When your land was a rubber plantation, the jungle trails and streams were enough for the slave labor to transport the balls of latex to the Amazon barges, but for alcohol you will need big tank trucks and the assurance of good roads. Are you quite certain that the new highway will touch your land?"

"Absolutely. Yesterday in Brasilia I consulted with the commissioner of roads, who showed me the Trans-Amazonian Highway system plans. The highway is projected to run close to the very portion of my property that I intend to clear."

"*Bom.* Without the highway, I would not consider lending a large amount of money. And it is still a risky investment."

"All business has an element of risk, *senhor.*"

"The degree of risk is greatly dependent on the character of the borrower."

Raul felt heat rise to his face. "Do you find faults in my character that make you doubt my integrity or my capability?"

Da Silva smiled and waved his cigar in a magnanimous gesture. "Not at all, my young friend. Had I any doubts, I would not have agreed to meet you for this little talk. I already know everything I need to know about you. I know, for example, that for the past few years you have been doing an excellent job as the manager of your father's export house here in Rio. I know that you do not drink too much or use drugs, that you are not a skirt-chaser like your younger brother, that you aren't deeply in debt—"

Raul's blue eyes darkened with anger. "Then you hired an investigator to snoop into my private life?"

"A mere business precaution. Simply knowing you are the son of an old friend is not enough. I will be blunt and say that if your younger brother Eduardo came to me for a loan, even a small one, I would have to say no. With you it is different. You are solid, responsible, intelligent, and ready to settle down. You have had your fling with the girls, like any average young man, but I have learned that you are now engaged to *Senhorita* Odete Bandiera e Xavier, who comes from a fine family—"

"*Senhor!* You have no right—"

"I have every right to know these things. I happen to be Odete's godfather. She is the daughter of dear friends of mine. She is a lovely, vivacious child with the impetuosity of youth. I think you will make a good match. She will bring joy and light into your life, and you will provide the stability she needs."

Raul, still simmering with anger that da Silva had secretively probed so deeply into his personal affairs —even his love life!—grudgingly conceded to himself that under the circumstances the older man may have been justified. The truth was, Raul had enjoyed many of his bachelor years exploring his sensual urges with a wide assortment of the delightful girls of Rio. But when he had met the unspoiled young Odete, fresh from São Paulo and a sheltered background, he had decided to win this lovely creature for himself exclusively, to help bring his dreams to fruition and to share his life. She had accepted his proposal.

"Therefore," continued da Silva, lifting one of the fresh drinks that had been brought by a waiter, "I will admit that all along I had intended to grant you the loan, in any amount that you require. But I wished the personal contact of a brief talk with you. The loan will be paid in installments—contingent on the new highway, of course. So put a smile on your face and raise your glass. We can drink to the success of your new venture and to a long life of happiness with your prospective bride."

As the two men clinked glasses, Raul's mood soared. Part of it was in anticipation of having dinner that evening with Odete. Eduardo would be there, too. Raul had invited his younger brother to meet his future sister-in-law for the first time.

But a small cloud lingered over his high spirits. What was it that da Silva had discovered to make him so distrustful of Eduardo?

TWO

Eduardo de Carvalho awoke in a sun-spilled room on silk sheets, his face pillowed against fleshy softness. For a few moments his glazed eyes tried to focus on the vision, only inches away, of a satiny brown mound of breast, cherry-tipped at the crest. Who was she?

It mattered not. Inching closer, his tongue reached out and started licking at the nipple. The sleek brown fleshscape stirred.

"Eduardo!" she murmured peevishly. "Not now. I wish to sleep."

Ah, he remembered now! Chica. A popular entertainer from the club Erotika, one of the sophisticated strip-show *boîtes* in Copacabana. She was a *chula*, a mix of Negro, Indian, and Portuguese, with a flawless skin the color of burnt sugar, an exquisite figure, and a face of exotic beauty. An impoverished poet had once described her as having the grace of waving palms, the delicacy of a rare jungle flower, the zest of sparkling waves, and the smoldering fire of a tigress. Nature, however, had created such allure for poets to admire only, not to touch. That intimacy was reserved for the rich.

Eduardo included, for he gave the impression of being a young man with an indulgent father and an unlimited supply of cash. His fashionable high-rise apartment overlooking the sea on the Avenida Atlantica in Copacabana had cost over a million—still being paid for—but none of his friends knew that the money needed to keep up his lavish life was increasingly harder to come by; his debts were growing more onerous by the day. He held an executive position in the Rio offices of his father's export company, which was managed by his brother Raul. Though little more

11

than a figurehead, Eduardo was fortunate in having a competent staff that handled all the difficult work and took the blame for his blunders. Apparently Raul had no inkling that his kid brother was as worthless in business matters as he was in almost everything else.

Except with the girls; there he excelled.

He had competed for Chica against richer young men last night at a cocaine-sniffing party. At least half of the girls there had been *morenas, mulatas, chulas,* or *crioulas*—every shade from palest tan to almost black—for despite the social stigma of black blood, or because of it, rich young Brazilian men were compulsively drawn to dark-skinned sex partners. Many envious white women were known to list themselves as *mestiças*—those with at least some strain of a darker race in their blood—to enhance their appeal for white males.

Chica, with her spectacular beauty, was queen of them all. She had arrived late in the escort of Sergio, a handsome older man and well-known rake. By this time most of the others, fueled by coke-heightened lust, had stripped and were entangled in a mass orgy. Eduardo himself had sniffed coke heavily up both nostrils and was performing beyond his usual capabilities. Orgasm after orgasm with several girls.

Until Chica arrived, after which he lost interest in the others.

His first approach was scornfully rebuffed, as had been the overtures of others.

"I do not converse with naked strangers," she told him haughtily. "Nor do I have any desire to participate in a circus for animals."

"Then why did you come?"

"Only as a favor to Sergio."

Sergio was standing a few feet away, plainly deriving great voyeuristic pleasure. Somewhat puzzled by the man, Eduardo still had wits enough to quickly dress, make himself as presentable as possible, and return to Chica. Sergio was still avidly drinking in the activities with his eyes, and Chica was obviously bored and a bit miffed. Eduardo had little difficulty in getting Chica aside and striking a deal.

Her price was a diamond-studded wristwatch she had seen that day in Maximino's, but which Sergio had been unable to buy. It would have been too crass to ask the cost, though Eduardo knew it could well be over $20,000—money he had no idea how he could raise quickly. But he had no choice. His compulsion to possess this high-priced merchandise was too overpowering.

Back in his apartment with his prize, he had a big letdown. When they were both stripped naked on his oversized bed, he found himself unable to perform. Even after Chica's expert manipulations with mouth and tongue, his organ remained limp.

She laughed softly. "How long have you been sniffing coke?"

"What the hell difference does that make?"

"I must warn you, *amante*. With some men into it heavy, it is sad. After three or four years, sometimes sooner, sometimes longer, it is *terminar*. No more fucking. *Impotência*."

"You're crazy! I'm still young and healthy!"

"Ah, it is not the age, but how bad and how long you have had the habit. Tonight you saw me with Sergio, who was once one of the greatest studs in Rio. Now he is *fino*—and only thirty-eight! There is nothing any doctor, any man, or even any woman skilled in love can do to bring his little joy tool back to life. It is the more terrible because the desire still burns in his head, but all he can do is watch."

A chill went down Eduardo's spine. He had indeed heard all the scare stories about impotence being one of the risks of cocaine. But it was something that only happened to others; at worst, nothing to worry about until the dim future.

"Never will that be my problem!" he said heatedly. "Already tonight I have had four orgasms. How many men can do that? It is only that perhaps I have overdone myself."

"Then sleep, *amante*, and in the morning—"

"No, no! I want you now. All I need is a little more coke. You'll see—"

"More tonight? You'll kill yourself! Like Sergio."

"*Que diabo!* Get the coke!"

She shrugged. "Very well, then. We'll call on the devil for help."

Rolling off the bed, she moved with limpid grace to a banquette stand against a wall. Taking a small silver box and tiny silver spoon out of her purse, she returned to the bed.

"But remember," she said, extending the silver box and spoon, "the devil always demands his price."

"To hell with the devil. I'll pay him when I get there."

With practiced skill he lifted a spoonful of the white powder beneath one nostril, holding a finger over the other. He snorted deeply, felt the familiar searing passage of the drug up his nose. He knew such overuse was bad; it was destroying the mucous membranes, but what the hell if he did lose his sense of smell and taste? Having Chica all to himself was more important, and he wanted his money's worth. He put the spoon under his other nostril and sniffed vigorously.

Almost at once there came that delicious surge of power. Once again the seethe of blood in his veins, the quiverings of nerves and flesh, lifting him toward those ecstatic heights where as a sexual giant he could overpower any female.

Then he became aware that his penis had only slightly awakened and was still hanging limp.

"*Pelo amor de Deus!*" he cried. "Help me! You know how to do it."

She smiled at him with hard eyes. "I, too, have my price—"

"You'll get your damned watch tomorrow or the next day, as I promised. Now *vamos para a frente!* Get on with it!"

14

Curling her torso downward, she began exerting all her erotic skills; for several minutes she worked with considerable lingual dexterity, aided by delicate fingers that knew unerringly just where to tickle, fondle, stroke. To his delight, the phallus began swelling, stiffening.

He fell upon her with rapacious lust, thrusting in so brutally that she let out a soft whimper of pleasure. Ah, now he would get his money's worth, no matter what the cost! She responded with practiced passion, with all the honeyed hot sexuality he had hoped for.

But after a few moments he was aware that it was not the same; a numbness in his organ persisted; the pleasurable sensations were muted. Perhaps it was from too much coke after all, robbing him of half the joy.

Or maybe it was her fault, for now she was strangely passive, barely responding to his thrusts. His first surge of anger changed to chagrin with the realization that she could no longer feel him; he was losing his stiffness.

Frantically he increased his tempo, ramming into her with all the force he could muster. At one point his shrinking phallus slipped out, and only with embarrassing difficulty did he manage to reenter.

"*Amante*, perhaps you should rest for a while—"

"*Não!* I want to climax!"

Doggedly he continued. A kind of fury seized him, a frenzy of lust that seemed to burn ever more fiercely in his head as his only organ for its gratification steadily diminished in size. Sweat poured from his face, torso, and limbs, trickling onto her nakedness.

Even when he slipped out again and knew that reentry was utterly hopeless, he kept thumping against her mechanically, crazily, until she rolled away from beneath him. He slumped forward, facedown on the bed, his shoulders quivering jerkily from muffled sobs.

Gently she cradled his head against her breasts and

began crooning an exotic but soothing melody that was part of her repertoire, a tune from the show *Anjo Negro*, Black Angel.

Relaxed against her perfumed warmth, he had finally slept. Fitfully.

That had been last night.

Now it was morning and the fire was reawakening in his blood. His hands began sliding over the sleek brown body, seeking out the intimate places.

"*Meu Deus!*" Chica protested, peering at him through sleep-heavy eyes. "So soon again?"

"But I didn't finish last night. It's never happened before—"

She looked down at his flaccid organ and laughed softly. "After a first time, there's always a second. I can see at a glance that you need more rest. Besides, I have not the time—I have much packing to do because I am leaving this afternoon for a few days' cruise."

"On a cruise! With whom?"

"With friends on Vinicius de Onis's yacht."

Feeling a deep stab of jealousy, he watched sourly as she padded off to the bathroom. Vinicius de Onis was one of the five wealthiest men in Brazil and a notorious libertine.

Later, sheathed in last night's saffron silk dress, one gleaming bronze shoulder and half of one breast bare, she looked at him with hard eyes. "The diamond watch—when will I get it?"

"As soon as you give me my money's worth. Call me when you get back from your cruise." Even as he spoke he knew it was a bad mistake; it was not a gentleman's way of speaking. And if he reneged on the watch, all the important people in Rio would soon find out and hold him in contempt.

The slam of the door punctuated her last scathing look.

Covering his head with the sheet—a childhood habit held over from the numerous times he had been

16

ordered to bed after a severe paternal scolding—he escaped into sleep.

Somewhat shakily, Eduardo stepped from the shower, vigorously drying himself with a towel as he crossed over to the large mirror above the lavatory counter top, which was of greenish black marble, as were the bathroom walls and floor. Anxiously he peered at his reflection, seeking but trying to minimize any signs of his recent excesses.

Except for an undue pallor, a pinkish tinge in the eyes, and a trace of darkening shadow beneath them, he thought he looked little the worse for wear. His rumpled damp hair hung in dark curls above heavy-lashed dark eyes that more than one girl had called "soulful." His red lips and cleft chin were beautifully shaped, and he considered his thin nose with flared nostrils to be most aristocratic. A few girls had even called him pretty, which was flattering yet secretly disturbing as it suggested effeminacy; could anyone be more *macho?* True, he was not as tall and ruggedly built as Raul, but his slender body was supple and strong. He danced superbly. Women were always attracted to him.

No, it was not his looks that bothered him; it was the way he felt. Since being awakened by the telephone about fifteen minutes ago—the call had been from Raul, reminding him that they were to meet for dinner—he had been troubled by a low-grade headache, an uncomfortable pressure, as if his head were overstuffed with cotton. Also in his loins was an intangible sense of unease; again not pain but more a seminumbed feeling of emptiness. It was a recurrent sensation, usually coming the morning after an orgy.

He had once consulted a doctor, who told him with a knowing grin, "You've been overdoing it, Eduardo. Even for a superman, there is a limit to everything, you know. The symptoms you describe are caused by prolonged sexual excitation. Unless you ease up, you are due for early prostate trouble. Maybe something worse. I would advise you, my friend, to give the girls a rest."

Maybe Chica and the doctor were right. From now on he would try to go easy on the coke and the screwing. Besides, both were expensive. He grimaced. His cash on hand was low.

He would have to depend on his big brother to bail him out. Good old Raul was always generous, always understanding. And with the huge loans Raul would soon be getting to finance that crazy energy plantation project, he could well afford to share some of it with his kid brother. Eduardo didn't look forward to sitting through a boring dinner with his stodgy older brother and the kind of prim and proper wifely type Raul doubtless had picked to marry, but it was a necessity. He would be as agreeable as possible and turn on all his charm for his future sister-in-law.

Finished rubbing himself dry, he raced back to the bedroom to select his evening's attire. He didn't want to ruffle Raul's mood by being late.

A half hour later, impeccably garbed in a dark silk evening suit, he stood beside the wide curved entry drive of the apartment house waiting for the parking attendant to bring up his Ferrari.

A voice accosted him. "*Senhor,* a word with you, *faz favor—*"

Frowning, Eduardo swung around. A short, ugly man with coal-black hair and a face like a mean-tempered porcupine was approaching. He wore a rumpled white suit and had only one eye, which darted about frenetically as if doing double duty, taking in all details around him as he sidled closer. His voice rasped irritatingly. "For the last delivery, *senhor,* you owe me ten thousand *cruzeiros.*"

An icy sensation slithered down Eduardo's spine. The swarthy-skinned man blocking his way was a *malandro,* one of the underworld characters who infest Rio's slums. Ordinarily someone of Eduardo's class would be outraged at being annoyed by such an unsavory type, but this one was no stranger. He was Eduardo's chief contact for obtaining cocaine. Known as *Ameixas-sêcas,* or "Prunes," both because of his appearance and the effect that fear of him was reputed to have on his enemies' bowels, he was said to be as fast and deadly with a knife as a striking rattlesnake.

Without a word, Eduardo extracted his wallet and counted out the money—more money that he couldn't afford. It left him with scarcely enough cash to get through the evening, even as Raul's guest.

"There's another small matter, *senhor,*" added Prunes. "I will expect delivery of the diamond watch no later than three days from now."

"How the hell do you know about the watch?"

"Chica is a good friend of mine. She calls on me whenever she wishes to collect money or gifts from those foolish enough to forget their obligations." With a nasty grin and a brief nod, he turned and scuttled away.

Whooshing along amid the thick traffic on the Avenida Atlantica behind the wheel of his white Ferrari, Eduardo soon shook off the spell of fright cast over him by Prunes. Problems that could be cured by money were never too serious, and he could always manage to get extra money. Never from his father, who was always scolding him for his extravagance, but as a last resort from his mother, if she could get it to him without his father finding out.

Twilight was just beginning, like blue dust sprinkling gently from the skies. His spirits lifted, as they always did with the approach of evening and the anticipation of unknown adventures ahead. He only came fully alive at night, and where were the nights more glorious than in this gay tropical city of wealth, gorgeous girls, and a multitude of sinful pleasures? Rio, generally acknowledged as the most beautiful city in the world, was as much a part of him as the very air, food, and drink that sustained him. On his left rose a wall of hills and shafts of granite that ringed the city on the offshore side, opening seaward onto a crescent of ocean and wide beaches that were thick by day with sun-browned bathers in string bikinis and of such heartbreaking beauty as to send the blood fizzing through his veins like champagne. Rio, a blaze of color and desire by day; by night an illuminated necklace of jewels promising secret fulfillment of illicit joys. And towering above it all, the Corcovado, or Hunchback Mountain, with its giant statue of Christ sorrowfully overlooking this paradise of corrupt pleasures.

Ah, this was his element! Even the shape of the city, stretching out along the sandy shores of the ocean as it did, was said to be like a beautiful female basking in the sun, somnolent, enticing. Her head formed the downtown section, her hair streaming in northerly directions; the rising mounds of topography and curved shorelines from the residential areas of Flamengo, Botafogo, and Copacabana were supposed to make up her voluptuous torso; and her legs spread invitingly at Arpoador Beach, reaching out to enfold the neighborhoods of Ipanema and Leblon.

Eduardo's own beach apartment, as he often told his guests, was situated in the very center of the pelvic area.

By the time he reached the magnificent Leme Palace Hotel and turned his car over to a parking attendant, his mood was almost back to normal. Jauntily he headed through the crowded lobby to Le Cordon Bleu restaurant, and guided by the maître d', he found Raul and his fiancée seated at a palm-shaded table in a corner of the terrace overlooking the ocean.

Even as he was shaking hands with his smiling brother, Eduardo could scarcely hide his astonishment. One glance at the svelte girl seated at the table had stunned him. What perfection of face and figure! How had stodgy old Raul managed to capture this one? She had flawless milk-white skin and gleaming black hair that was severely coiffed to set off the delicate elegance of her features. Her jewels and ice-green gown had obviously been picked to enhance the brilliance of her green eyes that sparkled and seemed to mock him as she looked him over.

"Eduardo, I wish to present Odete Bandiera e Xavier, my fiancée. Odete, my brother Eduardo."

"*Senhorita,* what a delightful pleasure," said Eduardo with genuine sincerity as he took her outstretched hand and lightly touched his lips to the back of her fingers. "My respect for my brother's good taste has risen a thousandfold."

Her laugh tinkled. "I have looked forward to meeting you, *senhor.* Raul has told me many nice things about you, but not that you are such a flatterer."

"I have many sins, but flattery is not one of them. Has Raul not told you about how bad I can be?"

"Oh, no. Raul is too much the loyal brother to say an unkind word. The bad things you must tell me yourself."

"It would be a great pleasure, *senhorita—*"

"Please! As my future brother-in-law, you must call me Odete."

"With pleasure, Odete—and you must call me Eduardo."

"Splendid," said Raul, flashing his grin at them. "It pleases me to see that you have both taken such a liking to each other."

There was a silver ice bucket on the table containing an open bottle of Cliquot's, from which a waiter had already poured a glass for Eduardo. He sipped at it nervously, wondering if his brother had sensed his powerful surge of attraction to Odete and was subtly warning him to cool it. Then he decided that Raul was much too straightforward for subtleties, too trusting to harbor suspicions.

Raul continued. "Shall we order? And after we have dined, I am anxious to talk about how my new plans will affect your future, Eduardo."

Eduardo groaned. "More work for me, no doubt."

"But at a higher salary."

Eduardo brightened. Plainly Raul was in a fine mood. He scanned the *cardápio,* noting that caviar Beluga Malossol, at 620 *cruzeiros,* was the most expensive of the appetizers, and he automatically selected that.

"I'll begin with the Beluga," he said, shoving the menu aside. "The rest I'll leave to you to order for me, Raul."

"I'll do the same," said Odete, adding with a laugh, "I must start practicing at letting my future husband do the thinking for me."

Raul beckoned the waiter and placed the order.

The caviar was followed by *gazpacho à Andaluz.* Conversation at this point, as custom mandated, was restricted to inconsequential or amusing topics, with no reference to business. Next came the entrée: *iscas de vitela com creme e batatas à Bernesa,* accompanied by *palmito.*

Raul ate voraciously. Eduardo ate with far less gusto, consuming but modest portions of everything. Odete only dabbled at her food, but she ordered *doces brasileiros,* Brazilian sweets, for dessert, with *cafézinho* and a sweet liqueur.

As the two brothers were finishing with coffee and brandy, Raul's voice turned serious. "Eduardo, I wished to speak to you on business matters tonight in front of Odete because all of our futures are necessarily affected by the plans we work out."

Eduardo laughed. "How different from our father, who would never dream of including a wife in a discussion of business matters!"

Raul didn't smile. "He hasn't changed in that respect—but he is still our father, and I still need his approval before I can go ahead with my plans for the energy plantation."

"But why? The property is yours." A sudden doubt clutched at Eduardo's hope for borrowing from Raul. "Have you had any trouble getting the capital you need?"

"No. Da Silva has pledged the money. My problem

is father's disapproval—and his dependence on me to manage our Rio export office. He feels I will be letting him down. It is my obligation to prove to him that you are very capable of taking over as the new manager—"

"Me!" Eduardo was truly surprised and a bit dismayed. He knew his own inadequacies, and he dreaded responsibility.

"Yes. I am counting on you to prove that you can work just as hard as anyone else when it is necessary. We have good people on the staff who will help you. Up until now you haven't had a real chance, but I'm sure that once you have been entrusted with full responsibility, you will take hold and make all of us proud of you."

Eduardo saw at once that the position might well afford opportunities to get his hands on company funds—borrowed only temporarily, of course—when hard pressed for cash. To cover his nervousness, he turned to Odete with a wry smile. "So now I have to pay a heavy price to help along Raul's dream of becoming an agro-industrial giant—all this extra work piled on me! Talk him out of it, Odete. I'm sure you aren't looking forward to hiding away in the middle of the jungle with only the alligators, snakes, and bugs for neighbors."

She shuddered fastidiously. "I do not wish even to know about such things. Perhaps after a while I can persuade Raul to hire managers to run his plantation, and we can live in town."

"I must warn you, Raul can be very stubborn."

"But so can I—and I have months to work on him, since mama will never allow the marriage to take place too soon after our engagement is announced."

Raul laughed, taking it all in good humor. "And I, too, will have time to convince Odete that the jungle is the most beautiful place left on earth. She will learn to love it just as deeply as I do."

Eduardo spread his hands in mock resignation. "You see, Odete? Raul has always been a stick-in-the-mud who has no appreciation of the excitements and fun of city life."

"Can we consider it settled, Eduardo?" said Raul. "You will agree to take over the managership? I must know because tomorrow I am flying home to talk it over with father."

Eduardo sighed wearily. "I accept, brother, and I will try hard to justify your faith in me."

"Splendid. Now one more thing. I shall be away most of the time for the next several months, and I am asking you as a great personal favor to look after Odete and help do what you can to alleviate her boredom."

"It will be my pleasure."

Odete smiled at Eduardo. "And then you can tell me all the bad things about yourself."

"That would take a long time."

"Who cares how long it takes?" she said.

Raul had turned away to signal for the check, and for a moment Eduardo could hardly believe his eyes. She had winked at him before fluttering her eyes downward, sipping her liqueur through her smile.

THREE

The Amazon is the giant of rivers. Two hundred miles wide at the mouth, seven miles across in other places, it is so deep that oceangoing liners can navigate 2,300 miles upstream. Its total volume is twelve times greater than the Mississippi.

It is a murky river, ranging in color from yellowish brown to almost black, and walled in on either shore by a barricade of jungle green that is astonishingly vivid and of a microstructure so closely knit in a confusion of growth and so bound together by the cordage of looping vines that the very sight of it conjures emotions of mystery and vague threat. Men forced to journey by boat day after day, week after week, over this colossal body of sullen water, running silently between its sinister green walls, have been known to go out of their minds.

Ensconced in a reclining deck chair aboard his 167-foot yacht, the *Rainha do Mar,* which was lazily cruising up a broad stretch of the lower Amazon, Vinicius de Onis was in a state of relaxed anticipation. His private plane was en route from the government seat at Brasilia, a thousand miles away, bearing news of great import. The plane, carrying one of his key men, Barbosa, was due any minute now. De Onis wondered whether the news would be good or bad.

He sighed. If it was bad, he would have to find ways to cope with it. There were always ways. More money, more bribes, at worst a quiet killing to dispose of any opposition stubborn and *estúpido* enough to hold out against him. But that would mean more delay, which was one of the things de Onis could least tolerate. He was a man in a hurry; he had always been in a hurry. That trait, added to ruthless ambition, animal cunning, and no encumbrance of morals, had propelled him to his present eminence.

At fifty-four, de Onis ranked as about the fifth wealthiest man in Brazil, and he hungered fiercely to rise to number one. Yet even if he achieved that (a certainty in his mind), it would not be enough. Nothing would ever be enough. For de Onis was the kind of man whose lust for power and money was so compulsive, so insatiable, that not even the greatest fortune in the world could end his craving. Among such men are the fortune hunters, the robber barons, the Mafia crime lords, the business tycoons, the financial wizards, the tricksters, and the thieves. De Onis was an amalgam of all these.

In appearance he seemed innocuous enough. He was short and squat, though powerfully built, and he was always trying to appear taller, using such devices as elevator heels, or drawing himself up importantly, ramrod straight, stretching almost on tiptoe when near anyone taller. His legs being disproportionately short and his trunk of normal proportions, he contrived to be seated whenever possible so that he could be taken as a man of average height. He had large brown eyes and strong white teeth in a squarish olive-skinned face that somehow missed being handsome. His most noticeable feature was a full head of straight black hair, down the center of which ran an irregular stripe of white. Because of its similarity to the fur of a common small obnoxious mammal, his bitterest enemies referred to him as the *jaritacaca*, or skunk. Friends and females, however, flattered him that the anomaly in coloration added much to his look of distinction.

The sudden screech of a long-tailed macaw followed by the outraged chattering of a flight of parrots, then deep silence, drew de Onis's amused attention shoreward. What was it this time? A slithering anaconda suddenly snapping up its prey? One of the things he most enjoyed about the Amazon was the

life-and-death drama. The cough of a prowling jaguar, the bellow of a caiman from one of the side
channels, the screams, the chokings of death. Here
was nature at its most primitive. Here, predators
reigned supreme, unhampered by laws to protect the
weak and stupid.

Here, he reigned supreme, the most powerful of
all.

With pride he looked down the vessel's long teak
deck at the polished brass gleaming under the heavy
afternoon sun. A large butterfly hovered and flickered
like lambent flame. Dragonflies were suspended over
an awning like jewels in shimmering colors. Off to one
side, a pair of curious wild ducks were keeping pace
with the boat which, set at its lowest speed, glided
over the glassy river surface with scarcely a ripple.
None of the guests were in sight.

The *Rainha do Mar* slept fourteen guests and employed a full-time uniformed staff of twenty-seven—
seven officers and twenty crew. Specifically designed
for the tropics, it had an air-conditioning system so
energetic that if turned to high at night, electric
blankets were required. Doubtless the guests had
retired to their staterooms to cool off. Or heat up.

A hard grin touched his lips. De Onis never sailed
without an assortment of girls—at least one for each
male guest. Such costly consideration for the guests,
most of them being business associates, was repaid
many times over in the way it smoothed out sticky
business deals.

Hearing the drone of a plane, he lifted the binocu-
lars slung around his neck and focused the ten-power
lens. As expected, it was the Falcon, one of his fleet of
eight planes of varying sizes and makes. Barbosa
would be on it.

His grin broadened. Whether the news Barbosa was
bringing would be good or bad, one consolation was
certain, for Barbosa was also bringing along a delightful passenger: Chica.

De Onis had a greedy appreciation of the charms of

all females, whatever their color or shade, but his
preference was for cinnamon-skinned women. Of that
category, the one he prized most was Chica. Her
erotic skills were superlative.

Soon the small plane, pontoons lowered, was
swooping down to land as closely beside the yacht as
possible. Crewmen were quickly assembling at their
stations to lower a small launch to pick up the arrivals. The roar of the plane motor was also bringing
some of the guests from their staterooms, most of the
men gaudily clad in shorts and sport shirts, the girls in
string bikinis—or partly so. Several were still drawing
their minuscule coverings into place and tying them
as they padded over to the railing to see what new
excitement might be in the offing.

Chica, stunning in a lime green sundress with
bright golden ornaments suspended from her neck,
wrists, and ears, was the first one helped aboard. She
rushed at once toward de Onis with a dazzling smile.

"Ah, Vini, *namorado*—how heavenly to see you
again!"

Without rising from his deck chair he accepted her
peck on the lips, then shoved her aside rudely. "You
wait, Chica—first I have important business to talk
over with Lúcio."

Pouting, Chica flopped down in a nearby deck chair
and began fumbling through her bag for a cigarette.

Lúcio Barbosa was a large and somewhat chunky
man, but graceful in his movements. He had curling
dark hair and the whimsical affectation of an old-time
mustachio, waxed and twisted out to stiletto points.
His expression oozed friendliness, competence, slip-
periness. He was well known in Brasilia, having
wined and dined most of the powerful members of
the Senate as well as of the lesser Chamber of Deputies. As lobbyist and chief troubleshooter for de Onis,
his talents ranged from being able to supply any kind
of girl—or boy if need be—for any kind of erotic
taste, to knowing how to bribe an official or arrange a

murder. Even more indispensable was his input to the National Department of Highways (DNER) and the Superintendency for the Development of Amazonia (SUDAM), where his influence had been most useful for the de Onis enterprises.

"Ah, my dear Vinicius," said Barbosa as he approached with an outstretched hand. "How well you look! How do you manage to look younger each time I see you?"

De Onis waved aside the flattery with a frown, secretly believing at least part of it. His barrel-deep voice was slightly more cordial. "Your trip was pleasant, I hope?"

"Most pleasant. How could it be otherwise?" Barbosa smiled, a most respectful smile, in the direction of Chica.

"And how did the other matter go?"

"It has been a difficult undertaking. I had endless conferences with the important officials of DNER and SUDAM. At great expense of time and money. Frankly, the majority are negative on the matter. Still, you know I am never one to give up. I argued, pleaded—"

"*Diabo*—don't tell me of your troubles! Just tell me the results!"

"Well, concerning the leg of highway through the de Carvalho property—"

De Onis held up a hand to cut him off and turned toward Chica. One of his traits was an animallike alertness to everything around him. Chica's head, he noted, had jerked up almost imperceptibly at the mention of the name de Carvalho.

"Ah, Chica my dear—so you know the de Carvalhos?"

She looked momentarily startled. "Only the younger one. Eduardo. He is just a casual friend."

Tucking that item in one of the file cabinets of his brain, de Onis made a gesture of dismissal. "Go to my suite, Chica, and wait for me there." No need for her to overhear anything more about a matter of such crucial importance. Shrugging, the girl got up and stalked away like a puma with its tail switching. De Onis scowled at Barbosa.

Barbosa smiled back, a smile now exultant with the pride of accomplishment. "After much sweat and agony, I finally got through to Hygino de Faria and won his agreement. The price will be high, of course, but I have his promise—"

"Then the highway will be diverted?"

"Exactly as you wished it, Vinicius. That leg of the highway will never go near the de Carvalho land. Work will be stopped at once while surveyors replat it to swing directly through your property."

Already de Onis was feeling a familiar thrill of victory warming his spine. Again he had scored! This time in a move that would bring him millions, perhaps billions. The cost of bringing a highway to his huge Amazonian tracts of land—land that was totally unfit for road building except at astronomical expense that even he could never have afforded—would now be borne by the government. It was land rich in bauxite, manganese, and other mineral wealth, waiting to be mined, but all locked away there virtually worthless unless there was easy access.

Which was now assured.

He put on his broadest grin. "You've done well, Lúcio. Now you can relax. Find yourself a girl and enjoy yourself."

With another of his autocratic gestures he dismissed the man and glanced down the deck at the scattering of guests. They appeared a bit bored. It was time for a new diversion. He beckoned to one of the nearby officers and snapped out an order.

"Drop anchor and bring out the pigs and rifles."

The piglets, four of them, squealed in fright as they were tossed overboard one by one. Meanwhile, the girls lined up along the gunwale had been supplied with small-caliber rifles, all loaded. Smiling with anticipation, they waited until de Onis gave the signal, then began shooting.

The squealing sounds in the water intensified with pain and terror in cruel counterpoint to the sharp poppings of the rifles as the bullets hit their targets. The girls were shrieking in joy. One screamed, "Look —they're coming now! The piranhas!"

De Onis himself left his deck chair and went to join the guests, for this was the kind of thing he enjoyed watching, just as in Mexico or Spain he always went to bullfights. For one of his sadistic temperament, the sight of blood and death acted on his genitals like a strong drug, heightening his sensuality.

The piranhas swarmed crazily around the stricken animals, churning the water into red froth. Most of the girls watched avidly, mouths open and eyes shining. A few of the men, their sado-eroticism whipped into urgency by the spectacle, were openly playing with the girls, who made no objections as bikinis were pulled down, breasts pinched and fondled. One of the men, a *norte-americano* oil executive, had turned away in disgust, his face pale and sickish. No *macho* in that one, de Onis concluded contemptuously, filing the item away for future use. Such squeamishness would make the man an easy mark in business.

The erotic horseplay was in full fever now, several of the girls already naked, laughing, shrieking like children at a circus as couples began returning to their staterooms.

De Onis himself was keyed high, seething with the double excitement of another big financial coup and sexual lust. He felt the giddy sense of giantlike power translated into his loins, in the enlarging and hardening of his male organ as he hurried toward his private suite where Chica would be waiting with all the voluptuary pleasures she had to offer.

But even in the ardor of his financial-sexual greed, his brain was busy devising ways to handle Hygino de Faria, who would be expecting a huge sum of bribe money in exchange for diverting the highway. It would be easy to stall the man with small payments until the highway actually reached his land, after which . . .

He grinned. What could Hygino do when no more money was forthcoming? Whom could he appeal to without cutting his own throat?

De Onis was as expert at screwing others in business as he was in bed.

FOUR

In Brasília, Hygino de Faria was in high fettle. Seated behind his fine desk of polished black jacaranda in his office on the top floor of the imposing glass-walled government building that housed the *Departmento Nacional de Estradas de Rodagem* (DNER), he shuffled busily through the pile of official reports, memos, letters, and other data stacked in front of him.

But none of the printed matter registered in his brain. His thoughts were elsewhere. His facade of hardworking executive was purely mechanical, a reflex acquired through long years in government service, during which he had accomplished virtually nothing for the vast majority of taxpayers who bore the burden of his high salary, but a great deal for a number of select lobbyists, and for himself. Mostly himself. Hygino was a shining example of a familiar principle rooted in all government jobs, regardless of the country: by sheer methodical persistence, complete lack of initiative, discreet ass-kissing, and not stepping on the toes of others, he had been steadily promoted to ever higher levels of incompetence.

And ever higher rewards.

Such as the deal just made with Vinicius de Onis, through Barbosa—the reason for Hygino's present mood of elation. The favor that de Onis had requested —the rerouting of a two-hundred-mile leg of the highway—was a relatively minor change, of no practical significance to the government in terms of the eventual nine-thousand-mile network of Trans-Amazonian Highway. For Hygino, as a key official of DNER with extensive bureaucratic powers of arbitrary decision, it was a favor that could easily be

33

handled. A half million in Swiss francs had been offered.

He had handled it shrewdly, knowing the stakes involved, knowing that de Onis would benefit by untold millions. He had stalled, citing numerous difficulties, vague risks. The offer had been doubled to a million.

For Hygino this was the apex of his career, the greatest opportunity ever to come his way. Once he had been smugly content with his good salary and the assurance of a generous pension—but that had been before elevation to his current position brought him increasingly in contact with the big industrial movers, multimillionaires, whose lavish lives made his own envisioned future with a boring matronly wife in a comfortable but modest country house seem paltry by comparison. At fifty-five, Hygino was also painfully aware of the accelerating years, the thickening of his once-slender waist by a half dozen inches, and the loss of much hair, the remnants of which were too skimpy to cover the bald areas. Once he had thought of himself as a ladies' man, and he still prided himself that with his suave manners and charm, all women found him attractive. With sufficient money—money his wife would not have to know about—there would be endless opportunities for delightful dalliance with young females in the private apartment he kept in the city.

Accordingly, he had seized this chance to make a tax-free fortune.

There was a small risk involved, of course. But not too much. After nearly thirty years in government service he was well acquainted with all the key subordinates, the trusted ones who were closely tied to him by favors given and received. He knew all the conduits of influence to be kept well oiled by bits of money sprinkled here and there. Nobody could question his decision to reroute the highway except possibly a few engineers. And who were they? Minions that he could hire, transfer, or dismiss at will. At worst, if his decision were ever criticized, he could be accused of nothing more than bad judgment.

Still, it meant discretion. The less anybody knew about it, the better. The road engineers might grumble, but they would follow orders, and once the highway had reached the de Onis land, it wouldn't matter. For the present, it would be wise to keep a lid on the change in the road plans.

Which reminded him of a small annoyance. The letter.

The letter had been referred to him by the Ministry of the Interior as coming under his jurisdiction. It was a letter from a woman reporter from the United States who planned to do a series of articles about Brazil that would be syndicated throughout the world. She was particularly interested in doing an article about the Trans-Amazonian Highway.

Hygino's opinion of *norte-americano* women was that they tended to be bold and brassy, jangling all over with cheap jewelry, and the kind who would want to be a reporter would most likely be lanky, scrawny, with a pointed, snoopy nose. She would ask too many questions, delve into all sorts of things that were none of her business.

He snorted derisively. He could handle her kind. The letter stated that she would be arriving today, so it would be circumspect to take steps now. He would close off all avenues of information concerning the highway and divert her with many other aspects of Brazil of far more interest for her silly articles. First of all, she would need a guide to escort her around to the wonders of Brasilia.

Chuckling, he reached for the phone.

The desk clerk at the Nacional Hotel, a slim gentleman with curly black hair, the dreamy dark eyes of a poet, and the brisk manner of an accountant, slid the registry book across the counter.

"Welcome to Brasilia, *Senhorita* Carpenter. You will please to sign here, and the boy will show you to your apartment."

Peggy Carpenter, just arrived by jet from Rio, shifted back the fatly packed red canvas tote bag that was slung over her shoulder and leaned forward to sign in the vigorous upright script developed during her Radcliffe days as an indication of a positive personality not to be pushed around by male chauvinist types. From her other shoulder hung a large and equally heavy camera case. The desk clerk eyed them with faint disapproval. Brazilian women, other than Indians and *pretas,* did not carry their own luggage.

"Another boy can carry your shoulder luggage, *se-nhorita.*"

"I can manage it quite well by myself, thank you."

Two of the uniformed "boys" were already carrying the rest of her luggage, which consisted of a portable nonelectric typewriter and a rather large battered leather suitcase—one boy for each piece. That should be enough, she thought, to salve their sense of Latin gallantry without assigning another to struggle along under the burden of her shoulder bags for the added tips that she would be expected to pay.

It was not that Peggy Carpenter was short of money—or chintzy about spending it; it was simply that female independence had become almost the essence of her existence. Nor was there anything unfeminine about her appearance. At twenty-three she was fairly tall, slim, and shapely. Almost the ideal picture of a leggy American blonde. She had skin the pink-white of fine Dresden, clear blue eyes, and pale wavy hair worn shoulder length. Her nose was small and slender, just slightly turned up at the tip; and her well-shaped mouth was generally quirked at the corners in an expression of lively amusement at the world and perhaps also at herself. She knew that her air of bravado was just a bit phony, but she hoped others could not discern it.

She had come from an upper-middle-class family in a medium-sized town in the Midwest, had gone East to attend college as a journalism major, and was now bent on proving to her family and the world that she could survive quite well, thank you, without the usual husband and family. She had bigger aspirations. Thus she had found employment with a large international news service, and she had wangled this assignment to Brazil for a series of articles.

Turning away from the desk she started toward the elevators, only to find her way blocked by a roly-poly little man in a crumpled white suit. His round face of palest brown was creased with an ingratiating smile.

"You are *Senhorita* Peggy Carpenter, the writer of articles?"

"Yes."

"Ahhh—" Waddling a step closer, he caught one of her unsuspecting hands, raised it to his lips, and deposited a kiss. "I am Graciliano Toronja of the Ciclone Hinterland Turismo Agency," he went on. "I was informed by our government of your arrival here to write beautiful stories of our great country, so I am here, *senhorita,* to offer my services for the grand tour of our fabulous city."

"I thank you, but I have no desire or need for the tours planned for tourists. I prefer to snoop around in my own fashion."

"But, *senhorita,* we offer you not the usual tour, but for me personally to drive you wherever you wish and explain most interestingly all matters you ask. I have been select for this honor because my English is of the most excellent. I can assist you most importantly to describe our most modern in the world city, so that you can write more beautifully of our many wonders. For you there will be no charge."

Free transportation? A free guide to the city? What more could she ask?

"It is so kind and generous of you, *senhor*—" She scrunched her brow trying to recall the name.

"Toronja," he supplied. "In English that means 'grape.'" His smile broadened. "I am like, how you say, fruit of the grape."

"You mean grapefruit?"

"Ah, yes, that is the way it is speak in your country."

Peggy smiled. "I appreciate your generous offer, *Senhor* Toronja, and accept with pleasure. Since it is already late in the afternoon and I must spend hours at the typewriter translating my notes into prose, could we make it for early tomorrow morning?"

"Ah, yes. Whatever hour you select, *senhorita.*"

"How about eight?"

His smile grew uncertain. "*Oito!* So early? Perhaps nine would be more suitable?"

"Nine it is then, but I'll have to cram everything into one day, since I intend to leave the day after tomorrow."

The round face registered dismay. "But it will take many days to show you everything! After seeing Brasilia, the marvel of all cities in the world, what is left to see? *Nada!* All else would be much boring and waste of time."

"To tell the truth, my main reason for coming to Brasilia is to get government permits to visit the highway construction camps and Indians in the jungle. Brasilia has been written about many times, but the highway through the jungle is new and exciting, and the whole world is curious about what will now happen to the Indians."

"Permits to visit the Indians? Highway construction? *Impossível!* For even a man it would be difficult. For a lady, never! The jungle, the Indians—they are much too wild, too dangerous."

Peggy smiled serenely. "I'll accept nothing as impossible, *senhor*, until after I've given it my best try. Until tomorrow morning, then?"

After a little bow and the assurance that he would be there faithfully at nine, *Senhor* Toronja waddled away.

* * * * *

Two days later, Peggy was no longer so confident.

At first she had been overwhelmed by the beauty of the city, which had been built, incredibly, in only three years—from wild brush country to its present magnificence in accordance with a well-worked-out plan by world-famed architects. All this despite the necessity of flying in each bag of cement, every steel girder, the pipes, the glass, the tiles, everything, because there were no roads or waterways to reach Brasilia.

The futuristic architecture enthralled her. It was a space-age fantasy set in the middle of nowhere. All the buildings were lavish yet tempered by the lean lines of understatement. Soaring arches; geometric tapestries in concrete; glass walls. The *Palácio da Alvorada,* the president's home, was a work of art, as were the fabulous government buildings, designed like two enormous bowls, one inverted, with twin twenty-eight-story towers seemingly floating on air above reflecting pools. Separating the many elegant buildings and the superblocks containing elite apartments, theaters, churches, schools, supermarkets—everything required for a self-contained city of the future—were wide spaces of green lawn, native trees, extravagantly lush water gardens, and a network of virtually accident-proof high-speed freeways.

At night the city blossomed into something even more fantastic under artfully placed illumination of white marble, shimmering fountains, walls of glass dramatically highlighted against the black velvet jungle sky. From her suite on the tenth floor of the Nacional Hotel, Peggy got an incomparable view, the entire city seemingly strung with necklaces of light, diamonds and rubies in a crisscrossed arrangement that Hollywood might have designed for a cosmic window display.

But Peggy's appreciation had been dimmed somewhat by her failure to achieve her primary objective: permission to visit a section of Trans-Amazonian Highway under construction.

At the headquarter offices of the National Department of Highways, the Superintendency for the Development of Amazonia, and the Foundation for the Preservation of Indians, she had repeatedly met with the strongest resistance. A woman venturing into such dangerous country? Did she not realize, said the officials, that the jungle was teeming with deadly animals and snakes, that some of the Indian tribes were hostile to outsiders? There had been, in fact, a recent outbreak of Indian attacks against the roadworkers, resulting in deaths from poisoned arrows.

No, senhorita, *we are deeply regretful, but*—a commiserating smile and a shrug of hopelessness.

Peggy had complained bitterly to her self-appointed guide, Graciliano Toronja, who was very sympathetic.

"I expected full cooperation from the Brazilian government, and all I get is the brush-off! You must help me, *Senhor* Toronja, please! You must know of someone who has the power to overrule all of the bureaucratic flunkies and give me the permits I need."

Reluctantly, Toronja gave her the name of Hygino de Faria.

The desk phone shrilled and the button indicating his secretary's extension flashed.

Irritated, for he was in the midst of complex computations concerning hypothetical investments of one million Swiss francs, Hygino de Faria snatched up the receiver.

"*Sim?*" he barked.

"Oh, *senhor*," came his secretary's excited voice, "there is a lady out here who insists on seeing you—a *norte-americana*. I told her you were too busy to be disturbed, but she would not listen. I tried to stop her, but she pushed past me and is on her way to your office at this very—"

The door swung open and a woman stepped inside, her blue eyes flashing with anger, her red lips drawn in a tight line. She had lovely blond hair and a nice figure sheathed in a navy blue summer frock. She was also, Hygino could not help noting, very attractive.

"*Senhor*, I demand that you talk to me and answer a few questions!"

Hygino rose to his feet, frowning sternly. "Young lady, I am in the midst of an important matter."

"So is my matter important! I've wasted two days trying to get a little cooperation around here, and all I get is the old runaround. The least you can do is spare me a few minutes!"

She had a full bosom, Hygino noted. Nice legs. A most beautiful pale complexion. He gave her his best smile. Unconsciously one manicured hand smoothed back a few strands of skimpy black hair. "Please sit, young lady, and I'll try to explain." He indicated a low modern sofa with a chrome frame and orange upholstery.

"I've heard too many phony explanations already, *Senhor* de Faria," she said as she seated herself, "and no honest answers. There is no valid reason why your government cannot grant me the permits I need to travel to the construction site of the highway. I am quite capable of taking care of myself. As much as any man. I'm willing to sign waivers, so that no one will be held responsible should anything happen to me. There is no reason to deny me such a simple request."

Hygino sighed. "Ah, yes. I have heard much about you already. Many department heads have called me and told me about your insistence, your anger. You have upset many of them. They said that at times you talked in a most unladylike manner." Hygino tempered his words with a smile, drawing a chair close to where she sat, and seating himself.

"You've heard nothing yet! I'm just beginning to get mad."

He leaned toward her and put a pudgy hand over one of hers as it rested on the arm of the couch. "My dear young lady, there is no need for getting excited. I am only a servant of the government, trying to do what is best. You see, there are many regulations, many laws, ordinances that we must adhere to. But I am always willing to do my best for a young lady who is so enchanting—"

As he spoke, his hand still cupped over her hand in a warm fatherly way, one of his knees had strayed as if by accident against one of her knees. He made no effort to move it away. "You see, my dear young lady, I am quite busy now. But I think there might be a way of solving your problems, later—after I have talked to various officials. In fact, I am quite sure that I can get you what you desire. But it is a matter I would have to keep very quiet from others, very secret. I could be greatly criticized for giving you such a special favor—so it would be more discreet if you could come to my apartment this evening, where over a private little dinner we can discuss the matter. It is very pleasant in my apartment, relaxing—a beautiful view of the city, with beautiful music. I am sure that out of the harmony we could create between us, I could definitely promise you—"

Whack! The stinging slap of her hand against his cheek jerked his head back, leaving him astonished and chagrined.

She stood up. "*Senhor,* in my country, that cozy little knee game, the invitation to dinner in your apartment, and your whole line of gab means only one thing. I'm sorry for the blunt way I've given my answer, but I wanted to be sure you got the message."

"B—but, *senhorita,* you misunderstand me most unfairly. Perhaps you do not realize how importantly I can help you."

"Forget it. I'll get the help I need, even if I have to go to the president of your country and tell him the whole story."

Spinning around, she went clicking out on her spiked heels.

Hygino watched her go, angry at himself for his clumsiness, but far angrier at her for failing to perceive the great benefits he could give her, for failing to appreciate his masculine charms.

And threading through his fabric of emotions was fear.

It was ridiculous to think that she could gain audience with the president! On the other hand, her imperious personality might well manage it. Apparently she had no respect for official importance. Had she not boldly invaded his own office? Had not all the departments been complaining about her persistence, her embarrassing questions?

And what if she did get to the president? She was not only smart, but attractive. Very attractive. The president surely would listen. And perhaps wonder why she had met with such lack of cooperation. An investigation might even be made.

Alarm stabbed through his mind. It was getting more dangerous to have her here in Brasilia than it would be to let her go out to the jungle country. For him at least.

As for the girl—he shrugged philosophically—if she wanted to risk her life for her silly articles, so be it.

Peggy was deeply ashamed. How could she have been so unsophisticated, so gross as to slap Hygino de Faria? How the poor man's ego must have suffered! She regretted that she hadn't reacted with humor, or cool aplomb. Perhaps even have accepted the invitation to his apartment, where she could have warded off any unwanted attentions firmly and gracefully, and still have achieved her objective. But thanks to her residual puritanism, she had blown it all.

Going down to the hotel lobby the next morning, she felt a twinge of embarrassment when she saw that the faithful *Senhor* Toronja was there waiting for her. Quite likely he had heard about her unseemly behavior.

But the rotund little man's face was beaming with a smile wider than usual.

"Ah, *Senhorita* Peggy, I have the fine news for you!

You have been granted permission to visit the Indians and the road building. You are to come to the offices of FUNAI and DNER today to sign papers and pick up the official permits."

"But how wonderful!" She could scarcely believe it.

"It was most difficult to change their minds, but for such a friend like you I go everywhere. I have influence. I say, 'Why you not do this for the so sweet young lady who is great friend of mine?' At last they say, 'For you, Graciliano, we will do this favor.'"

"I am grateful for all of your help, *senhor.*"

"It was most pleasure for me, *Senhorita* Peggy my dear. It has been exquisite joy to make such acquaintance with so beautiful as you. I have done all this because for you I feel much affection."

"You are sweet, *senhor.* I shall always treasure the memory of your generous efforts in my behalf."

His smile grew hopeful. "I would be even more pleased to make your memories more treasureful if Peggy my dear would kindly be my guest for dinner tonight in my very nice *apartamento.*"

"Perhaps during another visit, *senhor.* Tonight I shall be too busy writing all about the enjoyable stay you have made for me in Brasilia." Bending, she gave him a light kiss on the cheek.

Toronja beamed, kissed her hand, bowed, and then waddled away.

FIVE

Raul de Carvalho's birthplace, to which he was presently en route by Learjet, was known as the Granja do Sol. Situated in the middle of the wild grasslands of the Mato Grosso, the manse was surrounded by a high whitewashed wall that was topped with shards of glass set in concrete and a wide iron-grilled gate armed at the top with sharp spearpointed rods. These architectural features, adopted by many wealthy Brazilian families in the nineteenth century and still commonplace today, are said to be, primarily, expressions of male sexual jealousy, for the purpose of keeping out Don Juans. The women in the old patriarchal homes were as safeguarded by the iron grilles, lattices, screens, shutters, and locks as the master's own jewels or money that was hidden underground or in the thick walls.

Within the fortress walls, which encompassed about twenty acres of grounds, was a small self-contained community. Beyond the long horse-hitching rail was a row of what had once been slave cabins, but were now occupied by employees and servants. At one end of the property was a chapel, a kitchen house, a pigsty, a dovecote, a carriage house, stables, and a modern garage. Behind the manse were sizable vegetable and flower gardens and incredible arrays of shrubbery surrounding a flagstoned inner court with a fountain and flowing water. Pergolas of trelliswork were thickly hung with colorful climbing plants, brilliant orange red flowers, and plumeria blossoms. Giant lily pads, beneath which drifted brilliant tropical fish, graced the pools. Masses of palm fronds and other growth added a touch of the jungle, an aura of fecundity. The gardens were the special domain of the women, who spent much of their time there.

Beyond the gardens were the small orchards of trees imported from the North: guavas, cashews, oranges, coconuts, mangoes, jackfruit, and breadfruit. A small stream—an artificial stream fed by a canal that had been spaded out by hundreds of Indian slaves, diverting water from a river several miles away—flowed through the grounds. Drinking water came from a well house over a hand-driven well more than two hundred feet deep.

The mansion itself was a sprawling structure covering about an acre of ground. It had gabled red tile roofs and whitewashed walls, one story high for the most part, but rising in the center to two stories to accommodate the large airy bedrooms for the master and his family.

Despite its extravagance, the estate fronted on a narrow dirt road that was virtually impassable, and in any case led nowhere but to a few outbuildings and the airplane hangar. There was no need for roads or, for that matter, automobiles. The saddle horse was still the most convenient way to get about on the *campos*. For longer trips, the modern jet plane could take the de Carvalhos or their guests anywhere in the world within hours.

Afonso Sequiera e de Azvedo de Carvalho, the master of Granja do Sol, was in a somber mood. Pacing slowly and thoughtfully over the oriental carpeting of the large central hall, he puffed gently on the long slender cigar, which was of his own private brand made especially for him in Bahia. He was a most impressive man. Tall and handsome, at fifty-nine he was still as erect and graceful in his movements as he had been at twenty. He had a mane of graying hair, a formidable moustache, and luminous eyes that fluctuated in color from gray to hazel. He wore a white silk shirt, white riding pants, and highly polished black boots. A red cummerbund added a dash of flamboyance. His bearing was that of a young man mellowed by the air of authority, seasoned with experience, and accustomed to command.

Now and then as he paced, he cursed softly. His annoyance was directed at his elder son, Raul, who would be arriving within the hour to seek approval of his crazy plan for alcohol farming. Afonso's approval was a necessity because of a provision in Raul's grandfather's will, of which Afonso was executor, giving Afonso the power of decision as to whether it would be wiser to bequeath the old plantation and acreage to Raul intact or to sell it at currently appraised prices and give Raul the cash proceeds from the sale. It was a terrible responsibility for Afonso. Knowing of his son's enthusiasm for the energy project, he had tried to look at it as favorably as possible. But all his common sense cried out against it. It was true that others had begun manufacturing alcohol for fuel from trees, plants, garbage, and so forth, but no one was making any real money at it. They were merely gambling on a future shortage of petroleum supplies that would send prices zooming.

Afonso did not believe it would happen. This alcohol, or gasohol, product, or whatever they wanted to call it, was only another symptom of the hysteria filling the world—the fear that oil fields controlled by the Arabs would dry up, when in fact they were virtually limitless. Even in Brazil, new wells were being discovered every day. The high prices were temporary. A world recession was due any year now, and then prices would drop again to a reasonable level. And the high costs for the equipment and the new technology needed to produce the alcohol fuel would price it out of the market. It was all foolishness!

Also angering Afonso was the embarrassment of Raul going to a family friend, Cosme Almeida Branco da Silva, to borrow money! Not that Afonso himself would have lent the money to his son for such a silly venture—and if the truth were known, his funds at present were too low to have afforded it—but it was demeaning to a father's pride when a son sought financial help outside of the family, thus advertising it to the whole world.

Why couldn't Raul be satisfied with the family business? Raising and exporting beef. Afonso was of the old school who believed only in the things proven by time. Cattle was one of them. Beef was the preferred food of the classes as well as the masses, and with the proliferating world population, there would never be too much beef, not even enough. Why wasn't Raul satisfied to follow in his father's footsteps and, if he wished, expand their present land holdings in the Mato Grosso, instead of risking his youthful years by going deeply into debt on a venture that was only for idiots?

Over and beyond all that, Afonso's deep pride in the importance of his bloodline was at stake. He was ruefully aware that his younger son, Eduardo, did not have it in him to make any notable contribution to the family worthiness. Raul was the only one with enough drive and initiative to add honor to the family name—if he could be prevented from undertaking harebrained schemes that would only diminish its luster. Family names were badges of prestige, of integrity, to be revered and preserved for all time.

His own full name, Afonso Sequiera e de Azvedo de Carvalho, was an example of the Brazilian custom of adding surnames from members of the family ancestral tree who were held in highest esteem. Sequiera had been his grandmother's family name; Azvedo was his mother's. This was called the *parentela* system, a method of retaining not only the proud heritage of the patriarchal side, but also of honoring those of distinction on the mother's side. Sons and daughters were free to ignore the surnames of those lesser members of the clan and select only the more exalted surnames, even if but distantly related, to gain all the prestige possible. Such accretions of names had more than mere snob value; the more illustrious the names, the more doors they opened.

Afonso had married a de Corvo—another distinguished name—and both Raul and Eduardo were free to add it to their full names if they wished. Raul had declined, considering it too ostentatious to use anything but the parental name de Carvalho—another example of his intransigence when it came to family custom!

Still pacing, Afonso glanced up at the row of family portraits adorning the long wall of the entrance hall. Beginning with his grandfather, Jorge de Carvalho—the first of the family line to settle in Brazil—all members of the family down to the present day were portrayed, including Eduardo and Raul.

Afonso paused in front of the portrait of Jorge. Something about the face, the faintly mocking smile, seemed vaguely puzzling. In truth, Afonso rarely bothered to look at the painting of Jorge because he detested everything he knew about this particular ancestor, and he only kept the portrait hanging in a place of prominence so that he could document the family bloodline. And after all, Jorge had founded the family fortune.

Founded it on crime. Jorge, who had fled in disgrace from his homeland of Portugal to escape punishment for killing a man, had been the scapegrace member of the distinguished Portuguese de Carvalho clan. He was a blackguard, an adventurer, a ruthless murderer, and Afonso bitterly resented being descended from his seed.

Suddenly it came to him that what had struck him when he glanced at the portrait was the mocking smile. During his last serious talk with Raul, Afonso had seen the identical expression on his son's face. Raul was now about the same age as Jorge had been when the portrait had been painted, and Raul had grown to resemble Jorge remarkably. The same eyes, nose, chin, the same air of private scorn when it came to the opinions of others. How odd that he had never noted it before. As he continued pacing, he began to wonder, could it be that some of the ruthless, adventuresome traits of Jorge had surfaced in Raul? But *não!* It was unworthy of him to harbor such thoughts about his son. Still . . .

The voice of a servant obtruded. *"Patrão*—the plane is landing. *Senhor* Raul will soon arrive."

"Bom. Take a jeep out to the landing field at once."

Puffing gently on his cigar, he made his final decision. It behooved him as a fair man to be as charitable as possible. He would first do his paternal duty by using careful, cool reasoning to dissuade Raul from going ahead with his ridiculous scheme.

If that failed, he would exercise his authority to quash the whole reckless venture.

He glanced again at the portrait and again felt unease. The resemblance of Raul to Jorge de Carvalho was indeed striking.

SIX

Except for Jorge de Carvalho's hot blood and a freakish chain of circumstances, the Brazilian branch of the de Carvalho clan might never have existed.

It was in October of 1889 when Luis Felipe, king of Portugal, also holding titles as king of the Algarve, duke of Oporto, and duke of Saxony—and perhaps overly exhausted from such a plethora of royal responsibilities—dropped dead at the age of fifty-one. His eldest son, Carlos, age twenty-six, promptly succeeded to the throne, thereby indirectly setting in motion events leading to the founding of Raul's distinguished family.

The beginning was not all that distinguished, arising as it did from a sordid duel over a beauteous but lowborn tavern wench. One of the amorous antagonists was Henrique da Fonseca, a young nobleman and dear friend of the new king. The other was Jorge, the profligate son of a highly esteemed rich family. His reputation for fast living and carousing with loose women was the talk of Lisbon. His only talents—aside from lavish spending and bedchamber acrobatics— were his dueling skills with sword or pistol. So good was he that even Henrique, well known as an excellent swordsman, quickly fell mortally wounded under Jorge's cold steel, and a grieving but irate king at once issued a royal edict for de Carvalho's arrest and trial for murder—almost certain to mean execution.

Jorge de Carvalho wasted not a moment on the uncertainties of angry justice. He fled that same day, paying dearly in gold coins for passage on a Brazilian-bound frigate. Brazil at the time was a Portuguese possession with an emperor of its own, but still under

Portuguese rule. Jorge hoped to find a haven of safety among the noblemen of the Brazilian royal court.

However, owing to the inexorable workings of destiny, or, perhaps, simple cause and effect, Jorge arrived in Rio on November 15, 1890, exactly one year to the day after the Brazilian populace—in open revolt against the new king of Portugal—had liquidated the Brazilian empire and declared Brazil a free country. His Majesty Dom Pedro de Alcántara, the emperor of Brazil, abdicated to save his neck, and taking over military rule as chief of the provisional government of the just-born Republic of Brazil was Marshal Manoel Deodoro da Fonseca.

Fonseca, the strict new military ruler, was a relative of the very same Henrique da Fonseca that Jorge had killed in Portugal.

Fearing vengeance, Jorge turned to the only tools he had at his command: his sword, his pistol, his wits, and an adventurous spirit. History is vague at this point, but it is believed that Jorge fled as an exile to the trackless wastes of the jungle and the savannas and joined the *Caudilhismo,* the dreaded guerrilla bandits, soon becoming a chieftain of his own band.

The seven horsemen rode slowly in single file over the winding jungle *estrada,* a narrow trail cleared by the *seringueiros,* the rubber collectors. For hours they had been riding, crossing streams and swamps, breaking through brush with a rustling and snapping of branches that sent flocks of birds shrieking into the air ahead of them and monkeys whistling and howling from the treetops. It was getting late in the afternoon, and the normal greenish haze of day—for no sunlight ever penetrated the fantastic overhang to the jungle floor—was deepening into murky twilight.

The second rider, a big muscular black man, grumbled, "*Chefe,* I don't like this. I think it was a mistake to come. Already we have had to shoot three deadly snakes hanging from the trees and a caiman skulking in the water hole where I went to drink. Soon it will be dark. How will we know what awaits us?"

The lead rider twisted in his saddle to look back. He was clad mostly in leather, with boots, spurs, and two ammunition belts, one looped over a shoulder, the other around his waist with a holstered revolver. He wore the wide-brimmed hat of a *vaqueiro,* and his scraggly bearded face was burned so dark by the sun and the elements that one might have taken him for an Indian, except for the hard blue eyes. On his lips was a mocking smile.

"Your job is not to think, Nilo," said Jorge de Carvalho. "However, if you wish,.you are free to turn back and we will proceed without you."

Nilo cast a brief angry look backward at the murky trail and was silent.

They continued through the green labyrinth. The trees, with their enormous twisting roots, seemed to grow more threatening. Thick vines with immense leaves crept up the tree trunks. Palm leaves long enough to roof a small cottage jutted overhead. Everything was oversized; giant plants striving against other giant plants in competitive harmony. A silent steam rose from the ground, a tomblike silence pervaded the atmosphere, broken only now and then by the whistlings and chatterings of birds.

Nilo, who was more accustomed to the open prairies of Urucuia, the steppes of the Jequitinhonha, and the far-flung grasslands of the *sertão,* ventured more grumbling words. "I liked it better back where we could see the sky and the sun and the moon."

"And where our enemies sometimes see even better than we can?" Jorge retorted with a sour grin. His reference was to a trap they had fallen into several days ago that had almost led to their capture by a company of *soldados de cavalaria* out on special detail to rout out bandits that had been terrorizing the countryside. Jorge and his men had escaped, but at the cost of nearly half their band.

"The dangers there, I think, are less than here. This

jungle—*pitiú!* It stinks! Where do you expect to find jewels or gold in this foul place?"

Jorge wheeled his horse off to one side and stopped next to a strange silvery-barked tree. Its strangeness was primarily in the way the bark had been incised with a series of spiral knife cuts slanting downward in a fish-bone pattern. At the base of the last cut was a small tin cup attached to the tree by a lump of wet clay, and an enormous drop of milk-white latex was oozing into the cup. Jorge pointed.

"*Veja*—there's our gold. White gold."

Nilo scrunched his brow. "*Não compreendo, chefe.*"

"You will soon enough."

As they rode on, the numbers of silver-barked wild hevea trees increased. All of the trunks had been heavily scored by knife cuts until the beautiful bark was scarred and warty, and rubber sap was oozing into cups. The upper trunks were no larger than a man's waist, but where the bark had been incised year after year by rubber tappers, the trees had bloated out to grotesque shapes.

Soon the men began seeing scatterings of *seringueiros* busy at their job of rubber collecting. They were dressed similarly in white shirts, white shorts, hats, and sandals woven of dried palm fronds by their womenfolk. Each had slung from his shoulder a long-handled *machadinho* for cutting the bark and a gourd of lemon water for quenching thirst. Jorge reined in near several of them.

"Which direction is it and how far to the *fazenda* of the *seringalista?*"

The man spoken to, after a brief frightened glance at the armed men, doffed his hat and bowed jerkily. "Straight ahead on the *estrada, capitão,* about two kilometers."

Without a word of thanks, Jorge spurred his horse on.

Manoel Sequiera, with his wife Dolores and their three children, Emilio, Cláudio, and Alzira, were seated around the long rosewood table at their evening *jantar* when they heard the drumming of approaching hoofbeats.

The father stiffened in his chair. "Who can that be?" he said. It wasn't neighbors, he was sure, because the nearest one was ten miles away and feared to ride the jungle trails. Besides, from the sound, there were too many horses.

"Perhaps," said the wife, "they are *soldados.*"

"Why would the *soldados* come here, hundreds of miles from the nearest town?" As they well knew, the forest was almost impenetrable on horseback. Difficult even for one wise in the ways of the jungle and with knowledge of the few trails. Only a rider very brave, very foolish, or very desperate would risk so much danger and discomfort to come so far. It was better to travel the usual way, by river and streams in a canoe, and then to proceed the rest of the way on foot.

An authoritative knocking resounded against the heavy oak door.

"Perhaps," suggested Cláudio, the elder son, "we should get our guns. They could be the *bandidos.*"

"Don't be foolish. No *bandido* would come this far. There's nothing to rob except our heavy *bolãos* of rubber, which would pay them too little to carry away."

Striding to the door, Manoel pulled it open.

Three men stood just outside the door facing him, and four others were in the background, still mounted. All but the slender one in front, apparently the leader, had rifles slung over their shoulders.

"*Boa noite, senhor,*" greeted the slender one. "You are the *fazendeiro* here?"

"I am the owner, yes," Manoel said guardedly. The slender leather-clad man had spoken courteously enough in an educated voice, but the pale blue eyes were chilling. Next to him was a big soot-black *preto* with a frightening face despite his idiotic grin. The third man was a scrawny Indian with the eyes of a lizard. He wore a crimson rag around his black hair, badly soiled garments, a long knife under a snakeskin belt, and fine leather boots. He was grinning too, as if to show his yellowed teeth that were filed to sharp points.

"What is your name?"

Manoel told him.

"And how many *alqueires* do you own?"

"Five thousand," Manoel said, puzzled, wondering if this strange and obviously educated man was looking for land to buy. If so, he could find it anywhere in the jungle, cheap. His own five thousand *alqueires*, equal to over a quarter million acres, was a relatively modest tract that had cost him only five *contos de réis*. But of course with the market price of raw rubber going up . . .

"And much of your land is heavily forested with the hevea rubber trees, is it not?"

Manoel frowned. "Why are you asking all of these questions, *senhor?*"

The blue-eyed man wore a mocking smile. "Because, *senhor*, as I must regretfully inform you, I am the new owner of this *fazenda*."

"You are certainly joking, *senhor!* I have my land grant from the government. It is valid."

The slender man shrugged, speaking softly. "But the government is many hundreds of miles away, *senhor*. I am here. My men are all well armed. If you are wise, you will sign over the papers of ownership to me."

"*Não, senhor, não!*" Manoel cried out hoarsely, at the same time striving to slam the door shut, a futile effort against the combined weight of the three outside. They crowded in.

The son Claúdio rushed forward with a rifle. "*Saia!* Get out before I—".

A sharp blast of gunfire silenced him. He stumbled, his rifle clattering to the floor, then fell with agonizing slowness, as if resisting the pull of gravity, one hand clutching at the blossoming crimson liquid coming from a dark hole in his neck. The mother screamed. The younger boy and his sister huddled together in terror. Manoel let out a bellow of rage and pain and knelt beside his dying son.

"Murderer! Filthy animals!"

"The papers—the ownership papers—bring them to me."

"*Nunca*—never will I sign over my ownership to such beasts!"

The blue-eyed man shrugged. "It matters not. I do not need the papers to take ownership." Turning, he snapped an order to his henchmen. "Take care of the parents and the other boy. Throw the bodies to the piranhas. But leave the girl to me."

Even as the shots were being fired among screams of terror, Jorge was dragging the hysterical seventeen-year-old Alzira into one of the bedrooms.

A half hour later he rose from the bed, rearranging his clothing as he looked down at her naked body and the virginal blood staining the sheets. Her head was turned, sobbing into the pillow.

"Your tears are a waste, little one," he said. "Tomorrow I will send a man to bring a priest and make you my legal wife."

The son that was born to Jorge de Carvalho and his captive wife Alzira was a strange one. Never was he known to cry. Even when he began to crawl, and soon to walk—or if he happened to get in the way of his father and get roughly booted aside—he never made a sound. The bright blue eyes merely fixed on his father and followed Jorge's every move, the boy's face utterly expressionless. Sometimes Jorge wondered if there was something wrong with the child's mind. Alzira wondered, too, because often she would sweep him up in her arms to comfort him, but young Júlio was not the cuddly type, and he escaped from his mother's arms at the first chance.

But Júlio was a healthy child. And smart. At the age of two, he could speak long sentences when he chose. Though Alzira guarded him jealously, she could not keep him out of the hands of de Carvalho's rough band of *pistoleiros,* who doted on the child. His stoicism was to them a sure sign of manliness, and they played crude games with him—tossing him like a ball from one to the other, pretending not to catch his fall until the last moment—still, the child never let out a cry.

When Júlio was four, Jorge gave his men instructions. "You, Nilo—put my son on a horse and let him grow up in the saddle. Give him a gun as soon as he can pull the trigger, and teach him how to shoot. Train him in the use of the knife and sword.

"And you, Xuxú—teach him all the wiles of the Indians, all about the jungle, all about the animals and the dangers, how to use the poisons, how to use the bow and arrow and blowgun. Teach him these things until he knows as much as you do."

Jorge began importing tutors from Manaus to teach his son reading, writing, mathematics, geography, and other academic subjects he deemed suitable for a young gentleman. The tutors were of the best, and they were paid extravagantly.

Jorge could well afford it, for now the rubber boom was at its peak, and Brazil, the only country in the world where the wild rubber tree was known to grow, had a world monopoly in a fast-expanding market that was begging for all the rubber it could get. Owners of previously poor rubber plantations were becoming overnight millionaires. Little attention was paid to land titles at that time, so Jorge and other bold land robbers were able to lay claim to thousands of additional jungle acres, and no one dared dispute it except at the risk of their lives. Jorge now had fifty *pistoleiros*—hired killers—working for him. They were necessary for recruiting his army of rubber collectors and keeping them under discipline.

His method was to take his pack of killers to one of the Indian tribes, lavishly distribute cheap gifts, then get the Indians drunk on raw alcohol. After a day or two, the party was over, and while the *pistoleiros* surrounded them with guns, Jorge made a speech. To pay for the gifts, the tribe must henceforth gather balls of *borracha*, rubber.

A lesson in terror drove the point home. Those Indians who tried to give back the beads and other junk were tortured to death; some were burned alive, others had their limbs hacked off and were left for the insects.

More terror awaited the rubber collectors who failed to fulfill their quota—which was one hundred kilograms of coagulated latex every moon. One sport was to tie the Indian to a tree as a target. The first *pistoleiro* to shoot off his penis got a prize. Soon the Indians were so well trained that if the needle of the scales didn't reach the quota mark, they would throw themselves facedown for a whipping—the most merciful punishment they could hope for.

The fact that slavery had been abolished in Brazil in 1888 made no difference, for the government seat was two thousand miles away and the law was rarely enforced in any case. Without slave labor, such fantastic rubber fortunes could not have been made, and such wealth could afford to ignore the laws. Manaus, once a poor backwater village, became the center of rubber trading and in a few short years mushroomed into a fabulous city of palaces and grand mansions designed in the European style and built with materials imported at great cost: glazed tiles from Lisbon, hand-carved doors and stairways from Italy, Empire furniture from France, and rich paintings. The sudden fortunes created a hunger for instant culture; world-famed singers, actors, and actresses such as Sarah Bernhardt were imported to perform in the Teatro Amazonas. The nouveaux riches, despite a glut of servants in their palatial homes, sent their laundry to Paris. Indolent wives didn't bother to have their costly Parisian gowns cleaned but simply threw them out and kept replacing them with new ones from Paris.

Young Júlio knew little of all this—except that his father spent lavishly to enlarge and refurnish the *fazenda*.

Jorge also imported a steady stream of gaudily
gowned expensive whores. They came by riverboat
from Manaus for most of the distance, and the rest of
the way in a small carriage over the narrow jungle
trail used for hauling rubber. Usually they stayed
about a week—often several at a time—until they
were replaced by new ones. Jorge spent little time in
the saddle now and much time romping with his
trollops in bed. Or wherever he felt the urge: on a
living room sofa, on the carpet, even on the dining
room table. He was like a sexual drunkard who could
never get enough.

It mattered not that Alzira, the servants, or Júlio
were exposed to his depraved behavior. Was he not
the master of the house in a Brazilian patriarchal
culture that was at the time openly and even proudly
polygamous? As for Alzira, she was not neglected.
After a session with one of the whores, he often
dragged her to bed, finding stimulation in the revul-
sion on her face when he embraced her.

As for his son, he thought it was good for the boy to
observe such realities. Jorge himself had lost his virginity at the age of twelve, and since Júlio was now at
that age, it was high time for Júlio to be initiated, as
part of "becoming a man." Júlio was invited, then
ordered, to consort with any of the whores that ap-
pealed to him.

But Júlio was not interested. No amount of coaxing,
scolding, or direct orders accompanied by paternal
slaps and kicks could force him to touch a female. He
had heard and seen too much. He had heard his
father cursing over the discovery that he had con-
tracted the dread pox syphilis, then ordering his men
to bring the traditional cure—mercury and a young
black virgin to "cleanse his blood." Júlio had heard
the black lass sobbing after she had been used by his
father and then turned over to the *pistoleiros* for their
enjoyment. He had heard his mother crying softly
after learning that she, too, had been infected with the
same disease by her husband, and for her there was

no cure. Thereafter Jorge shunned her, kept her locked in a remote room of the manse. Júlio had heard and seen all sorts of corrupt sexual antics. For him, sex was indescribably vile.

Jorge was terribly worried. Could it be that he, the most masculine of men, could have begotten a son who was one of those despicable creatures—neither male nor female?

Xuxú offered advice: *"Chefe,* my people have much wisdom in such matters. We have fertility rites to turn young girls into full women and rites of manhood that quickly make strong men from the weakest boys."

Jorge was ready to grab at any straws. "Xuxú, find a friendly tribe, and arrange to have my son go through the manhood rites as soon as possible."

Júlio had glorious visions. In the small *tapiri*—a rude Indian hut thatched with banana fronds—he lay on a huge animal skin that was stretched tightly between four stakes in the ground. He had the sensation of floating through a dream. Beautiful pictures in brilliant colors drifted indolently through his head. Exotic fantasies of things he'd never seen and knew could not exist, like strange melodies to delight the eye as well as the ear, composed of fluid colors, the sounds of winds, rippling streams, laughing female voices.

Júlio knew they were only artful creations of his mind, caused by the juice of the datura mixed with the juices of other jungle fruits and given to him to drink from a small hollow horn by the *wishinú,* the tribal medicine man. It was the same potion given to warriors and hunters to lift them to a dreamlike trance that enabled them to commune with the spirits and foresee the future.

It had also caused all the pain to leave his body, which now seemed as numbed as if his flesh had ceased to exist and it was only his mind floating around in the *tapiri* where he had been resting since last night's ordeal of the dance.

For a week Júlio had been going through the mandatory endurance tests as part of the manhood rites. First he'd been made to find a wasp nest, smash it with his fist, then suffer the angry stings and the fever that followed. Afterwards, his body and face still swollen from the stings, he'd been sent off with the warriors to prove his hunting prowess with the bow and arrow and the blowgun. For several days they had hunted and slept in the jungle until he finally found and killed a jaguar.

When Júlio was brought back to the village, the sharp teeth of the jaguar were used to scratch his legs until they bled profusely, to assure that he would grow up strong. Then the warriors tied up the foreskin of his penis, cut off most of his hair, and painted his body black with the juices of the unripe *genipapo*. His face and feet were painted red with dye from the *urucú* plant. Then he was given a red macaw feather diadem to wear on his head, and he was commanded to dance for the next twenty-four hours to the music of rattles, bamboo ground-thumpers, and the chanting of the women of the village.

That had ended last night, and exhausted from the ordeal of nearly a week of pain, almost no sleep, and very little food, he had been brought to the *tapiri*, where he fell instantly into a deep sleep.

He was awakened in the morning by several women who were ornamented with necklaces, belts, and garters of coiled shell beads. They were quite old, at least twenty or twenty-five, but all were smiling and pleasant as they bathed him, put ointments on his cut legs—the swelling from the wasp stings was by this time gone—and brought him clay bowls of sweet potatoes, peanuts, pineapple, mangoes, and palm fruits.

He ate but lightly, finding he had lost his hunger. It was because of his growing fear. Until now he had endured everything bravely, but this final phase was most terrifying, for he knew that one of these women, picked from among the most respected wives in the tribe, would be selected—as a great honor—to teach him the rites of sex. Which one would it be?

Then had come the *wishinú* with his hypnotic potion of datura, after which all his pains and fears had melted away.

Now, as twilight was thickening in the *tapiri*, the dim light from the entry was briefly cut off by one of the women returning. He recognized her as the youngest of the women, the one called Quechua, the name of a plumlike fruit. She had smooth skin the color of honey and snuff, rounded hips and breasts, and a comely face. Except for shell earrings, gold bracelets, and intricate geometric designs painted here and there on her torso in bright colors, she was completely naked. Her skin gleamed from having anointed herself with sweet-smelling palm oil, and she carried a small wooden bowl containing *aninga* fruit and a small clay cup. Kneeling, she extended the cup and commanded, "Drink."

Júlio drank, and at once he felt a change in his body. The numbness slowly decreased, to be replaced by a flow of warmth, a surging of strength that tingled pleasurably through every part of him. Meanwhile Quechua had picked up one of the *aningas*, a fruit from a white aquatic plant that Júlio had often seen growing luxuriantly on the banks of the river. Xuxú had told him that all Indians knew that the plant had a "strong soul": when it was sliced off with a knife, it would grow back quickly, and because it had a banana shape similar to a man's erected penis, it was used to increase the size, strength, and reproductive energies of the male genital organ.

Smiling mischievously, Quechua began gently beating at Júlio's penis with the *aninga*, softly chanting a melody of simple lines, each one ending with an expressively exclaimed, *"Ahow!"* At the same time, her free hand was stroking him with knowing fingers in the most private of places. Normally this would have embarrassed or angered him, but now he was aware only of the sensations, the most wonderful he had ever experienced. He wanted her never to stop. She was so nice.

Finally, smiling widely, her eyes shining like black gems, she put aside the *aninga* and crouched over him with spread thighs. Caressing fingers guided his greatly enlarged, stiffened penis to the lips of her vagina. Slowly, softly, she lowered herself, making a series of little birdlike exclamations of pleasure as their male and female organs locked deeply together.

For Júlio, the sensations were indescribably pleasurable, accelerating to excruciating heights as her hips rolled and churned against his crotch, and when finally the exquisite delirium of his climax went shooting up his spine and all through his body like fire and lightning, he almost swooned from sheer ecstasy.

For three days and nights Júlio and Quechua did not leave the *tapiri*. They barely partook of the food and drink brought to them but mostly just made love, slept, awakened again to start all over with new variations and positions that Quechua taught him. When she had taught him everything she knew and he was too exhausted to continue, her assignment was finished.

She slipped out on the third night while he slept, never to see him again.

Xuxú and Nilo came, leading an extra horse, to bring him home. Júlio had lost weight; the rounded boyishness of his face was gone, replaced by a lean tightness.

Nilo noted the changes with a shrewd grin. He chuckled. "So at last you have found pleasure in a woman. You liked it, hunh?"

Júlio said nothing.

"The Indians said you were brave and strong in the endurance tests. They said you would make a great warrior. Your father will be pleased."

Júlio looked at the big *preto*. "Nilo, let me wear your gun."

"Why do you want my gun?"

"I want to practice."

"Practice? You already shoot better than I do, better than Xuxú, maybe even as good as your father."

"But I want to shoot even better than my father."

Silently Nilo unbuckled his gun belt and revolver and handed it to Júlio, who hung it around his shoulders because the belt was too large to draw up around his slim waist.

When they got to the *fazenda*, Júlio walked into the vast living room and saw his father seated at the dining table with one of his latest whores, a gaudy young blonde from Manaus.

"Ah, Júlio, so you are back!" Jorge called out jovially. "Did you learn everything I sent you to learn?"

"Yes, father, I've learned everything." Indeed he had learned far more than he could have anticipated. He had learned to his astonishment that male passion for a woman's body could be beautiful; that even a good woman could offer herself in a loving, kind way, giving her body with the purity of a holy sacrament.

That it did not have to be selfish, vile, or hateful, as his father made it with his whores, or turned into bestial cruelty, as toward his mother.

"So now you are a man!" said Jorge.

"Yes, I am a man."

"As a reward, you may take Gini to your room and enjoy her for as long as you like." Jorge indicated the blonde, who fluffed a hand through her hair and looked at Júlio with a practiced smile on her carmined lips.

"The only reward I want, father, is to see you dead. But I'll give you one chance. Draw your gun."

Jorge started laughing, thinking it some kind of joke, until he saw the look on his son's face. Júlio's hand was lingering close to the holstered gun slung over one shoulder.

"You crazy young fool! What are you saying? I'll have you horsewhipped. I'll—"

"Your last chance, father!"

Jorge's hand flashed down, and the booming *whock* of a large-caliber revolver filled the room.

Jorge was propelled backward by the impact of the heavy slug, blood from the ragged hole in his forehead already dribbling down over his frozen expression of disbelief.

Even as Jorge was falling, Júlio whirled toward Xuxú, whose hand was hovering with uncertainty near the butt of his gun.

"Any objections, Xuxú?"

The Indian let his hand drop away quickly. "*Não.*"

Júlio turned toward the *preto.* "And you, Nilo?"

"Never do I interfere in a fight between relatives."

"*Bom.* Now take this slut to the river and put her on the first boat back to Manaus."

"*Sim, chefe.* Right away."

The three horses and riders stopped on a hillock. For most of the day they had been riding through grass so tall it brushed against their mounts' shoulders. The youngest of the three, a lean and sinewy young man with hard blue eyes and a shock of wavy dark hair beneath the brim of his sombrero, showed white teeth in a smile.

"Looks like the kind of land I'm looking for, Nilo."

The black man took off his hat and scratched his woolly hair, which was now salted with gray. "It's sure more to my liking than the jungle, *chefe.* Here there's plenty of sun and sky."

Xuxú, the scrawny Indian whose scraggly hair was turning white, said nothing. He just kept chewing on his cud of maté while his alert black eyes swiveled slowly over the waving grass and the dottings of cattle here and there. For several days they had been riding through the wildest country of the Mato Grosso, circling the huge Pantanal area, which was largely swamp, fording brown, piranha-infested streams, skirting vast purplish lakes, but mostly riding through grass, grass, grass. Today was the first time they had seen cattle, the only evidence that humans must be near.

"Watch sharp for the *fazenda*," said the young man, giving his horse a touch of a spur. "It shouldn't be far away."

Júlio de Carvalho was finished with his rubber plantation. It had made him very rich, but in the year 1915 the Brazilian rubber boom had dwindled until it was no longer profitable to collect rubber. Many thousands of seeds of the hevea tree had been smuggled out of Brazil and planted extensively in Ceylon, Malaysia, and Indonesia, and once these efficient new rubber plantations had reached maturity, the crude and laborious rubber collecting system in the jungle of Brazil could no longer compete. The rubber monopoly was ended. Manaus, once the richest city in the world, again became a poor backwater community.

Júlio's mother, Alzira, had suffered the full virulence of her syphilitic infection. Quickly the dread disease had reached stage four, reaching her brain, bringing on insanity, and two years later her agonies were mercifully ended by death.

Now, in his mid-twenties, his rubber fortune intact, Júlio was seeking new ventures.

The Granja do Sol, "rancho of the sun," was the most imposing *fazenda* Júlio had ever seen. A uniformed black servant met him at the door, then summoned the master. Dom Octaviano de Azvedo was an impressive man with graying hair and a fierce mustachio. He was clad in the usual leather breeches and vest of the *vaqueiros*, and his manner was courtly, his voice hospitable as he invited Júlio in and inquired as to his errand.

"*Senhor*, I do not wish to impose on your time. It is only necessary to find if you would consider selling your ranch. If not, I must proceed on my journey, as I am seeking land such as yours to begin a cattle ranch of my own."

Dom Octaviano's eyebrows arched. "You do not look like a fool, *senhor*, so I presume you speak in earnest. In answer to your question, no, I would not sell my property. Never. But I could advise you. Perhaps you do not know what a risk you take in buying land for the cattle business. Why not rest here for the evening, and I shall tell you all that I know about the region and where it is best for raising cattle."

"You are very kind, *senhor*, but I could not presume—"

"*Absurdo!* It is too close to darkness for you to travel on. Besides, my wife and daughter, who rarely see visitors, would make my life miserable if I allowed such a personable young man to leave before you have dined with us and spent at least one night as our guest."

"But, *senhor*, I also have two of my men with me."

"They will be provided with food and lodging with my *vaqueiros*."

Júlio was a bit awed by the vastness of the manse, the richness of the paintings, the tapestries, the furnishings, and the book-laden shelves. The warmth and cordiality of the queenly *Senhora* Rosa de Azvedo charmed him, but most enchanting of all was the daughter Luísa, a lovely dark-haired girl with luminous eyes that at times seemed gray, at times blue, and sometimes green, depending on the lighting. Although, in accordance with proper custom, she spoke little to the male guest, her expression told much. After the first electric impact of their eyes meeting, Júlio felt that he had known her from somewhere, perhaps in one of his vagrant dreams.

At dinner the main dish served was the *especialidade* of the house, grilled *pacú*, a local fish known as a great delicacy. Though there were numerous servants, it was Luísa herself who undertook to serve the *pacú* to Júlio on a silver platter.

Júlio much enjoyed the dinner, but Luísa looked at

him with a hurt expression. "But, *senhor,* you have not eaten the heads of the *pacú,* which I myself cooked especially. The heads are the most delicious part."

Obligingly Júlio ate the heads and commented extravagantly on how tasty they were.

The next morning Júlio rose early, thanked the parents for their hospitality, and asked them to convey his respects to Luísa, who was nowhere in sight.

But when he went to saddle his horse, she was there waiting.

"You are leaving so soon?" she asked.

"I wish it were not necessary. I have much business to attend to elsewhere, but I shall always carry pleasant memories of my stay here and of meeting so lovely a young lady."

She smiled. "It will not be necessary to carry such memories for long, *senhor.* You may come back anytime you wish."

"I fear that may not be possible, *senhorita.*"

"It will be," she said confidently. "You will be back soon. I know. *Até mais ver.* Till we meet again."

Brooding, Júlio rode off with his men.

After a while, Nilo intruded into his thoughts. "You seem sad, *chefe.*"

"I feel strange, Nilo, as if I were coming down with a sickness."

"Is it possible that last night you were served *pacú* at dinner?"

"As a matter of fact, yes. Why do you ask?"

"Because, *chefe,* it is very dangerous."

"You mean poisonous?"

"Not poison. Worse. I was warned by the *vaqueiros* last night that a stranger should never eat the head of a *pacú.*"

"*Que diabo!* Why not?"

"Because when a stranger eats the head of the *pacú* he will soon marry a Mato Grosso girl."

Júlio returned to the Granja do Sol within two weeks, and soon after that his engagement to Luísa de Azvedo was announced. In the privacy of their own quarters, Dom Octaviano and Rosa danced with joy, and a few months later gave Júlio and Luísa a most lavish wedding that was attended by relatives and neighbors from hundreds of miles around.

Exactly nine months and two days later, Afonso Sequiera e de Azvedo de Carvalho was born.

SEVEN

As the Learjet started losing altitude, the drone of its motors lessening, Raul peered out of a window and saw the distant speck that would rapidly enlarge to the recognizable dimensions of Granja do Sol, his birthplace. A wave of nostalgia tinged with sadness swept through him. Homecoming always brought a flood of memories of his happy boyhood, especially of the long hours spent riding through the grasslands with his grandfather, Júlio.

He had adored old Júlio, who had been equally fond of his older grandson. Júlio's tragic death a few years ago at the age of eighty-two had been quite a blow, for the old man had died of a broken neck after being thrown from a wild young bronco he was trying to subdue. Grandmother Luísa had died of a broken heart about a year later.

Along with Raul's fond memories of his grandparents was an emotion of quite another kind: a tensing dread of the coming confrontation with his father, whose support he so badly needed for going ahead with the alcohol project. Afonso had inherited all of Júlio's toughness but very little of his venturesome spirit. However, the fact that the hardheaded businessman da Silva was willing to invest in the alcohol venture should surely convince Afonso that Raul's plans were sound. Raul was pinning his hopes on it.

The jet banked grandly over a vast purplish lake, swooped past a brown river coursing crookedly through green lowlands spotted with brilliant masses of flowers, then zoomed down sharply until it was scarcely a hundred feet above a sea of waving pampas grass. Ungainly cattle as wild as the Mato Grosso itself went plunging in all directions from the plane and its ear-piercing scream. A scattering of *vaqueiros* spurred their mounts in a brief vain race with the sky monster, shouting and shooting at the clouds with drawn revolvers.

Raul and Pio laughed. It was their usual welcome.

Moments later the jet was a mile past, touching down on the landing strip.

Braz was waiting in the jeep for Raul. Braz was a grizzled man with a heavy drooping moustache adorning a wrinkled, weather-worn face. He wore leather garments that had weathered three decades and looked it. As did the .44 revolver, its handle worn to a dull polish.

"How is my father feeling today?" said Raul as he and Braz gripped hands. "I have important business to discuss, and I hope I haven't picked one of his bad days."

Braz shook his head somberly. "I would advise that you speak softly and with care." Then he shrugged and grinned. "On the other hand, he is after all almost my age, and *bem passado*." This was a *vaqueiro* idiom meaning "well done." "If you are careful, I think he will keep his temper under control."

"You think he's angry with me?"

Braz shrugged again. "*Quem sabe?*"

The ornately carved front doors swung open even before Raul had crossed the wide flagstoned *átrio*. Two Indian servants uniformed in pink cotton blouses and pale blue trousers had anticipated his approach from the windows.

Raul greeted them pleasantly and continued down the long marble-floored entrance hall past century-old tapestries, statuaries, a decorative frieze surmounting both walls, and the row of family portraits. He walked through the central hall, the reception room, the banquet room; past the music room, the long unused playroom, the yellow room, the green room, the family dining room, and the billiard room, finally reaching the study, where the head servant had told him his father was waiting.

Afonso was seated at his desk. The study was floored with dark mahogany, inset at the borders with mosaics of Dutch tile, the only frivolous touch. All the rest was overwhelmingly masculine: beamed ceiling, oversized leather-covered seats and couches, rugged bookcases weighted with ancient volumes against the dark wainscoting, a gory painting of two bulls in battle, a coiled *vaqueiro* whip, and a collection of old guns and swords.

Rising with a proper paternal smile, Afonso came forward to embrace Raul and exchange perfunctory greetings. He gestured toward a chair.

"You will sit, please, while we have a talk."

Sighing involuntarily, Raul seated himself, knowing from his father's tone that rough sailing was ahead. Afonso remained standing, and with his hands clasped behind his back, he began pacing, glaring at the floor.

"I had a call from Dom Monteiro, who is part of the consortium headed by da Silva. He advised me that a large loan to you has been approved. I find it very disturbing."

"But why, father? It is purely a business matter."

"You are inconsiderate enough to ask why? Da Silva and Monteiro are old friends. You not only embarrass me by going to them, but in doing so you advertise to all Brazil that my son runs to others for money that he cannot get from his own father."

"But, father, you were the first one I discussed it with, and you turned me down. You said you strongly disapproved of the whole project."

"So I did, and so I do yet. The idea of an energy plantation, or whatever you wish to call it, is craziness. At best, it is as big a risk as the gambling wheel, with no guarantee of ever winning. If you took this risk and failed, you would become a laughingstock. You would make our name something to ridicule in Brazil."

"But surely if da Silva and the others are willing to lend me money—"

Afonso laughed harshly. "What have they got to lose? They get high interest and the property as collateral. Even so, I doubt that they would have been so ready to lend to you did they not know I would be honor bound to pay your debts, even if it impoverished me."

"I'm sorry you have so little faith in me, father."

"It is not a question of faith or lack of faith in you; it is your scheme for squeezing alcohol out of trees that I deplore! For such a silly enterprise, you are also giving up your responsibilities as manager of my export offices in Rio—leaving it all to your inexperienced brother. Have you considered the great inconvenience it will cause me?"

"Eduardo's inexperience is no fault of mine. I have tried hard to teach him everything about the business, but thus far his interest has been lukewarm. My hope is that when given the opportunity to shoulder full responsibility, he will meet the challenge. In any case, our top people are very capable. They will help him develop."

Afonso threw up his hands as if putting himself at the mercy of God and the fates. "Why, why—I keep asking myself that—why is it that you cannot be satisfied with doing things the way our family always has? Someday you will be the master of Granja do Sol. You will have to carry on with the cattle, which are getting more profitable all the time. I ask you, I beg of you, I implore you one last time: give up this crazy alcohol plantation idea!"

Raul squirmed and tensed inwardly. He loved and respected his father. He wanted with all his heart to please him, win his approval, but all the dreams he had nourished for so many years were too insistent. He remembered his grandfather Júlio first telling him about the old rubber plantation, that it was still maintained by a skeleton crew because he was convinced that someday it would come into its own again. The world was changing fast, Júlio had said, and the day would arrive when new ways would be found to

74

exploit the riches of the jungle land. It was then that he had confided that someday the rubber plantation and its million acres of land would belong to Raul, and that it would be up to him to find ways of making it profitable.

With great difficulty, Raul spoke. "I am sorry, father, but I cannot give you the answer that you want."

Afonso's eyes chilled. "Then I will give it for you. A codicil to my father's will—something I prevailed upon him to add—empowers me to change the bequest to you: if in my mature judgment it is more economically prudent to sell the rubber plantation at its current appraised value rather than permit you to risk money to operate it, I am free to do so. All money from the sale, of course, would belong to you. Therefore, I have made my decision—"

A soft feminine voice intruded. "Before you speak too rashly, Afonso, I have something to say."

Raul's mother, Florbella, stood in the doorway. She was a beautiful woman of about fifty with smooth olive skin, snapping brown eyes, and straight black hair combed back to a chignon at her neck. The simplicity of her gray silk gown enhanced her distinguished appearance and statuesque figure.

Raul rose quickly to embrace his mother. Afonso held back his anger, then said, "So you've been eavesdropping?"

"How can I eavesdrop in my own home? Are there secrets here to be hidden from me?" As she spoke, she patted Raul fondly on the cheek.

"This is a matter only for a father and his son," Afonso said peevishly. "Women don't understand such things and should remain silent."

Florbella smiled serenely. "A good obedient wife I have always been, but after all these years you should know better than to expect me to remain silent in matters where my sons are concerned. Yes, I overheard everything, and I know you are wrong. Instead of scolding Raul, you should be proud—"

"Woman! I forbid you to say another word!"

"Forbid all you want, but I shall speak my mind. My elder son has inherited the blood of your father and grandfather. He can never be satisfied to follow only in your footsteps, no matter how many riches it brings him. He wishes, like all real men, to do something on his own, to prove that he, too, can perform something new and useful for the world. I have seen this in him since childhood—always with his nose in a book learning about other countries, science, people. Our Eduardo is different. He will be content to take what is given him, with as little effort on his part as possible. But not Raul. He can know happiness with nothing less than following his dream and making it a reality. I am very proud to have given birth to such a son."

Afonso spoke with strained patience. "Have you finished your little discourse, my dear?"

"I have not. I only wish to add that if you are unwise enough to alienate your own son by selling his plantation and frustrating his dearest dream, I will come to his rescue with my own money and buy him all the land he needs."

Florbella had enough money in her own right to do this, as Afonso well knew. He was too proud a man ever to have touched any of her money and rich enough so there had been no need.

"Don't you realize what you are doing?" he half shouted in exasperation. "After I've tried so hard to knock the silly ideas out of Raul's head, you come around to undo everything!"

"Isn't it possible, Afonso, that it is your ideas that are wrong?"

"Wrong? Wrong to pit my long experience against my son's inexperience? Did it ever occur to you, for example, that if the highway fails to reach Raul's property, no amount of money short of the government treasury could make his plans successful?"

"But the highway plans passing through my property have all been approved, father. That is certain."

"Nothing is certain in this insane world of ours. Not even," Afonso added bitterly, "a father's authority over a bullheaded son."

Still smiling, Florbella walked up to Raul and embraced him again, kissing him on the cheek. "I give all my blessings to you, my dear son, and I know in my heart that your wonderful plans will be very successful."

"Thank you, mother."

Giving him another embrace and kiss, she turned and started out, adding, "And I'm sure your father will soon see it our way."

Afonso was scowling furiously. "I have nothing more to say, Raul, except one last bit of advice: never, *never* marry a woman who has too much money, for as God in heaven can witness, for the rest of her life she will always be able to talk back."

EIGHT

A battered green jeep was waiting when the Cessna 206 skimmed over the top of the dense jungle growth and settled down on the meager landing strip.

Peggy Carpenter emerged, decked out in full jungle regalia: safari-style khaki shorts and shirt, boots (in case of poisonous snakes), and a pith helmet crowning her blond tresses. Slung over her shoulders were a bulging red tote bag and a camera case.

The pilot, a debonair elderly Brazilian wearing a World War II flight jacket, a helmet with earflaps, and a parachute nylon scarf that somehow gave him the dashing air of one fond of flying upside down, followed with her portable typewriter.

The dusty jeep had crawled forward, stopping a dozen feet away. A lithe and lean young man with a mass of dark hair and angry dark eyes jumped out and strode toward her, eyeing her skeptically. On his T-shirt was emblazoned the acronym, FUNAI, and beneath it in smaller letters, *Fundacão Nacional do Indio.*

"*Senhorita* Peggy Carpenter? I am Carlos dos Santos, the FUNAI team leader for this area. I was informed by radio of your arrival and have come to take you to the only available lodging for the night." His whole attitude and expression bristled with resentment.

"I am delighted to meet you, Carlos." She stepped forward and took his hand in a firm handshake, manlike. "It is very kind of you to allow me to come here, and I promise I won't be any bother at all."

He gave her a sour grin. "I must be frank and say that I strongly registered my disapproval of a woman coming here, but headquarters would not listen."

"That's utterly ridiculous. I'm perfectly capable of taking care of myself. In any case, I signed a waiver in Brasilia absolving FUNAI and your government of responsibility should anything happen to me. So you see, you have nothing to worry about."

The pilot had set down her typewriter case and with a final *"Adeus"* returned to the Cessna, which had an overload of beef, beer, and other provisions that were going to another destination. Carlos, still glowering, picked up the typewriter and led the way to the jeep. Peggy followed.

Getting into the jeep she let out a yelp and yanked her hand away from the hood, where she had reached out for bracing.

"I forgot to warn you," said Carlos. "Here, close to the equator, you must never touch metal that has been long under the open sun."

As he started the motor, she felt a burning sting just above one knee and slapped frantically, too late to hit the bluish insect that zoomed away. Several others were buzzing close to her. "Good heavens! I've been bitten!" A drop of blood and a red welt was forming, beginning to itch furiously.

"It was just one of the *borrachudos*. Here—this will help keep them away." Reaching into the glove compartment, he took out an aerosol can and heavily sprayed the bare portions of her legs. The chemical odor rose searingly to her nostrils, bringing tears to her eyes.

"What are the *borrachudos?*"

"The biting flies. We have the *pium* flies, the *motucas*, the *carrapatos*—hundreds of varieties. They all bite."

"Why didn't they bite you?"

"I have Indian blood. Indians and blacks are not bothered. Mixed-blood Brazilians like me aren't much bothered. It is only the whites—especially with fair skin like you—that are most sensitive. I would suggest that the *senhorita* should wear pants." He was grinning. "I mean the kind that come way down

79

and can be stuffed in your boots," he added hastily.

Not an auspicious beginning, she thought ruefully, as the jeep went growling and bumping over a narrow road through tall trees, tangled vines, and broadleafed plants that seemed to be leaning inward, as if threatening to swallow back this puny strip of cleared red earth. She felt an uneasy foreboding. Strange birds shrieked from the trees.

Soon she saw on the side of the road a sign on which was crudely lettered, INCHACO. Translated literally, Carlos told her, the word meant a "swelling" in the road. It was one of FUNAI's staging areas, swiftly becoming a jungle boomtown.

Inchaco looked for all the world, Peggy thought, like a Hollywood set for a western movie. Most of the ramshackle wooden buildings lining both sides of the dusty main street had false fronts rising two stories. Many, judging from the sounds of drunken revelry inside, were saloons. It was a strange contrast, coming only a few hours ago from the ultramodern, sparkling Brasilia.

Adding to the wild and woolly frontier atmosphere was what appeared to be a street brawl. Carlos had slowed the jeep to a crawl to get past a noisy, rough-looking group collected around two men fighting a bizarre fight. Peggy caught a glimpse of the antagonists leaping about in a crazy kind of dance, sometimes using fists, sometimes knees, heads, or feet to attack each other. Bright objects flashed against their ankles.

"Are they really fighting or just playing a game?" Peggy asked.

"No game. It's a deadly form of combat called *capoeira*, something like jujitsu, only bloodier. If you look closely, you can see razors strapped to their ankles. Arteries often get slashed, and some of these men bleed to death before they can be helped. I've seen others with bellies sliced open and intestines hanging out."

Peggy shuddered. "They must be insane!"

"It is a common way of settling an argument. Usually over a woman."

"But how in the world can that settle anything?"

"It is settled when one of them passes out from loss of blood, or dies."

"How horrible."

"As you have been advised, civilization has scarcely touched this area." He paused, then went on bitterly, "And what it has touched, it has only contaminated!"

"How do you mean?"

"As you just saw, drunken louts trying to kill each other. The bars here are full of such roughnecks—the kind who would shoot Indians just for the sport of it. You will find that Inchaco, like all the *agrovilas*—which is what we call the new towns along the highway—is a mecca for criminal scum who come to prey on the honest workers. You will find crooked gamblers, whores, disease, plenty of whiskey, and no regard for the law."

"Are you saying you don't approve of the new highway?"

"I must be honest and say I do not. The highway is mostly for the benefit of the very rich, who have robbed the Indians of all this land. Once the Indians were a proud, happy people who lived beautiful lives, and what did civilization bring them? Disease, poverty, cruelty, and death. The early white settlers rounded them up, took their land, and forced them at gunpoint to be slaves. When they found that Indians couldn't survive long as slaves because they quickly grew sick and died from the white man's diseases, the settlers imported black slaves from Africa. The Indians were shot down by the hundreds, by the thousands, as if they were wild animals, just to clear the land. Of course they tried to fight back—they still do—but what can frail arrows do against guns and bulldozers?"

"But isn't it against the law to kill an Indian?"

81

"Of course. At long last, after most of the tribes have been exterminated and with the eyes of the world watching, the few Indians left are under government protection."

"Isn't that your job as a FUNAI representative, to protect the Indians?"

"Not armed protection. We don't carry guns. Our job is only to help the Indians in every way possible. I am the leader of what we call a 'pacification team.' We are called in when there has been serious trouble with the Indians—such as a few days ago when several road construction workers were killed by an unknown Indian tribe. It is our job to somehow make friends with the Indians and try to persuade them to move to the Xingú National Park, an 8,500-square-mile reservation set aside by the government for displaced tribes."

"Isn't it dangerous dealing with angry Indians when you have no guns to protect yourself?"

Carlos smiled grimly. "We've lost quite a few FUNAI workers to poisoned arrows and darts."

"It's a shame the Indians don't realize what's best for them. I'm sure they'd be so much better off in a government reservation."

The jeep had stopped, and Carlos turned to look at her, his dark eyes burning. Belatedly Peggy remembered that he was part Indian and feared that somehow she may have offended him.

"Would you like it if you or your family were taken from your traditional homeland against your will and moved like cattle to some parkland—like a zoo with invisible bars—where you must live out your lives as mere wards of a benevolent government?"

"No, Carlos," she said quickly, "I would not. Apparently you wouldn't either. Don't you feel a little guilty about your part in persuading them to give up their homeland?"

"Not guilty. Only sad. I do it because for the proud Indians of Brazil it is the only hope they have left.

* * * * *

Above the wide batwing doors was a roughly painted sign: CASA HOSPITALIDADE, and below it, *Atende-se Dia e Noite,* which Peggy took to mean, "Serving you Day and Night." Because the drive to the FUNAI camp was too long to set out this late in the day, Carlos had made room reservations for the two of them in this "Hospitality House," which was the only hotel in town.

Entering the stale, hot atmosphere inside, Peggy was greeted by a huge crocodile standing upright on its hind legs and holding in its mouth a large red electric light bulb. Only a stuffed crocodile, to be sure, but with the lighted bulb adding a bloody glow to the gaping cavern of mouth and rows of sharp teeth, it gave her a momentary fright.

Her state of mind was not helped by the sight of a huge anaconda coiled among the rafters overhead—a fat serpent at least thirty feet long, its head hanging down, mouth open, balefully eyeing with its glassy jet eyes the activity along the crowded bar below.

"It's not alive," Carlos reassured her, grinning at her expression. "The owner collects these things. He thinks it attracts customers."

The next gruesome exhibit were three dried human heads, no larger than those of newborn babies, with prune-wrinkled faces and black hair hanging all around that looked hundreds of years old. They were suspended from cords behind the wide plank bar, which ran the length of the room.

"Are they fakes?" she asked.

"They're real enough. Or were. They probably date back eighty or ninety years, when it was common-place for an Indian to kill an enemy, cut his head off, and shrink it."

"How did they get them so small?"

"They boned the heads, stuffed them with spices and gums, and put them through a secret shrinking process that only the Indians know about. It got to be quite a business, selling them to the whites. You could place an order, and an Indian would go out and lop off somebody's head and deliver it a week or two later. So many people started buying them as curios that the government had to put a stop to it."

Peggy shivered. In a sinister way the three heads reminded her of the classic trio of Chinese monkeys: see no evil, hear no evil, speak no evil. Certainly they would never bear tales.

Carlos guided her past the long bar, which was crowded with the roughest-looking bunch Peggy had ever seen. The grimy bearded faces ranged through all shades of skin color, their dirty garments reeking with the fetid odors of sweat mingled with the sourish fumes of beer. Almost all had knives at their belts; some had holstered guns. Liquor-thick voices cursed and argued, laughing raucously as they spat on the sawdust-covered floor. They jostled each other for a better place at the bar and openly fondled the sprinkling of females among them.

The women for the most part were gaudily gowned in soiled silks, satins, or bright cottons of low décolletage to best display their ample upper charms, the skirts daringly slit up one side almost to the waist. Yet, oddly enough, all the arms, thighs, and legs were concealed under woolen coverings or stockings. Protection against the biting flies and mosquitoes, Peggy guessed. Their skins, too, were of varying hues, as was their hair, worn long and in some cases dyed an improbable red or garish yellow.

"Why are so many people here?" Peggy asked.

"This is a collection point for the unemployed *caboclos* who wait here for days, sometimes weeks, for labor contractors to come around and give them jobs. It is also a Saturday, and many of the prospectors, miners, settlers, bushwhackers, and plantation and highway workers have come in for a big time." As he talked, Carlos glanced around the room. "Ah," he added, "there is the desk clerk working behind the bar. Wait here a moment while I go and get the keys to the rooms."

84

Carlos walked away, and moments later a hulking fellow with a scrubby beard, his face burned red from sun and booze, lumbered up and dropped a hairy hand on her arm.

"*Olá, senhorita. Como vai tudo? Como se chama?*"

Peggy flinched. "*Senhor,* I don't speak Portuguese."

"Ah, you Engleesh, *norte-americano?* Engleesh me speak good. You dreenk weeth me, *sim?*"

"I'm sorry, *senhor.* I am with another gentleman who will be back shortly."

"*Maldito! Não importa,* that one! Me beeger, better. You come weeth me—" His fingers closed like a vise on her arm, and he started hauling her toward the bar.

"*Senhor*—remove your hand! I insist—"

"You 'ave speerit, ha? I like." He yanked her along.

Carlos appeared in a rush. "*Senhor!* Release the lady at once! She is in my escort."

The big man snorted scornfully. "*Vá para o diabo!* Go to the devil!"

"I ask you once more!"

"Out of my way, *sertanista!* Indian lover! Before I—"

Swiftly Carlos slashed downward with the edge of an open hand against the other's wrist.

Letting out a yelp of pain, the big man released Peggy and looked at his numbed wrist in surprise and anger. His glowering eyes focused on Carlos.

"So leetle shreemp wish to fight, ha? I feex—" His hand went to his belt. A knife blade flashed and he swaggered toward Carlos.

Peggy got in front of the big man. "Leave him alone! You're twice his size and he carries no weapons."

Grinning, he knocked her aside with an easy swing of his arm. He sheathed the knife. "Leetle shreemp—I give him chance. We fight the *capoeira.*"

"The *capoeira* is only for brainless animals," said Carlos. "We'll fight with bare hands and fists—"

Whoooumpff! The big man had lunged forward

85

with astonishing speed and kicked Carlos full in the groin. With a cry of pain, Carlos doubled over, staggering backward.

The big man laughed. "You forget the feet, *não?*" He advanced at a rush.

"Getúlio!" One of the bar girls, a buxom *mulata* with wild blond hair, had scampered forward to block the man's charge. When he tried to push her aside, she caught his arm and clung to it with all her hefty weight. "You are only making a fool of yourself, Getúlio! Can't you see everyone is laughing at you for picking a fight with such a small man—who is also brave enough to defend his woman?"

·"Generosa—geet your ass away!" He tried to shake her loose from his arm, but she only clung tighter.

"*Não*, Getúlio. I know you to be a good and brave man, but others will think you only a bully, a coward who seeks to steal the women of smaller men who have no weapons."

"But he is a *sertanista*, a lover of Indians! His balls I should cut off!"

"Why should you care, Getúlio?" Her words crooned in his ear. "All you should care is you don't act like a fool. Come with me and we will go upstairs together, *sim?*"

Grudgingly, Getúlio allowed her to lead him away.

Carlos came over to Peggy. "Thank you for trying to intervene, but it was foolish. You might have been hurt."

She laughed. "No harm was done, thanks to Generosa. She certainly knows how to handle men. Maybe she could teach me some of her tricks."

"No! Tricks are not for a lady! But I think from now on you should wear long pants."

"I will. I promise."

"Now let us look at our rooms. I warn you, don't expect too much. There will be bugs—but not as many as you will have to put up with at the FUNAI camp."

* * * * *

Carlos dos Santos was long in getting to sleep that night, and when he did sleep, it was badly. He was too brimming with anger, shame, and other emotions.

He was angry at headquarters officials in Brasilia. Against his strongest opposition they had ordered him by radio to allow Peggy Carpenter to visit the camp of his FUNAI team. Because of that, he had lost a full day at a crucial time, a most dangerous time, when they were investigating the outbreak of poison arrow ambushes against the road builders.

Now he had been forced to endure the shame of trying to protect the girl—and of course failing—against a powerful brute who could easily have broken him in two. What an unfair position for one who did not believe in fighting—whose whole life was dedicated to pacification between hostile parties.

Carlos was a true *sertanista*—"wise in the ways of the jungle," and he had an almost mystic love for the Indians he was trying to help. He hated the new highway with a passion, but he saw it as inevitable as volcanoes erupting or the advance of a glacier. He had been through the University of São Paulo, having majored in anthropology and the study of primitive peoples, which was how he had reached his present position as a FUNAI leader. Although thus far, his best efforts had done little to hold back the forces of "civilization" that were destroying the last of the tribes.

But mingled with his anger was an even more disturbing emotion.

For Carlos, who had a wife and child back in Manaus, had discovered himself not invulnerable to Peggy's charms, and it only added to his bitter resentment about her presence. It was crazy that she should be up here among women-starved men. Never for a moment would he allow his own wife to come here. And loving his wife as he did, the knowledge of being trapped in close proximity to the attractive young woman brought angry blood rushing to his head.

He had first become aware of it in the jeep when he had leaned close to spray her sleek bare legs with the insect repellent—and felt the gathering heat in his loins. *Deus do céu!* God in heaven! For a man like himself who loved his wife, it was the greatest of sins to be so attracted. He could hardly blame Getúlio for the bad behavior. His own primal feelings, like Getúlio's reactions, might be expected from almost any man who looked at her.

Indeed, much of his wakefulness had been partly out of fear that drunken men might try to break into her adjoining room. For most of the night his jungle-trained ears had listened to every sound. There had been coarse laughter, curses, the uproar of fights—and in other rooms along the hallway the vigorous squeaking of bedsprings. He wondered if Peggy had heard the same sounds.

He sighed. Yes, up at the FUNAI camp near the roadhead, amid so many crude men such as the road builders, she would be a problem.

The bed in her tiny room at Casa Hospitalidade was the most horrendous she had ever known—lumpy, hard as sand, and smelly—but Peggy had slept well. If there were bugs, she didn't know it. Carlos, the dear man, had fumigated the bed and the entire room with a bug bomb before taking her down for *jantar*, which had consisted of a bowl of turtle soup, fried tapir, and yams, served with a sour murky wine made from the *maracujá*, a jungle passion fruit. The water, he said, was unsafe. Doubtless the wine had helped her sleep, and it was a sweet sleep. She had felt quite safe, almost like a queen among all these primitive males to whom her latent romanticism attributed qualities of protective gallantry. Their very unconcealed desire for her made her feel more fully like a woman—so unlike the way it was back in the eastern United States, where many of the boys had seemed only half men, only half interested in her as a female.

This morning, stowed away in the jeep with Carlos at the wheel, she was keyed high with anticipation of the adventures ahead. As the jeep sped along the two-lane strip of new highway at a sedate 45 mph, her alien eyes soaked in the strange scenery. This section of highway, Carlos told her, had been completed for just about a year, yet the dense jungle was already crowding in. Parasitic plants crossed the reddish gravel roadway surface with exuberant vines. The recently torn earth bordering the road was asplash with spectacular flowers whose brilliant colors rivaled the plumage of strange birds seen amid the green canopy of treetops. Huge butterflies in all hues fluttered about, occasionally splatting against the windshield in miniature exotic explosions of death.

Carlos seemed oddly reserved this morning, unbending only enough to answer her questions curtly. Yes, the shimmering green birds were parrakeets; the swift heavy-bodied bird that had just plummeted across the road ahead was a *jacú*, a kind of pheasant; that outlandish bird standing nearly five feet high, the white stork with black legs and head and a scarlet throat, was called a *jaburu;* the small deer leaping gracefully into the trees was a *veado.*

All was delightfully absorbing until she saw her first Indians standing haphazardly along the road's edge, a dozen or more of them. Men, women, and children, all stark-naked except for colored paint on parts of their bodies and faces. Carlos told her that the irregular patches of inflamed pink covering some sections of skin were not paint, but skin infections. All of them looked haggard, sad, and hungry. They stretched out their hands in supplication as the jeep approached. Peggy reached for her purse.

"No," Carlos said firmly. "Their begging is not to be encouraged."

"But won't they starve?"

"Our trucks will come later with food, and our men

will try again to persuade them to move to the Xingú National Park where they can be self-sufficient. And again they will refuse."

"Who are they?"

"They are some of the few members left of the once-fierce Kranhacarore tribe. The highway has ruined their ancestral lands. They have been decimated by the diseases of the civilized world, demoralized and corrupted by the proximity of the highway. With their tribal fabric destroyed, they have left their sweet potato patches unharvested. They are too sick of flesh and spirit to carry on their traditional way of living. I have little hope for them."

Peggy felt a rise of anger. "No hope for them? It seems to me that the very least you could do would be to move them, by force if necessary for their own good, to this great national park you talk about, where presumably they could get medical attention and a decent chance at living."

"No! If we forced them to move, it would quickly get back to the other Indians, who would interpret it as our taking prisoners. Then the other tribes would resist vehemently. It would wreck our only chances of winning over the last few tribes left in the jungle. You must understand that once the Indians in Brazil numbered four million. Now there are fewer than a hundred thousand, and that number is dwindling fast. Ninety-six tribes have disappeared forever. The Indian culture is precious and must be preserved from complete destruction, and our only weapons are kindness, gentleness, verbal persuasion. If we fail, the world will have lost something pure and wonderful that can never be replaced."

Surprised by the heat in his voice, Peggy modified her tone. "But perhaps gentleness and verbal persuasion are not enough. You say they have responded by killing some of your men."

"We have lost twelve FUNAI representatives to poison arrows and darts in the past three months."

"Then I'd say they must be savage people."

"Not savage! For generations they have known nothing but slavery, rape, disease, robbery—every kind of brutality from the white man. Who wouldn't try to defend himself against such evils? Since they can't fight bulldozers and road graders, they take it out on us. They don't know that FUNAI people are different. That is what we're trying to prove. It is a complex, delicate mission, like dealing with high explosives, where one small mistake could be your last."

"Forgive me for my ignorant questions," she said humbly. "I think I'm beginning to understand."

The jeep sped on. Now and then trucks rolled past. There was no civilian traffic; it was too far forward for settlers to have moved in and established farms. Distant heavy rolling sounds, punctuated by the booming of dynamite, were becoming audible.

"We're getting close to the roadhead," Carlos announced. "Soon we'll have to leave the highway and follow a jungle trail."

"Isn't the FUNAI camp at the roadhead?"

"No, we're a few miles past it in the unbroken jungle where we think it will be easier to make contact with the Indians and draw them out of hiding."

Or draw their poison arrows, Peggy thought with a shiver.

The sounds of the road builders were now thunderous. Ahead Peggy could see a turmoil of ponderous activity: mammoth power shovels, tractors, bulldozers, graders, slow-moving chains of yellow dump trucks. Explosions rent the air. Black smoke boiled into the sky. Huge trees toppled with a crackling and crashing of limbs. The very earth seemed to shake.

"We turn off here," said Carlos, wheeling the jeep onto a narrow trail that, judging from the fresh ax and saw marks on the stumps, had been only recently cleared through the jungle.

After another fifteen minutes of the roughest, most spine-jarring transportation Peggy had ever endured, the jeep stopped. The makeshift road had come to a dead end.

Carlos got out. "We walk the rest of the way," he said.

"Is it far?"

"About a mile."

Quickly fashioning a rope sling, he hoisted her typewriter on his back along with his own khaki duffel bag. A knapsack hung at his hip. Peggy slung her red tote bag on her back and kept her camera suspended from her neck in front, ready for instant picture taking.

Carlos led the way through the green labyrinth, following a skimpy path that was almost obscured by the luxuriant herbage along the way. The sun seemed to have gone out, roofed off by towering trees. It was cellar cool in the greenish murk. The air was palpitant with brooding silence that was violated only by the hum of insects, the occasional whistling of a bird, and the stealthy rustling of leaves.

Entranced, Peggy paused now and then to snap pictures. At one point something black, shining, and sinuous slithered across her path. She let out a muffled scream.

Carlos whirled. "What's wrong?"

"A big snake! It almost touched me."

Carlos grinned. "Since it didn't, you have nothing to worry about."

Trying to calm her jumping nerves, she leaned against a tree. It was a large tree covered with a flaky bark that suddenly turned to crawling life. She jerked away, her heart thudding furiously.

Carlos laughed. "They are nothing but mantises. You see, nature has camouflaged them so well that their wings look just like bark, until some disturbance makes them move. The mantises are harmless; but you shouldn't lean against trees—because there are also furry tarantulas, whose bites can be deadly."

"If you're trying to scare me, you've succeeded. I'm almost afraid to move a little finger."

"Have no fear. The jungle is dangerous only to the unwary. The general rule is that no wildlife, even poisonous snakes, will try to hurt you except when they think you're trying to hurt them. This doesn't apply, of course, to anacondas, crocodiles, and piranhas, but even they can be avoided if you keep your wits alert and your eyes open."

His words were not very reassuring to Peggy, who thought that a hundred eyes would scarcely be enough to see everything around her. Carlos started forward again, and she followed timidly.

"It's no worse than your own civilized jungle," he went on, warming to the subject. "In your cities you can be killed in an instant in an automobile accident, a plane crash, or a street mugging—or you might be robbed to the grave by bureaucrats and sneaky tax laws too complex to understand."

"I get your point, Carlos," she said, her glances racing hither and yon, from the path ahead to the trees, skimming up the looping lianas that looked for all the world like slender snakes, jerking nervously from one side of the dense foliage to the other. A strange prickling had started up her spine.

She knew it was but an outgrowth of her neurotic fears of the unknown, unintentionally stirred by Carlos's words. Or perhaps he had intended to frighten her, as a way of punishing her, a mere woman, for having the audacity to impose herself on his world. Still, this odd sense of unease was increasing, as if her own thought of needing a hundred eyes had been turned against her. The feeling grew that many eyes were watching her every move.

Meanwhile Carlos was acting silly. From his knapsack he had taken a red rubber balloon, which he was blowing up as he walked. When it was about the size of a basketball, he deftly twisted the end of it into a tight knot and then tossed it to one side to waft gently to the ground. From the knapsack he took another balloon—yellow this time—and started to repeat the procedure.

"Carlos! Why in the world are you doing that?"

"I'll explain later."

She debated with herself whether to say more, then decided it was the only way to relieve her tensions. "Carlos—I have a terrible feeling that somebody is watching me."

He turned, grinning. "It may interest you to know that you are blessed—or cursed—with the sixth sense, the survival sense. The fact is, we are being watched every step of the way. That is why I am blowing up balloons to leave along the trail. It is one of the FUNAI ways of signaling friendship to hostile Indians who might otherwise, out of fear, give in to their normal reflex to kill intruders." He finished blowing up the balloon, released it, then started with another. In the next ten minutes he had left a trail of floating spheres of yellow, orange, green, red, and purple.

Peggy's eyes were now straining to the utmost, darting from side to side in a vain effort to penetrate the screen of greenery. At times she thought she saw the vague outlines of a figure, but the curious quality of jungle sunlight made her unsure. The light, sifting through the branches to be reflected from breeze-stirred leaves, tended to blur and camouflage instead of illuminate. But once, for just an instant, she did see a face—an eerie black mask with pale rings for eyes.

She let out a muffled gasp. "Carlos—I saw a face!"

"Was it black?"

"Yes."

"With a red feather in the hair?"

"I—I think so."

"When they dye their faces black with genipa juice and wear the red macaw feather—the symbol of war —it means they are out to kill their enemies. I think now is the time to—" He started laughing, then burst into lusty song.

"I fail to see the joke!" she called out tartly.

"No joke. I am only responding to the Indian way of thinking: when a person approaches laughing, sing-

94

ing, or making any kind of unnecessary noise, he cannot be an enemy. I advise you to sing, too."

Peggy tried to sing. Her voice came out a squeak. She tried laughing; it jetted out more as a spasmodic hysterical giggle. She settled for pasting on her broadest and best toothpaste smile, angling it in all directions.

After another timeless but tense interlude of walking, she ventured a question. "Are they still following us, Carlos?"

"Who knows? If they are undecided, they may have left. If they appear suddenly, with weapons, then we are in trouble."

"If my sixth sense is still working, I no longer have the feeling they are watching me."

"Let us hope you are right. In any case, the camp is just ahead."

The FUNAI advance pacification camp consisted of several smallish green wall tents with nylon screen windows. They were grouped in a semicircle facing a central campfire, and nearby was a tripod of poles from which was suspended a Lister water bag. Four men wearing FUNAI T-shirts were hunkered near the fire, eating from aluminum mess kits. They watched curiously as Carlos and Peggy approached.

Carlos made brief introductions, to which each man responded with a broad smile and a *"Bom dia, senhorita."* One man rose and gestured toward an iron pot sitting on an iron grill positioned over the campfire.

"You are just in time for *lanche*. Is *senhorita* hungry?"

"I'm famished, and the food smells so good!"

Carlos helped serve her. The main dish was *feijoada*—black beans, rice, and dried meats with a kind of spicy dressing. There was also a bowl of fruit gathered from the jungle. One man went to fetch a canvas folding chair for Peggy, which she politely declined, preferring to sit cross-legged on the ground so as not to give the impression that she had to be pampered. She thought the food was very good, really, for jungle fare.

"Have you checked the trails to see if the Indians have accepted any of our gifts?" Carlos asked one of the men.

"*Sim*, but they haven't touched a thing."

Carlos shrugged in a resigned sort of way and turned to Peggy. "You see, to make contact with hostile Indians, we place gifts along the jungle trails as peace offerings. Sooner or later—it could take days, weeks, months, or maybe never—they will let us know. If and when they do accept our gifts, they will then make overtures of friendship. If not—" His voice faded away, and Peggy saw that he was not looking at her, but at a point past her head.

She turned to follow his glance and almost dropped her plate.

At least a score of Indians had appeared and quickly encircled their group. These Indians were totally unlike the pathetic creatures she had seen begging along the highway. They were ramrod erect and well muscled, and their faces were dyed black, with red macaw feathers adorning their heads and bodies.

Each man had a bow taller than his body with feathered arrows fitted to the drawn strings and pointed directly at the FUNAI group and Peggy.

NINE

The Cessna 206 skimmed over the treetops, swooshed lower, and landed with a series of jarring bumps on the rough field of cleared jungle land. Pio, at the controls, grinned sourly at Raul. "It flies like a dream but lands like a nightmare. What you need is a good landing strip. The ground leveled and the surface packed down with clay."

"I'll get some men working on it." On the whole Raul was pleased with the Cessna, a used craft in excellent condition that Pio had purchased for him in Rio. A plane would be necessary for his new agro-energy business, and his father's Learjet was too far distant to borrow.

The two men and the other passenger, Braz, climbed out. Another pilot had been hired to fly the Learjet, and both Pio and Braz were now on loan to Raul for as long as he needed them. They were men he could trust.

Since there were no horses waiting for them, they began trudging the quarter-mile walk to Casa de Ouro Branco. Raul had attempted to reach Cardosa, the plantation foreman, by radio to advise him of their coming, but there had been no response. He wondered if the radio-receiving equipment that had been installed in the manse—at high cost—was in operational order. If not, why hadn't it been repaired? Such matters were the responsibility of the Plantation Management Company, with offices in Manaus, who were paid for proper maintenance of Casa de Ouro Branco.

Braz paused to kick at the ground, raising a puff of red dust. "It is very dry."

"That will be corrected by the next rain. We have plenty of that."

Braz leaned down and scooped up some of the soil, touched a pinch of it with his tongue, and rubbed it between his fingers. "It is *infecundo*. Too poor for good crops to grow."

Raul was well aware of the soil's shortcomings. Contrary to the expectations of the first jungle settlers, land in the Amazon basin was far from being as rich as its lush rain forests had led them to believe. The very plenitude of rain—eighty inches a year—had wreaked damage by a constantly downward movement of water that dissolved and bled away soil nutrients and silicates having a high degree of solubility. The less soluble sesquioxides of aluminum and iron left behind were of little worth to vegetation. And once trees were cleared away, the damage was completed by sun and heat. After two or three years of exposure to the direct rays of the tropical sun, such soil became virtually sterile.

"But I intend to fertilize and replant with fast-growing pines and *Gmelina*—a weed tree from Asia. They can flourish in such soil and will slowly improve it."

As they walked, a sense of unease was beginning to plague Raul. Where were the newly cleared acres of jungle land he had expected to find? True, the primary functions of the skeleton crew of five men and a foreman hired by the management company were to keep the plantation buildings in good condition and to supervise the several dozen Indian families kept busy collecting rubber. Since many of the wild rubber trees had been ravaged by the Brazilian leaf blight, harvesting latex at current low market prices was only of marginal profit at best, but it made enough to pay the workers and the overhead, with some surplus that was supposed to be used for clearing more jungle acreage.

Nearing the manse, his apprehensions grew. When last he had been here, about a year ago, the gardens had been luxuriant. Now, through wavering breaths of heat rising from the dry ground, he could see the seared stalks of untended rare flowers, last year's withered vegetable patch, and fruit trees whiskered with unpruned sapsuckers. Wild vines wound their way up the trunks, looping heavily through the branches. Coarse weeds were proliferating everywhere, and the jungle was moving in with a vengeance, as if determined to choke out the less hardy plants of civilization.

Why hadn't someone been assigned to properly care for the gardens?

The house itself had the same general look of decay and disrepair. It was a long, rambling building, a wing having been added here and there seemingly on whim. Its overall style was rustic, being constructed of various rough-sawn woods and massive beams, with squared-off pillars supporting a tiled roof over the gallery. Yet the weathered gray wood and the overscaled dimensions gave the manse a certain grandeur quite in harmony with the brooding jungle.

The obvious things amiss were a broken windowpane, a sagging shutter, a tilted pillar.

Inside, the wide-planked flooring of black jacaranda was littered with debris, some of the paintings on the walls were askew, and on the marred surfaces of once-elegant tables were dirty glasses and empty liquor bottles. Sounds of booze-coarsened laughter boomed from the grand living room ahead.

Several men were lounging around the long dining table, two tilted back in fine hand-carved chairs with their boots on the tabletop. One was guzzling from a bottle. Another was lying on a nearby couch having a snooze, his spurs heedlessly dug into the velvet fabric.

"*Diabo!*" Raul roared at them. "What is going on here?"

One of the men, lank of figure and wearing a revolver strapped to his hip, rose languidly from a chair. He had a sallow face, a drooping moustache, and stringy black hair hanging low behind his neck and tied with a rawhide thong. His yellowish eyes fixed their stare on Raul in a show of offended innocence.

"What concern is it of yours, *senhor?*" he blustered.

"I am Raul de Carvalho, the owner. Are you Cardosa?"

"Ah, yes, I am the foreman here."

"Then explain all this outrage."

"Outrage?" The foreman's eyes widened in greater innocence. "*Senhor,* I do not understand. We are merely relaxing from our work."

"What work? I see no trace of any work being done around here! No forest has been cleared; none of the open fields has been planted. The gardens, the house, everything is a mess!"

Cardosa spread his hands. "But *senhor,* we get no orders. No one tells us what to do. So we wait."

"Weren't you given instructions by radio?"

"Alas, *senhor*—the radio, it does not work."

Probably because of careless handling, Raul thought angrily, realizing that it had been a mistake to leave thousands of dollars worth of expensive electronic equipment in the hands of ignorant men.

"In any case, your original orders should have been enough. There's no excuse for such irresponsibility. Cardosa, you're fired!"

"Fired, *senhor?* But I have not yet been paid."

"Paid for what? For not working? For ruining so much of my property? Now get the hell out of here!"

Cardosa drew himself up proudly. "You may fire me, *senhor,* that is your privilege. But how can you give me orders when I am no longer working for you? I will not leave before I have been paid, and also furnished with a horse and saddle."

"You'll get out now, or—!"

A commotion drew Raul's attention. A drunken man was dragging a struggling naked Indian girl out of a doorway. The man bellied out a laugh. "A real *fêmea do tigre,* this one. Who wants her next?"

Raul's outrage exploded. "So you're even allowing

your men to rape Indian women! No, Cardosa—you're not going anywhere! I'm locking you up until you can be turned over to the police!"

Cardosa's hand slid down. His gun came out. He grinned.

"*Não, senhor.* Nobody locks up Cardosa. Now I give you a chance to take out your fat wallet and pay the *dinheiro* you owe me—or I pull the trigger and help myself—"

Crraaackk!

A long snakelike whip flashed through the air to lash its fiery tip around Cardosa's hand. He yowled in pain as the gun spun from his hand and clattered on the floor. Cardosa looked at his numbed hand in astonishment, then at Braz who was holding the whip he usually carried coiled and hooked to his belt. Braz's skill with the whip was legendary. He could kill a fly or snap off the head of a snake at fifteen paces, never missing.

"Pio—" Braz called sharply. "Get the gun, and keep the others covered."

As Pio raced to get the gun, Cardosa let out a roar of rage.

"Lopez—Sebastião—*matar* the *bastardo!* Kill—"

The whip cracked again, straight across Cardosa's mouth. His scream was muffled in a bubbling of blood.

Pio had recovered the gun, and he was pointing it in the direction of Cardosa's crew. Considerably sobered, they showed no inclination to fight. The Indian girl was cowering against a wall.

The whip continued streaking through the air, bringing more screams and guttural moans. Cardosa was now rolling around on the floor. Blood welled from his face, soaked through his shirt. Relentlessly the whip kept slashing.

Raul was loath to interfere. He knew it was the Indian blood that ran in Braz's veins—as it did in Pio's—that had been stirred to such primal vengeance. Still . . .

He put a restraining hand on the *vaquerio's* arm. "Braz—I think he's been punished enough."

"Even to kill him would not be enough, but I do not wish it on my conscience." His face expressionless, Braz began coiling the whip. "As for the others, I cannot hold them responsible because they are just filthy dogs, animals who are no good unless led by a good leader. I will punish them by working them until their asses drag to the ground."

Meanwhile, Pio had gone over to the Indian girl and was speaking to her in the *Lingua Geral,* a generalized Indian language composed of words from many tribes in a modified form. It was used by the Indian-European mestizos as well as by white teachers and preachers throughout Brazil, and it was more or less understood by all Indians. After a few moments, Pio came over to Raul, leading the girl by the hand.

"She is of the Atroari tribe. Her name is Elena. She says she was alone walking in the jungle when they captured her; she expected to be killed when they were through with her."

Raul looked at her sullen face, strangely attractive despite the bruises and swellings on her honey-colored skin. There was no fear there. Anger sparked the jet eyes, and her head was held high with pride. Her golden nudity was lissome, graceful; it was easy to see how it would arouse the animal lust of brutish men.

"We've got to get her back to her village. Can you handle it?" said Raul.

Pio shrugged. "I can try. I'll take a couple of horses and let her guide me. I think she trusts me enough so that I won't become a pincushion for poison arrows."

"Then get going. Take food and water with you, but no gun. It would make the Indians suspicious." Raul turned to Braz. "Do you think you can make good workers out of these men?"

"If not, they will regret it."

*　*　*　*　*

Raul rode slowly toward the green wall of jungle. A day had passed since their arrival at Casa de Ouro Branco, and Pio had not yet returned. Raul hoped that the pilot hadn't met with trouble. Braz had already brought Cardosa's men completely under his iron-handed control, winning their respect, and they didn't resent him. Cardosa had been locked in a room and would at first opportunity be turned over to the police.

Raul's present mood, now sobered by his full realization of the magnitude of tasks ahead of him, was no longer so ebullient. An examination of the small refinery that his grandfather Júlio had installed in one of the outbuildings for sugar processing and distillation into alcohol revealed it to be so rusted and out of repair that it was almost worthless. Raul had hoped to revamp the ancient facility for experimental purposes in the distillation of alcohol fuel—and perhaps he could, but only with the aid of a competent chemical engineer.

That was one of the first, most vitally important things he had to do—get to Rio and hire such a man. That would be expensive.

The association of thoughts brought Odete to mind, touching off an inner glow. What a stroke of luck it had been to meet and win the love of one so unspoiled, so fresh with youth, so beautiful! The only small bone of contention between them was her professed love of city life. But that was because she was inexperienced. Once she had been exposed to the beauty and the awesome majesty of the jungle, he knew she would be enthralled. As for material comforts, he would give her free rein to have the manor redecorated and refurnished, to add all the luxuries she desired. Their life together could be idyllic.

Reaching the edge of the jungle, he directed his horse into a narrow trail among the trees. He wanted to make a preliminary inspection of the vast forested domain he had inherited but never seen from the ground. It would take many days, perhaps months, to see all of it, owing to the impenetrability of some areas, but eventually all would be accessible by a network of logging trails as the trees were felled acre by acre.

Raul had the sensation of being instantaneously lifted back into another world eons ago. Under the soaring roof of sun-soaked leaves it was suddenly pleasantly cool. As if done by an artist's brush, light filtering through in a mosaic of exquisite greenish golden tints added beauty and magic to everything below. The ascending tree trunks, the vaulted ceiling of greenery imparted the atmosphere of a celestial cathedral, inviting the spirit to soar. Golden shafts of light breaking through added an aura of glory. There was mystery, too, in the sinuous vines, lianas that looped from tree to tree in a tangle of eerie intimacy. It was an enchanted world that was created by the witchery of light, air, and moisture brought by time itself into harmonious balance with the earth—after millions of years of continuous battles of tiny life-forms for survival.

It was a world virtually unchanged since the day after creation, now doomed to destruction by man.

During moments like this Raul had qualms about being an instrument in bringing about the devastation of all this natural beauty—transmogrifying it into barren red earth that had to be artificially revitalized under a punishing sun. Could this be what God had intended?

Raul's jaw clamped tight. That was the way of the world. Of progress. Idealism, the fanciful dreams of youth sooner or later had to give way to the realistic world of adulthood. Yesterday the jungle had been an unconquerable giant. Today man was the giant, and the jungle—like an army of aged warriors—was doomed to fall under the swords of modern technology. Would it be a victory or a defeat?

It was sad. Death was always sad.

A sudden nickering from his horse made him tighten the reins. The horse balked a bit and pranced. Probably a nervous reaction to a snake or other wild thing, Raul thought. Soon he saw the reason.

Less than a hundred yards ahead was another horse, saddled but riderless, meandering among the trees in an uncertain way.

Carefully Raul rode on and caught the reins of the horse. His glance skimmed the trail ahead, seeking the rider, whoever he was, who would probably not be far away.

He came upon her after about another hundred yards of riding. She was limping along the trail. The sound of his approach made her whirl to stare at him as if uncertain whether to wait or flee. Her expression registered not fear, but astonishment.

Raul was equally astonished to find a white girl, sensibly garbed in a white gauze shirt, faded dungarees, and riding boots, alone on this remote jungle trail. He knew that there was a neighboring plantation a dozen or so miles from his own, but he thought it had been abandoned since the decline of the rubber boom.

He rode closer, leading the other horse, and saw that she was young—certainly no more than nineteen—and very attractive. She had long dark hair, a creamy complexion, and dark eyes piquantly slanted, suggesting a touch of Oriental blood. A short straight nose and full curved mouth set harmoniously in an oval face with a smallish firm chin completed Raul's first impression of the delicacy and smooth perfection of the fresh petals of a jungle flower. She was quite slim, yet curved in the best way that young ladies can be curved, firm breasts pressing to the limits of the thin shirt, hips snugged tight against the jeans—a manner of dressing much frowned on by most back-country Brazilian fathers. Even more surprising was that any Brazilian family would have allowed a nubile young daughter to ride unescorted in the jungle.

He held up the reins of the horse he had found and smiled down at her. "Your horse, I presume?"

She returned a dubious smile. "Your inference is quite correct, *senhor*. It is most embarrassing because usually I'm a good rider. If you can believe my alibi, which happens to be the truth, I was just ducking my head to avoid some vines when a snake crossed our path and my horse began bucking. I was off-balance at that particular moment, or I would never have been thrown, I assure you."

Raul quickly dismounted. "You're not badly hurt, I hope?"

"I've bruised a leg, and of course my pride, but I'm sure I'll survive. I thank you, *senhor*, for bringing back the horse."

"*Senhorita*, the pleasure is mine."

"It is also a pleasure for me to be saved from so long and miserable a hike alone through the jungle by so gallant a stranger."

"Neighbors shouldn't be strangers. I assume you live at the next plantation, *senhorita*—?"

"Viviane Vargas," she supplied. "My father is Dom João Abrais Vargas. Yes, it is true, our plantation adjoins this one, where I confess I am trespassing. You see, when I saw a plane land here yesterday and not leave again, my curiosity was aroused. Are you of the de Carvalho family?"

"I am Raul de Carvalho. I arrived yesterday, and I will be living here most of the time from now on. I'm surprised and pleased to learn that I have neighbors close by. Do you live here all the time, or are you just visiting?"

She frowned. "I have lived here for most of my life, except for some schooling at Manaus and more recently at the University of São Paulo, where my studies were interrupted owing to—my father not being in the best of health. I only returned home recently." With an easy grace showing long familiarity with riding, she mounted her horse. "You must forgive me for talking about so many personal things when I scarcely know you. Again I thank you, but now I must be going before father starts worrying."

"I will of course escort you."

"It is not necessary. I'm quite capable of riding by myself."

"While you are on my property, *Senhorita* Viviane, I am responsible for your safety. And with your horse so skittish, I will not be satisfied until I have seen you delivered safe and sound to your home."

She laughed. "Ah, like all Brazilian gentlemen, you are very *macho*. Very well, if you insist."

Their horses halted at the big iron gate while a sleepy Indian slowly opened it. One sweeping glance at the Mansão de Vargas and the surrounding grounds told Raul much. The mansion and its collection of outbuildings were pathetically run-down. Patches of stucco had cracked and fallen away from the walls; tiles were missing from the roof; gardens and orchards within the walled enclosure were unkempt; and the rows of former slave and servant cabins were in forlorn disrepair. Plainly it had once been a grand establishment, built by wealth and slave labor, and now it was being maintained by only a trickle of the original owner's income.

After they had dismounted, Viviane touched his arm. "I must warn you, father has lived for many years as a recluse and is not cordial to strangers. You must forgive him if his manner is brusque."

"You have no mother?"

"She died many years ago. Father is the only family I have."

Old and decaying as everything was, Raul was still much impressed as they walked into the entry hall, which was a full two stories high. Obviously, at the height of the rubber boom, Mansão de Vargas had been one of the grandest in Amazonas, in an era where opulence was not only possible but commonplace. A pair of waist-high terra-cotta lions with curling manes, which Viviane told him had been brought all the way from Pernambuco, guarded the foot of the curved staircase. Intricately carved dark wood paneled the walls. The floor was of black and white mosaic tiles set in a swirling pattern similar to those in front of the opera house in Manaus. Never mind that one of the lions was cracked, that spider webs formed lacy patterns among the beams, or that the tiles were dingy and graying. The whole aura was of former magnificence; of boom and bust—a part of the history of the Amazon.

By comparison, Raul's recently inherited plantation was humble. Whereas his own grandfather, Júlio, had wisely conserved his wealth—perceiving the coming end of the rubber boom—to later invest in the Mato Grosso cattle industry, Viviane's ancestors had doubtless poured their money out lavishly and sat tight, apparently believing the boom would never end.

"Vivi—so you're finally back."

The voice was reproving, and so was the expression on the face of the tall man who appeared in the archway. Dom João Abrais Vargas wore a black silk shirt, black boots, and tight-fitting black pants with a row of little silver buttons down the side of each leg in a style that might have been worn by a grandee of a century ago. His straight hair, too, was black, as were the heavy brows over the brooding jet-black eyes set in a face of pale tan, either from a lifetime of exposure to tropical sun or from heredity. The high-bridged nose and tight slit of mouth were arrogant. His age could have been anywhere from forty to a young fifty.

"And who," he added in a sharper tone, "is this stranger?"

"This is Raul de Carvalho, father. I had the good fortune to meet him while out riding." As she completed the introduction, briefly explaining her riding mishap and how he had recovered her unruly horse, her father's hot eyes stabbed at Raul in an imperious manner that was just short of insulting. With apparent reluctance, Dom João offered a hand for a limp, quick handshake.

"I know of your family, of course, *Senhor* de Carvalho, and I thank you for the aid you gave my daughter. If you care to remain for refreshments, Vivi will order what you desire from the servants, but I must beg you to excuse me, as I have duties that must be attended to." With a curt little bow of his head he turned and strode away.

Vivi bit at her lower lip. "You are most welcome to stay, *senhor*. May I offer you tea, or a drink?"

Raul felt a tug of sympathy for her embarrassment. He smiled. "I would much enjoy staying a bit longer, but unfortunately I am already overdue at my *fazenda*. My foreman is waiting to discuss matters of importance."

"Then I won't try to detain you." She turned. "I'll accompany you to your horse."

Outside, after walking a few moments in silence, she looked at him with apologetic eyes. "I hope you understand that father is so immersed in his business affairs that he scarcely has time to remember such things as social amenities."

What business affairs? Raul wondered. Even with cheap Indian labor it was hardly likely that Vargas could wring more than a scanty income from the blight-ravaged wild hevea trees. Was that why Viviane's studies had been "interrupted," forcing her to return home before completing college? Sheer lack of money? She had said it was her father's ill health, but he certainly appeared healthy enough. Or was his problem mental? His reclusive existence could have brought out paranoid tendencies.

"You can hardly blame your father for not feeling cordial toward a de Carvalho," he said. "From what I've heard about my family history, my great-grandfather Jorge was quite a scoundrel. He would have been capable of arousing great animosity in your great-grandfather."

"It's true that there was no love lost between our patriarchal ancestors, but I don't think father would hold that against you. It's just his usual way—always abrupt. He means nothing personal by it." Again she nibbled at a lip, and her lustrous dark lashes lowered as she continued. "It must be plain to you that father is a proud man who has fallen out of the mainstream of the modern world. He lives amid dreams of the past. As a child he was reared like a rich young prince—before the bubble burst. He still feels it is his right to be among the privileged men of wealth; he still owns much land, but it pays little. Now he no longer has the capital, nor is he able to borrow enough to do the things he would like to do."

"Perhaps I could offer him suggestions that might help him turn a good profit."

"I'm afraid father is much too proud to listen to your suggestions. He is pinning all his hopes on the new highway, believing it will revitalize the plantation."

"That's what we're all waiting for. I'm sure it will make a big difference. But enough of this talk, *Senhorita* Viviane—"

"You may call me Vivi. All of my friends do." At that moment her lashes raised, like a curtain letting in the sun, and for the first time their gazes locked. As they stared into each other's eyes, a kind of electric shock pierced him. He laughed lightly, turning away to break the spell, wondering if she had felt the same thing.

"I'm pleased and flattered, Vivi, to be included among your friends. I hope this means that we will be able to see each other again soon."

"Not for a while. I'm afraid that father would not approve."

He felt a flash of anger. "But—"

"You must wait until I come to visit you."

"*Não!* The jungle trail is too dangerous for you to ride alone."

"You forget that I am an expert rider, and I will not make the same mistake twice."

Once more their eyes met, exploring deeply, and this time he knew that she had read his first impulsive message and returned one of her own.

"When the time is right I will visit you. I promise," she said.

Not until he was riding homeward was he stricken with guilt. Odete! It had been too long since he had seen her. He resolved to get to Rio as soon as possible for a reunion with his betrothed. He would wipe out all memories of this brief jungle encounter with the enchanting Vivi.

TEN

As Peggy Carpenter swept a frightened glance at the ring of surrounding Indians, their arrows fitted to their bowstrings, Carlos called out urgently, "Sing, Peggy, *sing!* That is a friendly sign they understand." And he himself began an unmusical babbling, at the same time grinning widely at the Indian warriors.

Too scared to feel foolish about it, Peggy burst out with the first tune that came to her mind.

> America, America,
> God shed His grace on thee.
> And—
> *Da-dum* thy good with brotherhood
> From sea to shi-ning sea.

Although her voice quavered, never in her most fervid moments of patriotism had she ever sung with more feeling. Carlos and the others were following her lead now, gusting out with Brazilian words of their own.

And it was working! With a sense of relief she saw that the Indians were taking the arrows from their bows. Ah, the power of music!

Carlos hissed at her in a whisper, "It seems to have worked so far. Keep smiling at them. Act happy. Laugh—and make no sudden moves. From the symbols painted on their bodies, I think they are Atroaris —one of the most warlike tribes. We must be careful."

One of the warriors, a haughty fellow whose fierce expression was enhanced by the black dye covering

112

his face, walked forward a step or two and made violent motions with a pointing arm.

"He means we are to start walking in that direction," said Carlos.

Slowly, carefully, Peggy and the others began walking. The warriors arranged themselves on both sides and behind the small party, and one Indian walked ahead to lead them.

Peggy waited a minute or two before venturing to speak to Carlos. "What do you think they're going to do with us?"

"I don't think they intend to kill us," Carlos said reassuringly, "or we would already be dead. But you must remember that they have no love for the whites. Even more than we, they live in the memory of history, which is passed down to them by the tribal storytellers. All of them know as if it were yesterday that when the Portuguese began colonizing Brazil, the Indians were victimized. Since they didn't make good slaves, the Indians were a stumbling block to the first colonists, who showed little mercy—getting rid of them any way they could. Even in modern times some greedy *civilizados* have been known to machine-gun them, dynamite them from the air, and give them poisoned food. Keep that in mind and you'll understand why they are so hostile."

"My God!" Peggy exclaimed. "I'm surprised they didn't kill us right off."

"You must also remember," Carlos continued—quite nervously Peggy thought—"that they are just as human as we are—not untamable wild beasts. Primitive and fierce as they may be, they feel and respond to the same emotions we do. If we can convince them that we give them our full trust and love, they will return it."

"How do we do that?"

Carlos shrugged. "Let us hope that they are more charitable than most of the whites they have met. We

will have to—what is the expression you *norte-americanos* use?—play it by ear."

Arriving at the village—a collection of hivelike
dwellings constructed of wattles and thatch—they
were met by an inquisitive turnout of the entire tribe,
most of them naked.

As the warriors strutted in proudly, herding their
captives like so many sheep, they were greeted as
conquering heroes. From all sides rose exultant cries
of *"wooeee, wooeeeee,"* and hands and fists were
raised, shaking in the air.

Peggy shivered as a series of chills raced down her
spine. Carlos was affected differently.

"Meu Deus!" he breathed reverently. "This is the
first time I have ever seen an Atroari village. For years
I've tried to make contact with them, and they've
always evaded us. This could be our great success!"
He added dismally, "Or great disaster."

They were paraded to the center area of the village. A bizarre creature bedecked with colored
feathers, bright paint daubed over his face and
body, danced toward them with odd little hopping
steps while shaking what appeared to be a human
thighbone to which rattling teeth were attached by
cords. The warriors stepped back in obvious deference.

"He is the *wishinú,* the medicine man," Carlos said.
"He will examine us, and his decision will determine
how they treat us."

Chanting a weird tune, still shaking the thighbone,
the *wishinú* came close to Peggy and belched an
odorous breath in her face. Dancing over to Carlos, he
repeated the rude act, and then one by one he did the
same to the other FUNAI men.

"That is to rid us of all our *civilizado* diseases and
evils," Carlos whispered.

"He could make a fortune in my country," Peggy
said, trying to force back the trembling edge of hyste-

ria. "Now that we're cleansed, do you think they'll let us go?"

"That remains to be seen. Indians love ceremonies. They do almost nothing that can't be translated into some kind of rite."

Peggy's hysteria was pushing closer. She giggled. "Perhaps they'll adopt us into the tribe."

Carlos glared at her darkly. "I only wish I could be so optimistic."

Now a squat, muscular man of middle or advanced age was walking toward them slowly. His face was most ugly, made more savage by the black dye on his face. A thin wooden disk, at least six inches in diameter, had been inserted into a slitted and almost unbelievably distended lower lip, so that his mouth hung half open by the weight holding it down, showing yellowed teeth filed to sharp points. He wore a headdress of red macaw feathers, strips of jaguar fur around his loins and ankles, and necklaces of piranha teeth. One hand was clutched around a murderous-looking club that was inset with animal teeth.

Peggy shivered. "I don't like the looks of that horrible club!"

"That must be Chief Amaro, known for his fierceness. His very name comes from the *amaro* hardwood used by Indians for making war clubs. The whole tribe is conditioned and trained from childhood for war."

"War with the whites?"

"Primarily with their traditional enemies, the Txacatores. For centuries, the two tribes have refused to make peace. One of FUNAI's important objectives is to try to bring about harmony between them. As for the club he carries, I think it is mostly for show—the way some generals love to wear swords. I doubt we're in immediate danger. The chief will confer with the medicine man before making a decision. In such matters the opinion of the medicine man usually carries more weight than that of the chief, and since we've already been 'purified,' I think we're relatively safe."

The chief had in fact turned to jabber at the *wishinú*, who jabbered back, both gesticulating as they talked.

"What a sight!" she exclaimed. "Do I dare take out my camera?"

"Don't be a fool! They might think it's a weapon of some sort, or some mystical contraption that could steal their souls. Indians are volatile. One false move could bring sudden death."

Chief Amaro now stood in front of Peggy. Cautiously he raised a hand and touched the blond hair that was hanging wildly down her shoulders. With a timidity that seemed odd for such a savage, he took a few strands between his fingers and pulled tenderly. Peggy smiled at him. The chief smiled back and pulled harder. With an effort she kept smiling. Grinning broadly, the chief took a handful of her hair and yanked.

"Ouch!" she cried involuntarily. "Does he intend to scalp me?"

"I think he's never seen blond hair before. He wanted to make sure it was real."

Apparently that was the case, for now other Indians came forward to stroke her hair, then yank at it and start laughing.

With tears of pain streaming down her face, Peggy kept smiling.

Further indignities were in store, for now the old chief reached out a hand and began stroking her arm and her torso. He frowned when his hand came in contact with her blouse, and he pointed at her garments and began talking in an angry way.

"I can make out most of his words," said Carlos. "He's demanding that you remove your clothes."

Peggy was horrified. "Strip naked in front of all these leering Indians?"

"Nakedness means nothing to the Indians, Peggy. Most of the women are practically naked from the time they are born until the time they die. It doesn't create the same reactions as it does in us *civilizados*. Probably all they want is to see if your skin is as pale all over. They've never seen such white flesh. I think you'd better start disrobing."

Carlos was right. The warriors had begun pulling and tearing at her garments. Tactfully, Carlos turned his head and gave quiet orders to the other FUNAI men, who also averted their eyes as she began unbuttoning and unzipping. She took off her blouse, then the trousers, and her boots. When the warriors started plucking at her bra and panties, she hesitantly removed them too, remembering with apprehension that the *borrachudos*, the biting flies, also had a fondness for bare white flesh.

Blushing in humiliation, she stood tensed while the chief started pinching various parts of her body, including the most intimate, chuckling with great pleasure as he did so. Other warriors joined in the fun, all of them talking excitedly.

"Now I know what it must feel like to be a slave on the auction block," said Peggy, her voice cracking. "What are they saying, Carlos?"

Carlos's face was solemn. "As near as I can make out, they plan a tribal ceremony in your honor—"

"Oh, terrific!"

"More than that, Peggy. You see, the Indians have endless ceremonies to fit any kind of situation. In your case, you *are* the ceremony."

"Great! I'll sing, dance—anything they want. How many girls get a chance to be the toast of the Amazon?"

Carlos grimaced. "I'm trying to break it to you gently, Peggy. The Indians are very physical people. Most of all, they admire the human body, and yours is very beautiful . . ."

A horrible thought burst into her head, translated into a crawling sensation down her spine. She hardly dared put it into words.

117

"You mean they are planning—*rape?*"

Carlos looked miserable. "I'm afraid it's something worse."

"Worse! Is anything worse than being violated by a tribe of dirty savages?"

"For a modern woman, there are fates worse than rape. You see those women in the background? They are already preparing the ceremonial fires."

Peggy looked as the women piled wood on a fire, bringing it to leaping life. Some of them glared at her balefully. Her hysteria came bubbling out in zany words. "Jealous vixens! Can I help it if their men prefer blonds?"

"Peggy! This is no time for bad jokes! I must be blunt and tell you that the Indians were not pinching you out of sensual appreciation of your white flesh. They only wanted to see how tender it is. They admire your body so much that they think of it as possessing a kind of magic—white magic. The Atroaris are a cannibalistic people, and they all want a taste of it. The fires they are stoking up are cooking fires—"

Peggy swayed, but even as Carlos rushed over to prevent her from falling, she was gritting her teeth, determined not to show her weakness by fainting.

ELEVEN

For five days Hélio Rodrigues had been slogging through the jungle, often having to cut his way, using only his *adaga* to hack through the dense tangles of vines and other obstructive growth. He didn't know how far he had come, how far he had yet to go, or even if he had the chance of a virgin in hell of ever making it. Of the three of them who had started—all escapees from the miserable enforced labor conditions on the Vinicius de Onis plantation—only Hélio was left: one of his *companheiros* had been lost to the snapping jaws of a caiman; the other had collapsed from terminal exhaustion.

But Hélio kept going. He was stubborn, a rugged and formidable man. Squat, muscular, always with his dagger in his belt, he had a shaggy mane of black hair, a black beard, and black brows over fierce but large and sentimental eyes. A schoolgirl's concept of a dangerous pirate with a soft heart.

At thirty-three, Hélio had lived a dozen lifetimes, all in poverty. Although he was not overly ambitious, neither was he lazy. He never sought devious ways to cheat an employer unless he knew the employer was cheating him, which was nearly always.

The only work he had ever felt good about was when he was a *vaqueiro* in the cattle-grazing country of the arid *sertão*. The employer was a good man who permitted his *vaqueiros* to own a portion of the increase in herds under their care. Over several years, Hélio had acquired ownership of a half dozen scrawny cows—two in calf—and an aging bull. He was inspired into a brave attempt to start his own cattle ranch on a hundred *alqueires* of mortgaged wasteland, but two consecutive years of drought wiped out his meager beginning. Still owing money, he fled to Rio, where a friendly Carioca encountered in one of the *favela* cantinas tipped him off to a job driving a taxi and even spent two hours teaching him to drive. On his second day on the new job he smashed the decrepit taxi into a storefront and had to flee again, this time to the rubber forests of Amazonas.

It was on the de Onis plantation that he discovered slavery still existed. He toiled long hours, receiving no pay. He was told this was because he had incurred huge debts—the cost of bringing him there, the commission paid to the crew leader who hired him, food and clothing purchased at exorbitant prices from the company store, and other unknown charges. He must first work off his debt before expecting money, and he could not leave before paying off the debt, on threat of being arrested by plantation police and imprisoned as a criminal.

After a year of being worked to the tailbone and fed poorly while his debt to the employer only grew larger, he and the other two *flagelados*—the "whipped ones," as their class was referred to—made their escape into the jungle, into what others had warned could only mean certain death.

Maybe they were right; maybe not. He would soon know, for his strength was almost gone. His muscles burned, his bones were lame, his body fagged out. How much longer could he stick it out?

His shining goal was Inchaco, where he had heard that jobs could be found. It was said that at the Casa Hospitalidade one could obtain lodging and food on credit until the labor contractors came around and hired any man they could get to work on the new federal highway—an honest job that paid a man's food and shelter, with a few *cruzeiros* left over to spend on pleasures. A beer or two after work; now and then a woman.

Indeed, it was the thought of a woman that most sustained him as he struggled through the days of cutting, crawling, wading through clotted swamp water that was alive with squirmy things, and forcing passage by brute strength. He had never married, being of too honest a nature to burden a wife with his poverty, and he had only known women who gave their favors out of kindness or for the few *cruzeiros* he could borrow or scrape together. The visions of women that now filled his head were somewhat patterned after a brightly enameled effigy he had once seen in Rio of the spiritist divinity Pomba Gira, the sensuously smiling she-demon who wore a jeweled crown and rich queenly robes that were spread apart all down the front to reveal beautiful nakedness and breasts with crimson nipples tipped in gold.

Knowing that such sublime depravity was fantastically beyond his reach, his dreams included places loaded with a plenitude of more secular females, as in Rio, where all the women were as pretty as magazine pictures. All kinds, all shades of color. Some dressed in little more than strings around their breasts and crotch. Some leaning out from windows with inviting smiles.

Ah! All it took were the *cruzeiros.*

Such fantasies gave him renewed energy to plunge on, to bull his way through the seemingly endless jungle obstacles—at the same time feeling grateful for the irony of circumstances that had forced him to go so long without a woman. For early in life he had learned that a man's endurance was stored in his balls, and only a fool wasted it on women in times of stress.

But the time came when Hélio knew his rope was coming to its end.

He stood, wobbling, his legs ready to buckle. With a vast effort he raised a hand to mop his forehead in an attempt to keep more sweat from dribbling down to sting his eyes. For most of the day he had strained and writhed like a contortionist, fighting through networks of lianas that seemed to have a life of their own as they snagged his legs and torso. He'd barged through brambles with needle thorns that went in deep, caused swelling, and were difficult to cut out. He'd clambered over fallen trees and crawled under them. He'd sloshed across an *igarapé*, a narrow canoe stream, barely a few steps ahead of the protruding eyes and snout of a crocodile gliding toward him. He'd been scolded by the coarse-voiced *ciganas*, the hiss-birds clambering heavily in the branches above him, and he'd been screamed at by careening monkeys when he tried to stone one of them for food.

All he had eaten for many days were the perfumed fruits of the *capú-assú*, a few nuts hard to crack open, and tubers dug with his knife along the stream banks. He'd managed to catch a few rodents, and lacking matches for cooking, he'd skinned them and eaten them raw. To numb the gnawings of hunger he'd chewed on leaves of the coca tree—from which the *civilizados* made cocaine and which Indians and *caboclos* chewed for its stimulating effect.

Now he was beyond stimulation. He had sweated and bled and cursed until there was nothing left in him but the desire to lie down, and *se Deus quizer*, God willing, die as quickly and painlessly as possible.

He lay down. Ah, it was so pleasant to give up, to relax! After all, was it so bad to die? He remembered the face of his *companheiro* during his last moments of life, the little smile. Perhaps the smile was from seeing the face of God.

Sighing, he turned on his side, and he found himself staring straight into the unblinking, jewel-bright black eyes—only two feet away—of a large serpent, at least eight feet long. He recognized it instantly as a jararaca, a most deadly snake.

Oddly, he felt no fear as he watched the reptile draw its length into a looping coil, its spearlike head raised a few inches above the ground, regarding him with merciless jet eyes. Again he thought, death could be very pleasant. The paralyzing effects of the snake poison would be instant, killing all pain. He would simply drift off into forever—perhaps into the arms of a forgiving God who might admire him for his struggles to reach freedom.

Moments later, the slender head curved gracefully, and the long body went slithering into the underbrush, apparently deciding that Hélio was no threat, and certainly too big to swallow.

Hélio felt a tingle of excitement. It was a sign! Some great and mystical power was protecting him against evil!

As he lay there pondering the miracle, his ear, pillowed against the ground, picked up vague subterranean sounds. Rising up, he took his dagger, plunged it deep into the earth, and leaned down to clench his teeth around the haft. It was an Indian trick, a jungle telephone for amplifying through one's bones the vibrations of distant footsteps, hoofbeats, or approaching vehicles.

The sounds were now clearly distinguishable—it was the earthshaking road-building machinery! Perhaps only a few, perhaps many, miles away—it mattered not.

With a good rest he could make it.

He lay back and sank into deep, sweet sleep, blissful in the knowledge that he no longer had to fear any of the wild jungle creatures.

God was looking out for him.

At a back table in the Casa Hospitalidade, Generosa was seated alone, sipping from a bottle of warm beer, when the apparition of a man barged through the front door. He stood there for a few moments, blinking as he adjusted his eyes from the blinding sun to the dimness inside, and Generosa gave him her usual once-over.

Maldito! There was no money in this one. She had seen beggars young and old, cripples, the half blind, the sick, the crazy, all sorts of weak excuses for men who came in looking for work, but none so miserable as this one: His clothes hung in rags. He was filthy with mud and greenish swamp scum, some of it even matted in his beard and the wild tangle of his black hair. Ragged cuts scabbed with dried blood marred his hands, arms, and face, which was burned so dark he looked more than half Indian. Still, like all of them, he would want a woman. She began humming the tune of a *vaqueiro* folk song:

> Red bull, black bull, spotted bull,
> Each has its own hue,
> But in each horny head the same thought,
> A sweet cow for his love to prove.

Though it was a slow day, with only a scattering of *caboclos* along the bar, there were times when even Generosa drew the line. Dirty workingmen, yes—but not scum. Scornfully, she took another sip of beer.

From the far end of the bar the hotel owner bawled out, "Hey, you scarecrow in the doorway—over here if you've come to sign in."

Out of pure boredom Generosa watched the wretch walk toward the owner, limping slightly. Not from infirmity because he was not old, and where his shirt had been torn half away she saw the muscles were huge, the veins standing out against the dark skin in the way that came from hard work.

As if sensing her scrutiny, he stopped suddenly and looked at her. For several moments he just stared, entranced, as if she were a long-lost sister. Or lover.

She stared back, noting for the first time that those big eyes were quite beautiful. Eloquent with meaning. They were drinking her in, enrapt. Plainly he was woman-starved. It had been a long time since she'd seen a man look at her that way, and she felt a vague stirring in her belly and a sudden rise of sympathy.

Coitado! Poor thing, she thought, he looks like he's been swallowed by a crocodile and spit out again. He's not tall, it's true, but look at those broad shoulders. He looks strong enough to tip over a house. And that big knife in his belt . . .

"Hey you, *Senhor* Swamp Rat," the hotel owner called snappishly. "You want to sign up for work or don't you? If not, get the hell out!"

The man turned away and limped over to where the hotel owner stood with the big registry book. Generosa knew why the boss was so anxious to sign him in. It was plain as the blood and dirt on his face that the man had run off from some plantation job where he still owed a lot of money. Sooner or later the plantation owner would come looking for him, and the hotel owner would collect a big reward for turning him in. *Que pena!* What a pity that would be.

The owner was writing in the book. Ah, so for a while it would be all right. He would be given a place to sleep, food—at double the regular prices, which would be paid by the labor contractor, charged double again to the poor devil on his next job, and taken from his wages. Then, if the plantation owner caught up with him, all those new charges would be added to his old debt. *Diabo!* It would take him a lifetime to pay off.

Later she saw him seated at a table, old Rosa waddling to serve him with warm beer. His face lighted up as if he'd seen an angel, and he raised the bottle to his mouth and started guzzling. Rosa went back to the kitchen and soon came waddling out again with a large bowl of *feijão*. Never had she seen Rosa moving so fast. A ragged man like that!

It started her thinking. Someday she would be like Rosa—fat, waddling around making eyes at the lowest scum who wouldn't even look at her except as a piece of furniture. Generosa still got many customers because women were scarce up here near the end of the highway and lonely men weren't too particular. But soon the younger girls would start coming. Soon there would be too many women. The men would start picking.

Generosa often thought of these things, then quickly dismissed such depressive thoughts. It was too soon to worry about such things. She was making good enough money, had a tidy sum tucked away. Sooner or later she would find a good man to marry.

But so far, no good man had come along. None was interested in anything more than getting his money's worth for as long as he could stick it out in bed. And already she was almost thirty, getting too plump, sagging in places. Time was running out.

If the right man should come along—someone who really liked her—she'd go out of her way to be so nice to him that he'd remember her and come back again. And maybe . . .

He was looking her way again. He had shoved aside his empty *feijão* bowl and was just staring. Those big black eyes—so expressive!

With a good bath, cleaned up and in decent clothes, he would look quite nice, she decided.

Standing up, she brushed the crumbs off her slit skirt and started walking toward him, swaying her hips gently.

Hélio watched the approaching woman with unbelieving eyes. He knew she was just a tavern *puta*, but so beautiful! Like the Pomba Gira goddess in many ways. The same inviting smile, the sensual red lips, her slit skirt showing an enticing bit of naked thigh above the stocking. And of buxom shape, the way he preferred. Almost like his jungle dreams!

"Ah, *senhor*," she greeted. (How nice her voice!) "You look so lonely, so sad."

"My sadness, *senhorita*, fled like a shadow from the sun when I first saw you."

"Ah, and so romantic! My name is Generosa. My price is fifty *cruzeiros*."

He spread his hands apologetically. "But I have no money, nothing."

Her smile grew sweeter. "Today I am not busy. For this time I won't charge."

His dark face flashed with a show of white teeth. A grateful smile. "For how long?"

"For as long as you like."

Hélio got up and followed her upstairs, joy filling his heart.

God was still looking out for him.

TWELVE

In growing desperation, Carlos stared at the ceremonial fires, which were now roaring, snapping, and crackling as bundles of dried wood were heaped on by the Indian women. Through the billowing blue smoke the women's naked bodies glistened coal black from the fresh genipa sap they had been painted with. Salmon-colored lines had been painted across their cheeks and noses, and each wore a crimson bixa flower in her hair. Carlos knew that the women only painted themselves in that manner for the most important ceremonies.

After all, how often did they get the chance to broil the flesh of a white female?

Peggy pressed closer within his encircling arm. Striving to be brave, she had neither fainted nor sobbed, but when she turned her face against his shoulder he felt her body quivering and the warm moistness of her tears through his thin FUNAI T-shirt.

Mingled with his fierce surge of protectiveness was a strong primal awareness of her nakedness. It shamed him, but he could not help it. She had the body of a curvy young girl, small, lovely breasts with rosebud nipples, the whitest of tender skin, and a small focal triangle of pale golden pubic hair.

"Isn't there anything we can do to change their minds?" she murmured.

"I'm thinking hard, Peggy."

To attempt to fight—or to escape—was out of the question. The warriors guarding them on both sides had arrows fitted to their bows. Several held blowguns. Amazonas Indians knew the secrets of the dead-

128

liest drugs. Even a scratch from one of those poison-tipped arrows or darts meant quick death.

Reason with them? How could he reason against the age-old religious beliefs of an aboriginal people? Yet he knew that an undercurrent of logic ran through all their primordial superstitions, even if the original reasons for things had become so blurred by time, so instinctive or subliminal that they no longer understood why they acted as they did.

Clearly they believed they needed a sacrifice to one of their sternest gods—a *civilizado* sacrifice. Why? Perhaps to cast a spell or curse against the hated *civilizado* road builders who were destroying their ancestral homeland.

In a flash he thought he saw a solution—a terrible one, but still a solution.

Turning to one of the guards, he spoke in the *Língua Geral.* "I must speak to your *curaca.* Quick! It is important."

Doubtfully, after conferring with the other guards, the warrior went to fetch the chief.

Chief Amaro arrived, decked out in all his finery, showing the great import he attached to the ceremony in progress. He wore a brand-new *utiapa,* a wrap-around skirt, his bare chest and limbs dyed black. His face was striped with red and black; his hair was braided into strands, and waving above it was a diadem of toucan feathers.

"This innocent woman," Carlos said carefully, "cannot be sacrificed! It would anger your gods and bring great dishonor on your tribe because the woman is the mother of three small children who need her." His lie, which he felt was justified in such a life-and-death matter, was based on his knowledge that Indians loved children and revered motherhood. He continued, his voice faltering a bit, "I beseech you, great chief, to let me take the woman's place. You may sacrifice me to appease your gods, for I, too, am young, and my flesh is tender."

At once the chief burst into an angry torrent of words, shaking his head vigorously. The *wishinú*, he told Carlos, had already communed with the gods and they had demanded the sacrifice of a white female to atone for the loss of his daughter, who had been kidnapped by the *civilizados*.

So that was it! The chief had lost a daughter to some marauding *civilizados*—perhaps crude *caboclos* from a nearby plantation—and nothing but eye-for-an-eye vengeance would suffice.

The chief turned and stalked away, and Carlos knew his desperate plan to save Peggy had failed. His heart had gone out so completely to the girl—so beautiful, so brave in her fragile nakedness and vulnerability—that he would have gladly leaped in front of machine guns to shield her from the horrors that would now follow.

For as much as he loved and understood Indian ways—and he could even justify the cruelty and warfare—he found most repugnant the cannibalism that was part of the culture. He knew only too well what would come next: the rites of the cannibalistic feast.

First, Peggy would be clubbed to death. Then her warm blood would be offered around as a cocktail, and some of the women would smear it over their breasts to absorb some of the enemy's strength.

Next, her body would be quartered and roasted. The whole tribe would partake of the broiled flesh, with the delicacies reserved for the chief and his favorite warriors.

This vicious cruelty was in direct contrast to all of the Indian culture that Carlos most admired. In family life the Indians were loving and kind. Children and babies rarely cried, being permitted a great deal of freedom and almost continual bodily contact with mothers, siblings, and friends. Except for occasional tribal warfare, the Indians lived a peaceful, good life, planting their gardens, hunting until game grew scarce, then moving on in the abundant jungle to plant new gardens and hunt new game.

Their every act was in strict obedience to the complex set of ancient rules and laws of their tribal religions—as interpreted by the medicine man, who wielded the powers of a judge. Religion was the most potent force in their lives, and to break a taboo dictated by the gods or spirits was the greatest of crimes, often punishable by death.

Carlos stared at the blazing fires, his brain furiously at work. There were four fires—one for each quarter of Peggy's body—and the women were beginning to lay rows of flat rocks over the red coals. The rocks, some of which would crack and even explode from the intensity of heat, would serve as roasting pans. The licking red flames cast pinkish highlights on the women's faces, their wide smiles showing how eagerly they were looking forward to the feast.

Meanwhile, the tribal musicians increased the tempo of their beating on rawhide drums, the rattlings of clay and bone castanets, and the weird ribbons of mournful sounds coming from bamboo flutes. The subtle rhythms were becoming more frenzied.

Peggy lifted her head. "I wish I could tape that music. It's so—eerie!"

Carlos grimaced. Didn't she realize the music was a sacramental dirge preluding her imminent death? Did she expect a miracle?

Miracles played a large part in Indian religion, he thought, wondering what kind of miracle he could call upon to save Peggy.

Carlos was a dedicated student of the rites, customs, and mystic beliefs of the Amazonas Indians. In college he had majored in anthropology, specializing in Indian studies. He knew all the different gods and spirits of the various tribes. The tribes generally shared in the belief of a benevolent "father above" and a malevolent "Satan below." Their deities included the male Sun and his wife, the Moon. Their evil spirits mostly resided in the lower forms of jungle life, particularly the jaguar and the boa. Separate tribes worshiped scores of different gods, demons, and spiritist divinities.

In the case of the Atroaris who now held them captive, the most powerful divinities were Nungui, the earth goddess, and to a lesser degree Shacaimo, her husband.

The medicine man approached, chanting, and began a hopping dance around Peggy. After a few moments he produced a small brush and a clay dish of pigment and started daubing white polka dot spots all over Peggy's face and body.

Frantically Carlos searched through the Indian lore stored in his brain for the significance.

The white spots were symbolic of the cicatrices, or the unavenged wounds of the tribal ancestors. Dancing, chanting, and drumming, of course, were the favored means for inducing divinities or spirits to come from their other worlds to witness ceremonials and to communicate with medicine men, who were believed to be on a special wavelength giving them direct contact with spirits denied to most others.

Such arrivals of spirit gods were manifested by the *wishinú* being "possessed" by the particular divinity being addressed. The medicine man would suddenly go into convulsions, as if from electric shock.

But it could also happen to any devout believer, and it was a sign of great honor.

Finished with the daubing, the *wishinú* danced away. The flutes were wailing crazily, the fury of the drumbeats maddening, the rattles speeded to a tempo as fast as the whirring warning of a giant rattlesnake. Women had piled fresh pitch wood on the fires to produce boiling black clouds of smoke. Peggy started coughing. Carlos's eyes and nostrils stung.

Any moment now the *wishinú* would go into his hysterical trance . . .

Carlos suddenly let out an unearthly scream and staggered forward as if shot. He began shaking violently and groaning. His back arched. He tore at his hair, laughing crazily. His eyes rolled as if unhinged in their sockets while his face went into agonized contortions.

"Carlos—Carlos!" Peggy called. "What's wrong?"

As if not hearing her, he fell to the ground, rolled around convulsively, howling like a dog. Then he lay still.

All the music, all movement among the Indians had ceased. Only the crackling of the fires could be heard.

Carlos's voice rose to a harsh scream. "Oh, great all-powerful Nungui, goddess of the earth, goddess of fertility, and goddess of motherhood, and Shacaimo, greatest of all warrior gods who brings swift punishment to those who disobey the laws of Nungui, come you now to drive away the evil spirits who are conspiring against you to bring false sacrifice to this fertile woman, this symbol of motherhood, which will bring great harm to all Atroari women."

Carlos paused to gather breath, letting his tongue loll out. Then his voice rose to a trembling moan. "But I beseech you, Nungui, greatest of all gods and goddesses, to forgive the Atroaris, for they are like children and know not what they do. Tear the evil from their hearts and set them on the road to righteousness..." He let his voice trail away and lay stiffly, as in a trance.

In the somber silence, all Indian eyes turned to the medicine man, looking to him for an interpretation of the puzzling behavior and words of the *civilizado*, only a smattering of which they had understood.

The *wishinú* had begun jabbering at the chief, pointing angrily at Carlos.

"The *civilizado* is a sham, an imposter!" screamed the medicine man, himself an expert at fakery. "He knows nothing of our gods!"

"Then," responded the chief, "how does he know of Nungui, of Shacaimo? And a great spirit entered into his body. Never have I seen so strong a sign from our gods, even in you—"

Another outpouring of indignant words from the medicine man, whose tribal powers almost matched, sometimes overmatched, those of the chief. The two were often in rivalry for greater control of the tribe.

The chief's responses were less certain now, and soon a circle of subchiefs had gathered to join them in earnest conference.

From his position on the ground, Carlos had edged his head sideways to watch. The *wishinú* had produced a small pot in which he was burning herbs. His eyes were glazed, upcast, as he began intoning a chant in communion with the gods. The chief and subchiefs listened intently, plainly impressed.

Carlos's hopeful mood sank. It was clear that the *wishinú* was not about to be upstaged by a *civilizado*. The old fraud had his reputation to uphold and doubtless had endless arcane wiles in his bag of tricks.

Carlos felt that his desperate scheme to save Peggy had failed. All he had accomplished was to delay the execution.

He lay unmoving, resigned and depressed. Defeated. Knowing there was absolutely nothing more he could do to help Peggy, not even wanting to face her. But at least he had played his game to the hilt.

Minutes crawled past—how many he didn't know, for time seemed suspended—before the intrusion of one of the most unheard-of sounds in the deep jungle.

Hoofbeats!

He rolled to a sitting position just in time to witness the astonishing sight of two horses and riders entering the village. The lead rider was a naked Indian girl, the other a brown *moreno*. Loud cries of *wooeeee! woooeee!* rose from all the Indians. A chanting started, as did the drumming, the rhythms exultant.

Peggy, Carlos noted, had her camera out—against his strict orders!—and was rapidly snapping shots of Indians in all directions. The crazy, adorable minx— taking pictures at her own funeral!

But the warrior guards were paying no attention to Peggy. They had removed the arrows from the bow-strings, were gaping at the Indian girl, who had now slipped off the horse and was advancing toward the chief.

He met her gravely, with folded arms, and the girl talked rapidly, excitedly, gesticulating at the *moreno* and the horses.

After a while the chief approached Carlos. Tears swam in the old fellow's eyes.

"The gods have spoken. My daughter has been returned. You and your woman and your men are free to go."

Peggy rode the only horse on the procession out; the horse ridden by the Indian girl had been left as a gift. Carlos, his FUNAI men, and Pio walked.

Peggy smiled down at Carlos, who walked beside the horse. "You certainly put on a good act, Carlos. You even had me convinced."

"I'm not so sure it was an act, Peggy. After I got started, some great outside force seemed to take over and direct my words." His voice grew somber.

"Maybe—just maybe, the gods did intervene . . ."

THIRTEEN

Raul toiled long hours, feeling a touch of desperation. The house had to be cleaned up, repairs made, the grounds put in order. Many more men had to be hired and the proper equipment purchased for clearing more jungle land, fertilizing, and putting in a crop of weed trees. Most important, he needed a top chemical engineer to give technical advice and supervise construction of a prototype alcohol refinery. Perhaps his father had been right. At the very least, it may have been premature to attempt to get his project off the ground without considerably more advance planning.

In addition to Braz he now had only Pio to lean on. The half-breed pilot, who had returned a week ago with only one horse, had been trained to repair motors, and he possessed a natural affinity for all technical matters. He had repaired the radiotelephone equipment, finding only a loose connection. He and Braz had also made several flights into Inchaco to hire and ferry back more workers.

When asked how the trip with the Indian girl had gone, the taciturn Pio had simply shrugged. "No problems. The girl was returned safely."

"What happened to the other horse?"

"I left it with the chief as token reparation for what the girl had gone through."

"*Bom!* That was wise. However, I shall have to deduct the cost of the horse from your salary. In view of your many days of arduous journey, you will receive a bonus to compensate for it." Raul flashed a smile to show he was joking.

"My delay was caused only because I met a *norteamericana senhorita* and let her use my horse to save her a long walk back to her camp."

"You met an American lady in the jungle? That's insane!"

"All *norte-americanos* are *loucos*." Pio grinned and added, "But she was very beautiful."

And that was all that Raul was ever told about Pio's adventure.

At the moment, Pio and Braz were on another flight to Inchaco to bring back more workers, and Raul was in the ancient sugar mill building checking over its rusted machinery, some of which, Pio had ventured, might be cleaned up and salvaged for use in a small experimental plant for the processing of wood into alcohol.

"*O patrão—*" One of the workers had appeared in the doorway.

"*O que é que você quer*, Pedro?"

The *caboclo* grinned. "A beautiful *senhorita* has just come through the jungle on horseback to visit you."

The visitor was Viviane Vargas. Relaxed in the saddle, she smiled down at him. Her garb was casual: faded jeans, plaid shirt, a bright red scarf around her raven hair.

"I promised I'd visit you. Remember?"

"But, Vivi, such a long dangerous ride! I'm surprised that your father allowed it."

"Don't be silly. Both you and my father fail to realize that I ride as well or better than any man. Anyway, father is out in the fields today overseeing the planting of a shipment of hybrid rubber tree seedlings. I'll be home long before he gets back, so he won't have to worry."

"Nevertheless, on your return I will insist on escorting you."

"You may escort me part of the way if you must, but for now please satisfy my curiosity and show me how you turn wood into alcohol."

Inside the old sugar mill building, Raul waved a hand at the rusted machinery.

"All this outmoded equipment is for making cane

sugar on a primitive level. The stripped cane was first put into the big hopper of that ugly device over there, called the shredder, to be chopped up before passing through those heavy grooved rollers, the crusher, to extract the juice, which was then fed into the boiling vats—"

"But what has making sugar got to do with alcohol?"

"Sugar is one of the bases for making alcohol by the fermentation process. But I must confess I am not very knowledgeable when it comes to all the complex modern technology involved—especially the highly technical methods of producing methanol wood alcohol from trees. For that I will be dependent on hiring the best chemical engineer that money can buy."

"Where can you find such a person?"

"I am working through an engineering placement service in Rio, and they think they have located a well-qualified man for the job. They will notify me as soon as an interview with him can be arranged."

She glanced around somewhat skeptically. "And you think all this can be converted into an alcohol manufacturing plant?"

He laughed. "Hardly. Even to convert it into a small experimental installation will probably cost a hundred thousand or more. At best we might salvage the shredder and the vats. As for an actual alcohol production plant with the necessary huge holding tanks, the cost will run into the millions."

"*Bom Deus!* You dream big dreams! But how can you build such a factory way out here in the jungle?"

"The enormous machinery required and all the various components will be trucked in and assembled on the site."

"But the highway does not reach this far."

"By the grace of God, and the National Department of Highways, I am expecting the new highway to reach my land in the very near future."

"Then everything is dependent on the highway?"

He grinned wryly. "Without the highway, my dreams could not possibly be realized."

"Ah, *não!* Your dreams are so heroic. I shall pray for you. But I have other questions. Why did your ancestor who built this sugar mill not plant many fields of cane and keep on making sugar instead of closing the *fazenda* and moving away?"

"I can only speculate, Vivi. My grandfather Júlio built this during the rubber boom. By the time the boom ended, he'd probably discovered that the cleared land was not fertile enough to make money raising sugarcane, so he moved to the cattle country."

"Your grandfather was wise. If he had stayed, perhaps he would have lost all his money, as my grandfather did." She smiled. "On the other hand, if the de Carvalhos had remained here all this time, you would have been our nearest neighbors. Perhaps you and I might have been friends since childhood."

"We're friends now, Vivi."

"I meant a deeper kind of friendship—"

He broke into laughter. "You mean lovers?"

She flushed. "I didn't say that, but if I had, would it have been so funny?"

Immediately he was solemn. "All I meant was that I am at least ten years older than you are. Aside from that, my great-grandfather Jorge was an utter scoundrel who must have antagonized your ancestors. I gather from your father's attitude that bad feelings toward the de Carvalho clan still exist."

Her expression was grave. "He surely cannot hold against you any sins that might have been committed by your ancestors. Yet I must be honest and agree that what you say seems to be true. I cannot understand it. My father's dearest wish is to have me make a marriage with some nice young man from a good family— and what family today is held in higher esteem than the de Carvalhos? It puzzles me why he did not treat you with great cordiality."

Dom João's coldness puzzled Raul, too, and its very

unfairness brought out a welling of sympathy for this girl, who was even more directly affected by her father's strange temperament. How did Dom João expect his daughter to meet any potential husbands if he kept her penned up at home? Obviously she wasn't very sophisticated with men or she wouldn't have been so outspoken. Raul considered telling her that he was already engaged to Odete, but he decided that it would be presumptuous—certainly she hadn't the slightest romantic aspirations toward him, who was so much older. She was just a lonely girl with too few opportunities to meet boys and eager for any kind of companionship.

"Vivi—may I ask a personal question?"

"You may, but I do not promise to answer."

"You say that your father wishes you to marry well. Yet he keeps you virtually isolated in the middle of the jungle away from men. How do you explain the contradiction?"

A frown creased the smooth beauty of her face. "You must remember that my father is typical of the old school of patriarchal domination. Such Brazilian fathers do not think daughters should have much freedom—even to pick their own husbands. When the time comes, he will pick for me. That is why he does not wish me to continue in college. I was getting too many 'modern' notions, such as women having the right to make their own decisions. He fears everything modern, perhaps because he still lives in the dream of being a great grandee when in his heart he knows he is a failure. He is blindly hostile toward the modern world. He feels it has let him down and even threatened his control over his daughter. Even the way I dress—" With a graceful sweep of a hand she indicated her shirt and jeans.

"He is furious because I insist on riding horses and dressing in an unladylike way. Brazilian fathers of the old school believe that males and females must have the greatest possible differentiation in figure and dress. The man must be strong; the female weak. He must be noble; she beautiful, without a trace of masculine vigor or agility. Such fathers would prefer their daughters to be almost sickly, somewhat morbid—or plump and soft, domestic and motherly, with big hips and buttocks. Daughters are expected to be modest, retiring types who sit and read poetry or do needlework while contentedly waiting for a suitable marriage to be arranged."

Her heated outpouring surprised him. He grinned. "You've certainly given me a full answer, Vivi. It explains a lot. What it doesn't explain is why, with such a father, you have become rebellious enough to ride and dress as you do."

She shrugged. "Maybe it was the way I was born, but I think it is because fathers do not know how to force their daughters to obey. They know only how to handle sons. Only mothers know how to train daughters; they can easily see through all the wiles and artifices a daughter can use to exasperate a father and get around his sternest orders. But I love my father and try to compromise. I spend much time at home practicing on the piano, doing pretty little watercolors, or reading poetry."

"Do you write poetry, too?"

"Of course, I try. What girl too much alone with too much time on her hands doesn't? I write only foolish verse for my eyes alone."

Out of perfunctory courtesy he said, "One's inner thoughts, if honest, are never foolish. Would you ever allow other eyes to see some of your verse?"

"Are you sincere in wishing to read some of my verse?"

Realizing he had fallen into his own word trap, he said with forced enthusiasm, "I would consider it a great privilege."

Her eyes seemed to take on a deeper glow. "The time may come when I would want you to read some of my secret thoughts, but for now . . ."

She let the sentence hang, and their glances locked; again he felt the same electric contact he had felt the first time he had stared into the depths of her dark eyes. He sensed that she was probing for some signal from him, a response to the signal she was giving. He wanted all of a sudden to grasp her in his arms, kiss her, but he was restrained by his code of gentlemanly behavior, his sense of guilt, and an unbidden memory flash of Odete.

"Vivi!"

The harsh voice came from Dom João, who stood in the open doorway.

He strode in. Tall, straight, arrogant. He wore English riding breeches, spurs, a white silk shirt. His haughty jet black eyes stabbed at them.

"One of my men saw you riding in this direction, and I suspected where you were headed!"

Vivi's eyes flashed in anger. "Father, must you humiliate me by following me as if I were a delinquent child?"

"I'll ask the questions!" he thundered at her. "What in God's name are you doing here?"

"As you can see, I was engaged in conversation with *Senhor* de Carvalho."

"*Alone* with him in this—" his angry eyes swept over the rusting machinery, the cobwebbed ceiling, "in this abandoned place?"

Raul cut in. "Vivi was interested in how this machinery works, *senhor,* and I was just explaining—"

"Machinery is not for females to understand, *senhor,*" Dom João said coldly.

"She has every right to understand anything she wishes to understand," Raul shot back.

"*Veja!* She is my daughter, not yours! I decide what is best for her. Any gentleman should know that it is degrading to a young lady of fine breeding to bring her alone into a building of this sort, meant only for *pretos*—"

Vivi's words came in anguished appeal. "Father— you don't understand! *Senhor* de Carvalho brought me in here only because it was my wish—"

"And it is my wish to hear no more! Come—we will go."

Obediently, her head bowed forlornly, she went out, with Dom João close behind. Neither gave a backward glance.

Raul stood there in frustrated fury, flooded with sympathy for the daughter. And perplexed.

What was it about him or his family that Dom João so hated?

FOURTEEN

Manuel Gonzaga released his finger pressure from the trigger of the chain saw, allowing the motor to subside to a more tolerable level of sound. Hour after hour of cutting with the motorized saw, exposed continuously to its whining roar as its teeth chewed through the green wood, had left his ears ringing, beginning to ache. Also, he was much annoyed by two or three bees that had begun zooming past his head like miniature jet planes.

He guessed it was the sugarcane joint he'd been chewing. Bees were always attracted to sugar. Throwing the remaining section of cane stalk aside and spitting out the chewed-up cane fiber, he walked over to where he had put the jug of lemon water, wrapped in old newspapers for coolness, at the base of a tree.

While he was swigging from the jug, one of the bees swooped down and landed on the back of his hand. It was a black little bugger striped with orange, and Manuel brushed at it in annoyance with his free hand.

Diabo! Too late. The back of the hand holding the jug felt as if touched by the burning tip of a cigarette. With another slap, Manuel managed to squash the insect against the smarting sting. He put the jug down and returned to the chain saw. Now there were several of the nasty little bastards hovering close to his head. Maybe there was a nest nearby. Well, what was a sting or two? He would finish cutting this tree and then move on. He wanted to make a good showing for his new *patrão,* the crazy *Senhor* Raul de Carvalho, who paid unheard-of wages, even more than any of the highway workers were paid. A good man to work for, *graças a Deus*. With the money he could save, he could win the love of a beautiful *senhorita*. Ah!

With renewed energy he picked up the idling chain saw and positioned himself firmly by the tree to resume cutting. The opposite side of the trunk had already been notched, and it would take but a few minutes to send the tree toppling. The angry whine of the saw's motor rose and dipped and then roared higher as the racing teeth bit deeper into the tree. *ZrrrzzzzzZZZRRRRrrzzzzZZZZRRRRZZZZZ.* The sound merged with the crackling of wood fibers as the tree began to tilt.

But what was that swirling black cloud falling from the sky with a sound of its own? *Zzeeeeeeeeeeeuuuuuuuummmmmmmmmmm.* He glanced up and saw the beehive suspended from a branch.

Dropping the chain saw, he started to run.

It was no use. They were darting all around, enveloping him in a whirlwind of swooping black and orange shadows and a furious sound: *ZZ-ZZZZUUÜUUUUUUUMMMMMMMMMMMM!* Burning sensations were stabbing into him everywhere. Down his neck, back, chest, like red-hot coals sprinkled under his shirt. On his face and arms and hands. Like a thousand needles stitching into him from a hideous sewing machine run wild. On his arms, wherever he could see, they were massed like thick fur, pumping their barbed abdomens at him in senseless fury. Others were hurling their fat little bodies at him like fiery darts as the buzzing of countless wings stormed in his ears. *ZzzzzzzuuuuuuuUUUUUUMMMMMMMMMM-MMMMMMMMMMMMMMMMM!* They had gone crazy.

So had Manuel. He ran, flailing his arms, stumbling along like a wild man, his face already too swollen to see. He tried to scream for help, and at once they were in his mouth like hot rivets, bringing him to choking silence. They were tangled in his hair, in his boots, finding every part of his body, torching him with fire.

He fell, almost gratefully, into the whirling, enveloping black cloud . . .

"Diabo!" Raul swore softly when informed of the death of Manuel Gonzaga. "So now we have another problem!"

It was a most serious problem. He had heard about the Brazilian killer bee, the phenomenal product of a breeding accident. In hopes of increasing honey production, scientists had brought in a strain of the notoriously ferocious race of African honeybees, the *Apis mellifera adansonti.* In 1957, through an unfortunate error made by a visiting beekeeper who did not know the bees were dangerous, twenty-six African queens escaped from the genetics experiment station near São Paulo. The bees quickly intermixed with the gentler imported European bees then in Brazil, procreating a fierce new race, and they had since spread to many sections of Brazil and into other countries, bringing terror and death.

Raul, seated in the office he had set up in the manse, looked across his desk at Hélio, one of the new workers, who had brought the body in. "Did you see it happen?"

Hélio, a squat and powerful man, rolled his large, sensitive eyes. "I heard his screams and came close enough to see the *albehas* chasing him. Quickly I made a fire from dead branches and piled it with green leaves to make much smoke to keep the devils away from me. After they returned to their hive, it was safe to get Manuel and carry him here."

Raul looked at Hélio. Here was a man who could think and act quickly in an emergency, who even had enough consideration and courage to bring back the body, at the risk of being attacked himself.

"Did you see any other hives?"

"Não, but bees swarm often. There will be other hives near."

"Apparently you know something about bees. Do

you think it would be safe to take a few men with you and make a careful search for other hives on my land?"

"It can be done. It would be necessary to carry a can of oil and a bundle of dry wood to make a quick fire, as well as having thick blankets to protect us if any bees attack. But if we walk quietly and take great care not to disturb the bees, we will be safe."

Raul turned to Braz, who stood nearby listening impassively. "What do you think, Braz?"

"I think we should make a search for the beehives as soon as possible and destroy them. Until then, it will not be safe to send our men out to work. I myself will pick several volunteers, and we will go with Hélio to look."

"*Está bem.* But first make arrangements for Manuel's burial."

"That will be done."

"And remember, you are only to locate the bees, not try to destroy them. For that we will need expert advice."

"*Sim.*"

After Braz and Hélio were gone, Pio thrust his head in the doorway.

"Boss, there is a *Senhorita* Odete on the radiotelephone to speak to you."

Odete was petulant.

"You have not come to Rio to see me for so long, I think you must have forgotten all about me," she complained.

"On the contrary, I am counting the days until I can get away."

"If you count for too long, I shall be very angry with you."

"It is only that I am so flooded with work, it is difficult to find the time."

"You find work in the jungle so fascinating that you have forgotten your promise to me, yes?"

What promise? He searched his memory, could think of nothing. "Odete, I don't quite understand—"

"You see!" she scolded. "Already you do not remember your promise to take me to Carnival!"

Now it came back. Months ago, half in jest, he had given in to her entreaties to escort her to the Rio Carnival, which her conservative Paulista parents had forbidden her to attend, considering it too vulgar and uninhibited for a properly reared young lady.

But Carnival did not begin until four days before Ash Wednesday. He glanced at the calendar and got a mild shock—that was only five days from now!

"I confess I had lost track of the days, Odete, but now that you have reminded me, I promise to be in Rio this coming Saturday in time to escort you to the festivities."

She squealed in delight. "And do you still love me as much as ever, my sweetheart?"

"With all my heart."

Raul felt oddly depressed. He loved Odete most dearly, but could he honestly say "with all his heart"? His concept of romantic love was that it should be exclusive, centered on one love object only. There could be no room for thoughts of another.

His reason for doubt and nagging guilt was Vivi. There was no denying that she attracted him powerfully. Her nearness started his blood churning. Frequently her image floated through his dreams. Pleasant as such reactions to Vivi might be, they could be dangerous, and they could be devastating to his future with Odete.

Instead of being angry, he should be grateful that Dom João had moved in to put a stop to the situation before it progressed too far.

And it was just as well that he was going to Rio on Saturday for a long-delayed reunion with Odete.

But it still rankled him that Dom João had treated him with such cavalier contempt. Why?

* * * * *

The men had the look of alien beings. They wore cumbersome suits of heavy canvas and thick leather gloves, and their faces were shadowed behind veils of fine netting that encircled their heads from the brims of their hats to their shoulders. They carried collapsible ladders, boxes, large aerosol containers of smoke bombs and pesticide gases, and other paraphernalia. Some carried oily, unlighted torches.

Raul walked among them beside *Senhor* Humberto Cruz, the bee expert who had been, at great expense, flown in from São Paulo with an aide and all the necessary equipment. Humberto, a fussy little man with precise movements and an intensity of manner that reflected love of his profession, was explaining things as they walked.

"I shall first make an effort to capture the queen bees before resorting to other steps."

"*Capture* the queens?" Raul glared at the man through his netting. "I understood that you came to destroy the damn pests, and since I'm footing the bill—"

"You wish me to get rid of the bees, correct? By removing the queens and putting them in the special hives I have brought along, it will draw all the worker bees into the hives. The queen is much larger than the workers, and the hive apertures are too small for her to escape but just large enough for the workers to squeeze through. Then we can tranquilize the bees with smoke and remove them in the hives to the National Research Apiary."

"But why not just wipe out the deadly things and save all that trouble?"

Humberto Cruz sighed. "It is a complex problem. You must realize first of all that bees are an absolute necessity to the economy. Bees account for over 80 percent of all agricultural pollination. Without insect pollination of crops there would be no oranges, no mangoes, no soybeans, no alfalfa—not even much of a dairy industry, which depends on crops for cattle food. In the United States the honeybee's value to agriculture is estimated as high as six billion dollars.

"In Brazil, the gentle European honeybee has not adapted very well and does not produce much honey, which is why the African strain was imported as well, in hopes of creating a hardy high-production strain. An accident occurred before our genetic experiments were completed, with the result that the aggressive, vicious African strain has proliferated rapidly all through Brazil, killing scores of people and thousands of animals."

"Which seems all the more reason for eradicating them completely," Raul put in.

"It's too late to eradicate them all. They've spread too fast, too far. Our best hope now is that by capturing the African queens and injecting them with sperm from the gentle European drones, we will dilute the aggressive traits."

"And if that fails?"

"It will not fail, *senhor!* Our genetic laboratories are hard at work on the problem."

They were approaching the first of the hives. It was a hot day, even for Brazil, and Raul was sweltering inside the protective suit. Sweat rolled down his face, stinging his eyes.

"Now we must be very careful," Humberto cautioned. "No unnecessary noise, no sudden movements. The hotter the weather, the more easily the bees are provoked to attack. Once a bee is angered it releases a chemical alarm bell—secretions called pheromones. The odor triggers off a raging fury throughout the colony, and the bees will attack in swarms."

"How many stings does it take to kill a man?"

"A single sting has been known to kill people who have allergic reactions. A few hundred stings will kill anyone. As many as a thousand stings have been counted in some victims."

Humberto's assistant quickly but with great care unfolded the ladder and set it up near the hive. A few bees were buzzing around, darting here and there as if surveying the strangers. One alighted on Raul's head netting and crawled across it. A couple of others zoomed past.

"They're sentinels," Humberto said in a low voice. "We must do nothing to excite them."

The man on the ladder started ejecting spurts of vapor at the hive from his smoke bomb. More bees emerged, winging through the smoke, unfazed.

A few feet ahead of Raul, one of the *caboclos* made a loud smacking noise of one leather glove against the other. He let out an exultant cry. "Ah! I got the little *bastardo!*"

"*Idiota!*" Humberto called sharply. "Now you've—!"

He broke off as the bees came boiling out of the hive, braving the heavy doses of smoke being frantically discharged at them, descending on the *caboclo* like a sudden squall. The buzzing of thousands of wings filled the air. Other bee clouds were swirling down from hives in nearby trees.

Raul felt the heavy little bodies pelting at his netting and against the canvas suit, which was soon black with them. Clumps of them were forming on the protective net, obscuring his vision, their abdomens madly pumping their barbed poison into the mesh. A burning sensation needled his thumb as a stinger pierced a glove. He fought an urge to run. His stomach was queasy.

"Be calm, everyone!" shouted Humberto. "They can't hurt you through the suits."

But the worker in front of Raul was too rattled to hear or understand. The bees had converged most heavily around him, the turbulent black clouds driven into even greater frenzy as the man's arms flailed in a futile attempt to drive them away. One or two of the bees must have stung through his suit, for he yowled in sudden pain and started running.

Head and shoulders lowered like a football tackle, he weaved and plunged blindly—to ram solidly into Raul.

The solid impact sent Raul reeling for several feet before toppling backward. Into a thornbush.

As he struggled to free himself, he heard a ripping sound followed by a series of fiery stings along his neck and shoulders and down his arms as the bees streamed inside his suit.

Bom Deus! he thought sickishly. So this is how it all ends! What a ridiculous, ignoble, humiliating finale to all my fine dreams . . .

FIFTEEN

Vinicius de Onis glared out of the broad window, looking past the gleaming white futuristic buildings of Brasilia and across a glistening lagoon to the trio of buildings that housed the men who controlled the destiny of Brazil. The two giant bowls contained the Senate and the Chamber of Deputies, and towering close behind were the lofty twin shafts of the Congress building, where laws were written, the dispensation of billions in government expenditures decided upon, and endless other matters of administrative controversy resolved. Vinicius cursed softly.

The government had thrown a roadblock in the way of his plans.

Turning, he took from a slim leather case a long delicate cigar from Bahia and held it near his scowling mouth until Hygino de Faria scuttled forward to hold the flame of a lighter under the cigar's tip. De Onis took a powerful draw, letting a lazy plume of smoke drift from his lips.

"So you have failed!" said de Onis, making no attempt to conceal his anger. "After all the assurances you gave to Barbosa, after all the money that found its way into your pocket . . ."

De Onis's ire had been aroused by the jolting news that higher government officials opposed the change in plans—so carefully manipulated by Hygino—to divert a leg of the Trans-Amazonian Highway to the de Onis property.

Hygino nervously cleared his throat. "You must understand, Vinicius, it is not because I haven't done everything possible. At the time I was not aware that the route you suggested was through such difficult terrain. It would require so much additional blasting

153

and clearing. Additional grading. There are so many more streams that must be bridged. And worse, much of the land is so low that it would flood during high water and require endless loads of fill and gravel to bring it up to an acceptably safe level. The cost would be astronomically higher than for the road originally planned."

De Onis let out a sarcastic laugh. "When did our government officials ever worry about how much money they pour out?" He took a furious puff from his cigar. "But *I* worry about such things, Hygino! I think you have sold me a pig in a poke, and I shall expect a full refund of every *cruzeiro* of my money."

Hygino suppressed a groan and put a hand on the shorter man's burly shoulder. "*Acalme-se*, Vinicius. There's no need to be upset. I have been thinking deeply on the matter and am confident that ways can be found to convince the top levels of government that the route you wish is truly more desirable."

Twisting his heavy neck, de Onis glared at the hand on his shoulder as if it were an obscene pass, then roughly pushed it off. He glanced around Hygino's private office, seeking the most comfortable place to sit, his lips curling in distaste. Like all government offices, it was equipped with chrome and plastic furniture. Cheap, flashy crap bought at outrageous prices with taxpayers' money. His own taste ran to massive furniture upholstered in velvets or antique silk brocades.

Selecting an armchair upholstered in Dresden blue imitation leather, he slumped down on its hard cushion, saying, "What ways do you suggest?"

"There have been incidents with the Indians. Road-workers killed by poisoned arrows. A FUNAI team is now in the area to pacify the tribes, but it will be difficult because the road as presently planned runs directly through the tribal lands of the two most hostile tribes. The government is most anxious not to provoke the Indians—for the whole world is watching how we treat them—so they will go to great lengths to prevent trouble. So—if the road on its present course runs into more trouble with the Indians—*Compreende?*"

De Onis was thinking hard. Perhaps if Raul de Carvalho's energy plantation also ran into trouble, it would be easy to convince the government that a successful bauxite mine on his own land would do more for Brazil's economy than an unsuccessful energy plantation.

He stood up, frowning thoughtfully. "All right, Hygino, I'll give you more time to get the results I want. Keep in mind that I always reward those who help—and I never forget those who have failed me."

Barbosa was waiting for him at his private plane. De Onis was silent until they were in the air on the way back to Rio.

"Barbosa, I want you to start digging into the private lives of Raul de Carvalho and his *desprezível* brother, Eduardo. Dig for the shit. Pictures if possible. Got it?"

"Got it, Vini."

"Also, get in contact with that *malandro*—what's his name?—who does special jobs for us."

"Lobos."

"Ah, yes, the deadly one. Give Lobos enough money to interest him and send him to see me. Tell him I have a big job for him."

Lobos, the shifty-eyed guide, wore a wide-brimmed hat and an oversized, soiled white jacket. He herded the small group of nervous American tourists into the forecourt of the *barracão*, the large barnlike structure where the macumba ceremony was to be held. Lobos was most of the time a professional criminal, and the rest of the time—when hiding out from the police or fresh out of more profitable things to do—he was just another of the Carioca *malandros*, those sly loafers who are as expert with a knife as they are at charming the girls and who live by their wits to the heady beat of the samba. On this evening he was in the service of an *Exú* called Black Fire, one of the various personifications of the devil in the Quimbanda cult, a sinister offshoot of macumba spiritism that was devoted entirely to the practice of black magic.

"As you enter the *terreiro*," he bawled out to the tourists, "you will note behind the iron gate the one with the spear. He is the *Indio Mau*. In his body lives the spirit of evil, who is held in slavery by the *Exú*, Black Fire. You are to throw your offerings of money at his feet and he will leave you in peace. The more you give, the safer you will be."

The *Indio Mau* was a stocky, muscular Indian wearing only a necklace of black and red beads, a monkey-skin breechclout, and dirty sneakers. He held a fierce-looking three-pronged harpoon stained with what looked like dried blood, and he was chewing steadily on a cud of something presumably narcotic, since his eyes appeared glazed and lifeless, unaware of the scattering of coins that fell around his feet.

"You are fools to be so *avarentos* with the money!" Lobos said scoldingly. "I must warn you, the *Exú* must not be angered, as he holds over each and every one of you the powers of life and death. Be generous if you wish to live long and happily."

A much smaller scattering of coins and a reluctant couple of bills joined the first contribution.

"Next we will visit the house of the *Exús*, but walk carefully to avoid stepping on the sacrificial offerings."

Moving with fastidious care, the tourists followed the guide past the "sacrificial offerings"—rotting corpses of headless chickens scabbed over with flies and maggots, squashed toads, mice, and other unidentifiable objects in the last stages of decomposition. Mingling with the stench of decay was the cloying, perfumed odor from scores of flickering votive candles set about in the forecourt. Swarms of immense brown moths clustered around each candle, adding to the macabre atmosphere.

Among the tourists was one who weaved slightly as he walked. Plainly he was a *norte-americano*, a large and lanky man of about thirty with reddish-brown hair, hazel eyes, and a lightly freckled skin. He had not tossed any money to the *Índio Máu*—not from stinginess but because his alcohol-slurred brain was too confused by the surrealistic quality of his surroundings to be quite sure of what he was doing. How in the hell did I get roped into this farce? he thought, wondering if it were all real or only part of a crazy dream. For several weeks Matt Riordan had been living in a dull gray world, vacillating between somber sobriety by day and dead drunkenness at night.

The house of the *Exús* stank of death. Even with his half-numbed senses, Riordan almost gagged from the odors of putrefaction from long-dead chickens, a headless goat, and other loathsome objects in a roped-off corner of the room. Against the main wall was a kind of throne draped in purple velvet, on which sat a life-size statue of a pretty-faced man with ghastly pale rouged cheeks, long-lashed blue eyes, heavy black brows, carmined lips, and a most sinister smile. He wore a black top hat, a white collar with a black bow tie, a string of black and red beads, and a black robe. Placed around him was an assortment of liquor bottles, a bowl of popcorn, another of peanuts, and a platter of raw steak that was crawling with flies.

Lobos the guide made a low bow before the effigy, then turned and spoke in a funeral tone. "Here you are privileged to see the earthly representation of Black Fire, the king of devils, whose spirit resides here. On the wall across from him you will see a portrait of his woman, the she-demon whore called Pomba Gira, who sleeps only with the *Exús*."

Entranced, Riordan stared at the life-size portrait. Pomba Gira had a deepest-night allure. Pale face, midnight hair, a face of unearthly beauty glazed with a brazen sensuality that might have been spawned in the darkest hours of a sex-maddened hell. Though she wore a golden crown, a string of pearls, and a red robe, she was mostly naked, for the robe was widely parted, blatantly displaying the absolute perfection of her gilded pink breasts and torso. Her long-lashed eyes were heavily shadowed, glowing with forbidden passions, and her smile, dripping with honey, was wickedly enticing. Riordan felt a surge of warmth in his loins.

Maybe that's all I need, he thought miserably. A hot piece of ass.

But he knew it wasn't that. He'd already sought that out often enough, and it had only driven him deeper into the bottle.

"As you leave," said Lobos, pointing to a clay jar on a shelf near the door, "look well at the little jar on the left. In it are kept ten thousand spirits of the dead who were killed by the *Exú* because they dared to be his enemies. The earthly representatives of the *Exú* are licensed to kill anyone who displeases the *Exú*, and the spirits of those killed are kept imprisoned forever." He paused to point to another, larger jar on the right side of the entrance.

"In that jar as you walk out you will drop your offerings of money to the *Exú*. Take care not to offend him by being too stingy."

Riordan dropped an American nickel in the jar as he went out. Pomba Gira's smile was surely worth that much.

"And now," Lobos said reverently when they were all outside again, "by permission of the head priestess, the *Mãe de Exú* herself, you will be allowed to enter the Quimbanda Center and witness what few outsiders ever have seen—a spirit ceremony in progress. This way please."

Two of those following the guide were an elderly tourist couple from Owosso, Michigan. The woman dragged at her husband's arm. "Oh, Fred, I—I don't think I can take any more," she said in a hollow voice. "I feel like I'm going to be sick—"

"Oh, come now, Elvira, stick with it! A big cold martini back at the hotel will pick you right up again, and just think of the wild stories you'll have to tell to the women's club back in Owosso."

"You're right, Fred," she said, and with a determined lift of her chin she clung to Fred's arm as they proceeded.

The passageway into the large *barracão*, which had the look and smell of an ancient horse stable, was blocked by a large shirtless black man wearing a big knife in his belt, ropes of red and black beads hanging against his naked chest, and a ferocious expression. He held out his hand, palm up.

"You will now," ordered Lobos, "give the *Filho de Exú* fifty *cruzeiros* each, the special admission price for outsiders."

Riordan, who was considerably sobered, fished out his wallet and with a cynical grin paid his money along with the others. After all, it was cheaper than a Brazilian movie.

The scene inside was heavy with the atmosphere of black magic. Garish lighting from rows of large candles cast flickering shadows and highlights over effigies of the divinities—both saints and devils—set up in niches along the walls between pinned-up sketches in bright crayon of spirits of the Quimbanda. On a sacramental table in a basin pooled in blood lay the severed head of a goat, its dead eyes glistening like marbles. Crates of clucking chickens awaiting sacrifice were piled behind a long, low podium. The air was thick with the sickly smell of blood, the sweet perfume from heaps of pink roses strewn on the floor, and the odors of decay, dung, and smoke from the burning candles. From somewhere came a rhythmic chanting accompanied by tambourines and the throb of drums.

With a queasy sense of the imminence of evil all

around him—not the evil of supernatural forces, but the plain worldly evil of insecure humans pushed to the brink of insanity by hallucinations fostered by their cult leaders—Riordan stumbled through the dim light looking for a place to sit. Most of the seats in the rows that filled half of the room were already occupied by customers—apparently Cariocas, as the natives of Rio are called. Some were obviously poor, but many had the well-dressed appearance of the upper classes. All sat decorously, absorbed in the tableau onstage.

Wishing to disassociate himself as much as possible from the onus of belonging to the group of sightseers —for his travels had taught him that the natives of most foreign countries usually regarded gawking American tourists with amiable derision, if not downright contempt—he moved toward the rear and selected an empty seat beside an expensively suited Brazilian.

A suddenly increased tempo in the drumming drew Riordan's eyes to the podium. A half-naked youth with his hair shaved off, his face daubed with white paint, and numerous necklaces was kneeling before an altar on which was tethered a live rooster. Women robed in long white dresses and men in white T-shirts and black trousers were gathered on each side in two semicircles. All were chanting to the beat of a samba rhythm: *"Saravá, Nana e Oxumaré; Xango, Oxóssi, Oxalá e Yemanjá."*

Riordan was still somewhat drunk and therefore bold enough to turn to the man beside him and ask, "Sir, can you tell me what the words mean?"

The man, a handsome gentleman with pale tan skin and silvered hair, smiled apologetically. "I do not know all the words, *senhor,* as they are from the old tongues of the African slaves, but they are meant as a salutation to the spirit gods who will come tonight. The singers are the *Filhos e Filhas de Exú*—the sons and daughters of the devil—although on some nights they work for the saints."

"How can they work for both?"

"Later I will try to explain, but for now—" He nudged Riordan's arm and nodded toward the podium where there had appeared a hefty woman with skin the color of tobacco and straight black hair streaming wildly around her face. She was attired in a long black skirt and a frilly white blouse, and she wore many pounds of necklaces around her heavy neck. She was smoking a cigar, and in one hand she held a big knife.

The Brazilian whispered, "She is the *Mãe de Exú*—mother of the devil."

Striding over to the kneeling youth, the woman drew the point of the knife over his scalp several times until blood began trickling down his face. Then, turning, she deftly cut the twine holding the rooster and lifted it by its legs. It beat its wings frantically and let out a prolonged mournful squawk—which ceased instantly as a swift movement of the knife lopped its head off. With the bird's wings still flopping, she held it over the youth's head, and blood streamed rich and dark over his face.

"What is the significance?" asked Riordan.

"The young man is entering the priesthood. It is part of the initiation, to give him strength."

Riordan gave the man a quizzical grin. "Tell me honestly, do you really believe all this hokum?"

The response was a horrified expression. "No, no!" the Brazilian said earnestly. "It is not hokum!"

"Then you worship the devil?"

"Sometimes, yes."

"But the devil is evil. How can anyone in his right mind worship evil?"

"*Senhor*, you do not understand. Sometimes only evil can fight evil. Then it is necessary to call on the devils for help. When they fight evil for you, they do good."

"What kind of good?"

"I am a shopkeeper. I started out with only a pushcart, and I had many enemies who robbed me and kept customers away. I went to the *Exús* for help, gave much money in offerings, and my enemies were punished. One was killed in a street fight, one was drowned, and the others have disappeared. Now I am a successful man. I own several shops. I am no longer afraid to walk alone in the dark because I am protected." He paused to fish beneath his Dior tie, and after loosening a button of his silk shirt he drew out a small ivory object dangling at the end of a delicate gold chain. It was in the shape of a clenched fist with the thumb protruding between the first and second fingers.

"This is a *figa*," he went on. "An amulet against evil. Almost everybody in Rio wears one. You go to the beach at Copacabana and you see that even the pretty girls wear them between their lovely breasts when they swim."

Riordan smiled. "But I thought most Brazilians were Catholic."

"We are! All of us are Catholic. But there is nothing incompatible between Catholicism and macumba. The macumba *Olurun* is the same as God the Father in the Christian faith. *Oxalá* is the same as Jesus Christ. *Yemanjá* is Mary, Mother of Christ. The macumba divinities of the devil are the equals of the Christian saints."

"That's where you lose me. I don't grasp your connection of the devil with the saints."

"Ah, but devils and saints are opposites, like the positive and negative forces in electricity. Can you say that one is more powerful than the other? Or that one can function without the other? Of course, there is much more to macumba than that; for example, we believe in the transmigration of souls from this life into the next. But it is all too complex to explain here. I can only say that the macumba religion recognizes that the great power of the devil is equal to that of the saints and that it is as necessary to work with the forces of evil as it is with good forces to make happiness."

"Thank you, my friend. I have been greatly enlightened." And closing his eyes, Riordan leaned back and gave in to the tuggings of fuzzy exhaustion that followed heavy drinking.

But there was no escape. The hurt from the dissolution of his marriage several months ago was still unbearably present. All the security of six beautiful years—beautiful for him but apparently not for Jennifer—had vanished moments after he was served with papers notifying him that she had filed for divorce. She was restless, she told him, unfulfilled by their life-style; she had a great need to find her own identity. She had won custody of the kids: five-year-old Pam and three-year-old Bryan, and she had taken them to California.

After trying for a while to keep on with the torn fabric of his life, he had finally thrown in the sponge. He'd been granted a leave of absence from his lucrative job as chief chemical engineer for Apex Chemicals and had taken off to see the world. Brazil was his fourth stop after Paris, South Africa, and Japan. He liked Rio. It gave an entirely different emotional slant, with an emphasis on exuberance and the fun in life.

Of which he had known all too little. With a summa cum laude degree behind him, he had gone fresh from college into a top-level job and an intensity of work he loved so much that he took it home with him. In retrospect, he could see that Jennifer was right. Work had consumed too much of the part of him that belonged to her.

Now his savings were about gone and he would soon have to head home—or else find a job here. Out of curiosity he had investigated the Rio job market. The agency had one possibility that they thought was made to order for him—to help launch an energy plantation for the production of alcohol from wood. The salary was open. The catch was that it would be a thousand miles away, deep in the jungle. He had told the agency people that he would consider it, and he had intended to at least have an interview when the prospective employer came to town in about a week.

But on later reflection, he had decided against it. The thought of being shut off from the world so far out in the wilderness, a prisoner to his own broodings, was unthinkable.

Instead, he would stay in Rio for one last fling. He would enjoy the city's fantastic abundance of beautiful girls during the erotically superheated celebration of Carnival, only a few days away, and then he would fly back to the States.

A sudden frenzied increase in the volume and cadence of the drums roused him from his reveries. The *Filhas e Filhos de Exú* were singing and dancing to a lively samba beat that made the scene on the podium appear to be an amalgam of a spirited Negro revival meeting and a nightclub floor show.

Riordan's somnolence washed away under the electrifying fusillade of drums and jangling tambourines. The scene was affecting some of the Brazilian onlookers even more strongly. A half dozen or more had risen to their feet to start singing, undulating their torsos, and shaking their arms in the air convulsively as they danced down the aisles toward the podium. Most of them were white and had the look of smartly dressed upper-class people.

One in particular caught Riordan's attention. She was about eighteen, a beauty with pale skin and black hair, fashionably turned out in sleek black silk and pearls, as if attired for the opera or a soiree. Twisting and gliding, her shapely buttocks flexing this way and that to the beat of music, she moved onto the podium like a tigress slinking through a forest of velvet. There she swayed over the floor as if in the arms of an invisible partner, her eyes almost closed, her lips parted, lost in the rapture of whatever emotions possessed her.

The other dancers made way for her pliant body as she weaved among them seductively. Sinuous undulations ran up her supple torso; her hips vibrated;

ripples glided down her limbs. Always her graceful arms were caressing the air.

The dance grew swifter. Spinning, whirling, her agile hips began jerking with lascivious movements. Her half-closed eyes glistened, her teeth shone between soft blood-red lips. The dark hair shook loose from its careful coiffure and flew wildly around her flushed face.

It was a weird dance; more than a dance, it was an erotic ritual, an ovation to primal sexuality.

Suddenly, with the silken grace of a ballerina, she sank to the floor—still in her invisible lover's embrace—and went into movements even more unmistakably obscene. Lying on her shoulder blades, buttocks and lovely legs reared high in the air, her hips began thrusting and churning while her hands pulled on her dress until it was hauled above her waist. She wore no panties.

Now her rolling and thrusting, all her frenetic gyrations were lust-crazed beyond reality. Writhing and pumping her hips upward, her spread legs hooked around her invisible lover while her fingers clawed down his back. Her eyes were closed; perspiration glistened on her cheeks. Her pelvis vibrated.

A fierce shudder passed through Riordan. Blood pounded in his ears. His senses clouded. He ventured a glance at the Brazilian in the next seat. The man's lips were stretched back in a lascivious grin. He was breathing hard.

All at once a low animallike moan throbbed from the girl's throat as her erotic throes of copulation ended. She collapsed as if shot, to lie flat on her back in deathly stillness. Her expression was pure ecstasy.

The Brazilian turned. "She is in a trance," he explained to Riordan. "She comes here often to be possessed by Black Fire. Tonight his spirit came to her and entered into her body—and she is fulfilled.

"Of course," he added virtuously, "she is a virgin."

With a deep sigh, Riordan started to rise. He had seen all he could take for one night. The Brazilian put a gentle hand on his arm.

"One moment, my friend. I can tell by your eyes that you too are plagued by demons. Please honor me by accepting a little gift." And reaching in his pocket, the man withdrew a little ivory *figa* on a golden chain and extended it.

"I always carry one or two of these for such a purpose. As I was once helped by another, I wish to help you. Wear this charm and you will be protected. For you see, the *figa* is worthless unless it is received as a gift."

Riordan took the amulet, oddly touched. "I thank you, my friend, with all my heart." The two clasped hands warmly.

Leaving, Riordan had the illusion of still being trapped in a weird dream, a captive of his own demons.

But he knew where his salvation lay for tonight.

To exorcize the demons, he needed more than a mystic charm. He needed to find the loving arms of a hungry female such as the one on the podium.

Preferably one who was not a virgin.

The Quimbanda Center was emptied of all customers, and now the dancers and musicians were lined up to get their share of the take. Lobos was among them. Taking the money from a hollowed-out human skull, the hefty *Mãe de Exú* doled out some to each. Dissatisfied or not with their meager pay, none protested —except Lobos.

He let out a squawk of outrage. "*Diabol* The *turistas* I brought in gave many *cruzeiros!* You owe me many times this much!"

The *Mãe de Exú* expelled a lazy plume of cigar smoke. "I decide; you accept," she said.

"*Não!*" With the blurred speed of a striking snake, Lobos leaped forward. A razor had magically appeared in his hand, and a deft slash brought a bright ribbon of blood down one side of the woman's face. The cigar went skittering to the floor as she floundered backward.

"*Fora!* Out with him!" she shrieked at the giant *Filho de Exú* who stood protectively beside her.

Before the big *preto* could budge, Lobos made another lightning slash with the razor, and half of the black man's ear fell off. The big man bent to pick it up, staring in disbelief as blood gushed copiously from the stump of ear that remained.

"Now pay me the rest," Lobos told the woman, "before you lose a nose."

"*Valha-me Deus*, God help me!" moaned the devil-worshiper as she plucked a handful of bills from the skull and thrust them at Lobos. "And my curse goes with it!"

Lobos scooped up the bills and laughed. "I worry not, you old cheat. The devil is my best friend."

Lobos lived alone in one of the large *favelas*, a slum community of huts covering the hills between the Tijuca Mountains and the peak of Pedra dos Dois Irmãos, on the very edge of Rio. The *favelas* were first established after the abolition of slavery in 1888 when thousands of ex-slaves flooded the city with nothing to do and nowhere to go. Scorned by the whites, they built themselves shanties on the hillsides, and a few years later, soldiers returning from the campaign against rebels in Bahia, being equally poor, also built shacks on the hills in which to install the girls they'd brought back. During the campaign, they had been entrenched on a hill covered with wild flowers called *favela*, and thus the Rio shantytowns got their name.

Nowhere could individual creativity be more evident. Each shack was built in accordance with personal whim and extreme cash limitation. Old boards, broken bricks, stones, scraps of cardboard and cloth, corrugated metal—anything that could be scrounged up by begging, stealing, or sorting through junk heaps was used. Without benefit of plumb lines or carpenter levels, walls slanted, windows were askew; truly level floors didn't exist. Structures sprawled haphazardly, often leaning against neighboring abodes, but since all the residents were squatters, owning not a particle of the land they lived on, nobody complained.

The more prosperous residents of Rio never ventured into the *favelas*, which were said to be terribly dangerous, inhabited only by murderers, thieves, dope peddlers, and poxy whores.

Lobos continued his climb up the *favela* hillside. Although he had an automobile of ancient vintage, it could ascend no higher than the first level of the slum community. There was no road higher, only steep paths and crude stairways winding between garbage heaps and dribbling streams of sewage that filled the air with a stench to which he was too inured to notice. Lobos was fairly pleased with the evening's take but disgruntled that it had involved so much effort on his part. Work was only for *pretos*. Lobos liked the quick strikes, the fat rewards that came from wit and daring, not from sweat, although lately the pickings had been slim. The police were watching too closely.

Reaching the highest level, where his shack was located, he paused to catch his breath. Way above him loomed the gigantic statue of Christ the Redeemer looking down at him sadly, but Lobos never wasted a glance in that direction; his gaze was directed downward, past the avalanche of hillside squalor to the glittering rows of mansions that began scarcely a stone's throw from the edge of the *favela*.

All that wealth and glamour at his feet! The view always stirred strong emotions in his guts—envy, greed, and bitter hatred toward those who undeservedly had so much while he had to sneak around like a hungry rat to steal a few crumbs.

He spat in contempt and turned toward his own miserable dwelling, reassuring himself with the thought that it would not be forever. A man of his cleverness would find a way to outwit the stupid rich, and sooner or later . . .

He felt a clutching in his belly as he pushed the door open and immediately sensed the presence of an intruder.

Although there were boxes along the walls containing radios, clocks, watches, and bogus jewelry, as well as a wide assortment of personal items taken from unlucky tourists waylaid on dark streets, Lobos had never bothered to install a lock on his door. There was no need. His reputation in the *favela* was so fearsome that all residents knew better than to enter his shack, much less take even the smallest trinket.

The interloper sat at one end of the room smoking a cigar. Under the weak glow of a candle—there was no electricity—it was plain to see that the man was expensively dressed. A large, chunky man with dark hair and a moustache, his eyes widened with fright as Lobos approached with a knife.

"Ah, Lobos my friend—don't you recognize me? I am Barbosa. I have come from Vinicius de Onis to give you money—"

"It is not healthy to enter my home when I am not here." Lobos gestured with his knife. "Where is the money?"

"First you must agree to do a job for us. Then you will get the money as an advance payment on the job. When the job is successfully completed, you will be given much more."

"How much? I already have work to do and cannot be bothered with any Mickey Mouse shit."

"Ten thousand *cruzeiros* for now and another fifty thousand if you do the job right."

Lobos gave a low whistle. "And how many people do I have to kill for that?"

"Just a few Indians."

Lobos took a few steps and threw himself down on the biggest and most expensive piece of furniture in the room—a king-size bed piled with many blankets and pillows. Lying back, he grinned dreamily at the sagging ceiling.

"Tell me more..."

✿ ✿ ✿ ✿ ✿

Raul fumed with impatience. It had been only two days since the near-fatal attack by African bees, but it seemed like weeks of lost time..He had spent most of those two days in bed with a high fever, not to mention the pain and discomfort he felt from the score or more stings.

He owed his life to the quick thinking of the new man, Hélio, who had perceived the tear in Raul's suit from the fall in the thornbush and rushed forward with his canister smoke bomb to expel its contents into the suit through the rent. It had stupefied the bees (and Raul as well), but not before Raul had suffered a series of stings on his neck, shoulder, and back. The men had carried him to the *fazenda*, where the bee expert Humberto had stripped off Raul's clothes and managed to extract some of the stings simply by drawing a fingernail repeatedly across the sites of the sting punctures. Afterwards Raul had been put into a warm bath of a solution of baking soda to help alleviate the agony.

For the first day he had been barely conscious. Today, with great difficulty, he was able to hobble around, but it would be several more days, Humberto told him, before the anaphylactic reaction would subside enough for him to be able to travel. It would be impossible to get to Rio in time for the opening of Carnival.

Now, seated in his office with a pillow on the seat of his chair and another propped behind him, he put a radiotelephone call through to Eduardo.

"Eduardo, I've had a bit of bad luck that will delay my trip to Rio—" Briefly he told of the mishap with the bees.

"That's a shame, brother, but maybe it will teach you that it is a mistake to live out in the jungle."

Raul managed a feeble laugh. "It has taught me to be much more careful. But look, Eduardo, I have a big favor to ask of you."

"Anything within my limited range of capability."

"My problem is that I won't be able to get to Rio for the opening ball of Carnival, and I'd faithfully promised Odete—"

"Oh, she'll be utterly devastated!"

"I know it would be asking a lot—a major sacrifice, since undoubtedly you've already made your plans—"

"For anything important, plans can always be changed."

"What I'm requesting—could you stand in for me and escort Odete?"

Eduardo laughed easily. "I wish all favors asked of me were that easy. Don't worry, brother. *Terei muito prazer em ajudá-lo.* I'll be glad to help out."

"I'll be forever grateful. Of course, I expect to be there before Carnival is over, and I will make my amends to Odete. Meanwhile I'll call her and tell her of the change in plans."

"Don't give it another thought. She'll be in good hands."

SIXTEEN

A city gone mad.

To the boom-bam, boom-bam, boom-bam *of the* surdo, *the great bass drum of the samba band, Rio goes wild. With the beat exploding in their ears, all Cariocas, from the mansions to the slums, answer the call like moths drawn to flame. Down from the* favelas *stream the poor, their faces powdered or painted, opulently bedecked in fantastical costumes, costing as much as $1,500, for which they have scrimped and hoarded all year. Into the blistering streets, as humid and steamy as the Amazon rain forests, pour the middle and upper classes, garbed in their own bizarre and dazzling fantasias. Brazilian girls of privileged backgrounds—normally languid creatures who laze their days away on the beach and take long naps at home—are suddenly bestirred into strange frenzies, transformed into hyped-up images of super sex queens in costumes that reflect their secret aspirations.*

Following the fanfare of the surdo *comes the syncopated rhythm of tambourines, kettledrums, saxophones, trumpets, and trombones from scores of bands all over town, pervading every nook and cranny with the hypnotic samba beat, electrifying the populace. Everyone begins to sing and dance on the pavement. Inhibitions vanish. Hips wobble, shoulders sway, arms shoot out. Strange words of incantation swell from thousands of lips: "Oba! Oba! Obala-Ola-o-Baba!"*

It is the opening of Carnival, the pre-Lenten bacchanalia beginning at noon on the Saturday before Ash Wednesday and lasting through four days of sustained hysteria, each day wilder than the one be-

fore. It is mass insanity. A deliberate rebellion against reality. A joyful plunge into chaos. Reason is thrown to the winds. The whole point is not to think, but to sink into pure emotion.

It is a time when all dreams, erotic or otherwise, come true.

Briefly.

Luxuriating in her big marble bath, strange little thrills racing through her exquisitely shaped body, Odete Bandiera e Xavier listened to the booming of the *surdos*, the ebullient singing, and the inciting jungle rhythms echoing through the streets outside. All afternoon her very pores had been drinking in the delirious pulsating sounds, and now she was quivering with excitement. It was the first time in all her twenty-one, going on twenty-two years that she had come to Rio for Carnival.

She had always wanted to be among the golden girls and boys who flocked to Carnival each year like lemmings, but her strict São Paulo parents had forbidden it as improper for a single young lady of her breeding. The kind of rich and morally upright man they envisioned as a husband for her might well be dissuaded from marrying her if he knew her chaste sensibilities had been sullied by exposure to the orgiastic festivities.

But all that had been changed by her engagement to Raul, who was from a family even more distinguished than her own. If her fiancé considered it respectable enough to escort his betrothed to one of the exclusive Carnival balls, her parents had no objections. Aside from that, Odete's family, whose income depended largely on an extensive coffee plantation, had suffered a severe financial setback owing to a bad frost that had destroyed most of the coffee trees, and they were anxious to get their expensive daughter married off.

She had not bothered to tell her parents that it would be Eduardo, not Raul, who was taking her to the ball tonight, and her aunt and uncle, with whom she stayed on her frequent trips to Rio, thought nothing of it. They were far more sophisticated about such things and were charmed by Eduardo, who had taken her out to dinner and the theater quite often in the past couple of weeks. After all, was he not Raul's brother, and a gentleman?

Lazily she stroked her arms and torso with soap, enjoying the feel of her skin. She bathed three times daily, a ritual partly necessitated by the endless applications of suntan oil used on the beach. Lifting a tanned, sleek leg, she admired its precise curvature while examining it in a perfunctory way for any evidence of hair that she knew wouldn't be there. Only yesterday she had made one of her bimonthly visits to a depilatory salon that was patronized by the young smart set, where a special cream was used to remove hair on the limbs and paraffin was coated over the pubic hairs so they could be wrenched out in a brief ecstasy of pain. Otherwise, it would be unpardonable to appear on the beach in a skimpy *tanga*.

Her thoughts drifted to Raul, bringing a petulant frown to the cameo beauty of her face. How inconsiderate of him to go poking around wild bee nests just before he was supposed to come to Rio to take her to the ball! She supposed his handsome face was swollen into something ugly and he didn't want to be seen. Well, it served him right for wanting to hide away in the jungle.

Thank God for Eduardo.

In truth, she had a faint glimmering that her pique was mostly self-justification to cloud the fact that she was secretly glad Raul wouldn't arrive for another day or two. Eduardo was so much more fun.

It wasn't that she didn't love Raul. She was quite sure that she loved him. Hadn't she picked him over many other suitors? His family background, his good looks, and his aura of strength and dependability had attracted her. Besides, she was getting too old—how frightening to be almost twenty-two!—and she couldn't go on much longer looking for a better choice. Yes, she loved him as much as she could love any man, but how unfair of him to be more in love with the jungle than he was with her!

Angrily she sloshed water over her torso; then, dismissing thoughts of Raul as easily as kicking off an old shoe, she looked down at the perfect curves of her virginal breasts and wondered if her costume for the evening was not too bold. The gold-sequined *corpinho*—the only cover for her breasts—was scarcely wide enough to conceal her pink nipples and not likely to hide them for long if the activities got too wild. Except for the *corpinho*, she would be naked from head down to mid-hips, and almost as revealing the rest of the way down.

Her *fantasia* was intended to evoke the image of Cleopatra—as interpreted by her designer, Fernando. Her black hair had already been cut with a flat bang across the forehead and would be combed straight down each side. She would wear a golden diadem inset with jewels and a triad of emeralds suspended in the center of her forehead. Garish purple-blue eye shadowing and long fake lashes would enhance the brilliance of her green eyes. Below the naked torso was a hip-hugging floor-length skirt of glittering gold sequins, slit up the middle to reveal with every movement the nakedness of the rest of her body, except for the skimpiest of string *tangas*, also of gold sequins.

When she had protested to Fernando that it might be a bit too immodest for a ball, he laughed in her face.

"For you, *senhorita*, I have strained to be *very* conservative. When you see the others, you will feel positively Victorian."

"But are you sure it suits my personality?"

Fernando grinned mischievously. "Be assured it is perfect. You must understand, my dear, that for Carnival the costumes are disguises in role reversal. For example, many blacks paint their faces white and dress as whites; many whites paint their faces black.

The poor wear the fine clothes of the rich; the rich borrow their servants' cast-off rags and dress as beggars. *Compreende?* For you, an untouched *virgindade*, what could be more appropriate than to appear as a royal whore?"

She accepted that as a dubious compliment.

Yolanda the maid thrust her chocolate face through the doorway. Her expression was sullen. "*Senhorita* Odete, it is getting late. If I have to stay much longer to help you into your costume, my man who is waiting for me at home will get very mad."

"It is never a bad thing to make men wait."

"It be bad for me. If he mad enough, he'll beat me up."

"If he's that mean, why don't you leave him?"

Yolanda's eyes widened in astonishment. "And let the other girls grab him?"

Amused, Odete rose from the bath, reached for the towel Yolanda held out for her, and languidly began drying herself.

"You better hustle now," said the maid. "It take a long time to get your makeup on, and if you not ready when *Senhor* Eduardo come to pick you up, he be mad too."

Odete smiled. In her case, as she had discovered long ago, it was only bad for a girl *not* to make a man wait.

With darkness, the carnival was building into a full steam. Under a blaze of illumination from countless colored lanterns and television lights, the really big parades—representing top samba schools that were vying for prizes—had started down the broad Avenida Presidente Vargas, past the judges' stand, to the thunderous throb of drums and the blare of raggedy-ass jazz from two-hundred-piece bands: The *sambistas*—the common people who for months had been giving all their spare evening hours to be trained, choreographed, and costumed by the samba schools in preparation for the moment that would lift them soaring above their otherwise mundane lives—came prancing, dancing, and singing down the avenue with all the exuberance of their sudden release from long weeks of pent-up anticipation.

Behind the bands were the floats, displaying lovely girls wearing colorful plumes and fantasy finery of gold and silver lamé. Real rubies, emeralds, topazes, and aquamarines had been bought by the quart, polished by lapidaries, and mounted on skirts, capes, crowns, trains, or pasties covering the nipples of the generous sprinkling of near-naked beauties.

Next came the women in Bahia dress—billowing hoopskirts; jingling chain necklaces, bracelets, amulets; kerchiefed heads piled high with tropical fruits. There were black men in five-button Savile Row suits, derbies, spats, and white gloves; resplendent Harlequins and Pierrots; feather-bedecked Indians; plantation belles; and storybook conquistadores.

Parade after parade kept coming, extending for miles. A river of color, fantasy, and illusion. Nowhere else on earth has there ever been such an awesome spectacular. All the great extravaganzas in Hollywood history added together would pale by comparison with Rio Carnival and its cast of over forty thousand.

The people would march all night and all the next day, bringing traffic almost to a standstill, inciting the volatile emotions of all Cariocas into ever higher levels of frenzy.

The white Ferrari, purring softly, crawled through the garishly lighted street at a snail's pace. Good-naturedly, but in no haste, the revelers clogging the pavement moved aside to make way. Expressing admiration for the car—"Oh! Ah! Viva!"—some stroked their hands against the polished metal with an exaggerated show of deference. A brown-skinned girl, wearing only bright strings of beads crisscrossing her nudity and a jeweled turban of green satin, leaped on the sloping hood and began to dance, her flawlessly

rounded posterior, her *bunda*, jutting out and shim-
mying in front of the windshield. Another scantily
clad girl, a *preto*, thrust her black arms through the
window to pull the driver's head toward her, giving
him a big kiss on the lips to a roar of applause from
the crowd.

Grinning, Eduardo turned toward Odete, who sat,
arms folded, as far from him as possible on the
opposite side of the seat. She was in a snit because he
had been two hours late in coming to pick her up, and
even his extravagant praise of her costume had failed
to completely soften her mood.

"Now you can see why I was delayed. All the main
roads are blocked off for the parades, and I was
forced to take a roundabout route to reach your place;
every street is mobbed."

"And how many kisses did you get?" she said tartly.

He laughed. "I lost count."

Her ice-green eyes flicked a glance at his costume, a
royal purple tunic open to the waist to bare his torso,
worn over red tights. Numerous little red jeweled
hearts decorated the sleeves. "I presume your *fantasia*
is meant to represent all the hearts you have broken,"
she said.

"I am playing it straight tonight. Instead of hiding
behind a disguise, I am revealing to the whole world a
true reflection of my inner self."

"Is your inner self so greedy for love that it can
never be satisfied?"

"You misunderstand. It is not greed that motivates
me—but sincere dedication to a search to find my true
love. If I ever find her, I shall renounce all others."

"Perhaps you will find her at the ball tonight."

He smiled at her. "That is my hope."

She laughed lightly, her mood improved, whereas
Eduardo was finding it difficult to maintain his air of
gaiety. Too many troublesome thoughts were nagging
at him.

Foremost were worries about the money he had
embezzled from the family exporting business. Small

amounts, at first, to feed his compulsive love of gambling as well as pay his snowballing debts, then larger and larger amounts intended to cover past losses. By the law of averages, luck had to favor him sooner or later, and it would only take one big win to wipe out all he owed.

But the big win hadn't come, and now he was in so deep he had to cling to that elusive hope as his only chance.

Sometimes it seemed to Eduardo that he had been put on earth only to make a mockery of everything that most people thought of as good in life. He had lied, cheated, stolen, and gambled away money that wasn't his own. He lived in unearned luxury, abused his body with drugs, and lowest of all, he had plans for tonight, plans for Odete that would be a rotten betrayal of his own brother.

It was as if he were afflicted with an incurable moral perversity, a sickness, a weakness beyond his control. The overwhelming urgencies of the moment always blocked out any concern for tomorrow.

Odete let out a startled gasp. A big *preto*, naked to the waist and wearing a headpiece affixed with goat horns, had reached in to run a hand over one of her breasts.

"*Vem cá*, baby! Come to my arms!" called the grinning *preto*.

Odete flinched away and moved close to Eduardo, who laughed.

"Just smile and blow him a kiss," he advised her. "Fall in with the mood. We'll soon be out of the worst of the congestion and get on to the Yacht Club."

"I certainly hope so. How long do you think it will take us to get there? Won't we be terribly late?"

"Never fear, we'll be there in plenty of time. Carnival runs nonstop for four days, so it's impossible to be late."

He glanced down at her breasts quivering beneath the strip of *corpinho*, and he had one of his sudden changes of mood. All of his worries vanished. Eduardo took a certain pride in what he considered a talent—his ability to shift instantly to a more positive viewpoint, the clever adaptability to circumstances that all these years had enabled him to enjoy a free, heady ride through life and evade unpleasant consequences.

He knew he could always find ways to keep it that way.

And here was Odete, and the night was theirs to enjoy.

The Rio Yacht Club, located on beautiful Botafogo Bay beneath the formidable ramparts of Sugarloaf, was ablaze with life, blaring with the uproar of several thousand revelers. Being one of the most exclusive and expensive clubs in town—memberships cost $22,000—the club was privileged to call on the army to keep out unwanted gate-crashers. A cordon of white-jacketed troopers with determined expressions beneath their helmets and bayonets gleaming on their rifles stood ready to slice slum bums into mincemeat and to protect the throngs of people who would pay $90 to enter, $400 for a table, nearly $200 for a bottle of champagne, and $12 for a scant shot of whiskey.

Entering on Eduardo's arm, Odete felt tremors of nervous excitement race through her body. The animal vitality palpitant in the air was overwhelming. From several bands came thumping drumbeats that might have come straight from the savage heart of the jungle. Acres of tables had been extended out from the ballroom and over a wide lawn under a star-studded sky, and gushing into the soft night air were shimmering fountains changing hues under a play of colored lights. Frenzied hordes of moths clustered around the long rows of festive lanterns.

Everywhere was a bedlam of merriment, and it was always the women—the eternal goddess female as an object of sexual worship—who were the focal points of superheated attention. Whereas only about half of the men were in costume, most of the older ones dressed in tuxedoes—their boldness limited to pink, purple, or crimson bow ties—virtually every woman wore next to nothing. The costumes ranged from the slinkiest, skimpiest of coverings to complete nudity except for a bit of jewelry such as a necklace, a gem over each nipple, or several jewels over the pubic triangle. Society leaders were indistinguishable from expensive whores, who were in plentiful attendance as guests, and around the most stunning and most naked were the largest groupings of men, like drones in a fever to fertilize the queen bee.

In essence, it was a prolonged mating dance. Girls rode on men's shoulders, hot crotches wriggling against sweating necks. They danced on tables to applauding males. They vibrated to the samba. Couples danced sinuously, as close together as the barriers of flesh allowed, pelvic areas churning in sync. A couple dancing near the edge of the swimming pool fell in, continuing their undulatory movements in embrace as their bodies sank into the green phosphorescence created by the underwater lights.

During the hypnosis of Carnival, the bridge between reality and fantasy had ceased to exist. Under its camouflage, many a straitlaced wife, as well as many a normally faithful husband, would find sexual outlets with the inciting bodies of others.

Also during Carnival, the murder rate resulting from jealous passions would soar.

Odete and Eduardo had joined a large table with some of his friends, who had been calling to him from all sides—plainly he was very popular. Waiters hovered around, replenishing champagne bottles nestled in ice buckets on the table. Odete drank thirstily from one of the bubbly glasses thrust at her, for the night was hot and sultry.

"Let us dance," Eduardo crooned in her ear.

"I'd love to."

But the dance floor was too mobbed for any fluidity of movement. The crush of torsos, thighs, and buttocks kept them locked in place, for only the most mobile parts of the body could move to the explosive beat of the music. She felt the stirring of his male organ against her pelvis.

By 2:00 A.M. Odete was feeling more gloriously alive than she had ever felt before in her life. The magic night was a dream come true. She was admired on all sides; men lavished her with the praise and attention due a princess. The champagne, the continuous syncopated percussion, the very energy released into the atmosphere by the uninhibited frolicking of the best people had sent her mood soaring. She had danced and danced, drunk more champagne, nibbled at some of the elegant gourmet dishes, and danced some more—sometimes with Eduardo's friends—and she'd been kissed repeatedly by many men.

She felt marvelously attuned to the pulsating music, deliriously in unison with the whole universe. A warm sensuality throbbed in her veins, building higher and higher.

"Don't you think we've had enough of this?" Eduardo suggested during a dance intermission. "I brought you here only because Raul asked me to, but the action is getting pretty dull—"

"Aren't you having a good time?" She wasn't the least bit bored or tired, and she didn't want to leave.

"Perfectly marvelous, but I think I can promise you a better time yet to come." Slipping his arms around her, he held her tightly and gave her a rather more than casual kiss, to which she responded briefly but with ardor.

She drew away, her green eyes shining up at him while a roguish smile played over her lips. She had felt a momentary twinge of guilt, and then it was gone. The electricity of his touch was part of the night's magic. He was a most handsome man, she decided. Although he was not as tall or as muscular as Raul, he looked more poetic with his long dark lashes, his slender build, the almost too beautiful features.

"Do not expect to add my heart to the collection on

your sleeves," she chided. "Have you forgotten that I am engaged to your brother?"

"Ah, but am I not his stand-in for this evening?"

"I fear his trust in you is greater than mine. Tell me, what is this 'better time' that you say is yet to come?"

"Just a party at my apartment. It has been arranged, and many of my friends will soon be arriving."

"I don't think your brother would approve."

"I can't say with honesty that my stuffed-shirt brother would exactly approve of my kind of entertainment, though I am quite sure you will enjoy it. But since he's the one who stood you up for the evening, does it matter if he approves or not?" His mischievous grin was irresistible.

"Well then, *está bem,* as you wish."

Odete had never felt happier. It was a kind of euphoria charged with anticipatory excitement. It was the first time she had been in Eduardo's spacious multi-level apartment overlooking the pale sands of Copacabana Beach, and she loved every inch of it. From the black slate floor of the entryway to the lofty beamed living room. The thickly piled carpeting was luscious white, and the room was sensuously accented with low sofas in varying hues of crimson. Against the rich aroeira wood paneling hung colorful modern paintings by Brazilian artists, and one entire wall was of floor-to-ceiling glass, affording a splendid view of the bay and the tiers of glittering lights.

So different from the stodgy São Paulo town house where she had been reared! The heavy ancient furniture, the dark tapestries and heavy drapes to shut out sun, the religious paintings, the cloying perfume of votive candles eternally flickering in an alcove in memory of her grandparents. *Ughh!*

Soft music pulsated in the electronically cooled atmosphere, which was both sparkling with high spirits and murky with low lighting. The jollity came from about a dozen couples attired in a surrealistic fantasy of scanty costumes that apparently had been designed to adhere to only one rule: *Quanto menos melhor*, the less, the better. Most spectacular among them was a gorgeous black couple, Nubi and Zuzi. Nubi, a handsome young giant, wore nothing but earrings, bracelets, and in lieu of a loincloth, a gold chain supporting a jeweled bag over his bulging male organ. The shapely Zuzi wore a few fluffs of pink feathers here and there in a manner that artfully dramatized her gleaming black breasts, limbs, *bunda,* and other points of interest.

For Odete, the scene was glossed with the sort of sinful glamour against which—until her recent engagement—she had been scrupulously guarded by strict parents. This was the kind of fun life she hungered for. This was her element!

Nubi and Zuzi had sunk gracefully onto one of the sofas, and a jolting thrill raced up Odete's spine as she saw that as he kissed the girl, the black man let one of his hands play between her legs. The girl had reached down to fondle the jeweled codpiece at his crotch. Under the deft manipulations of her fingers, the codpiece began swelling, and then it burst aside to reveal the outthrusting male organ. Odete gasped.

"Are you shocked, my dear?" Eduardo had reappeared, holding a small tray. He had excused himself a few minutes earlier to give instructions to the several servants hired for the evening.

"I—I've never seen anything like it."

Eduardo laughed. "You've seen nothing yet. They're paid entertainers, very popular at the most fashionable parties for breaking the ice." He extended the tray, on which was a tiny silver spoon and a small silver bowl filled with white powder.

"But first you should have a bit of this mild stimulant, which is guaranteed to overcome any prudish inhibitions and greatly increase your enjoyment."

She let out a nervous giggle. "I don't think I need a stimulant. What is it?"

"Just a little snow—coke. It's perfectly harmless and

not habit-forming, safer than alcohol or cigarettes. Its only effect is to elevate your mood for half an hour or so. All the most important people take it at parties. Look, I'll show you how simple it is."

Taking some of the powder in the tiny spoon, he held it below one nostril, closed off the other nostril with a finger, and sniffed deeply. Taking more powder, he repeated the process with the other nostril. "See? There's nothing to it. But since you've never used it before, you'll get enough effect by inhaling it on just one side." He put more powder in the spoon and extended it.

She eyed the spoon, feeling vague fears. She'd heard enough about cocaine to know it was commonplace among jet-setters, but she also knew that Raul would not approve. On the other hand, Eduardo wouldn't offer her anything that would hurt her, would he? Besides, she'd always wanted to do daring things, things that were forbidden by her parents, and the Carnival hypnosis had emboldened her. With a gay little laugh she took the spoon.

"I'll try it just once." Imitating the way she had seen him do it, she sniffed jerkily from the spoon, feeling first a burning, then a faint numbness in her nose. And moments later, the explosive effect in her brain.

Waves of heat seethed through her like little electric currents on hot wires. Straight to her limbs, her tummy, her vaginal area, centering warmth there. She felt slightly giddy.

"How do you feel now?" Eduardo asked.

"I feel just marvelous!" she said, unaware of a new stridency in her tone. There was a faint strumming in her ears from the increased speed of her heartbeat, and her glance skimmed toward the black couple, now on the white rug furiously engaged in copulation. Others had gathered on the rug or on sofas, most of them embracing and tearing off the last of each others' costumes as they watched the erotic throes. Two brown-skinned servants were passing trays of cocaine.

Odete stared with glistening eyes. She found the tableau unbelievably outrageous, even depraved, but she was unable to pull her gaze away.

An arm slid around her and she turned to meet Eduardo's lips crushing down against hers. She responded with a long and passionate kiss, a kiss not of love but rising from the insistent heat of her genitals. At length she drew away, breathing hard, and her eyes drifted back to the pair on the rug. But it seemed that her vision was deceiving her. For it was a white female body entangled with the black man, and close by, the black girl was sprawled belly down over a naked white body, her face between the other's spread legs.

"You see," said Eduardo, "part of the entertainment is for the *pretos* to participate with any of the guests who desire it—" He felt her shivering. "But if it offends you, we can go to another room where we can be more private."

She moaned softly. "I—I don't know what I want."

She felt herself floating, being guided through the dim lighting. In a corner of her brain a tiny protesting voice was being snuffed out by the thudding excitement that inflamed her. Raul, what would he—? But no, she didn't want to think beyond the moment—not think at all—only feel . . .

The door closed quietly behind her, and then she was on the huge soft bed in Eduardo's arms.

He looked down in horror at the darkening stain on the sheets. Even in the dim lighting it was easy to recognize.

Blood!

A silent wail rose to his throat. *Deus do céu,* what had he done?

He had known that behind her relatively sophisticated facade she was an innocent. But a *virgindade!* Who would have dreamed, how could anyone suspect that in this day and age she was untouched?

Her eyes were closed, her head turned sideways, an

ecstatic smile on her lips. Her torso writhed slowly, her hips undulating. From her lips came murmuring pleas for him to continue.

Eduardo couldn't. He was too limp, and no amount of cocaine could have helped him regain stiffness.

Meu Deus! If Raul ever learns the truth, he will kill me!

From behind a wall a camera stopped whirring, and its protruding lens moved away from the aperture through which it had been focused. By a deft arrangement of strings and wires, a picture in the adjacent bedroom was shifted back a few inches to conceal the aperture.

The cameraman grinned up at Prunes, the *malandro* who had catered Eduardo's orgy by supplying all the coke and the speciality act.

"The pictures will be perfect, my friend! When de Onis gets a look at them, you will have a big bonus."

SEVENTEEN

Two thousand miles from the frenzied pleasures of Carnival, the roadworkers continued their sweating progress through the steamy jungle.

Plagued by sweltering heat, biting insects, poisonous snakes, and malaria, by the ear-jangling screech and thunder of gigantic machinery belching out sickening oil fumes, they toiled from dawn to sunset, then slept. Night shifts carried on the grinding drudgery in the blistering waves of heat that came from the seething holocausts of slash-and-burn fires that cast an eerie glow high in the sky for miles around, thickening the air with black smoke.

Night or day it was the same. Backbreaking, mind-dulling, spirit-numbing.

The overall dollar cost of the world's greatest highway—billions upon billions—would boggle the mind of any banker. But an audit of the greater human cost would never be made.

Displaced Indians; destroyed cultures. Sweat, pain, sickness, broken bones, blood; and a trail of dead men.

Whatever the cost, it mattered not. The road would go on.

Jaime Blasco, top construction boss over a section of highway that was but one bar of an enormous grid to be carved through a billion acres of rain forest, glared doubtfully at the group of men just brought in by the labor contractor. A sorrier-looking bunch he had never seen. Under the merciless white radiance of a molten forenoon sun, their hangdog appearance seemed magnified. They stood on the dozer-torn ground in the slumped postures of beaten men, apathy in their faces, eyes dull as mud. All looked hungry, physically defective, and none too smart. Good, healthy workers were getting harder and harder to come by.

One of the newcomers, a scrawny man with the eyes of a weasel, was garbed in flashy city clothes, and he looked particularly out of place.

"What's your name?" Blasco asked.

"Lobos."

"You don't look strong enough to lift a spade. Why in hell do you want to work on a road gang?"

Lobos put on a bored grin, delicately taking a sagging cigarette from between his thin lips. "My doctor told me it would benefit my health. You want references, write to *Presidente* Figueiredo. He's a pal of mine."

"Hah, a smart-ass! Well, we'll soon sweat that out of you."

Blasco turned away in disgust. Why a city-smart *malandro* would ever want to hide out in the jungle was no concern of his. He was too shorthanded to turn away any man able to walk. Besides, he had more important matters to contend with.

One of them was the exasperating *norte-americana* reporter, Peggy Carpenter, who was always getting underfoot. Another was . . .

An urgent voice interrupted his angry flow of thoughts.

"*Chefe—!*" Tomaz, the muscular foreman of the advance party, strode up. His black face, coated with the red dust roiled up by churning bulldozers and trucks, showed worry. "We caught an Indian—"

Blasco's anger soared. For days Tomaz had been insisting that hidden eyes were watching them. "My scalp prickles," he had said. "I look around quick. See nothing. Just the moving leaves where there is no breeze. I tell you true, *chefe*, the Indians are always watching." Blasco had scoffed, at the same time warning Tomaz that even if the Indians were watching, nothing must be done to scare them away. It could lead to great trouble.

"Caught an Indian!" said Blasco. "Haven't I ordered you not to molest or frighten the Indians in any way? Where is he?"

"I let him go. It was this way, *chefe*—" Briefly, Tomaz related how the crashing fall of a big tree had flushed an Indian from his hiding place in the bushes. Tomaz himself had been close enough to race forward and capture the aborigine in his powerful arms. Almost instantly he had been surrounded by other Indians with drawn bows.

"I thought my time had come," Tomaz continued, "although I was quick to let the Indian loose. Then an old Indian—tall with gray hair—came up to me and pointed at my *pistola*, making motions that he wanted me to give it to him."

"You gave him your pistol?" Blasco shouted. A quick glance at the foreman's holster confirmed it was empty.

Tomaz spread his hands apologetically. "It was a trade of my life for the pistol. Had I refused, I would now be dead, and the Indians would have the gun anyway. As soon as I handed over the gun, the old Indian motioned to the others and they all disappeared into the woods."

Blasco groaned. A gun in the hands of an Indian was dynamite, though under the circumstances he couldn't blame Tomaz for parting with it. The only consolation was that the Indians apparently knew so little about guns that they hadn't taken the ammunition belt. The gun would be dangerous only until the bullets in its chamber were exhausted.

But it only took one bullet to kill a man—or start a war.

"Do you have any idea what tribe the Indians belonged to?"

"No. Only that the old Indian pointed to himself and said, 'Me Xanqui.'"

Xanqui was chief of the warlike Txacatores. Carlos dos Santos, leader of the FUNAI Indian pacification team, had briefed Blasco on the nearby Indian tribes and the problems they posed, since the highway was now headed into the disputed borderland area claimed as part of their homelands by both the Txacatore and Atroari tribes—traditional enemies.

It was the Atroaris—fully as warlike as the Txacatores—who had killed several of Blasco's men and forced a temporary work shutdown. Thanks to Carlos and his pacification team, the Atroaris' friendship had been won, but the tenuous truce could easily be ended by one wrong move.

If any Indian trouble broke out again, strict orders would once more be issued from Brasilia to halt all road construction until the FUNAI team got matters cleared up.

Delay was the most hated word in Blasco's vocabulary.

"All right, Tomaz, get back to work."

Tomaz slapped at his empty holster. "*Chefe,* I need another *pistola* in case of poisonous snakes."

"*Não!* The Indians might take it from you again, and that's more dangerous than poisonous snakes. Remember, we're walking on eggshells." He made a mental note to double-check with the supply wagon and see that all rifles and handguns were kept locked up.

Tomaz still lingered. "There's another matter—"

"What now?"

"The golden-haired *norte-americana*—the men don't work when she's around. They just stand and show their teeth at her like lovesick caimans. When Estácio was crushed under the wheel of a tractor yesterday, she took pictures of him as he was dying. Questions, questions all the time she asks, and the men tell her everything, all the bad stuff—"

Blasco swore softly. Although not as important as the Indian trouble would be, the female reporter problem was more vexing. A young white woman to distract a crew of woman-starved *caboclos* was bad enough, but even worse was her continuous snooping for material to write for the newspapers. God only knew, road building was hard, dirty, dangerous work with a high rate of accidents and a miserably low rate of pay. Crude first aid was the only medical attention available. There was no compensation for lost wages, no disability, no death benefits.

But one's dirty linen should not be washed in front of the whole world.

"Don't you worry about it, Tomaz. Next time you see *Senhorita* Peggy Carpenter around here, let me know right away. I'll see to it that she drags her sweet *bunda* out of here."

The foreman's grin dissolved as he suddenly realized that his complaint had boomeranged.

Peggy Carpenter's typewriter desk was a section of upended log that had been cut for her by one of the men; her seat was a shorter piece cut from the same log. The typewriter was clicking in staccato bursts of speed interspaced with thoughtful pauses.

Yesterday she had filed another five-thousand-word article, the third of a series. Thanks to the courtesy of one of Carlos's men, it had been delivered via jeep to Inchaco, to be dispatched from there to her New York editor by air. Now she was hot on another story.

Part of her present concentration came from a bursting need to express her deeply felt reactions—critical as well as extolling—to everything exotic, exciting, heroic, shocking, or depressing that she had seen and experienced. She also feared there wasn't much time left. She had long overstayed her welcome.

Carlos's original opposition to a female visitor in the FUNAI camp—at first expressed only in gentle hints that it was unsafe for her and might complicate their work—had lately solidified into strong statements that she must plan to leave soon, before FUNAI headquarters ordered him to send her back, which would look bad on his record. She felt some guilt about it. The poor man was burdened with the instincts of a gentleman, incapable of being tough with her. Her sweetness toward him was sincere, for she had grown fond of him, and she was also well aware of his fondness for her, fueled, perhaps unconsciously, by a strong physical attraction. Though she felt slightly despicable about taking advantage of the emotional bond, she used it ruthlessly to gain all the time possible for her work. The completed series of articles on the emerging giant of modern Brazil might well make her famous.

A low exclamation of surprise from one of Carlos's men drew her attention.

"*Olhe!* Look—the Indians are coming—all with weapons! Get Carlos, *depressa!*"

About thirty Indians were advancing in single file, led by a haughty figure Peggy recognized at once as Chief Amaro of the Atroaris who had held her captive. All carried bows or blowguns. All had their faces dyed black.

A war party!

Carlos came rushing from his tent, where he had been working on a FUNAI report. Smiling broadly, he approached, open palms held up in a sign of peace.

"My friends, it gives me much happiness to see you," he said in the intertribal *Lingua Geral* (which Peggy was beginning to understand), accompanied by gestures: "But it saddens me to see that your faces are painted for war and that you carry weapons. Why is that?"

Chief Amaro held an arm outstretched as if it held a pistol and said, "*Boom-boom!* You give us the white man's weapons, and we go."

"You want guns?"

"*Boom-boom,*" said Amaro.

"Why do you want boom-boom? In the great Xingú National Park that our generous government has set aside for all Indians to live in, there is much land, many animals to hunt, medicine men for your sick.

There your tribe can prosper, grow fat, live in peace with all other tribes. You do not need the white man's boom-boom."

"We do not wish to leave. Our home is here. Our enemies are here. Today a party of the Txacatores invaded our land with a white man's boom-boom and forced our warriors to flee."

"They had a boom-boom? Was anybody killed?"

"No. Our medicine was too strong. But the next time, theirs may be stronger. Our arrows will not be enough. We must have the white man's boom-boom—many of them—to protect ourselves and punish the Txacatores."

Carlos spread his arms in dismay. "I have no guns—no boom-boom—to give you, my friend. I have only friendship and gifts." He signaled one of the FUNAI men, who quickly came forward with a blanket pack, which he opened to display bright plastic beads, aluminum pots, mirrors, colorful cloth, and other cheap trinkets.

Watching, Peggy had an uneasy recollection of Manhattan Island being purchased for twenty-four-dollars' worth of junk jewelry.

Carlos took up a bolt of crimson cloth and proferred it to the chief, who roughly knocked it aside.

"*Boom-boom!*" he said.

"But, my friend—"

Chief Amaro raised a fist in a menacing gesture, then swung around and strode off, his file of warriors following.

His face a study in pain and frustration, Carlos turned and saw that Peggy was holding up her camera, snapping pictures, and had doubtless been taking them all during the confrontation with Amaro.

"How can you think of pictures at a time like this?" he snapped at her.

"What better time?"

"Good God! Don't you realize what has happened?"

"I think I do, but I may have missed the significance."

Carlos squeezed his head between both hands in a gesture of magnificent exasperation.

"Don't you understand? We're sitting on a keg of dynamite, and it wouldn't take much more to touch it off into bloody warfare between the Atroaris and Txacatores. If that happens, all our long months of sweat and prayer trying to bring about peace between the tribes and get them moved to the Xingú National Park will be shot to hell—and the highway will have to come to a standstill!"

As he ranted on, Peggy ripped the sheet from her typewriter, tenderly setting it aside before inserting a fresh sheet. She began typing:

"Frail Indian arrows threaten to bring progress of world's mightiest highway to a standstill . . ."

Feverishly, she typed on.

EIGHTEEN

The sound of drums, tambourines, trumpets, and euphoniums still echoed through the streets of Rio, but tiredly now, for it was Tuesday, the fourth and last evening of Carnival. The wind instruments were more stridulous, their rich depth lost to weakened lung power; many of the drummers of the *bateria*, who had stuck it out with gritted determination bolstered by a heavy intake of drugs, were suffering numbed and bleeding fingers. The great sexual ballet—the heartbeat of the festival, at times breaking into headlong orgy—was winding down.

For Raul, who had arrived only late that afternoon, the day was depressive. His added delay of two extra days had been due to a slower-than-anticipated recovery from the anaphylactic reaction to the beesting poison.

He had called Eduardo, who had been strangely reticent about discussing Odete, which Raul had attributed to his brother's resentment at having been imposed upon. Odete herself had greeted him coldly, her displeasure more hurtfully expressed in tight-lipped silence than in words. She had discarded her Carnival costume, and for Raul was dressed primly in dark satin. Dinner at the Nacional Hotel, clogged with tired revelers and made more dismal by the shoddy service from exhausted waiters, had not improved her mood. Raul's suggestion that they repair to his hotel suite where they could talk in quietude and privacy had been rebuffed. Odete said she was not feeling well and preferred that they return to her aunt and uncle's town house, where they would have just as much privacy, since her fun-loving relatives would doubtless be out for most of the night.

Now they were seated, like two strangers, on a sofa in the living room, and Raul decided it was time to come to the point.

"All right, Odete—out with it. What's wrong with you tonight?"

She took a nervous drag from her cigarette. "Why do you think there's anything wrong? I already told you I don't feel well."

"Not feeling well is no excuse for your coldness toward me, your sulkiness—"

"You expect me to fall on your neck with joy after you stood me up?"

"But you know I had no choice. The bees—"

"So it's the bees you blame! If you felt it necessary to go poking into bees' nests, why didn't you order someone else to do it? *Trabalho é para cachorro e negro!* Work is for dogs and Negroes."

He frowned at her. "You're irrational tonight—"

"Irrational! Crazy, you mean? Because I am so angry at you?"

"Angry over a trivial matter that was beyond my control. What is so terrible about the fact that I was a few days late? You still had Eduardo to escort you."

"Oh, you are so blind! I wanted so badly to see Carnival with you, to walk hand in hand, to laugh together and love together—so long I had looked forward to it. Oh, if you had not been so stupid with the bees! It could have been different—"

In a flurry of rage she flung her burning cigarette on the carpet, then cradled her head in her arms on the back of the sofa and began sobbing.

Raul's impulse to put comforting arms around her and speak soothingly was arrested by the sight of the cigarette smoking against the pale beige carpet. As he snatched it up, a suspicion flashed through his head. Carefully he snubbed the cigarette out in an ashtray.

"Odete, tell me—did Eduardo offend you in any way?"

"Oh, no, no, no!" She whirled her tear-streaked face

toward him, the beautiful features contorted. "He was always the perfect gentleman! How can you think so badly of your own brother?"

Abashed, he dismissed the suspicion of Eduardo and stared moodily at the carpet, which showed a black spot from the cigarette. "I confess I'm mystified. I think you are hiding something. You must tell me what's troubling you."

"I don't know!" she wailed. "I feel like I'm changed. Like you are changed."

"I haven't changed."

"In my eyes you seem different from when you lived in Rio—all because of that terrible jungle you love so much."

"The jungle is my future," he said stiffly. "I had hopes that you would learn to like it."

"I am not the type to bury myself away from civilized people. I would hate it."

"If the jungle is so terrible to you, perhaps we are wrong for each other."

She gave him a startled look, her tone growing slightly warmer. "I do not think it is that. If you really love me, why could you not buy a house in Rio for me and hire a manager to run your jungle business so you could be here some of the time with me and some of the time in the jungle when it was necessary?" She added magnanimously, "I would even go to the jungle myself sometimes, to be with you."

He laughed wryly. "It would make for a marvelous marriage—me in Amazonas and you in Rio. Half a marriage—together only when you felt like it. If *you* really loved *me*, I would expect you to follow me wherever I lived."

"Of course I love you—it's just that I don't think that type of life is good for you either. It makes you so serious, for one thing."

"I am serious—I'm not a playboy."

"But there are limits. You might as well have no money at all if you can't enjoy it."

"Obviously we have different needs. Perhaps we'd better get things straight right now—"

"Please!" she moaned. "It is too upsetting to talk like this. I am too tired—not well . . ."

He stood up stiffly. "Another time, then—when you're feeling better."

She rose and flung herself against him, her face buried against his chest. "Yes, another time. I am so sorry for tonight. I am all mixed up, not myself. Now all I wish is to be alone."

He kissed her tenderly, but he was more deeply depressed than ever.

Alone, Odete smiled through her tears. She had enough experience practicing the hot-and-cold technique on smitten swains to know that he would be back tomorrow, probably with flowers and profuse apologies. Which she would accept, and she would change back into the sweet kind of girl he wanted. His love would only be stronger. Men were really so foolish, so easy to manipulate.

It wasn't that she didn't love Raul. At least she thought she did, and she knew she didn't want to lose him—but she also wanted more . . .

She went to the phone and dialed a number.

At the sound of Eduardo's voice, her genital area grew warm and moist.

"What's up, Odete? I thought you were with Raul tonight."

"He just left. I'll explain later. Can you come and pick me up?"

He hesitated. "I think it would be unwise while Raul is in town."

"Please! I must be with you tonight."

"I'd rather not, Odete—not until he's left Rio."

A fury seized her. "If you don't, I'll be so angry that in a rash moment I might even tell Raul what happened."

She heard his intake of breath. With obvious reluctance he told her he would pick her up in half an hour.

Glumly Raul picked his way along the street, stepping over drunks slumbering on the sidewalk in bedraggled costumes, scuffing through confetti, empty bottles, and other debris, detouring around a few couples still locked together tiredly squirming in the motions of lovemaking. Brown moths fluttered around the streetlights, and the concrete beneath was fluffed with insect bodies that squished underfoot. It was early morning of Ash Wednesday, and Carnival was almost over.

Raul felt equally as jaded. He had been going to bar after bar, drinking too much, trying to forget about Odete and all his problems, but he had been unable to dispel a heavy despondency.

"Veja sól" called a female voice. "Look at that—all alone! A beautiful senhor!"

Another chimed in, "Pst! Olá! Ó! Come to us, babee—"

He was surrounded by four or five women outlandishly made up in paint, spangles, bangles, a few strips of cloth, and little else. Their nakedness, ranging in shade from honey tan to black, was liberally sprayed with silver glitter. One wore pale blue plastic boots up to mid-thigh; another, black silk stockings, a garter belt, and an orange wig. The tangas and the string coverings over their breasts had mostly been torn away or hung loose. All of them closed around him, their ultrawhite teeth flashing.

"Ué, Vai! Nosso senhor!"

Other expressions of joy and admiration gurgled in his ears as he was pushed to the walk by the surging weight of sweat-slick limbs and torsos. Hands ripped at his trouser fly, avid fingers snatched at his penis. One woman was astride his head, her genitals working against his face. The air was redolent with the funky odors of stale perspiration and sexual juices.

"Ah! Nosso namorado—!"

With a sudden movement, using all his strength, he managed to roll over on his belly, rise to his knees, and then stagger up beneath a sliding pyramid of legs, arms, and buttocks.

He began running, trying at the same time to get his male organ tucked away. From behind him came a chorus of jeering catcalls.

"*Há, há, há! Que pena! Fora! Bolas!* Stupid man!"

When he was quite sure that they were not following him, he slowed down, breathing heavily as he got his pants zipped up, brushed off his wrinkled suit, and straightened his tie. Noting that he had fled into one of the darker side streets, he began walking fast, for at this hour it was not wise for a pedestrian to get too far from the brightest lights.

He had gone scarcely a block when he heard the scuffling of feet, a yelp of pain, and the muffled, meaty sound of blows against flesh. More trouble!

His impulse to flee was restrained by the sight of a big man staggering into the light of a festival lantern and flailing his fists at four or five *malandros* circling him like a pack of rats. Two were clinging to him from behind, and two in front, one of them brandishing a knife. They were taunting him with obscenities. Another man was emerging from the shadows, a short section of pipe in his hand. The big man—plainly a *norte-americano* with his gaudy sport shirt, pale freckled skin, and red hair—was putting up a valiant defense against impossible odds. The least he could expect would be a cracked skull, and he would certainly be robbed of everything.

Raul barely hesitated. All the night's frustrations came boiling up, seeking release with a reckless disregard for consequences. Rushing in, he caught the upraised arm of the *malandro* who was poised to strike with the pipe from behind. A furious wrenching of the man's arm sent the pipe clanking to the concrete. Just as furiously Raul brought up a knee with crushing impact against the man's groin. The *malandro* yowled and folded forward, gabbling in agony.

But two others were now upon him. Knuckles cracked against the bridge of his nose, followed by a warm gush of blood. The salty taste started trickling into his mouth as he swung a fist, missing. The thugs were nimble, darting around him like elusive shadows. One leaped on his back. As he bent forward in an effort to dislodge his assailant, he saw that the American had tripped backward over the curb. At once, the other two were on him, one with an upraised knife.

Crouched low and whirling, Raul managed to send the man tumbling off his back and to rebound quickly, ready for more fighting. The other man was crowding in.

"*Caramba!*" squawked one of the two *malandros* who were holding the dazed American down while going through his pockets. "*Escute!* Look here—he has the *figa!*" He held up a delicate gold chain that he had ripped from the American's neck, at the end of which dangled a small ivory fist, the thumb protruding between the first and second fingers. He let the amulet drop as if it were poison and abruptly stood up.

At that moment of distraction, Raul swung a fist with a lucky uppercut that sent one of his opponents reeling. The other held back dubiously.

"*Rua!*" called the man with the knife, backing away from the recumbent American. "*Pira!* Scram!" And moments later all the attackers were racing down the street.

Raul went over and helped the other man to his feet. The American, still groggy from bumping his head when he fell, managed a wry grin as he thrust out a hand.

"Thanks, pal," he said. "You turned the tide in the nick of time. I thought I was a goner."

Raul grinned back as they shook hands. "It's not every day I get a chance for such a good workout. It helped clear my head. But you look a bit worse for wear, my friend. Let us go to a coffeehouse and get better acquainted over a *cafézinho* and some breakfast."

"Suits me fine," said the redhead.

As they started off, a faint tinkling sound made the American turn around. He bent to pick up the golden chain that had fallen.

"I sure as hell don't want to leave my lucky piece behind," he said, thrusting it in a pocket.

They found a table in a small *botequim* that was crowded with played out but noisy revelers. Both men ordered coffee and double orders of scrambled eggs "*Ópera*" with bacon and hot muffins.

"By the way," said Raul, "my name is Raul de Carvalho. And yours?"

The American stared at him in astonishment. "You've got to be kidding!"

"What is so surprising, my friend?"

"Mr. Carvalho, you wouldn't know my name—which happens to be Matt Riordan—but it also happens that I was slated to have an interview with you, when I sobered up long enough, concerning employment."

It was Raul's turn to be astonished. "Then you must be the chemical engineer! I was given your hotel address by the placement agency and tried to reach you by phone after getting here, but you couldn't be located. What a coincidence!"

Riordan grinned. "It couldn't be coincidence, friend." Reaching in a pocket he produced the *figa* and held it dangling from its chain. "My little lucky piece arranged it. From now on I'm a true believer in *macumba*."

Raul laughed; then his face sobered.

"But the placement agency chief told me you no longer appeared to be interested in Brazilian employment. Is that true?"

Riordan sighed heavily. "That was a week ago—when I still had enough money to get out of Brazil. The pleasures of this country are very expensive—"

"I'm sorry to hear that your finances are in such bad shape, but perhaps—"

"Don't be sorry! The pleasures were worth every *cruzeiro*, and more. You know what the poets say: what can the vintners buy half so precious as the goods they sell? That certainly applies to the Brazilian playgirls and their delightful *bundas*. You know, I'm beginning to believe the *bunda* is the heart and soul of Brazilian culture. I mean that as the highest praise. This must be the last country on earth where women are still 100 percent female, and where female sexuality in its purest form is exalted on the level of religion."

"I'm surprised to hear you say that, considering that you come from the country that created Hollywood."

Riordan smiled bitterly. "It's not the same, Raul. You'd be surprised at how many of our most glamorous actresses are lesbian, or at least bisexual. Why, the reason that even my own wife walked out on me was because—" He sliced his words off abruptly, took a long swallow of coffee, and added, "Please, forget everything I said."

There was an awkward pause. Raul gave a short laugh. "We all have our problems with women—just as they do with us. But I doubt there are any real differences between women anywhere, or men either —only the surface differences of culture and individual responses to different expectations."

Riordan eyed him suspiciously. "Those are weasel words, pal. They could mean anything to anybody. You'd make a great diplomat. Myself, I'm too blunt. Fact is, I'm tabbed as a goddamn male chauvinist and react accordingly. I won't apologize. God made me this way, which I don't believe can be said for the goddamn female types who deny their own womanhood."

Raul grinned. "This is getting over my head."

"Mine, too."

"As I was about to say, regarding your finances,

perhaps if you're the man I'm looking for, the problem could be eased. As I understand it, you're a chemical engineer?"

"A damned good one, if you'll excuse my lack of modesty."

"Are you familiar with the principles of converting organic materials—such as wood—into alcohol?"

Riordan leaned back somewhat complacently and took time to light a cigarette.

"Raul, there's a volume in print called the *Biofuel Energy Primer*, put out by our National Energy Institute. In its latest edition, the section entitled "Principles and Practices of Methane and Methanol Systems" was written by me. I covered everything known or hypothesized about anaerobic and aerobic decay, every type of organic material that can be converted—from cow shit and fossil fuel to everything that grows."

"*Santo Deus!*" Raul breathed softly. "I seem to have blundered into precisely the man I need."

"And at precisely the right moment. I might have been out in the gutter right now with a broken head."

"Matt, how much do you know about the machinery setup and cost requirements for a commercially profitable alcohol-producing plant in the jungle?"

"About as much as is known by any of the experts, I think. The corporation I worked for dallied with the idea of going into methane, methanol, and ethanol production from renewable resources. They even paid me to design the overall system for a prototype methane power plant, but my designs were too advanced for the current state of the art. The plans were shelved because some of the hard-nosed directors decided that the chances of making a good profit were too uncertain."

Raul's expression clouded. "Then there's a big risk involved in making such a plant pay off?"

"In the States as of a couple of years ago, yes, but in Brazil it's a whole different ball game. Here you have abundant land, sun, and a surplus of relatively cheap farm labor. Your material source is constantly replenishable and also cheap. You're ideally situated. In view of zooming prices and the oil shortage, an efficient alcohol-producing plant here could make a killing."

"But the costs?"

"Costs would of course be tied to the size of the facility, but in any case would range from merely expensive to very, *very* expensive. However, there are many cost-cutting procedures. For example, instead of ordering—and waiting endlessly for delivery—the enormously expensive steel-fabricated digesters, you could save a bundle and achieve the same results more quickly with sealed concrete-block digesters that any competent mason could build for you from plans I would draw up. Here, I'll show you what I mean."

Taking out a pen and clearing off a section of the white tablecloth, Riordan began sketching in the rough and slightly lopsided but meticulously true lines of an experienced engineer. As he sketched he talked, explaining the various components: digesters, pumps, heat storage tanks, alcohol-fueled engine generators. The interconnected sketches kept expanding until the entire tablecloth had to be cleared to contain them. The scowling manager of the *botequim* came back to complain, but a large tip from Raul and a request for paper pacified the man and quickly resulted in a supply of paper.

Dawn had come and a sheaf of papers covered with sketches and scribblings littered the table before Riordan put his pen down and tiredly leaned back. "That's the general idea."

Raul's eyes shone with enthusiasm. He had been spellbound. "You've certainly convinced me that you know your stuff."

"I've done my homework," Riordan said modestly.

"Are you ready to work for me?"

"Why not?"

"If you do, you'd be stuck out in the middle of the jungle. Do you think you could forgo the pleasures of Rio for long periods of time?"

"The truth is I've had a bellyful of Rio pleasures. I'd like nothing better than to get away where there's enough solitude to think things through with a clear head—and to get my teeth into hard work again, especially a challenge of this sort."

"What kind of salary would you require?"

"For the present, I'd be satisfied with my upkeep and a little pocket money. When the project is far enough along to demonstrate that it works efficiently, and to your full satisfaction, you could either pay me what you think I'm worth—somewhat in line with my previous salary—or give me an equivalent amount of stock in your company."

Raul's eyebrows arched. "That's more than fair. How do you know you can trust me to honor such an agreement?"

Riordan grinned. "Women may be a mystery to me, but I pride myself in knowing something about men. I recognize you as a visionary. I'm one myself. And I'm willing to take my chances with you—if you are with me. Besides—" Reaching in a pocket, he withdrew the golden chain, and added, "I've always got my little *figa* to protect me."

Both men laughed.

Raul thrust out a hand. "Then it's a deal."

Almeida Branco da Silva's manner was oddly evasive, thought Raul as he seated himself across from the financier in the lush top-floor office overlooking the Avenida Presidente Vargas. Not that the big man's greeting had been anything less than courteous, but the warmth was lacking. Da Silva settled himself behind his desk, taking a slim cigar and rolling it in his fingers, and Raul sensed that he was stalling for time, as if he had something unpleasant to say.

Da Silva lighted the cigar and puffed, showing his white teeth in a smile. "Well, what can I do for you, my young friend?"

Raul's unease increased. This important appointment had been set only a week ago. The purpose was to present a breakdown of the estimated capital requirements for the energy project—and to obtain the necessary bank credits for a substantial portion of the loan money for initial expenses. Certainly the financier couldn't have forgotten.

"Here are the preliminary figures, *senhor,*" Raul said, sliding a fat folder across the large jacaranda desk. In that folder were all the estimated costs of overhead and initial purchases of capital equipment that he and Matt Riordan had sweated over for two days and nights since the ending of Carnival. "These include an estimate of the amount I will need now to get under way."

"Ah, yes, the money—" Da Silva took a long, gentle puff on the cigar, scratched his heavy neck, and sighed. "About that—there may be a few difficulties." He had made no move to open the folder.

"I don't understand, *senhor.* I was under the impression that the financing had already been approved."

"A conditional approval. The present doubts are but a reflection of the difficulties we understand you have been having."

"If your reference is to the wild bees, they are now under control, although they were an additional expense I could not have foreseen."

"A trivial matter. There are additional expenses in every business. Everything is not quite as simple in risk ventures as you had thought, *não?*"

"Granted. But that still does not explain why you entertain doubts as to the ultimate success of my plans."

"The fact is, some of my partners are not too pleased about risking their money in your enterprise in its present state. They feel we shall have to have more certainty of it working out profitably."

Raul felt momentary relief. "I think I can reassure them on that score. I have had the good fortune of finding and employing, as a possible partner, a recognized authority on the chemical and engineering problems relating to my project—"

Da Silva cut him off with an impatient wave of a hand. "Although I would approve of that as a wise step, I must be blunt and say that it has no bearing on the present problem confronting us."

"Which is?" prompted Raul.

"There is now considerable doubt that the highway will ever reach your land."

"*Absurdo!* I checked only yesterday with officials at the Department of Highways, and they reported no change in plans."

Da Silva gave him a condescending smile. "It is not the road commissioners, but the politicians who have the final say in such matters."

"Do you have knowledge of any political pressure to change the route of the highway?"

Da Silva consulted the glowing end of his cigar for several moments before replying. "Because you are the son of a man I greatly respect, I will explain something to you—on your oath that you will never reveal the source of your information."

"I promise—*valha-me Deus* if I lie—never to connect or implicate your name in any way with whatever you tell me."

"My young friend, unfortunately there are powerful interests at work to reroute the highway away from your land."

The information exploded like a tiny bomb in Raul's head. "Who are the ones behind it? What are their reasons?"

"One man only is behind it, and again I must impress upon you that I reveal it only in the deepest confidence, for he could be a deadly enemy. The man is Vinicius de Onis. He is determined—and his determination is backed by unlimited money—to see that the highway is diverted from your land to pass through his land, which is rich in bauxite, manganese, and other valuable minerals."

Raul frowned. "I know his land. It is far more difficult terrain for a highway and would be tremendously more expensive. How could they justify diverting the highway in his direction?"

"Enough money can justify anything, but there is more than that. The Indian problem gives all the justification needed."

"What Indian problem?"

"You must be aware that several road workers have been killed and that the lives of others are jeopardized by hostile Indians. I am told that the homelands of the two most warlike tribes are located in the forests through which the highway has been projected, which happens to be adjacent to your property. Rather than provoke the Indians into greater hostilities, the government would prefer to seek an alternate route."

"But our government has their FUNAI organization to pacify the Indians and move them to government reservations. Certainly such measures are more appropriate than going to the enormous expense of detouring through next-to-impossible terrain."

"FUNAI has thus far failed to pacify the Indians. You must keep in mind the position of the government. Because of a century of blindness toward our Indians, Brazil has been condemned for its insensitivity toward a minority race. It is now deemed of utmost importance that we polish our image and prove to a skeptical world that we are at least as kind and generous toward our Amerindians as the *norte-americanos* are toward theirs. You see, my young friend, the pressures of world opinion strongly affect all government policy. In politics, our Indians are virtually sacrosanct."

"Am I then to understand," Raul said gloomily, "that the loan will not be forthcoming?"

"Oh, not quite that—" da Silva said hastily. "It will merely be suspended until such time as the Indian and the highway problems are resolved to the satisfaction of my associates."

"Which may be never."

"*Se Deus quizer*—if God wills, the problems will be solved. But you must remember that was our agreement: everything was dependent on the highway running through your property."

Dejected, Raul stood up.

"However," da Silva continued, "I am ready to personally approve a modest amount to tide you over —say, a couple hundred thousand for now?—with the understanding that further moneys will depend on the conditions already mentioned."

Raul's first reaction was to decline politely. In terms of his grandiose plans, it was pin money. But he couldn't afford to let pride stand in his way.

"Your generosity will be much appreciated, *senhor*."

"*Bom.* Check with my bank tomorrow, and you will find that the sum has been credited to your account."

As the two shook hands in parting, da Silva added, "A final caveat—be warned that de Onis is as unscrupulous as he is wealthy. Be careful."

NINETEEN

Raul's dejection deepened. He had flown back to Casa de Ouro Branco yesterday in the lowest of spirits. Nothing was going as planned: da Silva was hedging on the money, Odete was hedging on setting a marriage date, and his father was upset about everything.

Working with Matt Riordan had so absorbed him that it had been two days before he got around to calling Odete. Again she had been in a snit of hurt feelings and tears from being so terribly neglected, and she was suffering another headache.

Raul's explanation of the urgency and pressures of his business situation only angered her further. Obviously his crazy plans for his silly business were of *far* more importance, she accused, than plans for assuring the happiness of their future life together. Although she loved him deeply, she told him tearfully, she thought it would be better to put off pinning down a wedding date until Raul could give more thought to *her* welfare.

Eduardo, who had been elusive and unreachable except for a couple of brief phone calls during Raul's stay in Rio, apparently had learned of the couple's difficulties and had conveyed the information to their father, who at once had called Raul and scolded him severely for having so deeply wounded the feelings of so lovely a girl, who came from such a fine family.

In Afonso's eyes it was an indication of immaturity in his son, a wish to escape the responsibilities of married life. And even more important, he pointed out sternly, he and Raul's mother were anxiously awaiting the grandson that they expected Raul and Odete to supply to assure continuance of the family bloodline.

All these worries, and now this . . .

Braz had appeared in Raul's office in the *fazenda* to make a report.

". . . the bee infestation has been fully cleared up on your land, *patrão*," he was saying, "but Hélio, whom I put in charge of the work, for he is the best of all your *caboclos*, has discovered that the bees have spread across the boundary of your land to nest in the woods of your neighbor, Dom João Vargas. Hélio did not wish to trespass on your neighbor's land, but if the bees there are not destroyed, they will soon be spreading back to your property, and it will be trouble all over again."

"I'll speak to Dom João about it and offer our help. I'm sure he'll see the wisdom of ridding himself of the bees right away and will be glad to cooperate."

"Let us hope so, *patrão*, but I have heard that he is a stubborn man to deal with."

Raul decided to go to visit Dom João. Matt Riordan had been left in Rio to research costs and suppliers of the materials needed for setting up a prototype plant, and he wouldn't be arriving for another few days. After that, there would be little free time to handle such bothersome details as the killer bees.

Besides, in the back of his mind was the pleasant prospect of seeing Vivi again.

Dom João Abrais Vargas faced Raul with a questioning frown. The two stood in the *vestíbulo* just inside the front door, where Raul had been left by an Indian servant while he went to inform his master. Dom João surveyed Raul from head to foot before deigning to speak.

"And to what purpose may I attribute your unexpected visit?"

With an effort, Raul held back his anger at this rudeness. As a social equal, he should at the very least have been invited into the drawing room to sit and speak his piece. "*Senhor* Vargas, my errand is motivated primarily for your benefit. My men have discovered the hives of wild killer bees on your property, and—"

"By what authority have your men trespassed on my property?"

Raul flushed, briefly explaining his own problem with the bees. "Only by accident did my men cross over to your land when checking to see how far our bee infestation had spread. I thought it something you should know, as the bees are a great danger to your men. Since we've had experience in dealing with them, I came to volunteer our cooperation in helping you to rid yourself of the bees."

"I thank you for your offer," said Dom João with strained courtesy, "but I do not wish to concern myself with bees."

"I don't think you realize what a serious threat they are, *senhor*. Every time your men go into that part of the forest, their lives are endangered. Unless the bees are exterminated, or the queens transported elsewhere, several more lives could be lost."

"The lives of *caboclos?*" Dom João allowed himself a sneering smile. "They are expendable. Rather than go to the time and expense of fighting the threats of nature, it is cheaper and more efficient for me to hire other men to replace them."

Raul's anger flared to the surface.

"In the name of humanity, have you no regard for human lives?"

"You're wasting my valuable time, *senhor*. If you have nothing of more importance to discuss than bees and *caboclos*, I shall have to ask you to excuse me." And bowing curtly, he turned away.

Seething, Raul spun around and walked out.

Outside on the *pórtico* he paused to glance around. Vivi was not in sight. Not until reaching the hitching rack did he see her standing near where he had tied his horse. She wore a simple dress of yellow cotton—a fitting color, he thought, as the very sight of her was like a ray of sunshine piercing the gloom of his mood.

"I was wondering when you would visit us again," she said, breaking into a smile.

"I needed an excuse. There was a little matter I wanted to discuss with your father—"

"I know." She sighed wearily. "I eavesdropped. I apologize for my father. I beg you to be as charitable as possible toward him. With all his worries, sometimes I think that mentally he is not a well man."

"Seeing you again more than makes up for—his misunderstanding of me. I only wish I knew what it was about, for perhaps I could convince him that he is mistaken. I'm not really that terrible."

"I know you're not, Raul. To me you're one of the finest—"

"Hold it." He laughed. "After all, you don't know much about me, either."

"I have no choice but to believe my female intuition." Her gold-flecked brown eyes glanced away as if fearing to look at his face. "Tell me honestly, if my father's attitude were not an obstacle, would you come here just to see me?"

At that moment Raul happened to glance past her. There was Dom João, staring at them from a window, his face tight with fury before he withdrew from sight.

"I will tell you honestly," Raul said, fueled by anger at her father, "that my main reason for coming here today was the hope of seeing you again."

Her face was again alight with the sunshine smile. "Now you have given me the courage to be bold."

"Now you've got me curious."

"I don't think it's right that my father should so control my life, keeping me here almost like a prisoner, away from one I would like to see again. I was going to suggest that we might have a picnic together. I would prepare a basket of food."

"It's a delightful thought, but wouldn't your father object?"

"Father is flying to Manaus the day after tomorrow in a plane he rents for business purposes. He will be gone all day."

"I can think of nothing nicer than a picnic with you—but where?"

"I would like to show you my secret little hiding place. It is near a beautiful stream that my Indian friends have cleared and made pleasant for me. I go there to be alone with my books and my dreams, and sometimes to write silly little poems."

Raul hesitated, thinking of Odete, but some of the sting of her cold treatment still lingered; besides, was there anything wrong with going on an innocent picnic with a perfectly nice girl?

"It's a date," he said, "but on one condition—that you let me read some of your poetry."

She laughed. "I'll do better than that. I'll write one especially for you."

The time and place of meeting—along the jungle trail where first they had met—was set. With a final *adeus* and wave of hands, they parted.

TWENTY

How can I tell how, or from where my love
Came into being, or what the future holds?
If some jealous goddess should take you from me
In all the glory of your sinew and strength,
And I'd be denied the sight of those eyes
Whose piercing look puts the sky to shame,
Still my heart would keep you just for me,
And me for you, what e'er the fates might bring.

Raul read the lines a second time, more carefully, and
was struck by a terrible sense of guilt. The poem that
Vivi had written "especially for him" was plainly a
declaration of love. Smiling shyly, she had handed it
to him a few minutes ago.

He looked across at where she was setting out the
picnic lunch on a blanket spread over the grass. Her
head was down, her eyes diverted. Her cook had
prepared cold grilled chicken, deviled *ovos, coração
de palmito frio, tâmaras, peras, frutas frescas*, and still
more was being delicately lifted from the enormous
basket she had brought—enough to feed an elephant!
In the center of the spread was the ice bucket and the
bottle of wine he had brought.

"Vivi—"

"Yes?" She didn't look up. Was she fearful of his
reaction to the poem?

"The poem is beautiful. Did you really write it?"

"Yes, but I must confess the style was influenced by
my love of the work of Luis de Camoëns, my favorite
Portuguese poet."

"Was the sentiment also influenced by him?"

She flushed. "Oh, no—that came entirely from my
own feelings. Now you see what silly thoughts are in

my head when I come here to be alone." With a light laugh, she changed the subject. "What do you think of my little hiding place?"

It was an idyllic spot—a grassy knoll high above a clear little fast-running stream, set off on one side by a glade of flowering trees and shrubs and on another side by a screen of brilliant green palm fronds. The air was fragrant with the scent of plumeria blossoms, and the sun filtering through the foliage cast an iridescent radiance over Vivi's ebon hair.

Raul laughed. "It's lovely—and very conducive to romantic sentiment."

Again she flushed. "You're making fun of me. Now I'm sorry I showed you the poem."

"Why?"

"It is embarrassing to expose one's deep feelings."

It was Raul's turn to be embarrassed. "I'm sorry if I appeared insensitive to the—uh, beauty of the poem, but I am not free to react as I would like ..."

"I don't understand."

"It puts me in an awkward spot."

Her bright face was unduly solemn. "If you have something to explain, say it. I won't bite."

"I should have mentioned long ago that I am engaged."

"Ah, but of course! A man as attractive as you—it would be silly to think that some girl would not have a claim on you." She laughed a bit too shrilly. "I think you misunderstand. The poem was all imaginary—like the fanciful games that little girls play when they are alone. It was not meant to be taken seriously. I've written many love poems to many imaginary men."

"Forgive me for misunderstanding."

"We talk too much foolishness. Come, let us eat."

But as they ate, seated on another blanket spread over the grass, their conversation grew strained. They talked of books, of the theater, of the terrible world situation—much as two strangers might. As if in collusion with their moods, a cloud passed over the sun, darkening the afternoon, and they continued picking at the food, neither of them really hungry.

"Is she beautiful?" she said unexpectedly.

"Yes, but no more than you are."

"She's like me?"

"Hardly. She's like a hothouse orchid—and you're more like some wild and lovely flower."

"Wild?" She laughed. "I think you are also guilty of romanticizing." She glanced around at the darkening shadows and crossed her arms, shivering. "But if you like things wild, I believe you will get your desire. It looks like we are going to have a storm."

Indeed, the sky was somber with sullen clouds. There was no motion in the sultry air, which had grown oppressively thick. The horses, tethered about thirty feet away, were restive, eyes rolling, ears erect, and then a clap of thunder came hammering down the river. It was the season when Amazon rainstorms came suddenly, unexpectedly.

Raul started to get to his feet. "I think we'd better make a run for shelter."

"The only shelter is home, and we'd never make it in time," said Vivi. "I'm used to these jungle storms. All we can do is sit it out." Looking down at her pale blue gauze shirt and her faded jeans, she added laughingly, "Water won't hurt what I'm wearing."

Punctuating her words came another rumble of thunder and a shuddering flash of lightning that whitened the whole world. The horses whinnied. Fat drops of rain began pelting down. It had become almost black under a sky of roiling purplish clouds, and the fresh breeze was rank with the odor of rotting leaves, logs, and damp earth. Soon came gusts of wind chilled by the sudden drop in barometric pressure. In a matter of seconds the temperature had lowered by twenty degrees.

Thunderclaps shook the air; lightning streaked from the heavens; the rain came down with accelerating fury.

Vivi had risen and was cowering under the on-slaught when Raul shouldered his way through the downpour to put a protective arm around her. Her thin wet shirt clung so close to her flesh she seemed almost naked.

"I guess we picked the wrong day for a picnic—"

"Ah, no! This is beautiful—this is life!" She yielded submissively to his embrace. He could feel her shivering.

"About that poem, Vivi. Please be honest, did you really write it for me?"

"Only because I thought I had sensed your true feelings, but I see now—"

"You weren't wrong."

"Nor was I right. You had already made the choice of another."

"Damn it! What I'm trying to tell you—" With a savage tightening of his arms he bent and crushed his lips against hers.

Under the whipping rain, the kiss was long and sweet. He could feel the thud of her heart, and he was acutely aware of her breasts and hardened nipples pressing against him. Her lips had grown blood-hot. He knew he should not continue. He would stop. Soon. But her body was straining against his, her arms clinging tightly, and his own hunger was like flame seething in his veins. Softly they sank to the blanket, still in an embrace.

With a vast effort, he drew away a few inches, his drugged sense of decency struggling against the clamorings of his blood.

"Vivi, maybe we'd better—"

"No, no!" she cried. "The moment that passes never comes again." And with twisting movements she be-gan removing her soaked clothing. He followed suit.

Kissing, clutching at each other's slippery-wet bod-ies, they gave in to the heedless frenzy of their fiery hungers, matching the fury of the storm. Lightning flashed. Blasts of wind shook the jungle, clattering leaves and limbs like rattles. Thunder rumbled as if from the bowels of the earth while the skies opened and torrential rains lashed at them mercilessly. It was an awesome spectacle of nature on a rampage. Their unleashed passions soared, as wild and abandoned as the elements.

A small plaintive cry of both pain and joy burst from her lips.

As suddenly as it came, the storm passed. Sun shafted through the dissipating clouds, turning the jungle floor a soft green and shining on the diamond droplets on the leaves. The insects, birds, and monkeys resumed their humming, chirping, and chattering. Mist rose from the hot soaked earth. All was at peace.

Except for Raul.

Dressed again, the pair lay on the blanket in each other's arms, unmindful of the wetness. Utterly relaxed, Vivi's face was turned against his chest, her expression pensive.

Raul was somber. He felt a deeper happiness than he had ever known. Or was it only transient euphoria born of glandular release? He had drunk greedily of love on the wing. Or was it only lust? Could the love act, stripped of total commitment, be anything more than that? *Yes,* he decided, *I love her.* But his commitment had been made to Odete.

Further troubling him was a disconcerting discovery.

He turned and kissed her hair. "Vivi—why didn't you let me know that you were a virgin?"

"I love you, my darling," she murmured. "Does anything else matter?"

He flinched inwardly. What kind of bastard am I? he asked himself. He loved her, yes—but he also loved another.

"I've already told you about my engagement."

"I regret nothing. If her love means more to you

221

than mine, so be it." She drew his head close and kissed him lingeringly on the lips. He felt her tears slide down his cheek.

"My love for you is greater than I can say," he began, "but—"

Cra-aack!

A long *vaqueiro* whip snaked through the air to lash across their limbs like stinging fire. Vivi screamed. Raul rolled to a sitting position, gritting his teeth against the pain.

"Foul slut!" roared Dom João, who sat astride a magnificent white horse as he coiled the whip back on his arm. "Knowing it was in your blood, I suspected you would sneak off for this purpose in my absence, so I returned early and beat the truth out of the servants!"

Again the whip whistled through the air.

Vivi's wail was pure agony.

Raul stared, appalled, at a diagonal line of blood that ran from her shoulder across one breast and down her torso, staining her wet shirt. He started toward Dom João.

"Sadistic brute—and you call yourself a father!"

He was stopped by the hissing of the whip and a fiery, choking sensation as the braided leather coiled and tightened around his neck. He began gasping. His vision blurred. Then he was spinning as Dom João roughly hauled back on the whip to unwind it from his neck.

"*Canalha!* Scoundrel! With this whip I could tear the flesh from your bones and leave you here to rot!"

Raul well knew that in the hands of an expert the whip was a deadly weapon, but in the grip of boiling rage, he plunged blindly toward the mounted man.

The whip snaked out again. Flinging up both arms, Raul managed to diffuse the lashing impact—but not enough. The flickering tip ripped across his face, tearing the skin, and blood dribbled its salty taste into his mouth. His arms, having taken the brunt of the punishment, were inflamed with throbbing pain.

But his fury was even greater.

Gripping the blood-slick whip entangled in his arms, he jerked back with all the weight and power of his body. Dom João, stubbornly clinging to the whip handle, half toppled from the saddle. Raul charged in and yanked him the rest of the way to the ground.

As Dom João was recovering his balance, Raul caught him by the front of his shirt and drew a fist back to smash at him.

"Raul—please don't!" Vivi's appeal came from the depths of an agonized spirit. "He is my father—"

Raul let his arms sag, then backed off, shaking his head to clear the blood-haze from his eyes. Dom João, breathing hard, stood beside his nickering horse, his burning eyes stabbing contempt. He spat on the ground close to Raul's boots.

"The next time I see you," he said coldly, "I'll have a gun—and I'll shoot to kill."

"Please, father—"

"Get on your horse, Vivi; come with me."

Head bowed, she obeyed.

Dom João paced moodily through his vast living room. He was sick with remorse, sick with shame, sick with a sense of abject failure. Vivi, after being bathed and having her whip cuts treated by one of the female servants, had retired to her room in a state of semi-shock. Doubtless she was as miserable as he was. But deservedly so!

Had anything really happened between the two? Dom João had feared to ask. The very thought of it made the blood rush to his head, and his hands clenched with the urge to murder.

Where had he gone wrong in the upbringing of his daughter? He had done everything possible to protect her from the traps set for the innocent in a world that was growing increasingly sick with immoralities. But since the death of Vivi's mother, Rosalina, it had been hard. After suffering from a miscarriage and exsanguinating hemorrhage, Rosalina had died, and he had also lost the son he had longed for—a live and healthy son that could have made the whole difference.

Without Rosalina, he had been severely handicapped. There were certain matters that a father could not discuss with a daughter, and he had been forced to depend on Olinda, the black nanny who had raised Vivi from babyhood, to carry on with the mother's role as much as possible. And Dom João believed sincerely that blacks by their very nature were without moral sense of any kind.

He had considered a second marriage, but there again he had been handicapped by fate. Because of the depleted family fortune, he had too little to offer the only kind of highborn wife he would have found acceptable, the kind who would never consent to living in the jungle unless fortressed by unlimited wealth. Even if such a woman would have consented to be his wife, there was another reason—a more compelling reason—why he dared not take the risk.

The family curse.

It dated back to his great-grandfather, Valentin Vargas, who first came to the jungle to make his fortune. Young Valentin had been endowed with all the strength and energy required of pioneers—perhaps too much, for he had come without a wife, and his strong sexual drive found its only outlets among the Indian and Negro slave women.

One of them, a fifteen-year-old black virgin, became his *minha nêga*—little Negro—a common term of endearment for the black mistresses of white Brazilians at that point in history. She was said to have the beauty of the rarest jungle orchid, which gave rise to his name for her, Orquídea. His passion for her grew into a mad love—and he brought her into his grand *fazenda*, then in the process of construction, and treated her as though she were his wife, though they did not marry.

When a son was born, out of consideration for the feelings of Orquídea, he did not make his slaves take the baby into the jungle and bash its head against the rocks—the customary solution to offspring of unions with slaves—but instead he allowed the mother to keep the infant for a while, intending it to be temporary. This was in the year 1871, when the princess imperial regent—in the name of His Majesty the emperor of Brazil, *Senhor* Dom Pedro II—out of the softness of her heart had established (with the weak emperor's permission) the Law of the Free Womb (*Ventre Livre*), declaring freedom for all children born of slaves.

With that as legal justification, but more because he had become as fond of his infant son as if the baby had been lily-white, Valentin took the unprecedented step of adopting the boy, who had been named Henrique, thus bringing him into the direct family line of descent.

Henrique, whose nature contained the enormous vitality and the hardihood of the two races that had created him, had been among the first to foresee the coming rubber boom. And profit by it. Despite the fact that slavery had been completely abolished by the Golden Law of 1888, he drove his Indian and Negro slaves as mercilessly as any white plantation owner, and like most of the plantation owners who resented and resisted the law, Henrique pushed his ex-slaves to the limit, never letting them know they were free.

With the snowballing Vargas fortune, the *fazenda* had been enlarged and enriched with imported luxuries, and Henrique had taken a highborn white wife. Despite his golden skin, with such wealth nobody questioned his ancestry too closely. Or cared.

Each succeeding generation had been the same. Each male Vargas heir had married white, progressively diluting the *preto* blood, and each had been told the story and sworn to secrecy about their black ancestor.

Dom João had never told Viviane. He no longer had the shelter of wealth to protect her, but he still yearned for the respectability of her marriage into the highest social level, where she belonged.

Still, if the secret of her *preto* blood were ever discovered, no man of noble lineage would dream of marrying her. One of the oddities of Brazilian culture was that a strain of Indian blood far enough back in one's ancestry raised one's status; whereas black blood, enticing as it was erotically, was a social stigma not to be forgiven in a marital prospect.

That was Dom João's secret.

Living far out in the jungle, the family had been successful in concealing it—from everyone expect their only neighbors, the de Carvalhos.

In the early days, Jorge de Carvalho had been most obnoxious. There had been disputes over the boundary line between their properties, and Vargas rubber gatherers had been kidnapped at gunpoint and put to work for de Carvalho. Later, when Jorge discovered that Henrique had been adopted, he never lost a chance to taunt the Vargas family as his *"preto* neighbors."

That was at the crux of Dom João's burning hatred of Raul.

In all justice to the de Carvalho family, Dom João had no fear that they might have discussed with others their knowledge of the Vargas black blood. After all, what highborn family didn't have a skeleton or two in the closet? The well-bred knew better than to gossip about such things.

But the de Carvalhos *did* know, and if their own son were involved in the possibility of marriage to a girl with the *preto* taint, they would be sure to react most decisively to prevent such a union.

Such a scandal could be advertised all through Brazil, thus forever dooming Vivi as persona non grata, an untouchable in high social circles, of value only as an exotic whore.

Não! Never, never would he allow that de Carvalho *canalha* to come near his daughter again. If he ever tried, if he so much as set a foot on the Vargas property, Dom João would shoot him down like a dog!

TWENTY-ONE

Squatting on a mat of reeds in his frond-thatched *tapiri*, Chief Xanqui, *curaca* of the Txacatore tribe, listened to the dull boom of dynamite, the angry roar of the huge "earthshakers," and the other road-building sounds in the distance. Each day they came a little closer.

Each day his tribe was closer to death.

Bitter anger trembled through his scrawny and somewhat withered six-foot body. He still possessed a leathery toughness from having survived nearly eighty years of jungle dangers, including evil spirits, disease, deadly beasts and snakes, and the deadliest of all enemies: men. He had survived at least two or three times as long as the average Indian, a longevity he attributed to the rigid training forced on him by a stern father—also a chief—and to the wisdom he had gained from the gods.

But now his strength and wisdom had failed him.

Lying white men would soon destroy their homes, kill them, or take them as prisoners to some far-off camp. Past experience had taught the Indians that whites took prisoners only to torture or work them to death.

Xanqui picked up the revolver that he and his warriors had taken from one of the road builders. Admiring its beautiful shape, he fondled it. The polished blue metal was cool and pleasant to the touch; its solid weight gave a sense of power. Curling a finger around the trigger, he pulled.

Click, click, click.

The boom-boom was gone. The short, heavy little arrows that made a big noise and killed quickly were used up. Five times Xanqui had fired the gun. Once against a hunting party of their hated enemies, the Atroaris, doing no harm but sending them racing away in terror. Another time he shot at a monkey, merely causing the animal to scamper higher in the tree and chatter at him angrily. The other three times, not realizing they were the last of the boom-booms, he had practiced shooting at a tree, succeeding in making only one small hole in the trunk.

A small hole that represented instant death.

Txacatore poisoned arrows and darts could bring quick death too, but they had been no match for the dreaded *fazendeiros,* the land robbers who had come with their bands of killers to murder, steal, or enslave. The Txacatores had fought and lost, as repeated murderous raids on their villages had driven them ever deeper into the jungle, reducing their villages and thousands of warriors to a single tribe of less than two hundred.

And now the road builders had come with devil-machines to drive the Txacatores out of their last homeland. With guns, with *civilizado* diseases that Indian medicines could not cure, and with strong drink that made warriors weak, the *civilizados* would soon destroy the last of the Txacatores.

Unless some power could be found to stop them.

Xanqui glanced around at the *tapiri* ceiling of crisscrossed poles, from which hung his many trophies of hunting and war. Among them were the *tsantas,* the dried heads of enemies he had killed. That had been the traditional way of gaining power, and he had about fifty of them, each shrunk by a secret process into diabolical caricatures the size of a small coconut. By this means, not only had he destroyed the evil directed against him by his enemies, he had also stolen their power for himself.

To shrink the heads of the white enemies was not possible. They were too numerous. War with them would be hopeless.

Only the gods could help him now.

Regretfully, Xanqui tenderly wrapped the revolver

in a monkey skin, set it aside, and began making his preparations. During his younger warrior days, when threatened by great dangers it had been his custom to pray to one of the gods, asking for counsel or favors timorously, out of fear that he might offend the god and thus bring punishment upon his head.

Now there was no timidity. The need for help to save his tribe and himself from destruction was too urgent. Moreover, instead of praying to an individual god, who might be too busy with other matters, he had decided on the bold step of seeking counsel simultaneously with *all* of the important deities.

He had begun preparations earlier that morning by dosing himself with *guayusa*, a purgative used by warriors to clear their heads. Then he painted half his wrinkled face with red urucú dye and stained the other half black with *genipa* juice. After that he donned his red toucan-feathered headdress and inserted two plumes through his pierced nose. Ornaments of shells and human bones were suspended from his neck and waist, as was his monkey-skin pouch containing his good-luck charms.

Readied for communion with the great spirits, he picked up a small ornamental clay bowl that was half filled with a mixture of certain animal juices, the saps of several plants, including the coca, and a potion extracted from the *chamico*, a plant known as the "devil's box." The concoction was a powerful narcotic used to induce a hypnotic trance that produced beautiful visions and opened the doors to the wisdom of the gods.

Taking a reed from another bowl, Xanqui thrust it into the liquid and slowly sipped.

Almost at once he began to relax. A warm, pleasurable sensation seeped into his limbs, through his belly, up to his head. Contentedly, he continued sipping.

When he felt the full effect lifting him from the mat, making him weightless, he began his appeal.

"Oh Cubanamá, supreme god and universal essence

of all things; oh sacred Nungui, goddess of the earth;
and Shacaimo, husband of Nungui; oh exalted Cupara
and your woman, who are parents of the sun, I
beseech you to listen to my plea . . ."

Xanqui was a boy again . . .

Beautiful visions floated through his head, scenes of
a lush world from long, long ago seen through fresh
young eyes, with all the joy, all the wonder of childhood.

His father was the *curaca*, straight and proud, all-
powerful. "You must grow up to be a mighty warrior,"
he said. "Greater than most men. You must grow up to
be respected, to be feared. I will teach you."

The teachings were many: All-important was intimate knowledge of the deities. He was taught how the
great god Cupara's wife had given birth to the sun,
for whom they made a wife called the moon, who was
very fair though created from mud. The celestial
couple then gave birth to many sacred children, both
animals and plants. Foremost among mother moon's
children was the sloth, the primal ancestor of all
Indians; the primary sacred plant was the manioc, the
Indian staff of life.

He learned about the supreme god, Cubanamá,
who, being too lofty for work, assigned all the chores
of running human affairs to Tsaratuma, who in turn
designated special duties to all the lesser deities under
his command, such as the rain god of the mountains,
the anaconda god of the river, the earth goddess, her
husband Shacaimo, and many others. It was imperative
that Xanqui know all of this, and that he know to
which deities he must pray to benefit from their
particular powers.

Along with these studies, Xanqui's boyhood was
filled with long hours of practice to master many
skills. He was taught how to weave baskets; how to
spin and weave and knit, using fibers from the cotton
trees; how to know all animals, birds, and snakes and

which of them were forbidden to do harm to and which were best for food or ornaments; how to use plants and trees for curing sickness. To give him pride, he was also taught the history of his tribe, all the legends, all their heroic exploits.

Xanqui detested such studies. The ones he most enjoyed learning were the arts of hunting and fishing.

For fishing he was taught to make astrocaryum palm fiber nets. An easier way was to dam up a small stream with rocks, gather barbasco (wild cinnamon) branches and beat them on the rocks until the sap oozed, then toss them into the stream well above the dam. Within minutes, the fish, stupefied by the paralyzing effect of the drug, were turning over helplessly on their backs.

For hunting, he was instructed in the making of his first blowgun. The two semicircular halves of a split piece of chonta palm were set up on forked sticks in the ground, and Xanqui spent tedious days grooving out the insides with a jaguar tooth. Next the two halves were temporarily bound together. The barrel inside was smoothed with a long chontawood rod worked back and forth with fine sand and water, which took many more days. Finally the two halves were glued snugly together with latex from the wild rubber tree, wrapped tightly with ivory-nut fiber, coated with resin, stained black with *sua*, then highly polished. The finished weapon would be capable of sending a *tsenac*, or twelve-inch palm rib dart, through a half-inch hardwood plank at ten feet, and it was almost as accurate as a rifle at a hundred yards.

To be assured of a quick kill, the darts had to be poisoned, for which Xanqui was taught the secret art of mixing curare, strychnine, vine saps, ground pepper berries, roots, leaves, mashed spiders, and sometimes snake venom. It made a sticky goo and was kept in a small gourd, to be smeared on the sharp ends of the darts. The blunt ends were wrapped with cotton to make a snug fit in the blowgun and to balance the darts in flight.

Most of all, Xanqui yearned to begin headhunting, and to begin the practice of head shrinking. He wanted to become a great warrior.

Though only twelve, he felt ready. Hunting expeditions had sharpened his skills with weapons. He had bagged many monkeys and once gotten a sloth he had found hanging in a cecropia tree. Proudly he brought it home, wishing to roast the meat to eat.

"No," said his father, "for by its expression it is plain that the sloth has the soul of an old enemy of the clan. Instead you will shrink the head to gain his power. I will teach you how."

To impress on his son the importance of head shrinking, his father had Xanqui fast for two days, after which he drank datura to induce a hypnotic state so that everything told him would remain indelibly impressed in his mind. Then, dangling before Xanqui's eyes the shrunken head of an enemy killed by his father, the whole reason for head shrinking was explained.

"A warrior must always avenge past killings of his clan brethren. Until your enemies are killed and their heads made small, your sacred ancestors will be angry at our whole tribe. Evil spirits will ruin our crops; our hunting and fishing will be fruitless; our wives will become barren. To kill an enemy is a noble deed. To shrink his head will bring security and prosperity to the entire tribe."

After learning how to shrink the head of the sloth, Xanqui was even more anxious to become a great headshrinker, and at the age of thirteen he was allowed to go on his first headhunting expedition.

He was shown how to paint himself fearsomely black like the other warriors and to adorn himself with shells and feathers. They all drank much *nijimanche*, manioc beer, after which they danced to the rhythm of a *tundui* drum. Then, armed with spears and ceiba-wood shields, they sallied forth.

Their attack on an enemy hunting party turned into

disaster. Xanqui's father was killed; the rest barely escaped with their lives.

The burden of vengeance now fell on young Xanqui, who began practicing incessantly with blowgun and spear. Finally Xanqui went seeking the killer, found him alone, drove a spear deep into his back, and cut off his head.

Alone in the forest he shrank the head. First, for protection, he put on his toucan feathers and braided a magic belt out of the dead man's hair. With a sharp bone knife, the thick fibrous skin of the head was slit up the back and peeled off the skull—hair, face, and all. Xanqui sewed the lips together with palm fiber and dunked the gory mess in a boiling solution of astringent saps. Then, putting hot stones and sand inside the skinned head, he started the shrinking process, which took two days to get it down to the size of a fist. With a wooden spatula and deft fingers, the features were pressed back into their original shape. The final step was to smoke the head slowly over a greenwood fire and polish the skin to a dull luster.

Back at the village, Xanqui was met with rejoicing. The tribesmen painted his legs with pigeon blood and black *sua* sap, and they did the *tsanta* victory dance. Xanqui danced, the head suspended around his neck, and at the same time shouted insults to drive away the evil spirits.

For the next six months Xanqui prayed and fasted in solitude while his dammed-up male forces built a great hunger for women. Already his eleven-year-old wife had given him one child and was heavy with another, but the blind instincts and customary mating rites that had brought them together were as nothing compared to the new and furious sexual desire that consumed him, for killing an enemy always stirred a warrior's lust.

After his long fast, he was installed as chief, replacing his father, and all the women of the tribe, including those already married, were put at his disposal.

Xanqui sighed softly. Even in his present drug-induced state, the visions of his many wives sent warm stirrings through his eighty-year-old male organ.

How many he had possessed throughout his life, he could not remember. They were too numerous, their life-spans too short. Those who failed to bear children were discarded or their lives sacrificed to the gods. Some died of strange woman diseases, some of old age. There were always new and younger ones, for he had become a powerful chief, with many enemy heads hanging in his *tapiri*. At present he had about a dozen wives. Some, who were less than a third his age, had withered into old hags, but they were kept to do the hard work. He had lost count, too, of his numerous children and their children and their children's children. He had outlived at least half of them, having proved himself to be the greatest of husbands, the greatest warrior, the greatest headshrinker, the greatest hunter, the greatest *curaca* his tribe had ever known.

Only against the whites was he powerless.

The visions flowing with rainbow brilliance through his head were beginning to break up into fragmented blurs that seemed to sum up, in incomprehensible symbols, his entire life story.

But the gods understood. They had shared all his visions and were now in the process of digesting them. Soon they would speak.

It was almost a day later when Xanqui emerged like a sodden log floating up out of murky waters, but his head was as clear as the sun breaking through a rain-washed sky. The deities had spoken.

All was as he had already known, but the approval and wisdom of the gods had clarified everything into law. Spoke the gods:

Never can you hope to hold forth in battle with the white man. They are too numerous, too skilled with more powerful weapons.

Your only weapons are friendship—and cunning.

All races have both good and evil leaders. With friendship, make peace with the good ones.

With cunning, seek out the evil leaders and destroy their power.

TWENTY-TWO

Tomaz, the black foreman of the highway advance party, gaped at the naked woman, unable to believe his eyes. She had emerged from the greenish light of the thick jungle wall into the sun-washed clearing where the men were working. Her straight black hair hung over the honey-colored skin of her shoulders. Her breasts were full, her figure slender and rounded. She walked as unconscious of her grace as a puma. Tomaz felt a stirring in his loins.

"*Santo Deus!*" muttered one of the *caboclos*. "See what heaven has sent us!"

"*Oh homem!* Man alive!" echoed another. "*Será possível.* I can't believe it. But look—she has children—"

Two small naked children trotted at her heels, their large round eyes darting fearfully.

"*Caramba!* And men, too—!"

Several Indian men wearing beads and feathered ornaments had stepped out from behind the trees to follow the woman. For a startled moment Tomaz unconsciously reached for his revolver before remembering that the holster was empty—and remembering too his *chefe*'s strict orders.

"Hist! *Silêncio!*" he called out softly but sharply. "Do nothing to frighten them. The presence of women and children means they are here peacefully, and the men have no weapons." He turned to the nearest *caboclo*. "Hurry back and tell the *chefe*."

Top boss Jaime Blasco received the news with surprise. In accordance with orders from Brasilia, he immediately assigned a man to relay the news to Carlos dos Santos, leader of the FUNAI party responsible for the pacification of Indians.

Upon receiving the news, Carlos almost danced with joy.

"Maybe all our efforts haven't been in vain after all," he said to Peggy. "I'm sure it must be the Txacatores, and plainly they want friendship. I think they are testing us to see if we are sincere. I'll take a few men up there immediately and begin giving out gifts."

"I'll go with you."

"No, Peggy, no! It could also be a trap of some kind—dangerous—"

"No more for me than for you."

"Peggy, I must be honest and tell you that I am getting more and more flak over you from headquarters. They wonder why you are staying so long and what kind of stories you are writing. I suspect they will soon order you away from here. And frankly, you are becoming a sore trial—"

"Carlos, I knew you'd understand," she said sweetly.

It was a gala day at the road builders' camp. A priest had been flown in on this Sunday morning to give a special service, and since visits of holy men were usually spaced months apart, the workers were in fine spirits. Almost to a man they were true believers, though they rarely had the opportunity, or the inclination, to attend church. But when mass occurred on company time, it had greater significance. It gave blessed reprieve from the monotony and sweat of the seven-day workweeks; it might even offer some salvation from their accumulated backlogs of sin.

For a pulpit, the priest had only the tailgate of a truck, but that was more than compensated for by the elegance of his pristine white- and gold-threaded vestments and the mellifluous flow of his voice.

"*Estote imitatores Dei sicut filii carissmi: et ambulate in dilectione sicut et Christus dilexit nos et tradidit semetipsum pro nobis—*"

The priest paused in his Latin rendering of the

admonitions from Ephesians and glanced around at the earnest but utterly blank faces of the roadworkers. He noted the presence of the naked Indian woman, the two children, and the few men. There was no need to impress these simple men and ignorant savages with his erudition, so he began again in the Brazilian tongue:

"Be ye therefore followers of God, as dear children; and walk in love together, as Christ also hath loved us . . ."

Three hundred yards away, Lobos heard the droning voice and made a grimace of disgust. "*Bôbos!*" he muttered. "Fools!" To emphasize his contempt, he spat at a small ant that was struggling along, transferring a big white egg from tunnels that had been destroyed by the road builders to a new colony site.

Lobos sneered at all religions and cults. His own philosophy concerning brotherly love was summed up in one of his many *malandro* tenets: Once you've got them by the balls, they'll kiss your ass.

Still, thanks to this holy day, he was being offered a perfect opportunity.

All the men were in attendance at mass—all but Lobos and the guard at the supply truck in the motor pool, where all the guns were locked up.

Lobos found the guard half dozing in the morning sun, propped against a tree trunk near the supply truck, a rifle resting in his lap. He knelt beside the man, grinning.

"Juscelino, I have come to do you a favor. I myself am not a Catholic, so I am willing to take your place so that you can attend mass."

Juscelino shook his head. "I dare not, Lobos. The *chefe* told me my ass would burn if I left my post for even a moment."

Lobos sighed. "Ah—it would have been better for only your ass to burn than to lose your last chance to make peace with God. However—" He made a lightning move and a razor flashed in the sun.

Juscelino's head sagged forward, the popping eyes striving to look downward at the blood bubbling from his neck.

Pushing the head back against the tree trunk, Lobos finished the job, slashing the neck arteries and then hustling back to where he had hidden a crowbar.

With the bar he made short work of prying open the rear door of the supply truck and ripping the lock, hasp, and screws from the wooden framework. Tossing aside the crowbar, he gathered up an armful of rifles and shotguns—all were loaded, he noted with satisfaction—and carried them into a nearby bushy section of jungle. One more armful was carried back to the same spot before he began the next step.

Working quickly, Lobos began dropping the weapons at spaced intervals along the jungle trails where he had seen the FUNAI men leave gifts for the Indians.

By the time he had finished, he was sweating heavily. But there was not a moment to waste. Taking the last of the rifles, he doubled back among the trees to a hidden position, close enough to give him a clear view of the religious gathering. Blood pulsed crazily through his veins from exertion and excitement. In a few more moments, his job would be done. All that was left was the long hike to Inchaco, most of it easy walking on the new highway. He had ample money hidden in his clothes, and it would be easy to buy passage out on one of the mail or supply planes. And when he got back to Rio—ah!—the big reward was waiting for him.

Taking careful aim, Lobos pulled the trigger. An Indian crumpled over and fell. Lobos continued firing as rapidly as possible and saw two more Indians fall, one of them a woman. Then the hammer clicked on an empty chamber. No matter. Enough damage had been done. All the roadworkers were milling around in fright, and the remaining Indians were fleeing into the forest.

In the midst of the confusion, a covey of poisoned

arrows suddenly hissed through the air—aimed by hidden Indian sentries who had been keeping watch over their naked ambassadors of friendship.

One of the arrows caught the priest. Still elevating the Host and chalice, he tumbled from the tailgate, the arrow protruding from his throat.

Lobos turned and fled.

TWENTY-THREE

In Brasilia, where architectural wonders explode from the red earth as in a futuristic fairy-tale, the government machinery was grinding along at its usual majestic but snaillike pace.

On today's agenda in the Chamber of Deputies was the question of highway diversion—somewhat unusual, since such minor details were normally decided by bureaucratic fiat. A vociferous minority opposing the diversion had insisted on pushing the debate up to the exalted ranks of Congress. The Senate had been evenly split, as well as uninterested, and had passed the matter down to the Chamber of Deputies for a final decision.

In the Chamber, the debate had gone on for long hours, until many of the people's representatives were half asleep from boredom. Then Mauro Luiz da Costa Monteiro rose to speak.

Monteiro was a small, meticulously neat man. He had a wisp of moustache, a full coif of gleaming silver hair, and lively gray eyes. He wore a gray silk suit, and his white shirt and silver tie were likewise of silk, as was his manner, for he had been a fine actor, until he discovered that the same talents could be more profitably applied to politics.

He paced back and forth, head down and hands clasped behind him, until the attention of the entire room had been captured by the silence alone.

He clapped his hands sharply, producing in the acoustically perfect room a sound like a gunshot. Every man present came alert. For another moment he paused.

"You have all heard, I am sure," he began smoothly, "of the shot that was heard around the world. I have just tried to symbolize such an act. I refer to the recent bloody massacre of one of our holiest emissaries of God, several highway laborers, and a few of our Indian brethren—an episode of savagery that has reverberated to the four corners of the earth." He gazed at them sadly.

"Let us devote a few moments of silent prayer for the innocents who were so needlessly slaughtered." And bowing his head, he made the sign of the cross while his lips moved inaudibly. One by one, his audience followed suit, and after a while, Monteiro raised his head.

"It is needless for us to point fingers of blame. Whether the guilt reposes in the Indians' innate ferocity or in some ignorant *caboclo*'s carelessness with a firearm—that is only for the police, the moralists, and the judiciary to decide, if they feel so inclined. As legal representatives of the people, our sophisticated viewpoints should be addressed solely to the importance of the barbarous incident as it pertains to the question of whether or not to divert the highway.

"Nor is there any need for more than a word or two about the innumerable arguments we have heard—most of them of little merit—presented by both sides of the question.

"Some say the alternate route proposed presents greater engineering problems. Perhaps that is so; perhaps not. What does it matter? Have we not the finest engineers in the world to solve such problems?

"Some also say an alternate route would be more costly. Perhaps they are right; perhaps not. Is that important?"

He paused again to let his stern gaze swivel over the key members of the assemblage, then he continued:

"I ask you, which is more costly—a few more *cruzeiros* for an alternate route, or the incalculable damage to Brazil's moral image in the eyes of the world if the highway is *not* diverted?

"If not diverted, the highway—which is presently

243

cutting through traditional Indian homelands—will only incite them to more bloodshed—not only against the road builders but against other tribes, for it is known that the aborigines have seized many guns, and their warlike nature will surely put those weapons to deadly use.

"Let me remind you that our own government, as well as the United States, England, and France, have spent—and are still spending—millions in the pursuit of anthropological studies of the Brazilian Indian culture, a great national heritage that must at all costs be preserved. Do we wish our international friends to think we are crude barbarians who will not take every possible step to protect our own Indians?

"Let me also remind you that we are involved with world banks, world politics, money consortiums that keep huge amounts of cash pouring into Brazil. Compared to the benefits we receive, the added highway cost would be insignificant to a mushrooming, fantastically rich developing country such as Brazil . . ."

For twenty more minutes Monteiro's rich voice rolled on, giving reason after reason why the projected diversion of the highway would be best for all concerned. Most of his audience listened respectfully, for Monteiro was a senior deputy who had the power of designating other members to politically influential committees.

When a roll vote was called, his view prevailed by a handy margin. The added costs of the highway diversion, after all, were but a small matter for such a superrich country.

But what a stupendous windfall in ultimate benefits, worth untold millions, perhaps billions, for Vinicius de Onis!

There was a new cockiness in Lúcio Barbosa's manner when he entered the lavish suite on the top floor of the Brasilia Palace Hotel. Vinicius de Onis greeted him impatiently.

"Well?"

Barbosa beamed. "It is done, Vini. They voted in your favor."

De Onis relaxed, smiling broadly. "And did you get the briefcase to Monteiro?"

"Ah, yes. He accepted it most graciously, without even counting."

"*Bom!*" De Onis produced a long fat envelope from an inner pocket and tossed it to his henchman. "A little bonus for your good work."

"*Muito obrigado.*" Quickly Barbosa examined the packet of bills inside, smiling in satisfaction as he stuffed them into his pocket. "By the way, I was accosted by Hygino, who is getting nervous about receiving the rest of the money you promised him."

De Onis made a gesture of annoyance. "Let him worry. His blundering has cost me a great deal of extra expense. Besides, the job is not yet finished."

"But now that Congress has already voted—"

"You have forgotten the American woman reporter, and the stories she has been writing. If she should start telling the whole world that the highway diversion is only for the benefit of private interests, it could cause many new problems."

"I am told she is a very difficult woman, Vini, and because the Department of Highways does not wish to offend the American press, they cannot order her to leave."

The muscles in Vini's squarish cheeks ridged tautly from the fury that always gripped him when something or somebody got in his way.

"Get *Coronel* Luz," he said. "He'll know how to handle her."

In his tiny office in the headquarters van, Jaime Blasco listened with disbelief to the change of orders that came through by radiotelephone.

"*Absurdo! Impossível!*" he half shouted through the airwaves to the highway officials hundreds of miles away. "To change the route in such a direction will require bridging a river wider and more treacherous than any we have bridged so far. It will also follow a geological depression through the *várzea*, where during the rainy season the road surfaces will wash out. They would have to be rebuilt and resurfaced every year."

"Nevertheless, Blasco, those are the orders. Your written orders, as well as maps of the new route, will be forwarded immediately, but meanwhile you are to reset your survey lines to conform precisely to the point of turn and new azimuth I have given you."

Blasco raged in silence. What kind of *bôbos* did they have back in Brasília playing God? What did they know of realities? Had they no common sense?

But of course, common sense had nothing to do with it. The whole matter had to be political. No kind of logic could support anything so utterly asinine.

And what was it to him, after all? He was just a *moreno* who had been honored by being given the responsibility for this section of the highway. And he was getting paid well. Grimly, he stifled his resentment.

If they wanted the road put through hell, he'd do it.

Tomaz thrust a head in the rear van opening. "*Chefe*, an army helicopter has just landed with a *coronel* who wishes to see you."

Everything about *Coronel* Luz was feral: the merciless glint in his obsidian eyes, the coarse hair curling from his broad nostrils and shadowing his shaven cheeks, the *pistola* strapped to his meaty hips. Even in his exquisitely tailored tan uniform, which stretched almost to bursting around his barrel chest, belly, and buttocks, he exuded an aura of the savage jungle. He showed his large animal-white teeth in a smile that seemed more designed to be a snarl.

"*Senhor* Blasco, I am *Coronel* Arsenio Luz, from the Bureau of Internal Security." He made no offer to shake hands.

Blasco felt a prickling go up his spine. Luz was well

known as a hatchet man for the powers that be in high government circles. His methods were ruthless and often without legal justification. To criticize him was dangerous. He was said to have arrested many innocent people on trumped-up charges, leaving them languishing, untried, for months or years in filthy prisons. Some died from torture—deaths recorded under the official euphemism of "suicide"—and some were gunned down during alleged attempts to escape. It was also rumored that Luz was a lecher who debauched female prisoners to gratify his depraved lust.

"What can I do for you, *coronel?*" said Blasco.

"I am here to check your security and make a report on the laxness of discipline that resulted in the recent attack by hostile Indians."

"It was not a matter of discipline, *coronel*, and the Indians weren't hostile."

"Not hostile? When they kill a priest and several of your men?"

"We have established that they were provoked by one of our own men, who murdered the guard of the supply truck where we kept the guns, and—"

"You have this man in custody?"

"No. Unfortunately, he escaped into the jungle before—"

"He escaped? And yet you fabricate a whole story of what happened without having him here to question?"

"But, *coronel*, the facts—"

"What facts? You bungling amateurs, who know nothing of the proper procedures of investigation, always jump to ridiculous conclusions. I shall ascertain the facts for myself and draw my own conclusions. But first there is another small matter I must attend to while I am here." He paused and gave a broad wink. "Where is the woman?"

"There is no woman here, *coronel*," Blasco said stiffly.

Luz arched his eyebrows. "A thousand pardons if I

have been misinformed, but I have been told that there is an American woman reporter, *Senhorita* Peggy Carpenter, who often visits your camp."

"She visits only because it is her job. She is a hardworking reporter writing articles about the highway and the Indians."

"Very interesting. And where is she now?"

"Probably at the FUNAI camp."

"Which is where?"

"Back in the woods a short walk from here."

"Assign a man to guide me there immediately."

The *coronel's* cold appraisal went from Peggy Carpenter to Carlos dos Santos, both of whom had been summoned from their respective tents for interrogation. His probing eyes rested on Peggy, his hard, thin lips bent into the suggestion of a smile.

"You have enjoyed your long visit to the jungle highway, *senhorita?*"

"*Enjoyed* is hardly the right word, *senhor*. I've found it exciting and instructive."

"I presume that by this time you have gathered all the material you need for future articles."

"Oh, far from it. Unusual things are beginning to happen. Indian tribes are on the verge of open warfare with each other; the highway route has been inexplicably diverted through impossible terrain—"

"I regret," Luz cut in harshly, "that you will not have the opportunity to write about such things. I have been instructed to inform you that your permits have been canceled. I have come to take you back to Brasilia."

Peggy's eyes widened in astonishment. "You—a full *coronel*—escorting me back to Brasilia! Why am I suddenly so important?"

"There has been displeasure aroused by the inaccuracy of certain articles written by you and published in the foreign press."

"*Senhor,* I am an accredited journalist. I research meticulously and write objectively only of the truth as I see it."

"The truth as you see it may not be the truth as seen by others."

"Granted, but that's no excuse for suppressing opposing opinions. I was assured that there is no censorship of the foreign press in Brazil."

"It is not censorship when irresponsible journalism is not allowed; we merely insist on proven facts. Back in Brasilia you will be perfectly free to write anything you wish, and our experts will be available to correct any inaccuracies."

Peggy's eyes grew cold. "I'm beginning to get the vibes. So it's all politically motivated after all—pressure from someone who has much to gain from the road's diversion. Someone important—"

Listening, Carlos dos Santos was appalled by her words. Little did she know of the ruthless powers possessed by such unscrupulous men as *Coronel* Luz, who could always find ways to twist good laws to suit their own purposes.

"Peggy—" he interrupted quickly. "Say nothing more. Brazilian politics are nothing you should speak or write about."

Luz let out a grating laugh. "It is good advice you give your blond *namorada.*"

Carlos flushed. "*Coronel!* I resent—"

"I am not a fool, dos Santos. The immorality of American women is well known. Why else would you encourage her to remain with you for so long? In the same tent perhaps, *sim?* But why be ashamed? When such opportunity is at hand, only an *idiota* would not seize it."

Carlos clenched both hands. "*Coronel,* if it weren't for that uniform—!"

"Carlos," Peggy said quietly, "I have his number now. He's deliberately provoking you."

Luz grinned at her. "You are intelligent as well as

beautiful, *senhorita*. You will now pack your things and prepare to leave with me."

By now Carlos had his temper under control. "There is no need for that," he said. "I will drive her into Inchaco myself and see that she is put on a plane to Brasilia."

"The *senhorita* is coming with me!"

"*Coronel,* your authority does not extend to dictating the means of *Senhorita* Carpenter's transportation. She has committed no crime. She's not a prisoner."

The *coronel* laughed softly. "I have sufficient authority to search anyone I may suspect of possessing illegal drugs. It is well known that all young Americans are marijuana-smoking hippies. I have only to order my aide to make a thorough search of the *senhorita*'s person and effects. If so much as a single marijuana seed is found, she immediately becomes my prisoner. Need I remind you that the penalties in Brazil for smuggling drugs are severe and there is no appeal from a drug sentence? The jails, I assure you, are most unpleasant. *Compreende?*"

Raging inwardly, Carlos glanced at the *coronel*'s aide standing a few feet away like a forbidding shadow. He looked back at Luz's mocking grin. Luz could rig up a false charge against Peggy if he chose, but would he dare risk it with an American journalist? It didn't seem likely. What bothered Carlos most was his own helplessness to do anything about it, in any case.

"Don't worry, Carlos," said Peggy, as if reading his thoughts. "I'm quite capable of taking care of myself. I'll start packing right away."

TWENTY-FOUR

The bad news reached Raul by radiophone. The informant was Cosme Almeida Branco da Silva.

"I am very regretful," came the big financier's blunt words, each seeming as weighty as a concrete block, "that the highway change will force us to change our plans for financing your business project."

"Sir, I don't understand."

"Have you not heard that the highway has been rerouted, as I warned you it might be? The decision has been made final by the Chamber of Deputies."

"That's crazy! They're making a terrible mistake!"

"That I don't doubt," da Silva conceded. "Mistakes are made every day in government."

"Mistakes should be corrected! Once I've presented all the facts—"

"*Não.* It would be useless to even try. Once a mistake is made in government it is almost impossible to change, since none of the lawmakers wish to admit they've erred. I wish you well, my young friend, but as it stands now I shall have to cancel any future payments to you, and, ah—we shall work out a repayment schedule for what you have already received. That was our agreement, as you recall. Everything depended on the highway."

Raul was sick about it. Already he and Matt Riordan had expended far in excess of the money received. A great deal of equipment and materials had been flown in. Orders had been placed with engineering corporations in the United States and Germany for specially designed machinery that was so large it would have to be towed on barges up the Amazon and hauled the rest of the way on rollers pulled by bulldozers along jungle trails.

Most of it was not paid for.

Otherwise, the project had been developing rapidly. Riordan and his crew of *caboclo* labor were working with zest and fury. It was the realization of the engineer's dream, an opportunity to see his ideas proven in operation. The first small prototype distillery—based on the system he had originally designed for a big U.S. corporation—was nearing completion.

And all of Raul's early dreams had been fired anew. What a stroke of luck to have found such a top engineer!

But now, all of it was about to end in dismal catastrophe, choked to death for lack of a highway.

Unless something could be done about it.

The first step, Raul decided, would be to find out all he could from the highway engineers, to pinpoint the problems, the obstacles, and the reasons. Then he could go to Brasilia and raise hell.

He sent for Pio to get the Cessna warmed up.

Jaime Blasco spread his hands in a helpless gesture as he talked.

"Why? I cannot tell you why, *Senhor* de Carvalho. I can only tell you that from a road engineer's viewpoint, the change is foolish. Stupid! They say it is because the road disturbs the homelands of the Indians, but why should that concern anyone when another branch of the government is trying so hard to move these Indians to the Xingú National Park? They say the road makes the Indians hostile, so that they attack us and are also stirred to warfare with each other. I cannot believe it is because of the road. All these reasons become even more silly when weighed against what any FUNAI man can tell you—that there are just as many Indians along the new route, and that they too will be disturbed by the highway. They also are slated to be moved to the Indians' national park as soon as possible, so eventually it will make no difference about the Indians. And we will be paying many extra millions to be stuck with an unstable road through bad country for endless years to come!"

Blasco paused to gather breath after his heated outburst, and Raul eyed him with new respect. Plainly the road boss was a sincere, dedicated man who was equally as outraged by the change.

At the same time, Raul was heartened. If the road change was really as illogical as Blasco had painted, perhaps there was hope.

"*Senhor* Blasco, are you familiar with the name Vinicius de Onis?"

"I have seen the name on the highway survey plans. He owns a considerable amount of property."

"The same property through which the highway diversion is now directed. Is that not true?"

"*Sim.*"

"Does that suggest anything to you?"

Blasco's lips clamped into a thin line. Then he spat on the ground. "It is not my job to speculate about such things."

"You're aware, I am sure, that if the whole truth of this matter were ever brought to the attention of enough honest men, it might blow into a scandal that could boomerang against all those important officials who helped contrive the road change. They'd all be frantic to make someone the scapegoat."

Blasco grinned. "I read you fine, *senhor*. But I've worked long enough for the government to know how to keep my ass covered. The first thing I did after getting my new orders was to write up a detailed engineering report on the situation, with my recommendation that a more exhaustive study be made. I had a bunch of copies made, with a list of the key officials to receive copies, and sent one to each, just to keep them out of the wastebasket files. Nobody can ever stick me with any of the responsibility for a bad decision. I'm documented for eternity."

"Would you allow me to read over the report?"

"I'll do better than that. I'll give you an extra copy—unsigned, of course."

It took Blasco only a few minutes to get the report, which he brought back in a brown envelope. As Raul was taking it, a voice accosted him.

"*Senhor* de Carvalho, pardon me if I intrude, but I would like a word with you."

The speaker was a rather good-looking young *moreno* wearing a T-shirt emblazoned with the FUNAI emblem. Raul raised his eyebrows, for he had never seen the man before.

"I talked to your pilot and found out who you are," the *moreno* went on hurriedly, "and I have a great favor to ask of you. It is an urgent matter."

"How does it concern me?"

"I am Carlos dos Santos, the FUNAI leader in this area, and I am appealing to you in the interest of a young American woman, a reporter, who must return to Brasilia. It would be greatly appreciated if you would take her in your plane back to your *fazenda*, and from there—"

"Hold it!" A harsh voice almost spat out the words, which came from a burly uniformed man wearing a *coronel*'s insignia. Slightly staggering along a few feet behind him with great aplomb was a lithe blonde burdened with a typewriter case in one hand, a bulging red tote bag on her back, and a camera case around her neck. She was very pretty.

"You will keep your noses out of official business," the uniformed man said brusquely, glaring at Carlos before focusing on Raul. "Your transportation service won't be required, *senhor*, since the *senhorita* is traveling with me."

Raul was confused, but he smiled amiably. "Whatever you or the *senhorita* may wish is okay with me, *coronel*, but if it is inconvenient for you, I would be more than happy to put my plane at the service of the young lady to fly her to Brasilia, or wherever she'd like."

"The *senhorita*," Peggy spoke up quickly, "most gratefully accepts the gracious offer to fly with the handsome young *senhor*." To anywhere, anywhere at all, her expression seemed to add.

Raul made a brief bow. "My pleasure—"

The *coronel's* jaw took on a bulldog look as he stretched himself to the limit of his five feet eight inches. "*Senhor*, you are interfering with my official duty."

"Official duty?" said Peggy. "Is it your *official* duty to threaten to disrobe American females to search for nonexistent marijuana seeds?"

"*Senhorita!* That is libel, slander, insulting—"

"Insulting it may be—I hope so."

"Peggy, Peggy!" said Carlos, clutching at her sleeve.

"*Não*, Carlos," she said with almost the proper nasal inflection. "You stay out of it. This is my fight. My vibes are giving me a handle on the story that *Senhor* Fancy Brass Buttons here—or his big boss—doesn't want me to write. My snooping has begun to pay off. I know the name of the big shot financier who's behind this whole—"

"*SENHORITA!* You are crazee—*louco!*" cried Carlos.

"The *senhorita* has made her own decision," said Raul, who himself was beginning to *compreender* a great deal. "She will travel with me."

Luz swiveled toward Raul. "Your name, *senhor?* I demand to know."

"Raul de Carvalho."

The *coronel's* belligerent attitude modified slightly. "Ah, that explains, but does not excuse, your arrogance. It is a shameful thing when a member of such a well-known family has so little respect for the law that he dares to obstruct an officer in the discharge of his duty."

"On the contrary, my respect for the law is so high that I dare to uphold it against its abuse. I know of no Brazilian law that permits discourtesies and high-handed measures against foreign visitors who have not knowingly broken any of our laws."

"For your information, *Senhor* de Carvalho, the exercise of my authority is backed by the highest official in the land."

"The *presidente*? When next I converse with him, I shall speak to him on the necessity of tightening up instructions to all those invested with petty authority, so that they don't overstep their bounds." It was bluff talk, since Raul had only met the president once at a social gathering, but he thought, what the hell. Anything to put this Neanderthal in his place. Turning, he signaled to his pilot standing in the background.

"Pio—help the *senhorita* get her luggage into the plane."

Luz glared at Raul with murderous hatred. His chest heaved from repressed wrath. But he made no move to prevent Peggy from moving off with Pio, who was carrying her typewriter.

"*Senhor*," Luz said harshly, "you are fortunate to have influential friends. However, there are some situations in which no friends can help. I warn you, this matter is not ended."

As he swung around to stride away, Peggy called, "*Coronel* Luz!"

He turned, his face still ugly with rage. Peggy's Nikon clicked three times.

"Oh, thank you so much, *coronel*," she called gaily. "I just wanted a picture for my scrapbook."

During the plane ride they talked about the highway diversion.

"So you see," Peggy was saying, after giving Raul a rundown on the notes she'd been taking for her highway articles, "I have every reason to believe that bribery is involved, but absolutely no facts to back up my theory, so naturally I wouldn't dare hint at such a thing for publication."

"For a man as important as de Onis," Raul said glumly, "nothing less than complete factual proof could touch him, and that's probably an impossibility."

Peggy gave a cheery laugh. "Have faith. A good reporter never gives up. Maybe I can dig something up when I get back to Brasília—which reminds me, may I use your radiophone when we get to your place to arrange for a charter plane to pick me up?"

"You may not! Not for that purpose. My plane can carry you anywhere you wish. But if there is no need to hurry, why don't you relax as a guest at my *fazenda* for as long as you like?"

"Do you really mean that, *senhor*?"

"Please—I prefer to be informal. It is Raul."

"Raul, you're a dear! And your hospitality overwhelms me. I was just thinking how much I would love to stay a day or two at your jungle *fazenda*, but I hadn't worked up the gall to ask. And of course you must call me Peggy."

Minutes later, as the plane was swooping over the rolling sea of green treetops toward the small landing field near the manor, Raul's eyes widened in surprise.

A sleek silver and green Beechcraft Baron was parked at one end of the field. Who, he wondered, would drop in from the skies for a visit without having given advance notice?

Walking the short distance to the house, Peggy was intrigued. "What a lovely place! It must be a hundred years old. Was it once a rubber plantation?"

"It was until most of the rubber trees were killed off by the leaf blight."

"Can't you plant new trees?"

"Rubber seedlings take ten years before they begin producing, and in today's market it wouldn't be profitable enough. We'd have to use the old methods of hauling the big *bolãos* of latex over many miles of rough jungle trails to the riverboats for shipping. The fact is, no plantation business this far out in the jungle can prosper without good roads."

"I see why you're so concerned about the highway."

Just ahead, a redheaded man emerged from the

workshop building. Seeing Raul, he grinned and started toward him, saying, "Got a surprise for you, Raul—" His glance shifted with interest toward Peggy.

"Let it wait, Matt. I've brought along a fellow American I'd like you to meet—Peggy Carpenter. Peggy, this is Matt Riordan."

Peggy thrust out a hand, and Riordan shook it in a businesslike way while they exchanged amenities.

"By the way, Matt, who's our other visitor?" said Raul.

Matt shrugged. "Beats me. I've been buried away in the workshop."

"Well, let's go in and find out. Come along, Matt—"

Peggy hung back. "If it's a business matter, perhaps I'd be in the way. I can wait outside."

"Nonsense! You're my guest." And taking her hand, he drew her along beside him as he pushed through the ornately carved door into the tiled entryway. He stopped in surprise.

A familiar figure stood at the end of the hallway, arms folded, an accusing frown on her face.

Odete.

"I see now," she said coldly and sweetly, "why you've been too busy to call me."

With an unconscious sense of guilt, Raul quickly released Peggy's hand, "What a nice surprise, Odete! But you should have called me first so I could have been here to greet you."

Striding forward, he caught her in a strong embrace and sought to kiss her on the lips, but she turned a chaste cheek instead. Riordan watched with amused eyes; Peggy maintained her usual aplomb.

As Raul made the introductions, Odete responded with a stiff snobbishness, and Riordan and Peggy were gravely courteous. Raul managed to catch Riordan's eye with a meaningful look, and Matt took the hint by sliding an arm around Peggy in an intimate manner. "Come, my dear," he said, guiding her back to the door, "I'm sure that Raul and Odete would appreciate a little privacy."

Peggy went him one better. "Sure, sweetheart—I remember how it used to be with us." She went out cuddling against his strong torso.

Alone with Odete, Raul gave her an aggrieved smile. "You see? There was no reason to greet me so coldly. You have no cause for jealousy."

He bent to kiss her again, and this time she allowed it on the lips, but her response was only lukewarm.

"You're still tense," he chided. "Did you fly way out here just to punish me for reasons I know nothing about? What's wrong?"

"I've been terribly unhappy. You've left me alone for so long!"

"My love, you know how hard I've been working, but anytime you really needed me you could have called and I would have come at once."

"You didn't come for the opening of Carnival when I needed you so badly!"

"You know there was no way I could have been there. And what difference did another day or two make?"

"It was so upsetting. I felt so abandoned, *degraded*—"

"But, darling, we've been through all of this. It's water under the bridge."

She appeared not to hear him. "All the beautiful moments with you I had looked forward to—and then, you, the one I had thought I could always count on as a solid rock to lean on, to protect me—"

"Protect you?" He caught her roughly by the shoulders, unaware that he was hurting her until he saw her flinch. "You had my brother Eduardo to escort you in my absence!" By Raul's code, any brother would protect the purity and safety of another brother's fiancée to the last drop of blood.

An ugly suspicion edged into his thoughts. "Is there anything you're not telling me? Did Eduardo—"

"Oh, no, no, no! Don't get crazy ideas!"

"Then you owe it to me to do a better job of explaining yourself. You're not being rational. Carnival is over and behind us. Something has changed you."

She turned her head aside as tears flooded her exquisite green eyes. "It is *impossivel* to explain. It is as if I was seized by a strange fever—but it is all over now. I am very sorry. I apologize for treating you so badly when you came to Rio."

He gave her a rueful grin. "You can hardly blame me for wondering if you still gave a damn about me."

"But now you know better. If I did not still love you, why would I charter a plane and pilot and come so far to visit you?"

"Without a chaperone, too! It's hard to believe. How long can you stay?"

"I can't risk mother or father ever finding out—they would be horrified—so I dare stay only overnight." She smiled up at him through tearful eyes, adding, "Perhaps that will be long enough to prove to you how much I love you."

He was at first slightly shocked by her words, until he remembered how innocent she was. She had no idea that the same words coming from a more sophisticated girl could be interpreted as a sexual promise.

"Wonderful! We'll make it a memorable evening of getting to know each other all over again."

She snuggled closer, her head bowed against his chest.

He tilted her face up. "And now for a real kiss . . ."

The kiss was hard and lingering, and slowly she began to respond with an ardor that matched his. He could feel the tightening of her arms around him, the increased pressure of her breasts. When after endless moments he drew back, he saw that her face was flushed, her eyes emerald-bright. He was hot with arousal.

"Tell me," she murmured huskily, "that you love only me. Tell me honestly—have you been truly faithful to me since our engagement?"

He was consumed with guilt. Thoughts of Vivi had haunted him night and day since that beautiful after-noon picnic that had ended in the nightmare of her father's whip slashing across her soft body.

He forced a laugh. "Is it not enough to tell you that I love you? Must I swear on a Bible and account for every minute of the days when we are apart? This is no time for foolish talk. I'll have my housekeeper Emilia prepare a bedroom for you right away, and one of the men can bring in your luggage. Then we can look forward to an enchanted evening."

Odete sniffed in disdain at the ancient four-poster and its ornately carved headboard. She watched Emilia, a plump *morena*, making up the bed with fresh sheets. The bedroom was large and pleasant enough, but the furnishings were horrendous. A faded satin love seat, two heavy chairs that might have been hewn with an axe, an age-darkened French armoire, a small marble table, a rococo gilt-framed mirror, split bamboo curtains. Still, the floor visible beyond the edges of the woven mat rug was of polished black jacaranda, the ceiling was beamed, and the walls were paneled in striped aroeira. A good decorator could transform it into something chic and lovely.

The whole manor, with its spacious rooms and its air of solidity mellowed by time, had undeniable charm. With money—a great deal of money—it could be turned into a sensational showplace, bringing gasps of admiration and envy from her Rio friends when they were flown in for spectacular parties.

But it would serve only for part-time living, of course. To keep her sanity, she would need a town house in Rio where she could spend at least half of her time. She would insist on it.

Finished with the bed, Emilia turned her kind brown face toward Odete. *"O que posso fazer para a senhorita?"*

"Nothing more now, Emilia. You may go. I'll call you if I need you."

The housekeeper bobbed her head in a semblance of a curtsy and bustled out. Odete went over to the bed and plumped both hands down with all her weight to test it. Ah—nice and soft. As it should be, having two mattresses, both doubtlessly stuffed with the finest down from wild swans.

Odete liked to be as sensuously comfortable as possible when enjoying the love act.

For that was her whole purpose in secretly chartering a plane and pilot to visit Raul. It was a purpose made necessary by the soul-shaking events that had derailed her staid and proper existence into an almost surreal but titillating fantasy world during—and since —Carnival.

Swept into a delirium of unsuspected and unreleased passions, fueled by youth, cocaine, and the heady excitements of Carnival, she had for the first time tasted, then gobbled at the sexual provender she saw others reveling in all around her.

Which all too quickly began to fade. Eduardo, who had taken her virginity, who had introduced her to corrupt parties and cocaine, who had kindled in her unholy desires she had never dreamed possible, could no longer satisfy her. Each time they were together, his performance had grown weaker, until soon he could do nothing. It was all psychological, he had explained, an outgrowth of deep guilts. He had apologized, begging her forgiveness, and begged her never to breathe a word of it to anyone.

She, too, had been overwhelmed with a backlash of shame, a sense of being dirtied.

And pervading it all was fear. Not only a fear of discovery but the more primal fear of pregnancy. On the night of her seduction by Eduardo, she had been unprotected by any kind of contraceptive. The very next day she started taking pills, which she obtained from a girl friend, but the fear lingered that it might be too late. The possibility of already being pregnant, remote as it might be, was terrifying to contemplate.

It was still much too soon to know, of course, but

by the time she would know—if the worst of her fears was confirmed—it would be too late. She would need an abortion. A most sordid operation, explicitly forbidden by the church. Something hard to keep secret.

It could mean the ruination of her whole future if it ever got out. *Não*—never, never abortion!

She had toyed with the idea of marrying Eduardo instead of Raul, but the circumstances of his sexual impotence, his great fear of Raul, and plain common sense made that impossible.

Raul was her only hope.

Raul was a strong and trusting man—but, like all men, he would be weak when tempted by an attractive female. She had not the slightest doubt that on this very evening, after music and champagne, when she became meltingly submissive in his arms ...

On sudden impulse Odete reached down and pulled back the bedcover, for she was very fastidious. Ah! The sheets were pristine white, sparkling clean.

The red stain of virginity would be most conspicuous.

For Odete had been told by her closest girl friend of a clever trick often used by brides who did not wish their husbands to discover they were not virgins. On her friend's advice she had gone to a macumba priestess, who for a high price had supplied her with a capsule that was to be inserted into her vagina early in the evening. The capsule would break at the first pressure, spilling a bloodlike stain on the sheets.

After that, Raul would be irrevocably committed to marrying her, and as soon as possible.

A soft knocking at the door startled her.

"Who is it?"

"Who are you expecting?" came Raul's chiding reply. "I thought that if you're at all interested, I'd like to show you the birth of the energy business we're working on—"

"I'd be thrilled, darling! I'll be right out."

Outside, as they started walking down the hallway together, Emilia approached hurriedly.

"*Ó patrão*—there is a visitor at the door to see you."

Raul grinned ruefully at Odete. "This seems to be a record day for visitors. Please excuse me while I see who it is."

Odete dawdled along the hallway, admiring the rare jungle wood paneling, the impressive sweep of living room ahead, all the decorator possibilities to be exploited. She heard the front door swing open and Raul's expression of surprise.

"Oh, my darling, my dearest!" came a female voice. "I've been just dying, wanting to see you again, but this is the first chance—"

The voice broke off as Odete, who had rushed from the hallway to the entryway, let out a shriek.

"Who is this woman?" she screamed at Raul.

Caught in the act of embracing the stranger—an exotic-looking creature, Odete had to admit, with streaming black hair and a most attractive face, but dressed tastelessly in faded jeans and a man's shirt—Raul was flushed with embarrassment.

"Uh—Odete, this is one of my neighbors, uh—a friend, Viviane Vargas. Vivi—this is my fiancée—"

Vivi looked stricken. "I—I'm sorry. I'm *so* sorry," she said helplessly. "Please forgive me." And turning, she fled.

Raul made a move to follow, then turned back toward Odete, his expression pleading. "Odete, please let me explain—"

But Odete was racing back to her room, in such storming fury that she had to open several doors before she found the right one. So he had betrayed her! So he had other lovers, perhaps dozens of them, out here in the jungle! Oh, she could kill him! And the girl, too! So that's the kind he was—a liar, a deceiving, two-timing rotten—

Unable to think of a strong enough term, with her *latino* temper flooding hot blood into her head, she rushed at the nearest object to vent some of her spite. Only to bang the big toe exposed in her open sandal against the hard bottom edge of the bed, bringing a yelp of pain and adding to her rage. She leaned toward the clean white sheets she had turned back and spat on them. She began shrieking, "EMILIA! Come here at ONCE! Get my PILOT! Get my luggage out to the AIRPLANE! Quick! QUICK! *Rápido!*"

In his office at Casa de Ouro Branco, Raul stared glumly across his desk at Riordan, who sat with Peggy on the leather sofa against one wall. Braz, who had helped carry Odete's luggage to her plane, lounged in the doorway.

"You're a man of the world, Matt—what did I do wrong?" said Raul. "Two lovely girls, and I certainly didn't want to hurt either one of them."

Matt guffawed. Peggy giggled.

"You did nothing wrong, man," said Matt. "You just overextended yourself. Two beauties like that, I don't blame you. But your timing is off."

"And I suppose," said Peggy, "that you love both of them with all your heart?"

"That's the problem—I do!"

"Matt," said Peggy, "how do we explain to this astonishingly naïve gentleman that in this broadminded age it's perfectly all right to have dozens and dozens of lovers—one after another like a row of falling dominoes—but never, *never* two at the same time. It just isn't done."

Matt nodded solemnly. "He's got to make a choice. That's for sure."

"I doubt that either of them will ever forgive me."

Peggy adopted a serious expression. "Being a conniving but always helpful female, with more wiles than I'll ever admit, I think I could help smooth things over for you—if I knew which one you wanted more."

Raul knew his choice, his only choice, but he wanted solid confirmation. He looked at the leathery-faced *vaqueiro* in the doorway. "Braz, how would you advise me?"

Braz removed a brown twist of cigarette from his

mouth. "There is an old *vaqueiro* saying that it is not by the spots on a cow that you measure the milk."

Tittering, Peggy grabbed her notebook and jotted that down.

Raul grinned. His choice was confirmed. "One more thing, Matt—what was that surprise you had for me?" he said.

Riordan reached down into a brown paper bag at his feet and drew out a gallon jug with an air of triumph. "Here it is—the proof that my system works. Two hundred proof, in fact—the first gallon of pure methanol alcohol produced from ordinary jungle wood feedstock in our little experimental plant!"

"This calls for a toast!"

"Oh," said Peggy, "can we drink it?"

Matt made a sour face. "Not this stuff. It's deadly poison."

Raul laughed. "We'll just have to settle for champagne."

But perhaps it would be more appropriate to drink a final toast of methanol, he thought glumly. Unless I can perform the miracle of overcoming the powerful Goliath, de Onis.

TWENTY-FIVE

The steady droning of the jet engines lessened. The smallish but graceful Citation I began swooping lower over the green sea of jungle.

"We're there, *senhor*," came the pilot's voice. "In a few moments we'll be landing. Better tighten your seat belt."

"Is there enough room down there? Going to be any landing problem?"

"*Não*. From here the field looks big enough, but it may be a little rough."

Vinicius de Onis casually adjusted his seat belt. Such details annoyed him. He hadn't risen from relative obscurity to his present importance by timidity, or by being overly cautious. He was by nature a gambler, a plunger who took great risks for great stakes.

On the other hand, when the stakes were high, he left no stone unturned in the pursuit of the big win. His mission today—a personal call on Raul de Carvalho—was to overcome one of those minor obstacles in a manner that he felt only he could handle properly.

As the plane skimmed lower, he sucked angrily at the cigar clamped between his lips. One foot tapped against the carpeted floor. He was impatient. Success had bloated his ego to the extent that it was an irritation even to travel in the Citation, one of the smaller jets in his fleet. His preference was the prestige and comfort of his seven-million-dollar JetStar—an exact replica of the customized four-jet made for the shah of Iran, including push-button porn movies, a built-in bar, a luxurious bedroom with a bed large enough to hold the several female bedmates Vinicius usually took along for amusement. Like many great entrepreneurs, he had a limitless sexual appetite that often outreached his capabilities.

He had been forced to forgo the JetStar today because the pilot said it would be impossible to land without a large, well-graded field, but such a small irritation was nothing compared with Vinicius's anger at *Coronel* Luz for having fumbled. Luz had been ordered to find ways to keep the American reporter from writing articles about the highway. Instead, the blundering *coronel* had allowed the woman to accompany Raul de Carvalho to his *fazenda. Estúpido!* Vinicius had read one of her articles in the foreign press. Her way of writing gave Brazil a bad name; and she snooped too much, asked too many questions.

Moreover, there was some uneasiness in Brasilia. Some of the officials who had helped him were fearful of a thorough investigation that might blow up in their faces. The muckraking female reporter and Raul de Carvalho—who would lose everything by the rerouting of the highway—might together dig up too much and broadcast it to the world. De Carvalho was a respected name that could win the support of other important families. It was a dangerous situation, which is why de Onis had decided to get personally involved.

He had two solutions worked out. The first and easiest would be the amicable approach. And if that failed . . .

Vinicius's teeth showed in a thin feral grin. His other method never failed.

Raul received de Onis with due courtesy in his private study. Peggy, who at Raul's invitation had been taking notes on the energy project, was intrigued by the unusual visit and had asked if either man would object to her sitting in on their meeting.

The financier gave her his most charming smile. "I understand that you are an accomplished reporter. For such a beautiful young *senhorita,* to be so industrious is unusual, but regretfully I must inform you that it is my strict policy never to discuss confidential business matters in the presence of reporters."

"Then it is business that has brought you here?" Raul prompted when they were seated.

"Always business. Is there anything else?" Vinicius winked knowingly. "Except beautiful women, of course."

Raul waited in silence while de Onis paused to bite the end of one of his long cigars and then light it.

De Onis expelled a lazy plume of blue smoke. "For your sake," he said, "I am sorry that the highway has been diverted away from your land—although, of course, it is fortunate for me. Still, that's the way of life. Win some, lose some. However, to lessen your loss and ease your disappointment, I am prepared to make you a generous offer for your property."

"Why would you wish to do that, *senhor?*" said Raul.

"It distresses me to see one of my neighbors in difficulties when I am in a position to help."

"Why are you so sure I am in difficulties?"

De Onis arched his eyebrows. "Without the highway your land is virtually worthless, and I happen to know that you are deeply in debt. Still, by improving the airfield, I may be able to find a use for it that would justify paying you a good price."

"My property is not for sale, *senhor.*"

De Onis considered the end of his cigar, his brow wrinkled. "Do you prefer losing it to your creditors?"

"I won't lose it."

De Onis smiled. "You are a miracle worker perhaps? My sources inform me that your father is displeased with your energy venture and would not bail you out with another cent. Da Silva has already turned you down. It would only be throwing good money after bad. By what miracle do you think you can save your property from foreclosure?"

"No miracle, *senhor.* I'm convinced that the majority of our lawmakers—and even most of our bureaucrats—are basically honest, and that they will move to correct an expensive mistake—when under enough pressure from public outrage."

"What mistake are you referring to?"

"The highway diversion, of course."

"*Ridículo!* The best engineers and the highest officials in the land have examined the question and approved it."

"And I have reason to believe that a considerable amount of money has changed hands in order to influence their opinion."

De Onis laughed. "Then you are accusing some of our most reputable officials of criminality?"

"Some of them, yes. But the biggest criminal of all is the one behind it all, the one who supplied the money."

"I think you suffer from paranoia, my friend. So full of suspicions! To accuse some of our finest citizens of bribery is a serious thing. If you were to mention names, you could be prosecuted for slander. And who do you think this big criminal is?"

Raul looked into the other man's eyes until de Onis looked away. The financier squirmed, unconsciously running a pudgy hand through his slicked-back black hair with its startling albino streak down the center.

"Let's dispense with the bullshit, de Onis. Your devious operations are obvious enough to anyone who bothers to look under the rug. You're worried that someone might kick up a big enough fuss to bring everything out into the open—which could force a reversal of the decision to reroute the highway."

"Nonsense! If your crazy aspersions were true, why would I offer to buy your land?"

"That in itself suggests that you know I am the only one with enough at stake to fight back. Your purchase of my land would remove me as your only obstacle, since I would no longer have any reason to protest the highway diversion. My very agreement to sell would be tantamount to clearing you of any complicity in the bribery behind—"

"Bribery!" Face reddening, de Onis rose to his feet with all the dignity his squat figure could muster. "I will take no more of your insults, de Carvalho! You will regret your rash accusations. Very soon, I assure you, you will wish you had accepted my fair offer. I am a man who cannot accept defeat."

"Nor can I," said Raul.

Spinning around, de Onis stalked out.

Beneath Peggy's cultivated veneer of sophisticated self-sufficiency was a soft but indestructible element of romanticism. Raul's dilemma with two lovers intrigued her, and she wanted to help. He was such a dear, so sweet, so generous, so vulnerable to scheming females. With the unerring instincts in all women concerning other women, she had at once seen Odete as little more than an expensive, ornamental pet. At best, Odete's capability for loving would be like the classic affection of a cat: Seeming to caress the leg of its master, all the cat is doing is voluptuously stroking its own fur. Such love would not be enough for Raul.

Vivi Vargas, on the other hand, seemed to be a sensitive, perhaps naïve girl who was genuinely in love. And from a few remarks that Peggy had extracted from Raul, she believed that his feelings for Vivi were just as solid.

Thus it was that Peggy decided to visit Vivi as an intermediary in Raul's behalf. He gave his permission reluctantly, with the proviso that she would be escorted by tough old Braz, since the trip would have to be made on horseback.

Dom João, not immune to female attractiveness, was aloof but courteous enough when she introduced herself as an American writer who was fascinated by old Brazilian plantation houses and would be ever so grateful for the opportunity to see the interior.

"I'll call my daughter," he said with an indifferent shrug, "and have her show you around."

Vivi, who through Peggy's romantic eyes looked as

exquisitely beautiful as any fairy-tale princess locked away from her lover by a stonyhearted father, brightened a bit after learning of Peggy's occupation.

"So you write for newspapers and magazines—how marvelous! How I would love to do something like that. I feel so useless."

Dom João, Peggy noted, was frowning in the background, and she decided not to broach the subject of Raul until a more opportune moment.

The manse enthralled her. The carved rare wood paneling and the domed ceilings of *faux-bois* parquetry told a tale of decaying opulence. The contrast of the old and the new was evident everywhere. Oil lamps that once burned fish oil were now wired for electricity. Dark tapestries from a bygone century hung side by side with a few colorful paintings by such moderns as di Cavalcanti or Consessa Colaço. The furnishings, though somewhat fallen into disrepair, were elegant period pieces.

"How fantastic to have grown up amid such magnificence!" cried Peggy. "And with the beautiful jungle right outside your door."

Vivi smiled her melancholy smile. "But so lonely. Rarely do I have anyone to talk to. Out here I have no friends."

"I am your friend, Vivi. I'm only sorry that I can't stay long enough so we can really get to know each other."

"Perhaps you would stay here as our guest for a few days?"

"I would be delighted, but I am already a guest of Raul's."

"I know."

"There's a story concerning Raul that I would like to tell you, if I had the time and opportunity. If your invitation still stands, and if your father permits it, perhaps I could stay over for at least tonight—"

"Oh, I assure you that father would be most agreeable to having you stay! I could tell he was much impressed by you."

Peggy smiled. One hurdle overcome. "But of course I would have to let Raul know I was staying. And then there's his man Braz, who accompanied me."

"Braz can bunk with our foreman, and you can reach Raul by our radiophone."

"Wonderful! Then I'll stay."

TWENTY-SIX

Hearing the chopping roar of a helicopter circling above the *fazenda* roof, Raul hurried outside, filled with unease.

With a thunderous whirring, the clumsy aircraft set itself down into a miniature storm of swirling leaves and red dust, scarcely a hundred paces from the manor. Four men got out. Three of them were in the uniforms of the provincial *milícia*—open-necked shirts and dark green trousers, German army fatigue caps, black boots, and revolvers at their belts. The fourth, wearing the nattier uniform of an officer and a black-visored cap, was *Coronel* Luz. With the *coronel* leading, they strode purposefully toward Raul.

"So we meet again, *senhor*," said Luz with a nasty grin.

"For what purpose, *coronel?*"

"There are two matters. One is that I have come with special instructions to interrogate the American woman, Peggy Carpenter."

Raul felt a touch of relief, for Peggy was still visiting at the Vargas *fazenda* and had called earlier to say she would be staying for yet another day.

"She is not here."

"Where is she?"

"I am under no obligation to report on her whereabouts."

Luz glared at him for a few moments, then shrugged. "*Não importa.* I have effective ways of finding out. The other matter concerns a man named Hélio Rodrigues, who works for you."

"What about him?"

"The man is a fugitive. He was employed by the de Onis plantation and ran off owing a large debt to his

274

employer. We traced him carefully to Inchaco, and then here. By law he is subject to arrest. He must be returned to his previous employer to work off his debt."

"That is no problem. I will gladly pay off the debt myself. How much does he owe?"

"The previous employer does not wish the debt paid back in cash, only that the worker be returned to him for discipline and to work off his obligation in accordance with the signed agreement. Nothing else will satisfy the employer."

"That's not legal! Slavery was abolished here almost a century ago."

Luz laughed. "Obviously you know nothing of the laws of usury, which differ in each province. In this province a debtor can be imprisoned for his debt or forced to work it off—the choice belongs to the employer. I demand now that you bring this man Hélio to me to be placed under arrest."

"And if I refuse?"

"I hold you responsible. If my men are forced to make a search for the fugitive and do not find him, I shall place you under arrest."

Raul's anger flared. "You can't threaten an innocent man, *coronel!* You know damned well you are going beyond the law!"

"We are a thousand miles from Brasilia, *senhor*. In this province, *I* am the only law. I order you to bring the fugitive to me at once."

Raul brought his anger under control. The *coronel's* arrogance indicated that he felt free to break laws with impunity because he was under the protection of someone very powerful—de Onis, of course. It was all highly illegal, and perhaps it was some kind of trap, but for the moment there was nothing he could do about it except comply with Luz's demands.

He beckoned to one of the *caboclos* who were standing back listening, their faces reflecting fear.

"Find Hélio and tell him to come here."

* * * * *

Hélio first cast frightened eyes at the hard-faced *milícia*, then turned an imploring expression toward Raul. It struck Raul to the heart. This was the man who had saved his life from the wild bees. He was an honest man, a brave man, a loyal, hard worker. Was this his reward?

"I'm sorry, Hélio, but you will have to go with the officers because of your debt to your previous employer. I offered to pay it, but they won't accept my money. However, don't lose heart. I will retain a good attorney and pay whatever costs necessary to set you free as soon as possible."

Hélio hung his head. "I understand, *chefe*. Laws against the *flagelados* are strict and cannot be broken without terrible punishment. It would be a waste of your money to try to help me, but please not to worry. I am accustomed to being whipped."

"Whipped? Have no fear of that, Hélio. They won't dare harm you in any way. They know I'll soon have a lawyer to set you free."

Coronel Luz gusted out a hoarse laugh, and even the three soldiers allowed tight, evil grins to touch their lips.

"The fugitive knows more about the law than you do, *Senhor* de Carvalho. But soon enough you'll learn." Luz signaled to two of the soldiers. "Pedro, Sylvio—tie the prisoner to a tree."

With practiced speed the two men hustled Hélio to a nearby tree, turning his face toward the bark; they ripped his shirt until his muscular back was bared, then quickly bound him to the trunk. The third man had already uncoiled the whip that was attached to his belt.

"Whip him until the blood flows!" bellowed Luz. "Let this be a lesson to all those who have no respect for the law!"

As the whip began swirling toward its target, Raul leaped forward and caught the soldier's arm.

"Leave him be!" he shouted. "This is inhuman!"

In a surge of fury he wrested the whip from the man's grip, but in the next moment the other two soldiers had caught him from behind and were twisting his arms back until the fiery pain made his vision blur.

"Get him handcuffed!" bawled Luz. "He's under arrest for interfering with the performance of our duty. And get on with the whipping."

Helplessly, his hands cuffed behind him, Raul lay on the ground hearing Hélio scream as the whip came hissing, snapping through the air, ripping raw flesh. Again and again.

The provincial jail, though quite new, was a dismal structure with low fortresslike walls of gray concrete and narrow barred windows. Surrounding it was a high steel fence set in red clay ground that was burned dry and hard under a blistering sun, utterly devoid of a single blade of grass or any other green life.

Inside, despite the sunless murk, the air was even more sweltering, permeated with a stench that came from the open toilets in the row of cells along one wall.

"Bring de Carvalho to my office," said Luz. "Take the other one to the interrogation chamber."

Rough hands pushed Raul down a dim corridor past the cells, most of which were occupied. Miserable, beaten faces peered out; brown, beige, black, and a few white faces tinged a sickish yellow. A sprinkling of women were mixed in with the men. One was a sullen-faced Indian girl, completely naked, crouched like a cornered animal in a cell containing about a half dozen men. Raul wondered how many times she had been raped. A guard, holding a water hose that was thrust through the bars, was flushing down the cement floor of another cell, doing little to wash away the dried excrement encrusting the edges of a narrow oblong opening in the floor that served as the toilet at one end of the cell. Some of the spurting water carelessly, perhaps purposely, flooded over the scrawny figure of a silver-haired man whose naked torso was scarred and bloody from a whipping. He appeared oblivious, whimpering like a puppy drowning in a well.

The *coronel*'s office was a bleak room boasting a green metal desk, a radiotelephone, file cases, and several chairs. Luz plumped himself down in a foam-cushioned swivel chair behind the desk and indicated a folding metal chair opposite. "You may sit, de Carvalho."

"I'd like to use your radiophone to contact my attorney."

"*Não*. For such a serious crime you are not entitled to that privilege. Maybe later."

"Serious crime? I've done nothing but try to protect one of my men from your brutality!"

Luz shrugged. "*É nada*, that is nothing. It was only for the purpose of placing you under arrest. I did not wish to advertise the real reason in front of your men, for they might have taken steps to destroy the evidence."

Raul was bewildered. "What kind of evidence are you talking about?"

"You pretend innocence? It is the same with all criminals. But here, I will show you." Reaching down behind the desk, the *coronel* produced a potted plant about a foot high and placed it on the desk. It had slender rusty brown branches covered with elliptical leaves of a somewhat leathery texture and tiny clusters of yellow flowers. The *coronel* grinned knowingly.

"You recognize, *sim?*"

"I'm not a botanist."

Luz leaned across the desk, his face harsh. "It is a young coca shrub of the genus *Erythroxylon*, the Peruvian type that is most famous for yielding *cocaína* from its leaves."

"How does that concern me?"

"It was found growing on your land. Under cultivation."

Raul's fists clenched. Another trap! "Why play these games, *coronel*? Everyone knows that the wild coca shrub grows in many parts of the jungle. I've heard that it is cultivated by most of the Indian tribes. If it grows on my land, I know nothing about it, and any trumped-up charge you try to bring against me won't hold water."

"You think that is all we have? *Senhor*, we know all about your plans for building a jungle laboratory for the production of cocaine—using the alcohol business as a cover-up."

"Ridiculous!"

"Not so ridiculous. If I were in your shoes and had a criminal mind, I would do the same. What better way to get rich? Making alcohol is breaking your back for a living, but cocaine—ah! The big American market is begging for all they can buy at $15,000 and up a kilo. Ounce for ounce, that is four times more precious than gold. In most parts of the world it cannot be raised, but in the Amazon forest we have just the right soil, the right humidity, as on your land. And you have seclusion from the world, as well as the perfect cover-up of the alcohol business. For cocaine, you do not even need the highway, no big trucks, only a little plane to deliver the stuff to your brother Eduardo in Rio—"

"Eduardo? You're insane to try to drag my brother into this rotten little game you're playing."

"A game you call it? *Sim*—a most dangerous game! Your brother Eduardo is well known to our Rio police contacts as a heavy user of cocaine. He is also heavily in debt to certain *malandros* of the Rio underworld—who are ready to testify that he has approached them to help deliver the coke you manufacture for world-wide distribution."

Eduardo a drug addict? What nonsense! The whole mess was growing so ridiculous that Raul wanted to laugh, except that he knew it was deadly serious.

"I think, *coronel*, that you'd better watch your step. Sooner or later I will be able to get the truth to the highest officials, and then you will have to pay for your slander, your false accusations, all your atrocities."

Luz let out a single burst of laughter. "You are naïve. I can prove every word I say. Still, I am a fair man with no desire to destroy your future, and your brother's as well. For a reasonable consideration— only one million *cruzeiros*—I could be persuaded to drop all charges against you and forget the whole matter."

"You're asking *me* to bribe *you* with one million *cruzeiros* to keep you from smearing my brother's name and release me from false arrest?"

"You can afford it, *senhor*. Your family is rich. Of course I would first need your signed confession of the crimes, which I would keep locked up for my own protection."

"You're insane to think I would pay you, let alone sign a false confession."

"You must believe me, *senhor*, my offer is only to save you from much suffering. I give you one more chance. Your confession I must have, and will have. To give it freely is the only way to save yourself."

"Never!"

The *coronel*'s heavy face hardened. "Then you must suffer the consequences."

In the "interrogation" chamber, a naked man hung upside down. His knees had been hooked over a pole about six feet above the floor, his wrists and ankles lashed together. He was a skinny, gray-haired man, his ribs showing prominently in his frail chest. Blood dribbled from his slack mouth, and there was a crisscrossing of long red welts on various parts of his body. Despite his open, abnormally protruding eyes, he appeared to be unconscious.

Luz laughed softly. "This is his second day here. Soon he will talk."

Raul stared in horror. "*Deus do céu!* What has he done?"

"His son belongs to a band of National Liberation Movement guerrillas—radical scum who wish to overthrow our government and change the laws. We require him to reveal his son's hiding place, but he lies, he says he doesn't know. He is *estúpido*. We have put him on what we call the parrot's perch, to break his will. When he is conscious again, there will be something worse. I assure you that no matter how strong the will, it is only a matter of time before there is no will left."

Turning to one of the guards, he barked out an order. "Cut the trash loose and throw him back in his cell. Bring in the fugitive."

When the bonds were cut, the scrawny oldster clumped heavily to the concrete floor, and one of the guards dragged him out. Soon after, Hélio was brought in by two guards.

"Strip him and put him on the perch!" ordered Luz.

Quickly the experienced guards pulled off their prisoner's clothes and boots. They were grinning. One ran his hands over Hélio's buttocks. "Ah—*fino!*" he said. The other guard let his fingers nip playfully at Hélio's penis.

Beads of saliva played on Hélio's mouth.

Rage quivered through Raul. "*Coronel*, I demand that you put a stop to this outrage at once!" He started toward a guard, his fist drawn back.

The *coronel* moved with the speed of a cat. A heavy fist landed on Raul's chest. The blow was followed by other blows and kicks from Luz and a guard who had joined in the attack. Raul staggered and fell under the continued pounding and kicking, his head spinning crazily. He was sodden with nausea. He turned his head to retch, and through a roaring sound in his ears he heard Hélio call out, "*Ó patrão*—do not try to help me. It will only bring more punishment on you. I beg of you, say nothing, do nothing."

When his vision had cleared a little, Raul saw that

Hélio was suspended upside down from the pole. Luz stood near him.

"Answer me, dog!" said the *coronel.* "Were you not ordered by your master to plant the coca in a field you had plowed?"

"That is not true! You may whip me until I am dead, but I will not tell lies about my *patrão.*"

Luz nodded to one of the guards. "The electrode."

The guard uncoiled a black electric cord hanging from a wall and brought it over. On its end was a short rod tipped with a metal lozenge.

"We'll show how brave he is," said Luz. "Give it to him in the *bolas.*"

Chuckling, the guard brought the electrode against the exposed testicles. A rending scream burst from Hélio as his muscular body writhed and jerked.

Raul forced himself to a sitting position. "Rotten fiends!" he shouted. "This is inhuman, bestial!"

Luz walked over and looked down at him. The shining black eyes had a demonic quality. "Are you ready to confess?"

"I've already given my answer."

The *coronel's* boot shot out, thudded against Raul's jaw, knocking him backward.

"Off with his shoes," ordered Luz.

One guard threw himself over Raul's chest to pin him down. His breath reeked of onions and garlic mingled with some kind of male perfume. Raul made no attempt to resist as the other guard yanked off his shoes and socks.

"Now the hose."

Moments later a powerful jet of water hit him like a cushioned sledgehammer, slamming his head back, rolling him over the concrete. He began choking, gasping. Then it stopped. He lay in wetness, water streaming from his sopping garments, wondering what was next.

The *coronel* loomed above him. There was a sinister twist to his smile. "The water cooled you, *sim?* You are a lucky man, de Carvalho. We are careful with you because we do not wish to hurt you in ways that will show bruises. I expect you to be grateful. I now ask you to dance for our entertainment." At Raul's silence he arched his eyebrows in mock disappointment. "*Não?* In that case you must be induced—"

He signaled to a guard. "The hot wire."

The grinning guard was holding a fat black electric cable, and he lowered it until several inches of exposed copper wire at the end touched the wet concrete floor.

Instantly, thousands of prickling needles were shooting fire through every part of him. His involuntary reflexes started him rolling about frantically in futile attempts to escape the inescapable. The floor was a scorching frying pan. He tried to rise, one hand braced on the floor, and pulsating needles numbed his arm, searing his palm. Making an enormous effort, he managed to stagger to his feet.

It was no better. The jabbing hot needles raced up his legs. His heart was pounding crazily, thundering in his ears. He started yanking first one bare foot, then the other, from the electrified floor. Jogging, jumping about jerkily. Faster and faster.

Luz and the guards, insulated by the thick rubber soles of their boots, broke into giggles and guffaws at his desperate antics.

Through the vibrating red haze that fogged his vision he saw the *coronel's* head flung back, shaking with laughter. The thick neck . . .

With one leap he had both hands clutched around that neck. Luz let out a shriek of agony as the jolting voltage from Raul's bare hands poured through his chunky frame. The startled guards stumbled back a few steps, fearful of being touched. For a few moments Raul and Luz were locked together in a macabre dance, Luz croaking, "Off, off—!"

It ended in another instant when a guard snatched up the electric cord. Raul weaved about drunkenly, feeling drained of all life except for the frenzied beating of his heart. The *coronel's* face was red with fury.

"*Bastardo!*" he shouted. "I would have your fingernails pulled out and your body cut to ribbons if I didn't have to keep you alive! Instead, you must be humbled." He jabbed a finger at the floor. "*Engatinhar*, down on all fours! I will teach you that even the high and mighty can be made to crawl and beg forgiveness."

When Raul failed to comply, one of the guards said, "I think his brain is fried."

"We will see. Get the wire whip."

A short whip of braided wire was produced. Two guards took Raul's limp arms and held them stretched out, the palms facing up.

"*Não*—not the hands. He will need them to sign his confession. On the soles of his feet. Seventy-five lashes. It will make him crawl fast."

Roughly, Raul was pushed to his knees. His head hung loosely. The fog was creeping in, growing thicker, darker. He was barely conscious when the flesh-ripping strokes of the whip began, adding new layers of pain to the numbness of his agonized flesh and nerves. He began moving feebly in an unconscious drive to escape into deeper darkness—crawling. Someone was counting.

It went on for an eternity.

"*...setenta e dois...setenta e três...setenta e quatro...*"

But Raul could no longer hear. He had finally reached the edge, had fallen into a bottomless pit of hellish blackness.

TWENTY-SEVEN

In her private garden within a high-walled enclosure behind the Granja do Sol, Florbella Sequiera e de Azvedo de Carvalho sat on a white wicker sofa working on a design of flowers in needlepoint. The garden, which had been designed especially for Florbella by the renowned landscape architect, Roberto Burle Marx, was a masterpiece of soothing enchantment. A small artificial stream wended its way through exotic Brazilian flora, bubbling over a modest waterfall into a pool graced with floating flowers and lily pads. Shielding Florbella from the harsh afternoon sun was a graceful lath pergola roofed over with a variety of hanging flowers. As a maiden, Florbella had been a stunning beauty, and at fifty, she was still attractive, though a trifle plump. In bed, and when in the proper mood, she could still, with ease, arouse her husband into ardent lovemaking.

Which was farthest from her thoughts now as she sat deftly plying her needle and listening to Afonso's explosions of wrath.

"*Que desgraça!*" he roared as he strode back and forth over the granite slab walkway. "My own son under arrest as a common criminal—the most shameful thing ever to happen to the de Carvalho family!" He had received the news only minutes ago from Eduardo, who had been called by Matt Riordan, the engineer who worked for Raul.

"You fuss too much and too loud," she said placidly. "Raul could never be guilty of a crime. Plainly it is a mistake, nothing to worry about. As soon as they find out their error—"

"Woman, you know nothing of the world! Law is law. Eduardo checked for himself and found that

285

Raul is guilty not only of attacking an officer—a most serious offense—but far worse, he is charged with intent to traffic in drugs."

"*Absurdo*. Raul is not that kind. When you go to take care of the matter, I am sure they will apologize." Serenely she continued her crewelwork.

Afonso glared at her. "I have not yet made up my mind to intercede. If Raul is guilty, I can do nothing. Drug crimes are the most serious—worse than murder."

"Surely you do not believe such *calúnia* about Raul!"

"Eduardo says they have evidence, sworn testimony against Raul. Perhaps the jungle has changed him. He went there ignoring my better judgment, and who knows what corrupting influences and bad company he has fallen among? That wild jungle girl, for example."

The thought of the girl had also fueled Afonso's anger. He had heard a garbled report from Eduardo about Odete's visit to Raul—and her discovery that he was carrying on an affair with some strange woman who lived in the jungle. Raul's perfidy had broken Odete's heart. Such a fine girl, and from such a fine family. A disgrace! Raul deserved to be punished.

"If only the fool had listened to me, and shown more respect for my authority, none of this would have happened." He pointed an accusing finger at his wife. "And you were the one who encouraged him in that foolish energy project!"

Florbella stood up, her lips tight. Her crewelwork dropped to the sofa. "I've heard enough!" Rarely did she get angry. She had grown up happily enough in a patriarchal social system where the male, the husband, was all-powerful. Women had no voice in anything except running the household and other female matters. As for sons, the father's authority was so entrenched in Brazilian culture that, if a father chose to kill his own son for intransigence or serious disobedience, the law would not interfere. Afonso would never go that far, of course, considering himself modern and enlightened, but women were another matter. They were expected to remain in their place.

But Florbella had wealth in her own name, and hidden fires. When her favorite son was in danger . . .

"You call yourself a father?" she accused. "You who are always quick to think the worst of him and slow to believe in his innocence! You forget that he is also my son—more mine than yours, for he sprang from my womb, and my love for him has not once faltered all through his life. If you do not rush to his defense, I will."

"Wife—you stay out of this! I forbid you to meddle in matters that are only for men to handle."

"How conceited you men are! And what have you done to handle it? *Nada*. You have done nothing but condemn him. So it is up to me. My family, too, has influence. I will call upon my cousin Armando, who is now the minister of justice."

Afonso gave her an expression of disgust. "That swellheaded pig? Since he has risen so high in government—undeservedly, I might add—he does not even know that we exist. He has never once invited us to important government functions. He would be the first to condemn our son."

"His coolness is only because you were so rude toward him during our engagement."

"*My* rudeness? I responded only to his overbearing manners. He was a nothing then—a radical and a great danger to our government—and I could not stomach his insulting attentions to you, my betrothed."

"But he is only my cousin. It was silly of you to be bothered by his show of affection."

"Affection? To other eyes, his attentions were more that of a lover. I disliked him from the first."

Florbella smiled inwardly. She was familiar with male jealousy. During her maiden years she had done all possible to stir it in young men at every opportunity. It had been a pleasant game. But jealous of her

cousin? *Ridículo!* It was true that during her teen
years they had carried on an innocent flirtation. All
the girls she knew had secretly flirted with their
attractive male cousins. It was easy, and good practice. What was wrong with that, as long as they didn't
marry? A few sneaky kisses now and then, what did it
matter?

In truth, Florbella had been infatuated with Armando de Salles Salgado. His idealistic determination
to overthrow and "purify" the government (aside
from his handsome face) had great romantic appeal.
Armando had been a firebrand born into a rich family.
After education at Eton and Oxford, he had returned
to Brazil seeking adventure as a diamond prospector,
and finding no gems, he worked as an overseer on a
large plantation, where for the first time he became
aware of the miserable working conditions of the
poor. That had fired him into organizing groups to
work for improved laws, and he so offended the power
structure that he was arrested as a "communist." Despite Brazil's traditional reputation for tolerance and
mercy, he was sentenced to thirty years in prison.

Two years later, he was pardoned by the new
president coming into power. Since then, prison having taught him the need to adapt to political and
economic realities instead of battling them, his rise to
success had been rapid.

"Armando will surely do all possible to help Raul if
I request it."

Afonso bristled. "It would be demeaning to me for
you to go to another man to seek help for our son. I
forbid it!"

Her expression grew more determined. "I am an
obedient wife who has always deferred to your wishes
in every way but one: When it concerns my children,
I must obey my heart. I am going to call Armando."

"You would be making a fool of yourself! And an
ass of me. He always detested me as much as I did
him. We have ignored him for half a lifetime, and he

has long since forgotten that you even exist. He would laugh in your face."

Florbella swept past him, not deigning to answer. Armando would never forget, she knew. For, unknown to Afonso, it was she who had gained audience with the *presidente* himself and pleaded for Armando's pardon with all the persuasions of her charm and the love overflowing from her idealistic young heart. After his release from prison, she exacted an agreement from him that they must never again see or contact each other, as it would be too upsetting to Afonso.

But this was an exception.

At her usual table in the boozy interior of the Casa Hospitalidade, Generosa guzzled at her bottle of warm *cerveja* and silently cursed the *polícia*, the *hoteleiro* manager, and all men in general.

Beneath her sullen exterior, her mood was *triste*. Melancholy had become a chronic condition of her *puta*'s existence, to be perceived in the depths of her soft brown eyes like a cosmic tear, a somber moistness, even when she was laughing in the arms of one of her endless lovers. Sometimes business was brisk, such as when she got a run of jackrabbits from the work gangs; sometimes it was slow. Her average had once been about one customer per working hour. Now it was less, but the manager—who, like all *alcoviteiros* who suck the blood of women, was as cold and hard as snake turds—still demanded his fifty percent commission based on her highest average of years ago. On bad nights, she was lucky to make a *cruzeiro* for herself.

If it got any worse, she would be working for nothing, as well as sinking into debt to pay for the stinking room and the food she was furnished. She was free to leave—the manager could select from plenty of younger *putas* to replace her—but where could she go? Who cared what happened to a tired whore, no longer so young?

She could think of only one person who had seemed to have *compaixão*, who saw her not merely as a *puta*, but as a woman, a person with feelings of her own. Hélio. She remembered vividly the day he had staggered in from the jungle. *Deus do céu!* What a mess! All covered with swamp scum, bloody from cuts. It was plain that he was one of the *flagelados*—the whipped ones—who had escaped from his plantation master. Even she had scorned him at first, until she had looked into those big, beautiful, mournful dark eyes.

It was like looking into a mirror. The mirror of her own soul. His body had been trapped, just as hers was, by those who would squeeze it dry of every drop of blood before casting it aside. They were two of a kind.

And now he had been caught in the trap again. What a shame!

That was the cause of Generosa's deep depression today. All Inchaco knew of the arrest of Hélio and the *fazendeiro*, de Carvalho. That the important *fazendeiro* had been arrested was an astonishment, but for Hélio it was to be expected. It had only been a matter of time. Last week the officers had come, and she had heard them talking to the hotel manager. The manager had told them where to find Hélio, collected the reward, and that was that. Hélio would be punished. Whipped till he was half dead, then dragged back to be worked the rest of the way to the grave. *Que pena!* What a pity!

If only she could find some way of helping him.

The idea took seed in her mind and began to grow.

As she tilted her head back to gulp more beer, she found herself looking directly into the beady eyes of the enormous stuffed anaconda looped among the rafters. *Diabo!* How she hated that snake! As she hated everything else in the hotel. The glass eyes were like the mean little eyes of Pessalino, one of the guards on night duty at the jail. There were only two on duty at night. The other guard was Bastião, big and strong but not much brain. He thought of nothing but women, wine, and cards, which was sometimes lucky for her because Bastião was her best customer whenever he won at gambling. Bastião would be easy to fool, but Pessalino, *não*—he was too sharp, and he hated women. He liked best young boys.

Sometimes Bastião came to see her at night when he was supposed to be on duty. It was a deal he made with Pessalino, who liked now and then to go out at night to look for boys to arrest, or to pay if he had to, and then it was Bastião's turn to stay at the jail.

It was a crazy idea she was thinking about, but it was a slow afternoon, and she had nothing else to do. What if she could help Hélio escape? Then what? Hélio had nothing to lose. If caught again, except for an extra whipping or two, he would be no worse off than before.

If she got caught trying to help, God help her!

She'd be thrown in a filthy cell with only animal slop to eat, and she'd be raped by the whole *milícia*, if they felt like it.

She shrugged. Was that much worse than her life now?

But if Hélio did not get caught again, and if she wasn't suspected, there was just a chance—*se Deus quizer*—that he might find enough love in his heart to come back someday and take her away with him. She had a modest little sum of money hidden away, perhaps even enough to start them in some small business somewhere.

She gulped the rest of her beer with the passion of irrevocable determination. She knew the hour that Bastião was due for night duty at the jail, and she knew the path he always followed to get there.

Bastião rolled over like a sick hog and emitted a long, fat snore, his breath redolent of garlic and whiskey fumes.

Generosa stared at his hairy nakedness on the rumpled bed beside her, wrinkling her nose in distaste. Bastião had exerted himself mightily and was slick with sweat. Its sour pungency mingled with the sickish sweet odor of the lotion he used to keep his wavy black hair in place. Generosa herself sometimes rubbed the lotion over her body between bouts with customers to kill the animal and sex stinks.

So far it had been easy. Bastião had been flattered when she'd waylaid him and told him how much she yearned for him, and that she badly wanted him to visit her that night. He had pleaded lack of money, but she'd assured him that she would grant credit, as he was the only one who was able to give her joy. After making arrangements with the other jailer, he had joined her in her little bedroom, where she had a bottle of strong wine waiting.

The wine was mixed with a little of a potent drug obtained from a macumba priestess and kept on hand only to use when one of her customers became too obnoxious. A drink or two from the bottle would soon put one into a sound sleep for a couple of hours.

Stealthily sliding off the bed, Generosa quickly donned Bastião's uniform. She had cajoled him into taking it off completely, telling him she wanted this to be a night of love. Most of her customers did little more than draw down their trousers. Though the uniform was a bit oversized, her generous figure filled it out well enough. Balling her long hair atop her head with one hand, she worked the fatigue cap on. A glance in the mirror showed that the hair made a bulge, a trifle *extraordinário*, under the cap. People might think it was a bump on the head from a *heróico* fight with *bandidos*, she thought hopefully. On the other hand, who looked closely at the *polícia*?

She hurried out into the dark hallway, padded down the back stairway, and slipped out the back door.

Something furry slithered up one leg and over his chest. It raced across his face, dragging a rough, scaly

292

tail. In his nightmare thousands of rats were swarming over him, their sharp teeth ripping at his aching flesh.

Raul exploded out of sleep, his arms flailing. A weak flashlight beam was playing through the bars of the cell and over the bodies. A few heads raised from the concrete, reflecting fright when the light splashed over their faces. They had been aroused by a sibilant whisper.

"*Hélio—Hélio—where are you?*"

The light lingered on one face, followed by a gasp of horror. It was Hélio's face, badly swollen. His eyes shone like two spoonfuls of blood. "Who—wha—?" he croaked.

"*Psssst!* Quiet!" the voice hissed.

A key scraped in the lock. Seconds dragged past while key after key was tried. Then the door creaked open. In the dim lighting from a weak bulb in the corridor, Raul saw a figure in a dark uniform slip in and cross over to kneel beside Hélio. Hélio let out a grunt of surprise as the two started whispering. After a few moments he sat up. "But I cannot leave without my *patrão*."

"He can come, too."

Hélio crawled over and shook Raul's arm. "Come— let us go."

Raul tried to rise, scarcely able to suppress a cry of pain when his weight came down on one bare foot. He fell back. "I—I can't walk. My feet are too swollen."

Hélio didn't hesitate. Crouching low, he caught Raul's arm and expertly hefted him over a broad shoulder, quickly cutting off Raul's protests.

While Hélio was hastening out with his burden, Generosa hurried to the tiny front office where Pessalino was sprawled facedown over his desk, still out cold from the bottle she had smashed over his head. From behind. It had been easy.

Deftly she returned the ring of cell keys to the snap

fastener on his belt. Then she produced an object from a small bag slung around her shoulder. One of the most popular sellers in the huts of many a macumba priestess, it was a small straw-stuffed doll wearing the green uniform and fatigue cap of the *milícia* police.

Carefully she placed the doll on the desk. Through its head had been stabbed a long needle. It was her crowning touch.

Virtually all lower-class Brazilians believed fervidly in the terrible powers of macumba. Macumba could perform such miracles as opening cell doors; it could punish or kill. And woe to him whose effigy, in the form of a straw doll, had been mutilated.

Outside, Generosa caught up with Hélio and his *patrão*, who was complaining.

"Hélio, set me down! I'll manage by myself."

"*Não, ó patrão*—not until I've carried you far from this accursed place."

"Hélio is right," said Generosa. "He is a very strong man. I am sorry that there is no more I can do to help, but perhaps you can find your way back to your plantation and hide."

Hélio turned toward her, his large eyes glistening in the moonlight.

"Generosa, no matter what happens, what you have done, I shall never forget. My heart will be grateful until my dying day."

"If you live, will you someday come back for me, Hélio?"

"As God is my witness, I want nothing more than to come back if I am able and take you as my woman."

He grasped her. They kissed. Then Hélio swung around and moved through the darkness, staggering a little under his load.

"*Va com Deus*," she called after them. "God be with you."

Generosa watched with blurred eyes until they vanished into the dreadful jungle. What they would do now she couldn't imagine. But she had no regrets.

Anything that happened in the jungle, even death, was better than jail.

Behind her tears was elation. For the first time in all her life she had hit back at the hated *policia!* Whatever punishment might catch up with her was worth it.

Turning, she hastened off toward the Casa Hospitalidade.

It was important that she be back in her room, naked in bed beside Bastião when he woke up.

Morning came softly to the jungle, a bright sunrise that filtered through the dense foliage to light the secretive solitude below with a greenish-gold haze.

Throughout the night Hélio had struggled under Raul's weight, taking frequent rests, wanting to get as deeply as possible into the *cão-apoam*—the "great woods" of the Indians—before dawn.

"They will bring in the dogs," he said. "Bad dogs that can follow a man's trail anywhere, some say even through swamps. They are bloodthirsty and very fast, and it is said they often kill the ones they chase before their masters even catch up with them."

Now they were resting again. Raul stared gloomily at his feet, which were red with fever and still badly swollen. The lacerations on the soles from the braided wire whip were purplish from infection.

But all that was as nothing compared to the emotions festering inside of him. Though slow to anger, his outrage over the arrests, the whippings, and the torture had grown into so obsessive a fury that at times he literally trembled with a raging desire to kill—to strangle Luz and de Onis with his bare hands. Hate, the lust for vengeance, had been alien emotions to him, but now they dominated his every conscious moment.

Still, he knew that rage was energy, something that had to be controlled, not wasted. He would need every ounce of it just to stay alive. Long enough to reach his plantation, endless miles away.

Nor could he afford to waste a moment of time.

"Let's get moving again, but from now on I'll manage to walk by myself. You've exhausted yourself too much already lugging me on your back."

"*Mas não, ó patrão.* Without protection for your feet, it would be *impossível*."

Raul glanced down at Hélio's bare feet, which showed innumerable scratches and cuts from the rough ground and brambles. It was customary for the shoes of prisoners to be taken away, Hélio had said, not only to make it difficult if a prisoner escaped but because shoes gave the hounds the best spoor for following a fugitive's trail.

"You're not much better off than I am, Hélio."

"I am different. I grew up much of the time without shoes. The skin is tough, like leather."

Tough they had to be, Raul thought, and the sturdy *caboclo* had to be a marvel of endurance as well to have carried him so far without caving in. Several times during the night he had protested that he wanted to walk on his own, but Hélio had refused to let him try, insisting that it was much faster to carry him. But pride had its limits.

"I've made up my mind, Hélio, I'm going to walk." Rising to his knees, Raul gingerly touched one foot to the ground, started to rise . . .

And gasped out an agonized groan. Bringing weight down on the sensitized raw nerves of the foot was like stepping into fire. He rolled back.

"You see?" said Hélio. "You cannot walk."

"Then I'll crawl!"

"That is too slow. The dogs would get us." Without waiting, Hélio knelt and quickly hefted Raul over his shoulder. He strode on. "Soon," he added, "we will reach the *igapo*, where I think you may be able to walk."

Hanging upside down, his head jouncing with each of his carrier's strides, Raul was only mystified by the *caboclo*'s remark. How could he walk?

For a timeless interlude, this uncomfortable mode

of travel continued through a tumult of vegetation and monstrous trees. Frequently Hélio had to skirt around the boles of giant silk-cotton trees, their gray and brown trunks rising smoothly for nearly a hundred feet before branching out like umbrellas. Liana vines looped everywhere, intertwining among tall trees, scrubby palmettos, and all forms of green growth like a long-tentacled octopus. Flamboyants crowded in: bougainvillaea dripping with magenta blossoms, colorful frangipani, crimson passionflowers, startling flame vines intertangled with black velvet gloxinia. Their perfumed scents mingled with the humid rankness of the rich black soil and the rotting vegetation.

Hélio stopped, gently lowering Raul to the ground.

"The *igapo*," he said.

The *igapo*, or aqueous jungle, was swampy terrain webbed with small streams. Water reeds grew lushly in the greenish scum. Here and there in the deeper pools floated giant lily pads strong enough to hold the weight of a man. Bugs and winged insects were nuisance enough everywhere in the jungle, but here at their breeding grounds they were in such profusion that the air seemed to vibrate with humming. Brilliant dragonflies, damselflies, crane flies zipped past in erratic flight; deadly spiders and furry tarantulas were thick on the bark of cypresses. Mosquitoes, gnats, *borrachudos* of all kinds swarmed thickly around Raul in their greed to get at his flesh. He began slapping at himself crazily. Soon his hand was spotted with bits of blood from crushed pests.

"Put your feet in the water," said Hélio. "Mud, clay, wet leaves—they are soft and healing."

Raul plunged into the swamp, his arms flailing around his head to fend off the insects. He had waded several feet before he realized—he was walking! The coolness of the water and the soft mucky bottom were soothing to his feet.

"Now reach down and get handfuls of mud to spread over your face and arms. It will help keep the *borrachudos* away and draw the poison from their bites."

Quickly Raul began scooping up gobs of swamp mud and smearing it over his face and the exposed parts of his body. Ah, relief! Then he felt something squirming near one eye. Hélio came over, plucked away a three-inch bloodsucker, and threw it aside.

"The mud is full of *sanguessugas*. They do no harm, but I will check you over and pull away all the little *bastardos* I can find."

"Where do we go from here?"

"We must cross the *igapo*. It is the only chance of keeping the *policia* off our trail."

"How far across is it?"

Hélio shrugged. "I do not know. Maybe many miles. It could take many days."

"If we live long enough."

"We will live, *ó patrão*, because the *bom Deus* is looking out for us. But it will be dangerous. There are many poisonous snakes and the crocodile, but I think no piranhas because they like better the rivers, not too shallow. Have no worries. I will lead the way."

Hardly reassured, Raul floundered along behind the *caboclo*, who slogged steadily ahead, knee-deep in the mucky water. Raul's respect for Hélio had risen to the highest admiration. Here was one of the true heroes of the world. Hélio had broken off two dried branches, one to serve as a crutch for Raul and one as a weapon for himself. Frequently Hélio paused and poked down the staff to sound out the water depth ahead, and once when a large dark snake came skimming toward them, its beady-eyed head raised a few inches above the water like the elliptical point of a spear, Hélio beat at it furiously.

"Get away from here, you ugly devil!" he howled. "I'll smash you into a thousand pieces!" The snake swerved gracefully and skimmed off elsewhere.

Hélio was coping with the situation—for now. But what would happen when they had to rest? There was no place to sit, let alone lie down to sleep. Already Raul was weaving a bit unsteadily.

Hélio stopped unexpectedly, cupping a hand to an ear. Raul heard it then—a strange tinkling.

"The dogs," said Hélio. "They wear bells because they run far ahead of their masters. They are close behind on our trail."

"Won't they lose it at the edge of the swamp?"

"*Não*. They will follow. They are big dogs and can move much faster in water than we can. We have not gone far enough. Soon they will see us and come to pull us down. If it is only two dogs, maybe we have a chance. If there are more—"

A sudden eruption of howling and yapping sent chills slithering down Raul's spine. A whole pack! And they sounded so close.

Hélio turned, his swollen face and bloodied eyes looking more dismal than ever.

"*Diabo!* I can see them jumping into the water already—six or eight of the *bastardos*, maybe more. There are too many for us to fight off. God help us!"

TWENTY-EIGHT

Remorse weighed heavily on Afonso's conscience. He was a prideful, unbending man with a strict sense of justice. Any man who broke a law, regardless of his importance, should be punished. Otherwise there could be no stability in the social structure. He still believed Raul must be guilty of something illegal—where there was smoke, there was fire—but he was also his own son. A Carvalho! A proud name that must be protected. Throughout the night his pride had battled with his conscience, and as his anger cooled, he came to see that he had failed in his duty. Whether Raul was guilty or not, the Carvalho name must not be dragged through the mud.

In the morning, after an aggravating breakfast with Florbella, whose polite but chilly attitude was plainly meant to rebuke him, he retired to his study and put a call through to Raul's plantation.

A female voice responded in English.

"May I ask who you are?" said Afonso.

"You may. I am Peggy Carpenter. And you?"

Such effrontery! "I am Afonso Sequiera e de Azvedo de Carvalho, Raul's father," he said stiffly.

He heard a quick indrawn breath of surprise. "How nice to talk to you, *senhor*. Is there anything I can do to help you?"

"You have not fully answered my question. In what capacity are you staying in my son's home?"

"Oh, I'm just one of Raul's friends."

Some of Afonso's anger welled up again. How many females did Raul keep around the place? Had he become a debauched womanizer?

"I wish to speak to *Senhor* Riordan."

"He's not here just now. I expect him back in the next hour or so. May I take a message?"

"Advise *Senhor* Riordan that I wish him to fly as soon as possible to Manaus and engage an attorney to represent my son. My other son, Eduardo, will join him later to take over the responsibility."

There were a few moments of silence before she spoke again. "We assumed, after Mr. Riordan's call to your other son yesterday, that an attorney would have already been engaged. Mr. Riordan flew to Inchaco first thing this morning to visit Raul and to assure him that help was on the way."

Again the shame flung in his face. And by a virtual stranger.

"Ask Mr. Riordan to call me the moment he gets back," he said curtly.

About an hour later, Riordan called with the terrible news. Raul had broken from jail and the police were after him with bloodhounds.

Eduardo was reluctant to answer the phone, but its ringing had already awakened him from a nightmarish sleep and was too intimidating to ignore. Languidly rolling over on the black silk sheets, against which his slim nakedness appeared abnormally pale, he lifted the phone receiver from the bedside stand. There was a dull, hollow pain in his head, as if his brain had been marinated in acid. *Meu Deus,* why could he never learn that it was a mistake to stereo the effects of cocaine with alcohol?

"Hello?" he said with sleepy indifference.

"Why aren't you at the office?" roared his father, startling Eduardo to full wakefulness and exacerbating his headache. "I called there first and was told you hadn't arrived yet. You should have been there over an hour ago!"

"As a matter of fact, father, I'm not feeling too well, which is why I'm running a bit late today—"

"Not feeling well! At a time like this, when your

brother is creating a family scandal? Your responsibility is to think of family first and forget your own selfish feelings."

"You seem unduly agitated, father. I agree that Raul's arrest is a scandalous affair, but I'm confident that your attorneys will be able to smooth things over."

"You talk from ignorance," Afonso said sourly. "Attorneys would be wasted on such a rash fool as your brother has shown himself to be." He went on to tell of Raul's breaking out of jail.

Eduardo gave a low whistle. "That's beyond belief! Whatever possessed him?"

"Who knows? Perhaps because of drugs."

Eduardo winced. "Drugs? I didn't know that Raul was into that kind of—"

"That's beside the point. Until I get to the bottom of this matter, something must be done to salvage as much as possible of Raul's large monetary investment, for which I, as his father, will be ultimately responsible."

"But what can we do?"

"I want you to fly out to Raul's plantation immediately and take over full management. Find out what's been going on out there, and put a stop to it. The alcohol business was a mistake. Since I will have to bail Raul out of trouble and make up his losses, I will insist on more sensible ways to use the land. With the highway coming, there should be many better ways. Perhaps by planting cane, or reestablishing a rubber plantation."

"But, father, I am hardly qualified for that kind of thing."

"You will hire agricultural experts to advise you."

"Even so, it would be impossible for me to leave so soon. There are many things I must attend to first, and my office duties—"

"Your office duties," Afonso said scathingly, "have been too much neglected. I had hoped that in a position of responsibility you would shape up, but your record is shameful. I think it is because your Rio life-style is too frivolous. I am putting old Adriano, my most trusted employee, in full charge of the office, and I will expect you to leave for Raul's plantation no later than tomorrow morning."

"But I have many personal matters to clear up!"

"Forget your personal matters. This is far more important. In the jungle, either you will make good, or not another *cruzeiro* will you get from me. This is your last chance. I will send the Learjet to transport you. Be packed and ready to leave at the crack of dawn." He hung up.

Eduardo slammed the dead receiver back on its cradle and noted that the palms of his hands were moist. Delicate tremors ran through him. His father did not make idle threats. Why couldn't he be left to live his life in his own way?

The answer, of course, was money. Or lack of it. That was his number one worry. Unlike many play-boy sons of the rich, whose fathers lavished money on them unstintingly and did not expect them to work, he had been cursed with a strict father who had old-fashioned ideas about money and the work ethic. Why, if a family was rich enough, should a son have to work? Sooner or later the parents would die and then all of it would go to their children. But that could mean waiting many, many years, until one was no longer young enough to enjoy it. It was unfair.

True, his father had given him a fair allowance and a modestly generous monetary gift on each birthday, but it was never enough. Except for his mother, who secretly advanced him large sums of her own money when he begged for it out of desperation, he would never have been able to keep up his present life-style. But even she was getting more and more reluctant to give him money, fearful that Afonso would find out and berate her unmercifully. Sooner or later, she told him, his father was sure to examine her financial records.

Records...

Eduardo felt a trickle of cold sweat slide down his spine. To cover gambling debts and other pressing expenses, he had on several occasions "borrowed" money from the company, and it now amounted to a substantial sum. He had juggled a few figures to cover the deficit temporarily, and he fully intended to replace every cent—but what if an audit were made before he was able to get it back?

He shuddered, feeling the need for a snort. Coke had long been his quickest escape from unpleasant realities. Rolling off the bed, he padded across the lush carpet into the bathroom where he kept hidden a little silver matchbox full of snow and a snorting straw.

After a snort up each nostril—which he could no longer feel, for the mucous membranes had long since been destroyed—he felt a little better. Not good, but better. His rationale for using cocaine had been an outgrowth of his permanent party mentality. To get an instant high, to be able to rid himself of all worries, to function a little sharper, faster, a little crazier. And, ah! To heighten sex.

Except that it no longer worked.

Even Odete refused to date him—she whom he had introduced to cocaine and sex! After his first night or two with her, his lovemaking attempts with her had failed, and the astonishing sexual greed he had awakened in her had drawn her to other men. She was one of the most popular figures in the rich young set. It was fortunate for Raul that she had broken off with him, for her hidden nymphomania would have destroyed their marriage sooner or later.

Thank God that was one problem he no longer had to worry about. Raul would kill him if he ever found out about his seduction of Odete, but now that danger was past. She had started dating young Fabiano de Manguerio, who was soft, plump, and very rich, a marshmallow type she led around by the nose. It was rumored they were secretly engaged, and Eduardo knew that Odete was just as anxious as he was to keep their past buried.

Unfortunately, the biggest of all his worries remained.

He had consulted several specialists about his impotency, and out of all the costly garbage they gave him, they could offer no cures. The painful facts were that he had lost his sense of smell and much of his taste—senses he could dispense with—but most cruelly, heavy and continued use of cocaine had finally extended its debilitating effects to that most magical part of the central nervous system—all those thousands of delicate nerves, the sympathetic ganglia, that produced the wondrous sensations of sexual excitation. They were so far deteriorated, so numbed, that only occasionally had he been able to achieve the feeblest of erections, and soon that last whisper of life from his little love machine would be silent. Forever. Never again could such nerves regenerate and recover any of their sensitivity.

The worst of it was that his sexual hunger—all the greater for its lack of gratification—still burned like fire locked away in his head.

The hunger seethed in him now, a craving that had intensified since his father's upsetting call. Soon he would be shorn away from Rio and the life he loved. The excitement, the girls. Chica.

Her image was always the first to leap into his mind when the craving grew strong. The exquisite beauty of the cinnamon-skinned songstress, her silken movements, everything about her could stir him more than any other female he had ever known. Just thinking of Chica sent a hot flush of blood to his head, and he thought he detected a slight echoing arousal down below.

The doctors could be wrong. Most of them were just money-gouging quacks, and if anybody could prove them wrong, it was Chica. With her subtle, tantalizing lovemaking tricks, she was a top expert at arousing men, and beneath her elegant, hard exterior she was *simpático*. She knew of his problem, but did not laugh.

He could not leave Rio without seeing her again. And perhaps...

He raced to a phone and hastily dialed her private number. Doubtless she would still be sleeping and would be annoyed at so early a call; but there was little time left.

The phone rang on and on. Stubbornly he held on. To be rewarded, finally, by the angry slap of her voice.

"What the hell are you calling for in the middle of the night? Have they dropped the *bomba atômica?* Who are you?"

"It's Eduardo—"

"You! Have you been sailing snow up your nose again? What the fuck do you want?"

"You, of course. I want to see you—"

"You must be crazy!"

"Chica, please listen. I'm leaving town tomorrow, and I may not be coming back for months, or years. I've got to see you again."

"I cry for you, Eduardo, but there is no way! Now stop bothering—" Her voice sliced off, and for a few moments in the suspended hum he thought he heard a male voice in the background—then silence as a hand was apparently cupped over the mouthpiece. After a minute or so her voice was back.

"I'm sorry I was such a grouch, *amante*," she said in a softer voice. "When I am awakened too soon, I am horrible. Now what is this about you leaving town?"

"The old man is exiling me to my brother's plantation—a thousand miles from nowhere, off in the jungle. I've got to leave first thing in the morning, and—" His voice grew pleading. He was sweating profusely. "Just one more time, Chica."

Her voice grew seductive. "I've missed you, too, *amante*, but I'm all tied up for tonight. Only time I could spare is if you come over right away."

"I'll be there in half an hour." Elated, he hung up and began racing to get ready.

He looked down at her. The thunking of blood in his ears was frenzied, not normal. All the lyrical grace of her pale brown nakedness—the haunting allure of her face, her lovely breasts, her sleek torso melting into the sensual cleavage of her thighs—lay captive beneath him. It was the same body that drove many men half crazy with desire, accelerated passions to insane heights. She lay there passive. Waiting to be possessed.

Yet as unobtainable as if they were separated by a million miles.

He had tried and failed, and now he remained frozen in position, feeling caught in a bad dream, a familiar dream. Déjà vu. As if he were a tiny moth propelling himself again and again into an inferno of heat that would destroy him.

But he wanted to be destroyed. He would pay any price to be whirled away in the inferno of her heat, burned to ashes. Anything for just one more chance.

She looked down at his limp organ and laughed softly. "*Amante*, I am afraid your desires have again overreached your capabilities."

Shame washed through him. A hot tingling behind his eyeballs threatened unmanly tears. "Do something," he pleaded. "You know all kinds of ways—"

A bellow of laughter slammed at him from behind. He whirled around on the bed, feeling acutely vulnerable in his nudity. Grinning at him from just inside the bedroom door was a short, solidly built man of middle age. His squarish head, set on a muscular neck, was topped by a coif of thick black hair, down the center of which ran an irregular stripe of white.

"What the hell kind of sideshow are you running here, Chica?" squawked Eduardo.

"I am sorry, Eduardo. Vini—*Senhor* de Onis—was here as a guest when you called. I didn't want you to come, but Vini insisted, as he is anxious to talk to you about a business matter." Her voice was sorrowful. "But please remember, I first gave you a chance at what you came for."

De Onis took a gentle puff on his cigar and regarded Eduardo with a benevolent smile. "So you are about to go into the jungle to your brother's plantation. It does not make you happy. *não?*"

Eduardo scowled. Though he had never met de Onis, he knew of the man's importance. But he was fuming with too much embarrassment to be impressed.

Eduardo was dressed now and the two sat in the living room of Chica's apartment. Chica had withdrawn.

"My private life is none of your damned business, *senhor*." he said sourly.

De Onis chuckled. "You are angry that I saw too much, *sim?* It was but a joke. Is anything more comic than the sight of a man trying to mount a female?"

Blood rushed to Eduardo's face. "It may be comic to you, *senhor*, but most others would consider spying on anything so intimate the crassest of manners."

"Crass maybe, but still comic. Have you never watched others engaged in such intimacies? At an orgy, perhaps?"

"*Senhor,* what is the purpose of these silly questions?"

"You will soon find them not so silly. I was hoping to put you in a more humorous frame of mind, for I would prefer that we be friends instead of enemies."

"I have no desire to be either."

"Ah, but sometimes one has no choice. So far you have evaded my questions. It matters not, since I already know the answers. I am well aware, for example, that you have been to many orgies. I couldn't care less. I know many other things about you and your family. I was particularly interested in your brother's engagement to the lovely *Senhorita* Odete Bandiera e Xavier. What a shame that it is ended!

Which leads me to another question. Do you think your intimacy with your brother's fiancée had anything to do with it?"

"*Senhor!*" Eduardo's face flamed. "How dare you suggest such a thing!"

Ignoring him, de Onis turned his head and called out, "Barbosa, bring in the briefcase!"

The big frame of de Onis's chief troubleshooter hustled into the room, put a slim black attaché case on the carpet beside his boss, and departed. De Onis took the briefcase on his lap and opened it, smiling. Withdrawing a packet of photographs held together with a rubber band, he tossed it across to Eduardo.

"Perhaps your brother—or your father—would be interested in seeing a set of these photos, Eduardo. What do you think?"

After one glance, Eduardo's face went white. A trembling seized him. Cold sweat broke out on his forehead. Plainly they had been taken with a hidden camera at the party he had staged during Carnival. He had seen every type of pornographic picture, and they usually bored him, but never anything so vividly shocking as these—with himself as the star performer.

Most of them were of himself and Odete. Naked. In positions of wanton carnality. Whereas Odete's face, though turned to one side and shadowed, was a study in what might have been intense pain—or ecstasy— even Eduardo was sickened by the raw animal lechery distorting his own expression. *While befouling his brother's bride-to-be!*

If the pictures ever fell into the hands of his family, all hell could hold nothing worse than the explosions of rage—and the eternal contempt that would follow. The least of it would be violent death at Raul's hands, that is if his father didn't gun him down first. If his mother—God forbid!—ever set eyes on them, she would faint away in horror and forever after disown him as a son.

Alternating waves of shame, guilt, self-disgust, and fear curdled through him, leaving him drained. He could not even summon the appropriate anger toward the rotten *bastardo* who had trapped him.

"What do you want?" he said weakly.

"Nothing more than your full cooperation."

"To do what?"

"It is simple. I want you to destroy your brother's alcohol business. Plans, records, equipment, buildings, everything."

"I couldn't do that, *senhor*."

"But you will. Your brother is an escaped prisoner who may or may not survive and be free again. I take no chances. You are now going out to his plantation to run it in his absence. You know nothing about such things. Nobody can pin blame on you if, instead of running it you ruin it."

"What would you gain by that?"

"I offered to buy your brother's plantation, and he refused to sell. Now I am even more determined to get it. Cheap. It is a game I play with money. Like chess. I make sure that every square of escape is blocked. I have checked about the insurance. There is none. Why should any insurer take a risk on an unproven venture so far out in the jungle? Your brother is way over his head financially. I have paid off some of his biggest creditors so that I can demand payment and force foreclosure at an appropriate moment- of my choosing. I also happen to know that your father is disgusted with the whole alcohol fiasco and would like to wash his hands of any responsibility. And now that it is known that the highway will not touch your brother's land—but why am I revealing all this to you?" His expression hardened. "All I need from you is your agreement that you will fully cooperate."

"And in exchange. will you promise to give me all the photos and negatives?"

De Onis arched his eyebrows. "Don't be naïve. I will of course have to retain the photos to assure your continued cooperation. But I am not a difficult man to please. It's a two-way street. If you do your part, you need have no worries. I am waiting for your answer."

Eduardo buried his face in his hands. "I will do what you want," he said hoarsely.

"*Bom!*" De Onis gave him a sly smile. "About the photos—if you'd like a set for yourself—"

"Your contemptuousness has no limits, has it?"

De Onis laughed and got in a last thrust. "My thought was that you might wish to frame them as a testimonial to the time when you still had one of your balls."

TWENTY-NINE

Standing in the scummy water, Raul stared back in consternation at the pack of howling dogs. Several had already plunged into the swamp and were half leaping, half swimming toward them.

Then something mystifying happened. Beside him, Hélio breathed, "*Diabo me levem si!* I'll be damned!"

The dogs in the water, one after the other, had halted. They were kicking and thrashing, and moments later they were rolling over to float on their sides or backs, unmoving.

Raul's first dread thought—*piranhas!*—was quickly ruled out by the spectacle of something similar happening to the dogs still on the bank of the swamp. They were falling, going into brief contortions before lying still. The chorus of excited yapping and yowling whimpered off into silence. One of the dying beasts pawed feebly at an object protruding from its neck.

An Indian blowgun dart.

Hélio saw them first. "*Veja!* The *Índios!*"

They melted into view from behind the jungle screen as if by magic. Two dozen or more. All had their faces dyed black and streaked with markings of yellow and white, and they were virtually naked except for ornaments of shells, bones, and feathers. Some of them went immediately to the carcasses of the dogs and began tying them with rope slings. The rest rushed into the water and waded out in a curved formation. For Raul and Hélio, there was no escape.

"I think," said Hélio, "that they're a hunting party. It was the dogs' barking that drew them here. *Índios* are crazy for dog meat."

Raul watched the warriors sloshing through the water, rapidly approaching, and despite the heat he felt chills race down his spine. Some had blowguns; some held bows with arrows fitted to the strings. All pointed directly at them.

"If they're a hunting party, why are they coming after us?"

Hélio let out a moan. "Because, *ó patrão*, they're even crazier about human meat."

"Nonsense. If they wanted us for meat they would have shot us down already, as they did the dogs."

"The dogs were lucky. It is the custom of the *Indios* to save their enemies—to roast them alive as a sacrifice to their gods before eating them."

Now the warriors had them surrounded. The apparent leader, whose scowling expression looked all the more ferocious because of a red macaw feather thrust horizontally through his pierced nose, made jabbing motions for them to follow the Indians on shore who, with the dog carcasses slung over their shoulders, were filing off into the jungle.

Wearily, Raul and Hélio slogged their way back to the edge of the swamp.

"Now I'll carry you," said Hélio.

"No more of that! I'm going to walk, even if it kills me. Anyway I think the mud and water helped my feet."

Shrugging, Hélio pulled off his shirt. "Then I will try to make it easier for you, and do not try to stop me. Sit down—"

Tearing strips of different widths from the shirt, the *caboclo* quickly folded some of the cloth into pads, lined them with wet leaves, and bound them tightly against the soles of Raul's feet. The Indians watched impassively.

"You're a damned fool, Hélio. Now the *borrachudos* will eat you up."

"*Não*. My skin is too thick. Even the *Indios* will soon discover I am too tough to eat."

Drums started throbbing, and jubilant shouts erupted from the gathering of Indians who watched the hunting party emerge from the woods carrying the dead dogs and prodding two *civilizados* along in the vanguard. The warriors strutted proudly. Hélio staggered drunkenly, supporting Raul against his shoulder.

Raul, who could scarcely hobble, sagged frequently, saved from falling only by the *caboclo's* arm hooked around him. Most of the foot bandages had been torn off along the rough trail. The few still left were blood-soaked. Each step on the raw bleeding flesh was like walking over needles and fire, producing agony so intense that the screams ripping up his throat could only be muffled into convulsive gasps by gritting his teeth until his jaws ached. Mercifully, a numbness was setting in. His feet were beginning to feel like heavy lumps of clay. The numbness was beginning to pervade all of his sore muscles, his bones, his tormented flesh.

The only part of him fully alive was in his head, which burned with an undiminished fever. It was a sickness, a madness, a distortion of all his previous values, yet it had become his prime reason for wanting to survive.

To find de Onis and Coronel Luz, and to kill them. To destroy two such monsters was perhaps the best service he could give the world.

Slowly they wobbled along between rows of *tapiris* that looked like giant beehives thatched with palm fronds. Naked women adorned with shell jewelry and painted with geometric markings jeered at them. Naked children with fat little bellies threw pebbles or dashed in bravely to poke them with sticks. Drums pounded steadily in frenzied percussion.

At the largest *tapiri* they were halted in front of a tall, imposing figure who stood with folded arms regarding them balefully. He had a deeply wrinkled face that was dyed half red and half black, and his white hair was crowned with a feathered diadem that marked him as chief. Ornamenting his scrawny but sinewy body were splashes of bright paint, loops of shell beads around his neck, and bones and feathers hanging from a snakeskin belt. Thrust under the belt was a gleaming blue-steeled revolver.

Scowling, he jerked out the revolver and pointed it at Raul. The trigger went *click, click, click.*

"No boom-boom," he said.

"Thank God for that, you bloodthirsty old devil," said Raul, managing to smile.

Replacing the revolver, the Indian tapped a forefinger against his chest.

"Xanqui," he said.

Raul pointed his own finger at himself. "Me Raul."

Raising his head haughtily, the Indian again pointed at himself. "Me *curaca!*"

"*Curaca,*" said Hélio. "That means 'chief.' I learned that from one of the Indians who worked at the plantation I escaped from."

The chief's gaze flicked between Raul and Hélio. "*Curaca?*" he said with a questioning inflection.

Suddenly inspired, Hélio nodded vigorously, pointing his finger at Raul. "He *curaca!* Big *civilizado curaca!*" For emphasis, he stepped back a couple of feet and, both arms outstretched toward Raul, bowed low several times.

The chief showed great interest. He stepped close and began examining Raul from head to foot. He pinched his cheeks, arms, and torso where the dried mud was beginning to flake off. He stared long into Raul's blue eyes, stretched Raul's lips apart to examine the teeth, felt the muscles of Raul's biceps and thighs. Down to his bloody feet.

At that point, guttural words began pouring out of him. Jabbing a finger at the feet, he made chopping, slicing motions across Raul's ankles with the edge of his other hand.

"Good God," said Raul, "he's telling them to cut off my filthy feet! Plainly they hate the whites—and white chiefs most of all."

"I'm sorry, *ó patrão.* I told them you were a *curaca* thinking it would get you the best treatment."

"I think you succeeded, Hélio. Doubtless I'll be the choicest cut on the menu."

"*Não!* You mustn't talk that way!"

Now the chief was waving his arms and giving orders.

A cry of *woo-ahh! woo-ahh! woo-aahh!* burst from many throats as the crowd began to disperse. Everyone seemed gleeful. A number of chattering women scurried off to a row of smoldering fires at one end of the village and began stoking them with armfuls of dried wood, stirring them to leaping life.

The chief pointed at the captives and gave another order. Two warriors caught Raul by the arms, one on each side, and two others caught Hélio in the same manner. They were half walked, half dragged to a squarish *tapiri* constructed of heavy poles, indicating that it might be a jail, and roughly shoved inside.

Elsewhere, hollow log drums were beating furiously.

Splintered streaks of light squeezed through the chinks in the pole walls, creating a twilight haze. There were no windows, no furnishings, only a layer of dried banana leaves spread over a hard dirt floor.

"It is more comfortable than the *civilizado* jails," said Hélio, "but I am starving. If only they would feed us before—"

He broke off as a plump woman with graying hair appeared in the doorway. She entered carrying a large clay bowl. Behind her came another woman, much older, with stringy white hair and shriveled, pendulous breasts that flapped loosely as she trotted toward Hélio with another clay bowl.

The plumper one, whose nakedness was creased like crepe paper with myriad wrinkles, had already waddled over to Raul, and she knelt beside him. Her protruding belly hung in folds from many childbirths. Putting the bowl down, she set about trying to get Raul's shirt off. The buttons stumped her until Raul himself quickly unbuttoned the shirt and pulled it off. Whatever she was about, he decided, it was pointless to resist. Next she tried tugging his trousers down, but she was mystified by the belt. Raul released the belt and hauled his pants off, also his underwear, and tossed them aside. How could you be coy about nudity among nudists? He heard Hélio grunting and cursing softly.

"What is it they want from us?" groaned the *caboclo*. "And look—*olhe!*—here come more of them—"

It was true. A half dozen or more naked females of elderly appearance were crowding through the doorway, gawking at the captives.

"Maybe we're going to be raffled off. Maybe—" Something mushy and wet slopped against Raul's face. The one who had unclothed him held a handful of wet silk-cotton tree fibers with which she proceeded to vigorously scrub away at the dried mud. Frequently she paused to rinse the spongy mass in the bowl beside her, squeezing out the surplus water, and then she continued working down his torso.

Hélio's voice came sputtering through a mouthful of water. "W-why do they wash us, *ó patrão*, when they do not even give themselves a bath?"

By now the plumpish one had cleansed Raul, after a fashion, down to his most private organ. And there she lingered, playfully flicking his penis this way and that with one finger while washing around it. Little birdlike tittering sounds of amusement burst from her lips. The tittering, accompanied by choking gurgling sounds that Raul took to be giggling, swelled to a chorus that came from all the watching females, who had increased in number until the *tapiri* was crowded.

"*Ó patrão*," wailed Hélio, "now there are six of them pulling and feeling me all over! What do I do now?"

"Take heart, Hélio. I think they're just old maids looking for a little fun. If you please them, it could save your life."

"Ah, no, I would not want to be untrue to my

Generosa." After a moment he added, "But I must be honest and admit that I have been so long without a woman that even these *bruxas*—"

An angry voice silenced Hélio and the women. Xanqui had entered with two of his warriors. His fierce scowl and the scolding tone of his voice made his displeasure clear, and it was punctuated by a few kicks at the posteriors of the ladies as the whole flock made haste to scamper out.

Pointing at Raul, the chief gave a guttural command to his warriors. Moments later, Raul found himself being roughly dragged out of the *tapiri*, stark-naked.

Outside, the air was thick with woodsmoke and the odor of roasting meat. Off to one side Raul could see the row of fires and the skinned carcasses of dogs broiling on spits. Many of the Indians were dancing near the fires, chanting joyously, and the untiring drums were still pounding.

A shiver of terror raced up his spine as he was taken to a smaller *tapiri*.

They shoved him inside.

A naked young girl of perhaps fifteen sat cross-legged on a reed mat beside what appeared to be a bed made of animal skins stretched between stakes a few inches above the floor. She had long straight hair hanging down both sides of an oval face, a softly rounded figure, and skin the color of golden tobacco leaves that gleamed from rubbings of palm oil. Except for a simple shell necklace and wooden disks in her ears, her only adornment was a brilliant crimson flower in her hair.

Near her were woven platters of mangoes, bananas, and palm fruit; bowls of manioc, turtle eggs, and other edibles. Raul's astonished eyes stared at the girl, at the food, then back at the girl. Her large and lovely dark eyes were staring past and behind him, filled with apprehension.

Xanqui was entering. He strode directly to the girl

and roughly pulled her to her feet. She stood cowering, head bowed.

"Ninquita," he said, pointing at the girl. Turning, he pointed at Raul. "*Curaca.*"

With the introduction over, he reached down and patted the girl's tummy, making a curved motion through the air, showing how her stomach would look swollen out. Pregnant.

Then, using the fingers of both hands, he went through the gesture unmistakably symbolizing intercourse.

Raul was appalled at the idea. With this child? Impossible!

His mission accomplished, the chief stalked out.

Now the girl was kneeling, shyly offering him one of the platters. Raul grabbed a banana and was soon eating ravenously while questions crowded his head. What were the chief's motivations? Obviously he wanted the girl to be implanted with the seed of a white man—a white man he believed to be a chief. Why? Did he think that by so doing, some of the power of the whites, whom they perceived as enemies, would accrue to the tribe?

And what would happen to him afterward? Did the Indians not also believe that they gained some of their enemies' power by cutting off their heads and shrinking them? And by eating their flesh?

He continued eating, greedily sampling something from every tray and bowl. After all, it was doubtless his last supper.

He had bypassed one small bowl that was filled with a dark liquid. Ninquita lifted it and held it near his mouth, indicating that he should drink it. He took a tentative sip. It had a fruity herbal taste, not unpleasant, but nothing he cared to drink. How could he know what was in it? The Indians, he knew, for all their seeming ignorance and childlike nature, were skilled pharmacologists with uncanny knowledge of all sorts of drugs obtained from nature.

Noting his reluctance, the girl pushed his hand

close to his mouth again, urging him to drink. Why not? he thought. Obviously it wouldn't be poisoned if they expected him to perform the rites of fertilization —which he was definitely determined to have no part of. Imagine a child of his growing up among aborigines!

He took a long swallow, savoring the flavor. The girl's gentle hand was on his, still urging him to drink, and he finished all of it.

Almost at once he was overcome with a pleasurable languor. He yawned. It was as if all his exhaustion, his lame muscles, his frayed nerves were piling up into a great weight that was irresistibly pulling him down, down—down—into a soft, deep blackness.

A blackness swirling with sensuous colors, alive with nude females, shapely limbs, breasts, smiling lips. Glimpses of all the girls who had attracted him since adolescence ... the racing curves of slender bodies with virginally budding breasts and exquisite bundas stretched out supine on the beach in the passionate embrace of sun and sand. Hauntingly familiar but strange women, lovely composites of some he had known and many he had not ... Odete, Peggy, Vivi, beauteous strangers; a mingling of all of them into an ever-changing vision of female loveliness ... of welcoming smiles, arms, limbs spreading open like the exotic petals of some fantastically rare night flower ...

A furious lust seized him. He writhed and twisted with a seething desire that could not be denied.

He awoke sweating. It seemed that he had slept but a few minutes, but darkness had come. At first he couldn't remember where he was—until he was reminded by the heavy throb of drums and the eerie chanting that filled the night outside. The last fragments of his dream were fast melting away, but he was still afire with hunger for a woman.

Then he felt the soft body cuddled against him, the delicate fingers stroking his thighs, his pelvic area ... and he became aware of his hard upthrust organ.

In a surge of joy he rolled toward her.

❋ ❋ ❋ ❋ ❋

Two days later Raul awoke in the gray of early dawn to discover that he was lying alone on the animal skin bed. Ninquita had vanished like all the rest of his weird dream—or had it all been a dream? His head still felt a little strange, but his mind was clear enough to realize that he had been in a drugged state. Probably from some mind-altering mixture of tranquilizers, aphrodisiacs, hallucinogens, and who knew what else?

He glanced around, saw the residual scatterings of food, including a bone with bits of meat clinging to it that he could not remember eating. He shuddered and wondered about Hélio.

He looked at his feet, which seemed remarkably normal and gave him no pain, and he had a vague memory of the Indian girl applying a salve to them.

He strained to remember more, but as is the way with dreams, it was vanishing like smoke.

All he could remember was the loving female warmth. He smiled. Dream or not, he couldn't bring himself to regret whatever had happened.

Moments later, the last vestiges of the dream exploded into reality.

Xanqui and two warriors, their faces impassive, stood inside the *tapiri* staring down at him. The chief began an outpouring of angry words, and leaning down, made a vicious slicing motion with one hand, as if cutting off both of Raul's feet. In the chief's other hand was a heavy machete.

The two warriors gestured for Raul to get up and accompany them.

Raul rose slowly. With growing numbness, he left the *tapiri* and marched like a sleepwalker between the two warriors, Xanqui leading the way.

Their destination was an enclosure with low picket walls of poles and palm fronds. Drifting upward from within was the thin smoke of a dying fire—and a terrible smell. It was the stench of blood, burned flesh. Death.

As Raul was pushed through the crude gate, everything escalated into a nightmare.

A naked, hairy-chested white man was staked out on the ground, spread-eagled. Weakly straining against his bonds, he squirmed, gabbling inhuman, crazed sounds. Hordes of black flies were clustered on his legs so thickly that both feet were hidden.

Or where both feet should be.

Raul could see now that both feet had been chopped off. Apparently the charred stumps had been held over a hot fire, which would cauterize the flesh and stop the bleeding—as well as intensify the pain a thousandfold.

A sick haze swam in Raul's head. Poor Hélio . . .

The old chief's querulous voice was now sputtering at him. Pointing contemptuously at the man on the ground and then at Raul, he lifted the heavy machete and strode toward him.

THIRTY

The saffron glow of another sunrise was creeping through the blinds when Eduardo opened his eyes and blinked, looking around sourly at the plain furnishings of Raul's bedroom. His sleep had been harsh and unrestful, as if he were trapped in a kind of overwound exhaustion in which all the little cogs and wheels of his brain seemed to be racing out of control while his body begged for rest. Several times during the night he had awakened and taken a few gulps of brandy from the bottle beside the bed in hopes of knocking himself into deep slumber, but it had only seemed to heighten that odd strumming of his jittery nerves. Now, at dawn, he felt more fatigued than when he had gone to bed.

Meu Deus! He was going crazy for a snort or two of snow! Nothing else could end his torture.

He had left Rio without bringing a single line of cocaine with him, having made the rash decision to prove that he could do without it if he wished. How stupid! On his first night at the plantation the craving had grown so intense that only by drinking heavily was he able to get a few winks of sleep.

Alcohol had been the crutch that had pulled him through the next several days, but each day seemed a little worse. He had grown increasingly jumpy; his nerves skittered like grasshoppers on a hot plate. His head felt stuffed with cotton and much of the time throbbed with a dull ache that aspirin failed to relieve.

Pushing himself to a sitting position against the headboard, he glanced with displeasure at an opened book lying face down on the stand beside the bed. He had found it in Raul's library—it was a botanical treatise on the medical and chemical properties of plants and shrubs. Skimming through it, he had come upon an entry that had touched the very core of all his worst fears.

He picked it up to read again, to see if it were as horrifying by day as it had been by night:

Cocaine (kō-'kān). A colorless or white crystalline narcotic alkaloid extracted from the leaves of South American coca shrubs. Cocaine was first introduced into medicine as a local anesthetic in 1855, and at one time it was recommended as a cure for the morphine habit, with disastrous results, as it actually has a more violent action on the brain than morphine. It is one of the most habit-forming of drugs, and its habitual use often leads to confusional insanity which may bring on convulsions and death. One of its well-known effects is debility of the nervous system, with consequences such as impotence and . . .

Slamming the book shut, he flung it across the room. The book proved nothing. Plainly it was old and outdated. Insanity? What crap! If coke was all that bad, why were all the smart people—including doctors, lawyers, and successful young businessmen—taking it?

As for impotence—it was a word he tried not to think about, yet it had become the most omnipresent fact of his existence. It lived with him night and day like an ugly cancer squeezing the joy out of life. That he was suffering from the humiliating inadequacy—temporarily at least—he could not deny. But who could prove it came from taking coke? Or that it was permanent?

His main reason for leaving Rio without any coke had been in hopes that, after a few days without it, his little love tool would spring back to vigorous life and disprove the old wives' tale Chica had scared him with.

The blond American girl, Peggy, had been ideal for testing his physical responses, for she attracted him enormously, and when he exerted himself to charm her she plainly enjoyed it—but in a humorous way that seemed to draw an invisible line beyond which he was forbidden to cross.

Which was just as well, for despite all the emotions of desire that built up in his head, none of the *fervor o sangue* was reflected in his loins. Could women sense when a man was incapable of lovemaking?

Leaning back against the pillows, he stretched his arms and yawned, and after a moment's hesitation he reached over to the nightstand to pick up the brandy bottle. Two-thirds of it had been killed during the night. Shrugging, he uncapped it and took a long swallow. What the hell, he felt a lot worse without it, and he needed something to numb his conscience sufficiently so that he could do what had to be done today.

He had it roughly planned so that it would not arouse suspicion. The small plant constructed by Matt Riordan was now in production, distilling methanol. Already it was being used as fuel for the bulldozers, the jeep, the pickup trucks, and the generator that supplied all the electrical appliances for the *fazenda*. Raul's idea seemed to be working. It was a shame that it had to end.

Great vats and many barrels of the highly combustible liquid had been filled. It would take nothing more than a misplaced cigarette—a match—and poof! A grand inferno! The explosion might even scatter burning debris to the manor itself, which was dry as a tinderbox.

After that, it would be easy to convince the old man that the whole thing was a bust, and he could return to his beloved Rio. To the fun life. He clung to a childlike faith that somehow everything was going to turn out all right.

Rolling out of bed, he went first to the dresser mirror, as was his custom, to inspect himself. It was not reassuring. His eyes looked sick, bloodshot; his skin had a grayish pallor. The physical beauty that he so much admired was wilting. Even the proud arch of his eyebrows seemed to have sagged, and his thick black hair, disarrayed from tossing and turning during the night, had lost its gloss. It was the terrible heat. *Cristo!* How could Raul stand living here without air conditioning?

A warm shower did little to improve his mood.

Lazily he put on lightweight casuals, leaving his sport shirt hanging outside of his trousers. From the dresser he took the Walther PPK pistol he had brought with him, a blued-steel little beauty less than six inches long, 7.65 short caliber, with a seven-round magazine. For him it served the same purpose as a child's teddy bear. Sometimes he slept with it under his pillow. It gave him an immense sense of security. Once, during a night of self-loathing over his betrayal of Raul, he had held it against his temple with the full intention of pulling the trigger. Then he had laughed bitterly, conceding to himself that he was too cowardly.

Where was poor Raul now? he wondered. Lost somewhere in the jungle? Perhaps dead? Eduardo's eyes blurred. Despite the way he had wronged his brother in the past, and the wrong he would commit today by destruction of the alcohol plant, Eduardo loved his brother deeply and despised his own acts. However, with that facile knack for self-justification that so often accompanies a guilty conscience, Eduardo had been able to persuade himself that Raul would be far better off and happier back in Rio in the old man's business. And as far as Odete was concerned— good riddance.

In any case, to save his own neck he had no choice but to follow de Onis's instructions.

Angrily he snatched up the brandy bottle and downed a couple more slugs. Then, thrusting the pistol under his belt where it was easily concealed by the shirt, he headed for the kitchen and his morning coffee.

After several cups of thick black coffee, he felt primed enough to venture out and face the jungle world.

As he stepped outside, thick waves of humidity, so heavy it felt solid. pressed against him. Even this early, with the torrid sunrise barely burning its way above the treetops, the heat was suffocating. By noon any piece of exposed metal would be too hot to touch. *Meu Deus* how he hated it!

More than hated it. He feared it. The steamy jungle, crowding in from all sides. filled him with nameless dread. The cloying scent of flowers, the odors of the dark soil the rankness of growth, the very fertility of everything unnerved him. He was overwhelmed by a sense of everything multiplying by the trillions, reeking of unbridled sexuality.

He was as out of place here as a sour note in an orchestra.

But it wouldn't be for much longer. He had to make his move today.

Leisurely he strolled toward the alcohol building. A few of the *caboclo* workers near the toolshed were staring raptly at a distant point in the sky. What the hell was so enthralling?

Then his city ears heard what their ears had already heard—the faint chopping roar of two motors—and moments later he could see two specks against the blue. With astonishing speed the roaring sounds crescendoed and the specks grew larger. Two helicopters.

Eduardo's puzzlement grew as the awkward aircraft began to circle over the *fazenda.*

In the lead helicopter Vinicius de Onis chewed on his cigar, thinking hard. The fact of Raul de Carvalho's successful jailbreak had been incredible enough, but the failure thus far of the *polícia* to catch the fugitives was astonishing beyond belief. Even with the best trained hounds to follow their trail! And both fugitives barefoot!

Coronel Luz had been shamefaced and apologetic, blaming it all on the stupidity of his men, who would be punished by extra duty and fines deducted from their pay. The men in turn blamed it on supernatural forces. They muttered about macumba, *umbanda,* candomblé, or other cults dealing with black magic. How else could the prisoners escape from a locked cell? The straw doll with a needle through its head left in the jail office proved it. And the dogs—how could the whole pack go silent all at once and vanish into the air along with the fugitives?

In truth, de Onis was uneasy. Though he tried to convince himself that he was above believing in such cults of the macabre, neither did he disbelieve. He had dropped many a *cruzeiro* in the collection boxes at macumba and candomblé centers, just to keep on the good side of any diabolical forces that might be present.

He had been infuriated by Raul's escape, but on reflection he decided it could save him many headaches—if de Carvalho had really perished in the jungle.

If not, the *bastardo* could be more troublesome than ever.

De Onis couldn't afford the risk of uncertainty. By some miracle, Raul might have survived and made it back to his *fazenda.* Which was one of the reasons for this visit today—with two helicopters carrying a dozen of the *policía.*

The other reason was just as galling. Turning to *Coronel* Luz, who sat beside him, he put it into words.

"Remember, next to de Carvalho, the most important one to nail is that American bitch, Peggy Carpenter. The American papers are beginning to carry her articles about the highway. At all costs she must be silenced!"

*   *   *   *   *

The chattering of Peggy's typewriter was uneven. Sometimes it was steady, more often it was halting, spaced with pauses; at times it erupted into little bursts of extra speed, as if to ram home a point by fury alone, in counterpoint to the state of her mind. Her lips were set in a tight line. Her blue eyes had the gleam of ice. The outrage that had seized her when she returned from her stay with Vivi Vargas—to find that Raul had been arrested for trying to defend poor Hélio—had only increased with each passing day.

Watching her from a nearby desk, Matt Riordan waited for one of the pauses. The two of them were in the small office that Matt had set up in the alcohol plant. Peggy had moved her typewriter in yesterday because of Eduardo, who had been bothering her too frequently with unwanted attentions in her bedroom where she usually worked.

"Still working on the story of Raul's arrest?"

"Oh, no, it's gone far beyond that. I'm roughing out a piece about Brazilian justice as practiced in the provinces, particularly in the jails. I've queried the workers here, and you'd be surprised at how many of them have been jailed at one time or another for trifling matters—usually for crimes no more terrible than being too impoverished to pay for a loaf of bread. You wouldn't believe the stories I've heard! Whippings, torture—oh, I pray nothing like that happened to poor Raul and Hélio."

"Considering the importance of Raul's family, I doubt that they'd dare to be too rough on him. On the other hand, what pushed him to such an extreme act as a jailbreak? He must have known that if he sat tight long enough, his father's influence would get him out."

Peggy made an expression of disgust. "I'll refrain from comment on that. My big worry is whether Raul is still alive."

"He's with Hélio, who's tough as rawhide and knows the jungle. I have great faith that they're both

okay and will be showing up almost any time now."
Then they heard the approaching helicopters.

They were here to conduct a search for the fugitives, *Coronel* Luz told them. In short order the provincial *milícia* police had rounded up all the *fazenda* workers, who were briefly questioned by the *coronel*, and now they were being herded into the toolshed.

Riordan, who with Peggy had been watching in frustrated anger, strode up to Luz, standing beside de Onis. "Why are they being forced into the shed?"

"We wish no trouble with the *caboclos*, who are hot-blooded and might do foolish things. They will be kept locked up until we are finished with our business here." Swinging around, he snapped out more orders. "One of you guard the shed. Six of you search the house and grounds. The rest stay with me."

Eduardo appeared, his steps unsteady and his eyes glazed. "There's no need for this search," he said. "I assure you that my brother is not here."

Luz gave him a contemptuous once-over. "You, the brother of the fugitive, advising me how to conduct the search? I warn you, any interference—"

De Onis nudged the *coronel* sharply. "Don't waste time on him! He's a harmless fool. Get on with the other matter."

Eduardo flushed deeply and started to speak. Luz cut him off by calling harshly to Peggy, who stood in the background scribbling into a secretarial notebook. "Now, *Senhorita* Carpenter, we wish to interrogate you!"

She looked up, smiling demurely. "Fair enough—if I may also interrogate you, as well as *Senhor* de Onis, who appears to be running this sideshow."

"*Senhorita!* You will step forward at once to be interrogated!"

"Oh, no. In this fantastic *macho* world of great muscular men who carry guns and whips, surely I am entitled to a lady's prerogative. You come to me." She made her smile inviting.

Anger darkened the *coronel's* face. He spat out an oath. "*Senhorita,* as an officer of the law, I order you—!"

"I'll handle this," said de Onis. Smiling, he waddled toward Peggy on legs too short for the squat, powerful trunk of his body. He was elegantly attired in white silk trousers and shirt, white shoes with elevator heels, and a white Panama, which he doffed as he made a token bow of his head. "You must forgive the *coronel* for his stern manner, *senhorita*. He does not understand your type."

Peggy's eyebrows arched. "And what type am I?"

"An intelligent young lady—who has chosen a man's profession and is also courageous enough to come to the wildest part of the jungle where many men fear to come. It is most unusual. It is even more surprising to find that such a woman can be so beautiful."

"Thank you for the flattery, *senhor,* but what is your point?"

"I think it is shameful for a young lady with your talents and attractions to waste your time writing about wild Indians and filthy *caboclos* when there are so many more pleasant things to write about in much more comfortable surroundings." De Onis gave her his most charming smile. "I am inviting you, *senhorita,* to be my guest for as long as you like at my own *fazenda,* which is on the Amazon, where I have docking facilities for my yacht. I can offer you the most sumptuous quarters, the finest foods, wines, entertainment—anything you desire."

Peggy sighed. "Frankly, it is tempting. I'd love to see how the superrich live, but I have my job here to do."

"A job is only to make money. I will give you a job writing for me and pay you double—triple—whatever you are getting now, plus all your living expenses. However, I would require that you also sell to me all the articles you are now working on, for which I will pay generously."

"*Senhor,* are you offering me a bribe?"

"Why should I bribe you?"

"You are well aware that I am getting a handle on your involvement with the highway diversion, the arrest of Raul de Carvalho, your control of certain corrupt police officials—"

De Onis laughed. "A word of advice. You are intelligent, but unfortunately afflicted with a common female stupidity—you blab too much. Until now, I wasn't sure of the extent of your prying into my private affairs. Or perhaps you thought it would give you more leverage to raise the ante. I give you one more chance. What is your price?"

"I have no price, *senhor*. I am not a whore."

He smiled thinly. "Perhaps I offered the wrong inducements. Would you prefer to be turned over to *Coronel* Luz and his men, who have ways of guaranteeing cooperation from even the most stubborn?"

"I am aware of their methods, *senhor*, but you forget that I am a citizen of the United States. They would not dare to—"

"And you forget, *senhorita*, that you are no longer under the protection of your great, diseased country. This is Brazil, where women and *pretos* are still taught to keep in their places." He swung angrily toward Luz.

"She's all yours, *coronel*."

A cruel smile played over Luz's heavy lips as he stood in front of Peggy and held up what appeared to be a thin, crudely rolled cigarette for her inspection. "I'm sure you recognize this, *senhorita*?"

"Why should I?"

"It was found in your luggage, which was identified by your initials and letters. It is what you call a 'joint'—marijuana—which is illegal in Brazil."

Peggy looked at him with contempt. "Must you go through this charade? I realize it's pointless, but for the record, I'm not into marijuana or any other drug. Your alleged discovery of a joint in my luggage is nothing but a ridiculous trumped-up trick."

"Then you deny possession of marijuana?"

"Absolutely."

The *coronel's* smile broadened. "In that case we have no choice but to search for evidence that even you cannot deny." Turning to two of the grim-faced *policia* standing near, he jabbed a finger toward Peggy. "Strip her!"

There was a rushing movement, and Riordan appeared beside her, both fists clenched. "Over my dead body!" he shouted.

The two uniformed men converged toward him smoothly, warily. Both wore savage grins.

"Please, Matt!" cried Peggy. "Get back! Don't be a fool!"

The *policia* rushed. One neatly sidestepped Riordan's swinging fist; the other brought a knee up under his groin. As Riordan buckled in pain, a fist smashed into the pit of his stomach. Then both officers were efficiently pounding at his head. Riordan collapsed to the ground and lay still.

"Rotten beasts!" Peggy shrieked, flailing and tearing at the assailants with clawed fingers. They swung toward her. One caught her by an arm and twisted it with such savagery that she screamed. The other caught her blouse, ripping it down the middle. He snatched at the waistband of her denims and yanked them down.

Eduardo, his pallid face showing shock and consternation, stumbled toward them. "*Pelo amor de Deus!* For the love of God, show a little decency—"

De Onis chortled. "Are you shocked by the sight of a naked woman, my friend? You have but to close your eyes or turn your head."

Peggy gave in. Knowing it would only incite them to more brutality if she resisted, she bowed her head and numbly submitted to her undressing.

One man had kneeled in front of her, and thrusting a hand under her panties let it circle around to squeeze at the round curves of her rump; giggling passionately, he brought the hand around to send probing fingers up between her legs. "Nothing here," he moaned. "Only the hidden treasure." Saliva beaded his lips.

Oh, dear God, she thought; just let me have a gun, anything lethal . . .

The other one, whose goggling eyes shone with a demonic quality as his fingers prowled hurtfully under her bra, let out an exultant cry. "Hah—I have found it!" He withdrew a hand and held up a small glassine envelope. "A packet of seeds—I recognize! Marijuana!"

They are so unimaginative, she thought with sick fury. They could just as well have found a terrorist bomb up my rectum, if it so tickled their fancy. Both men, she noted, had bulging hard-ons.

Coronel Luz directed a smug smile of self-satisfaction at her. "It was just as I expected."

Peggy glared. "How could it be otherwise, since you directed the whole script?"

"Have you nothing more to say in your defense?"

"If you lent me that big pistol of yours for about a minute, I'd give you an answer you'd remember until the moment you dropped dead."

"Ah, the *senhorita* has spirit! You are angry, yes? I cannot blame you, but after I take you back to my jail, I will teach you to smile for me." His gaze ran over her nudity. "And if you show me the proper appreciation, I will treat you well. You will enjoy it."

"Here's my comment on that—" And stepping forward, she spat in his face.

Luz backed away, furious. "*Diabo!* Tie her to a tree and get out the whip!"

"No!" De Onis walked up, frowning. "There is no time for that now. Lock the Americans in one of the buildings and come with me. I have an important errand to do at the next plantation."

"But *Senhor* de Onis, I think I should stay here to make sure the prisoners do not escape."

De Onis gave him a sneering grin. "You are *excitado* by the girl, *sim?*" His gaze slashed at the *coronel*'s crotch. "It is too bad for you, but you must wait. You will have your chance when we come back—after I have had her first. Now go to the helicopter and wait for me. I must have a word with de Carvalho."

Tremulous with icy chills, Eduardo, watched the bulldoggish figure of de Onis waddling toward him. He had witnessed the appalling spectacle of Riordan beaten to the ground and the humiliation of Peggy. Riordan had been dragged into the alcohol building and Peggy, unresisting, shoved in after him. What was the next outrage going to be?

De Onis's harsh voice rasped, "What have you done about carrying out my instructions?"

"I had planned it for today. Uh—it was my intention to set fire to the alcohol building. It has many containers of alcohol inside which would explode into a conflagration. But now—"

"*Perfeito!* Such a magnificent fire would destroy all the machinery, everything—" He winked. "Even anyone so unlucky as to be inside at the time. It is working out even better than I had hoped."

"Certainly you don't mean the two Americans!"

De Onis shrugged. "We all have to go sometime. There could be no proof that it was not an unfortunate accident, so have no fear."

"I will have nothing to do with murder, *senhor*." Eduardo's voice was shaky. "I would rather die first."

De Onis let his jaw drop in mock astonishment. "You would prefer to join them? You think it would end all your troubles? *Ridículo!* Burning yourself to a crisp would not send you to heaven. If you were so foolish to try the easy way out, I assure you that those pictures of you screwing your brother's fiancée would get in the hands of both your parents, and forever after your memory would be held in loathing and disgrace. It could kill your mother. Even you would not want to do that to your parents."

Cold sweat popped out on Eduardo's forehead. He

felt it dribbling down his torso. The cool weight of the little gun under his belt felt sticky against his sweating skin.

If only I had the guts, he thought wildly, and knew that he did not.

"For the love of God, *senhor*," he pleaded. "I have agreed to carry out your instructions—everything but murder! What are you trying to do to me?"

De Onis laughed softly. "Relax. I like you, Eduardo. You are the kind I can take in one hand, like this—" He thrust out a hand, palm upward, and slowly began tightening it into a fist. "And squeeze, squeeze, until your bones scrunch and you squeal for mercy. But you are more important to me alive, as I have many uses for your kind, so stop worrying."

Luz approached. "The *piloto* is waiting, *senhor*."

"*Um momento.*" De Onis turned back to Eduardo. "I have to leave now, as I have a little business deal to negotiate with your neighbor, Dom João Abrais Vargas. We'll be back in a couple of hours. In the meantime, to relieve your tender sensibilities, forget about the fire. We'll take care of that when we return. I wouldn't want to miss the pleasure of watching the inferno."

THIRTY-ONE

Maniacal rage distorted the wrinkled visage of Xanqui as he slowly approached Raul. With one hand he gripped the heavy machete; with the other he jabbed a finger at the moaning white man with charred stumps at the ends of his legs. Wrathful words poured from the old chief's mouth.

Eyes blazing like black fire, the Indian paused in front of Raul and raised the machete. Thrust it at him.

Handle first.

In that instant, Raul understood. Xanqui's expression had suddenly transformed to one of pleading. His fury was only for the naked man staked out on the ground. The chief was offering the machete as a gift. He wanted Raul to have the privilege of killing the prisoner.

Numbly, Raul took the machete. Kill poor Hélio? Was this a hallucinatory nightmare resulting from the drugs they had given him? He walked toward the victim. Then he stopped as a thrill of relief raced up his spine.

The man was not Hélio. He was weasel-faced, and too scrawny. His half-closed eyes flared open as he saw Raul.

"*Deus Todo Ponderoso!* God Almighty! A white man! *Acuda! Socorro!* Help me, or I will die."

"Who are you?"

The man let his head roll sideways, as if not hearing, his face tightened in agony. Xanqui stepped close and kicked at the charred stump of one leg. The prisoner screamed and began babbling again.

"...name's Lobos—help me—help me get outta this hellhole! I'll pay—anything!"

Xanqui had picked up a stick, and pointing it like a rifle at some of the Indians peering in from over the low fence, he said, "Boom, boom, boom, boom!"

A glimmering of understanding came to Raul as he recalled the incident of a roadworker who had shot and killed several of the Indians who had been peacefully visiting the camp during a religious ceremony. The violent act had provoked the Indians to retaliate with arrows, killing a priest and other whites. It was largely over that incident that the highway had been diverted.

"All right, Lobos, you'd better start talking. You killed those Indians! Who paid you to do it?"

"I'll make a deal. Get me outta here—promise immunity, and I—I'll talk ..."

"I can't promise you anything except that I'll do everything possible to keep you alive and get you to a doctor if you tell me everything. Otherwise you'll have to face Indian justice."

Lobos squeezed his eyes shut. His moaning changed to blubbering sobs. Tears streamed down his cheeks. "I—I got nothing against the Indians. It was de Onis hired me to make trouble. He's in back of it all—"

A new voice startled Raul from behind: 'Graças a Deus! Thank God I got here in time!"

Raul whirled. "Carlos! How did you know—?" The FUNAI agent's face was flushed, and he was breathing hard, as if from running.

"Xanqui sent for me. My Indian guide told me the tribe had three white captives, and for a while I was afraid that—that the chief might mistake you for one of their enemies." His gaze swept to Lobos. "But I see they have the right one. I heard what Lobos just said—"

"Then you realize how important it is that we keep him alive and get him back to the authorities to make a confession. Apparently you can speak enough of the Indian dialect to make yourself understood. Will you please tell the chief that this man must be brought back to face the white man's justice."

"I'll do my best, *Senhor* de Carvalho."

"And please find out what happened to my friend—"

A familiar voice called out, "I am here, *ó patrão!*"

Raul turned and saw Hélio standing just outside the fence, his arms around two older Indian women, one on either side of him.

"I was worried about you, Hélio."

"Ah, nothing to worry about." Hélio sighed. "I have discovered that in the dark, even these old *bruxas* aren't too bad."

In his study, Dom João looked across the polished top of his massive baroque desk at his two visitors and tried to subdue his sense of unease. His reaction was silly, he knew, for the name de Onis was well known. It had been many years since such a distinguished person had visited him, and it was flattering. But why was de Onis accompanied by an officer? It was important business that had brought him, de Onis had said, something he wished to discuss in private, with only *Coronel* Luz present.

All three were seated comfortably. Cigars had been lighted. Brandy had been offered and declined.

"I am honored by your visit, *senhor*," Dom João said graciously. "What is the nature of the business you wish to discuss?"

De Onis exhaled a cloud of blue cigar smoke. "I want to buy your plantation."

Dom João smiled. "I am sorry, but I have no desire to sell."

"Perhaps I can change your mind."

"Nothing can change my mind—not at any price. My ancestors, who were the first pioneers in this part of the jungle, built this *fazenda* nearly a century ago. I was born here, and I intend to die here."

De Onis examined the tip of his cigar. "I don't wish

to embarrass you, but I have information that your *fazenda* is heavily mortgaged, and your debts are piling up."

"A man's finances and his debts are personal matters, *senhor*," Dom João said stiffly, "and I have taken the proper steps to remedy the situation."

"By borrowing? I am aware that you have made application to the Banco da Amazonia to extend your mortgage and advance you more money."

Dom João flushed. "*Senhor*, you have no right prying into my private affairs!"

"I have every right. You see, I have purchased your mortgage. The bank has washed their hands of it. From now on, you deal directly with me."

A cold, numbing sensation stabbed through Dom João. His whole world had hinged on the large bank loan he was expecting. It couldn't be true that it was being denied!

"*Impossível!*" he said. "It would be improper. The bank has committed itself. I was promised the money as soon as the paper work is completed."

"It is perfectly legal and proper. You must realize that at the time you made your application, it was not known by the bank that the highway would be diverted. Now that the highway will never touch your land, their agreement is invalidated. They are in business to make money, not to throw good money after bad."

The coldness in Dom João seemed to be shrinking him inwardly. "The highway is not everything," he said weakly, as if to himself. "My ancestors and I myself have lived here for many years without it."

De Onis shrugged. "Times have changed. Some win, some lose. Be that as it may, payments on your mortgage are long overdue, and I am empowered to demand payment for the entire balance of the debt you owe. If you do not pay, I can foreclose."

Dom João made a groaning sound. "No—never."

"You have no choice, my friend. However, foreclosure can be time-consuming, and since I am a charitable man, I am willing, out of sympathy for you and your lovely daughter, to pay you a good sum to handle it more quickly and without embarrassment to you. If I foreclose, you lose everything. If you sell to me immediately, it could be handled in a few days. I would give you a fair price, considering that the property is of little value without the highway and that you'd lose it anyway. I would pay enough so that you and your daughter could take an apartment in the city where, with her beauty, she could find a rich husband who could support both of you."

"*Senhor!* You are insulting! The law allows me time to raise money to pay off the mortgage. I have friends. I have never gone to them before, out of pride, but in a situation of this urgency—"

"If that is your decision, there is another matter I must bring up that might change your mind—"

"Nothing will change my mind. Further discussion would be wasted."

"I'm sure you will want to hear this. I refer to something of interest in your family history—a dark secret, so to speak—that is not generally known. I doubt that even your daughter knows of it."

Dom João sat as if frozen. "Explain yourself, *se-nhor.*"

"Bluntly, I have discovered that the illustrious Dom João Abrais Vargas is the great-great-grandson of a Negro slave woman. If your friends were to learn that you and your daughter are actually part *preto*—"

All the blood drained from Dom João's face. This final blow had slammed into him like a sledgehammer. For all these many years he had tried so hard to hide it from the world, from Vivi . . .

"Your beautiful daughter," de Onis continued, "while still desirable for a certain profession, would no longer be in a position to make an advantageous marriage—"

The study door burst open and Vivi rushed in, her face flushed, her eyes wild. "I heard!" she cried. "When I happened to pass and heard my father's voice raised in anger, I stopped to listen—"

De Onis laughed. "The little dove has big ears."

She whirled toward him. "I know about you, too. It is no wonder they call you the skunk!"

Dom João had risen to his feet. "Vivi—leave at once."

"Father—" Her voice was soft and pleading. "Please don't be upset. It matters not a bit to me if we have black blood, and it wouldn't matter to any true friends—"

"Go—go!" her father roared at her. "None of this is for you to hear!"

"But, father—"

"Out!"

Head bowed, she left meekly, shutting the door behind her.

De Onis spoke gently. "You still have a chance to accept my offer."

Dom João rose heavily, as if hoisting a great weight, and walked over to a wall where he kept a large bullwhip that his ancestors had used to whip slaves. Slowly, gravely, he took it down and turned to face de Onis.

"You contaminate my home," he said calmly. "Get out."

Hopping from his chair, de Onis backed away nervously. *"Está louco!* You are mad!"

Luz stood up too, reaching for his holstered gun. The whip cracked, and Luz yelped as the whip's end curled around his wrist.

"Diabo!" he yowled. "For that I'll—"

"Leave the madman alone," de Onis ordered. "Just serve the papers."

Scowling sourly, the *coronel* took a sealed envelope from an inner pocket and tossed it on the desk.

"That is the legal notice of foreclosure, Vargas," de Onis said coldly. "On the very minute that the time limit is up, if you have not paid the entire balance of the mortgage, with interest, the *polícia* will be here to evict you."

Keeping wary eyes on the whip, the financier and Luz backed to the door and went out.

Dom João returned to his desk and slumped tiredly in his chair. A few moments later, Vivi appeared in the doorway.

"Father, are you all right?"

"Everything's going to be all right, Vivi. Just leave me alone for a while."

She closed the door quietly, and he sat there for a long time brooding over the insurmountable problems that faced him. Vainly he raked his brain for possible solutions, all of them born of desperation, but he could think of nothing workable.

Only a few stark facts stood out clearly:

For him it was all over. His whole reason for being was gone. Even for Vivi, he was no longer of any use. She loved him, yes, but he had lost the all-powerful father image in her eyes. She could do better without him. She was young, beautiful, intelligent. A quick forced sale of the property would easily bring in enough to pay off the mortgage, with enough left over for Vivi to go out into the world unencumbered by an aging dependent and start a new life. She would be free . . .

Opening a lower desk drawer, he reached in and withdrew the Luger he always kept there. The cool feel of the heavy steel was oddly comforting.

Releasing the safety latch, he raised the weapon to his temple and held it there hesitantly.

If you do this, he told himself, it will be too late for another chance.

He answered himself at once: It is already too late. And he pulled the trigger.

THIRTY-TWO

Matt Riordan opened his eyes to a blurred world. His head throbbed, his belly churned, his face felt swollen, and various parts of his anatomy ached from the beating he had received. Through hazed vision he saw Peggy's face.

"Thank God you're conscious, Matt. How do you feel?"

"Rotten. Worse than all the hangovers I've ever had rolled into one. I could use a drink."

"Sorry, I can't accommodate you. I couldn't even find any water in here to bathe your face."

Bathe his face? He felt a childish surge of gratitude. No female other than his mother had ever done that for him.

"I was referring to booze. There's a bottle hidden in the lower left drawer of my desk."

Peggy rose from her kneeling position, and he became aware that he was lying on the little cot in his office in the alcohol plant, where sometimes he slept after working late into the night. He was even more aware that Peggy was wearing only bra and panties. What in hell had happened since he'd conked out?

She called from the desk. "The bottle appears to be empty, Matt."

"There's an unopened one hidden behind the file folders."

In a few moments she was back with a full bottle of brandy. "You have good foresight, Matt."

"With Eduardo out to consume Raul's entire liquor supply, I thought I'd better squirrel away an extra bottle." Breaking the seal, he offered the bottle to her. She declined. He tilted the bottle and took a long swallow.

"Did you also squirrel away a gun?" she asked.

"I'm not bloodthirsty. Why do you ask?"

"The guards out there have been leering at me through the window with dirty smiles, calling out remarks that I have to suspect are equally dirty, so I guess it's just as well I don't know enough of the language to understand."

"I don't think one gun would be of much use against the whole pack of them, Peggy." Sitting up, he stripped off his shirt and handed it to her. "Put this on. It might cool their interest just a bit, though I doubt it."

As she was putting it on, protesting words came through the window screen, against which were pressed the faces of the two guards.

"*Diabo!* She is covering with a shirt! I was hoping to see her in *pura nudez.*"

"Ah! *Que pena!* But it hangs like a very short dress that excites me to get my hungry cock under."

The crude ribaldry continued. Though they spoke in Brazilian Portuguese, Riordan understood most of the words, having briefly studied the language before coming to Brazil and absorbing a lot since.

"Matt, are they saying what I think they're saying?"

"It's about the kind of smut you'd expect from such pigs." His head jerked sharply toward the window at something one of the guards was saying:

" . . . could go in there now and screw her, but the *coronel* would kill us if we got her first."

"With *cachaça* to drink, I would be brave enough."

"Juca promised to bring us booze from the *fazenda.* He should be here soon."

"*Bôbo!* Juca is quick to forget his friends when he drinks. He is so greedy he will drink it all."

One of the guards turned his head away and gave an exultant cry. "Maybe you are wrong! All of them are coming from the *fazenda.* Juca too. But some of them are staggering."

Matt quickly rose up from the cot. Blood pounded in his ears, and haze swam before his eyes. He waited until his head cleared, and hiding the brandy bottle from view, he crossed over to his desk. Kneeling behind it, he got out the empty bottle that was there and poured it about half full from the one he had, spilling quite a bit in his haste. Next he took one of the jugs from a shelf where he kept samples of each new batch of methanol.

The jug gurgled as he poured the liquid into one of the brandy bottles until it was full. He filled the other bottle only about three-quarters full.

"Matt, what in the world are you doing?"

"I'll explain in a minute, Peggy." Placing the full bottle on top of the desk and concealing the other one close to his side, he went back to where Peggy was seated on the cot.

"Now listen carefully. I am very much afraid that we will soon have a bunch of drunks to contend with. For animals of that kind, booze and sex go together—"

"What you're saying, of course, is that there's a probability that I might be raped by all of those . . ."

"More than a probability. More like a certainty. Unless—"

"Unless what?"

Voices from the window prevented his answer. Chortling, giggling, alcohol-slurred voices had joined in the obscenities.

"Ah, for me I bet she would spread her legs!"

"*Está louco.* It is me she would prefer when she sees my big cock."

"The *coronel* would cut off your balls."

"He would not have to know. He and de Onis, those big pricks, plan to screw the girl only for themselves and then set fire to the building with the *americanos* inside. I overheard him saying that. We will not have a chance with her unless we take it now."

Matt brought the brandy bottle into full view, quietly saying, "Peggy, this bottle is heavily laced with methanol. It is our only weapon. I am going to pretend to drink by blocking it off with my tongue.

346

They're sure to take it away from me, and if they drink too much of it—"

"It could be murder, Matt!"

Matt's expression was savage. "Whose murders are you most concerned with—theirs or ours?" And tilting his head back, he raised the bottle to his lips.

Reactions from the window were immediate:

"*Veja só!* The *americano* has *bebida*—liquor!"

"*Maldito!* And we have not a drop!"

"*Diabo!* We must get it before he drinks it all. Hurry!"

The door burst open and the *policia* streamed in, snatched the bottle from Riordan's grasp, and rudely shoved him aside. The man who had grabbed the bottle lifted it to his lips.

"*Um pouco, um pouco!* Drink just a little!" warned one. "It belongs to all of us—it must go around so each gets a drink."

"But first give some to the girl. Then she will be better to us."

The bottle was roughly thrust at Peggy. Grinning faces watched while she lifted it to her mouth. She held it there for several seconds, then took it away and bent forward, coughing, gagging. Riordan went numb. Had she swallowed any accidentally? Or purposely, to escape what she feared was in store for her? Or was it just an act?

God forgive me if I've made a mistake, he thought.

Guffawing at her discomfort, one of them took the bottle and hoisted it to his mouth, taking two swallows. He made an expression of disgust and handed it to the next man. "*Arrrhhh!* The taste is *terrível*, but it is strong."

"It is not the taste, but the strength that matters." The second man raised the bottle. It gurgled. "The strongest *cachaça* I have ever tasted," he pronounced, handing the bottle to another.

In similar fashion the bottle passed from man to man.

Tensed, Riordan waited, wondering what would

happen next. He could only guess at how much of the methanol-laced brandy it would take to incapacitate them, or how much would make a lethal dose. In its pure form, between one and two ounces were usually fatal. Lesser amounts produced symptoms ranging from excitement, dizziness, vomiting, and headaches to delirium, blindness, and coma. His hope was that, diluted by the brandy, a couple of swallows would only make them violently sick, or unconscious. They would recover—unless they guzzled it like pigs.

With startling speed, the first effect—excitement—was becoming evident. Voices were louder, raucous laughter increased. One man broke into a bawdy song; another began hopping about in a crazy dance while unzipping his fly. "The blond female—I am ready for her!"

"*Não!* I am to be the first!" The speaker lurched toward her drunkenly.

Peggy cowered, but made no resistance when he caught at the shirt and yanked. There was a ripping sound.

"All of it—everything off!" someone howled. "I want her naked!"

Willing hands helped rip off her bra and panties. The first man had his pants lowered and wobbled toward her, one hand supporting his swollen organ.

"*Vamos para a frente!* Go it, man!"

"*Ande, ande,* on her!"

Now Peggy was battling; turning, twisting, kicking, clawing. Two men trapped her arms; two others caught at her legs, spreading them, pinioning her to the cot. The one with his trousers down lowered himself heavily on bent knees. The cot sagged.

In a sickish fog of horror and fury, Riordan had been struggling to break through the circle of men crowded around the cot. His head was woozy, his flailing fists weak. Almost contemptuously, the drunken men pushed him back, swinging careless blows to knock him out of the way. Off to one side a man was shaking the empty bottle and complaining that he had been cheated out of his share of the *cachaça*.

Another one swung toward Riordan, reaching for his holstered pistol. "This *americano bôbo* is too much the pest! I fix him for good—"

Riordan backed into the corner of the office as the man lurched toward him, raising the pistol. "But I have more *cachaça* for you," Riordan said, twisting around, grasping the brandy bottle, and flourishing it aloft. "See?" he shouted at the top of his lungs. "A full bottle of *cachaça!*"

His shout attracted the attention of others. Several men, their expressions elated, yammered senselessly as they staggered toward him, but the one with the pistol had already grabbed the bottle. Seeming to forget Riordan, he was clumsily trying to return his gun to its holster, and not able to get it in, he let it drop to the floor in his haste to drink from the bottle.

One of those headed for the bottle came to a wavering halt. "I am dizzy—very dizzy . . ." He slumped to his knees, his head and eyes rolling about stupidly.

Another suddenly bent over, the contents of his stomach gushing out in a foamy yellowish stream.

Next, a piercing cry of pain and agonized words: "My head—my belly—I am dying!"

The group around the cot had broken up. The man with his pants hanging loose clambered off the bed. He stood weaving, holding hands over his eyes. "What has happened?" he howled. "There is no light —I cannot see!" His penis had wilted.

Most of them were staggering about like grotesque puppets whose strings had broken. Cries of fright and pain filled the room; the air was putrid with the stench of vomit.

All around they were falling.

Except for one. He had staggered against a wall for support. His face was that of a crazed man facing hell's fire.

"It is he!" he screamed, pointing at Riordan. "He has poisoned us!"

His hand struggled with his gun, got it out. The gun whocked. A fiery sword stabbed at Riordan.

Then he, too, was falling . . .

THIRTY-THREE

Hands clasped behind him, Dr. Valentim Alves scowled at the vista of waterlogged terrain ahead. Great *acarembás*, cypresses, and other swampland trees towered like an army of giants on the splayed feet of their tangled root systems. A crew of about a dozen men, hip-deep in muck and water, were hard at work with chain saws, axes, and dynamite, determined to fell the monsters. It was rough going; the conditions were vile. This was the *várzea*, a wide stretch of land regularly covered by floodwaters, land so treacherous that without enormous amounts of gravel fill to stabilize it, the most powerful bulldozers were mired down.

Alves sighed and swiveled his blazing dark eyes back at the conglomeration of crawler tractors, vibratory rollers, bottom dump wagons, and other heavy equipment—all part of the advance army that was to ram a wide, smooth road through what long had been considered impassable jungle.

Beside him, Jaime Blasco, the superintendent for this leg of the highway, spoke bitterly.

"As you can see, Dr. Alves, much of our equipment stands idle because we can't use it on this ground until we bring in endless loads of fill that must be trucked from a long distance. And even when we get a roadbed established, it will be subject to considerable erosion from the flood periods. It is going to require expensive maintenance."

Dr. Valentim Alves listened patiently, but in silence. He had no answers. He was an energetic young man with enormous shoulders and a handshake like that of a professional wrestler. His dark hair jutted up in profuse disorder; his eyes shone with a zest for living.

Despite his youth, he was an important person, a special interventor from the lofty Ministry of Justice, dispatched by the minister himself. His errand was to get to the bottom of the trouble at the roadhead.

"There is no engineering rationale for this ridiculous change in route," continued Blasco. "It's insane!"

"*A Deus nada é impossível*," said Alves. "There is nothing impossible to God." With a wry grin he added, "Or to the gods back in Brasília. When they want something done, they have but to command."

"Are they all so *estúpido* that they could not read my report? Or so corrupt that they ignore it?"

"They're not stupid, Blasco. By and large they're typical career bureaucrats and lawmakers who, like trees in the wind, survive by bending to the strongest pressures. A few may be corrupt, and if so, we hope to find them and weed them out."

Idly he swatted at the *borrachudos* buzzing near his face despite the insect repellent he had doused himself with. He shifted his weight uncomfortably. In this hot and humid atmosphere, his feet, encased within rubber hip boots donned for today's inspection, were damp and itchy with sweat. What a dreadful place to live and work!

He didn't like this assignment. Normally any such controversy would have been shuttled back and forth among the lesser bureaucrats until some solution, satisfactory to no one, would be decreed. But when the minister himself, Armando de Salles Salgado, expressed his personal interest, it became an issue of primary importance.

Alves had been at the roadhead for two days, querying the engineers and workers, tape-recording their responses. He had visited the FUNAI camp, grilling them about the Indians. Later, he would visit the plantation owners whose land was close to the projected roadway.

"They cite Indian trouble as a major reason for the road change," Blasco went on. "But there is no Indian trouble—only misunderstanding. FUNAI had them pacified until they were stirred up by troublemakers. We all know who is behind it. Why can't something be done?"

"Because of one simple word—proof. Without solid evidence of bribery and wrongdoing, there's not a thing we can do."

Alves had heard enough and knew enough about de Onis to be utterly convinced of the criminal chicanery involved. It was outrageous, but what could he do? Was Brazil becoming as corrupt as the sick United States, where half or more of the country was in the grip of the powerful Mafioso crime lords who could not be touched by the law?

Trained as an attorney, Alves knew the futility of pressing a case without indisputable documentary proof. Galling as it was, it was a necessary part of democratic justice.

"Proof!" Blasco spat out. "It is only a word to shield the rich. For the poor, no proof is needed to send them to jail—only a rich man's word."

"*Chefe!*" The muscular black foreman came trotting up. "Come quick!"

"What's up, Tomaz?"

"The Indians are coming out of the woods with Carlos and three other whites. One of them, who is being carried on a stretcher, looks like Lobos."

The gleaming silver government plane, emblazoned on the side with colors of the Brazilian flag, sped like an arrow through fluffy white stratocumulus clouds high above the green forest.

"My plantation is just ahead," Raul told the pilot. "You can see the landing strip from here."

"*Sim, senhor.* I'll put you down there in a few moments." The plane swooped lower.

Raul turned to Alves, who was seated near. "And thank you for the lift home, doctor."

"*De nada,* my friend. You are the one to be thanked. You have made my mission a success. I have all the evidence I need to nail de Onis."

In nearly incoherent words, Lobos had told them everything, and Alves had tape-recorded his confession. Now Lobos was being taken back to Brasilia for medical care, to be held as a valuable witness who had done many other jobs for de Onis, through his agent, Barbosa.

The plane landed smoothly. Raul and Hélio disembarked, waved their good-byes, and started walking toward the *fazenda*. Both were wearing shoes and rough clothing lent to them by the roadworkers, but their bearded faces still showed the ravages of their ordeal.

Hélio caught at Raul's arm, holding him back. "Look—a helicopter near the *fazenda*. It could be the *polícia*."

Raul's suppressed anger boiled up. "We have nothing to fear, Hélio. We're no longer fugitives, and we have a score to settle."

A sudden racketing sound drew their attention toward the green canopy of jungle, over which another helicopter had appeared.

"They are coming to land," said Hélio. "Perhaps more *polícia*. What will we do now?"

"We'll continue on to the house and find out what's going on."

Nearing the house, both stopped in astonishment at the spectacle ahead. Uniformed men, a half dozen or more, were lying on the ground, some crawling or rolling around. Moaning, groaning, hoarsely calling for help.

"*Nossa Senhora!*" exclaimed Hélio. "What has happened?"

"They're acting very drunk, only worse—" The truth suddenly hit Raul. "Good God, they must have been sampling the wood alcohol!"

As they started toward the stricken men, a powerful downdraft laden with dust particles blasted at them from behind. The helicopter was landing.

At the same time, a familiar voice was hailing them from the doorway of the manor. Raul turned.

Eduardo! What in the world was his brother doing here? Eduardo propelled himself from the doorway and approached at a staggering run.

"Raul!" he shouted. "Watch out—look behind you!"

Raul swung around in time to see de Onis and *Coronel* Luz getting out of the helicopter. Both wore dumbfounded expressions, glancing from the incapacitated *polícia* to Raul and Hélio.

"It's the fugitives!" howled de Onis. "Get de Carvalho before he escapes again! Shoot to kill!"

A gun appeared in the *coronel's* hand, followed by the *whock* of a .38-caliber bullet.

Something heavy slammed into Raul, and at the same instant Eduardo let out a sharp cry of pain. He had tackled Raul to get him out of the line of fire, and both were falling. Eduardo rolled about on the ground, fumbling under his shirt, which was rapidly staining with a blossoming splotch of crimson. His hand jerked into view gripping a small pistol, and twisting toward Luz and de Onis he started shooting.

Luz screamed. He stood wobbling a few moments, with de Onis trying to hide behind him, then fell, still clutching his gun.

Eduardo's pistol was clicking on an empty chamber. He let it fall from a lax hand and tried to speak through the blood that was frothing from his mouth. "I—I'm sorry, Raul. I—" His mouth remained open, the rest of his words unspoken.

He lay still.

"Eduardo—Eduardo!"

Raul's eyes blurred as he knelt and embraced his dead brother.

An enraged Hélio, who had left Raul with Eduardo while he plunged toward his most hated enemy, was distracted by the toolshed door bursting open. The *caboclos,* aroused by the shooting, had used their collective strength to smash the door off its hinges. They flowed out, led by Braz, who was holding his whip.

Hélio rushed up to the grizzled *vaqueiro*. "Braz—lend me your whip, and tell your men to keep that *bastardo* from getting on the helicopter, but not to hurt him. He belongs to me. I have suffered the most."

Braz handed him the whip, and Hélio started after de Onis, who had turned and started running blindly toward the woods.

Hélio ran behind him. Hélio could easily have overtaken the short-legged financier, but he urged him on with frequent crackings of the whip. Hélio was an expert at using it, having grown up as a *vaqueiro* herding balky cattle in the grazing country of the *sertão*. When de Onis lagged, the flicking tip of the whip against his buttocks produced a yelp of pain and increased his speed. If he veered in the wrong direction, a warning crack of the whip on the appropriate side brought him back on the course Hélio desired. Soon de Onis was puffing and sweating.

"P—put down the whip," he called hoarsely over his shoulder, "so we can talk—"

"No talk; no talk! Keep running!"

"Look, my friend—I—I'll pay—much money if—if you—"

The whip lashed viciously across his back, tearing away some of his shirt. De Onis yowled. "A million *cruzeiros* I'll give you!"

"Would that pay me for the years of my life slaving on your plantation, forcing me all the time deeper into debt? For all the whippings? The torture? For all those you have ruined and killed?"

"Two million I'll give—"

The whip came with more fury. De Onis screamed, spurting ahead faster.

"Have—have you—gone crazy, Hélio? W-where are you driving me?"

"You'll find out."

De Onis was beginning to wobble, and after a while he stumbled and fell forward. He rolled around, facing Hélio, gasping for breath. "I—I—can't—run any farther—"

"Then walk!"

"Can't—even—walk."

"Then crawl, you *bastardo!*" The whip started lashing at his torso again and again, ripping away the rest of his shirt. Red welts oozing with blood appeared across his chest and his fat little belly. "Get moving before I tear all the flesh from your bones!"

De Onis began crawling, guided by the relentless whip and Hélio's commands. Now and then he would clamber up and run a few stumbling steps to escape the flicking whip, then fall again.

"I—will give you—half my fortune, if you—"

"Not for all your fortune."

"For the—love of God—have mercy on me, Hélio!"

"What mercy have you ever shown?"

Still crawling, de Onis turned his sweating face toward his tormentor. "If—if you spare me, I will change my life. I—will be different—become a—good man."

"Your word is worthless as *borrachudo* shit."

"As God—is my witness, I—I tell the truth."

"If you speak the truth, then I will leave it to God to show mercy. You can stop now."

With an astonished expression, de Onis turned, still on his knees. "I knew that—as a man who has reverence for God, you—you would show pity."

"The same pity that God will show you." The whip came curling, whistling through the air. With a cry of fright, de Onis cowered, shielding his face with his arm.

But the whip wasn't for him. It streaked out overhead, lashing through the conical beehive suspended from a branch above.

Letting the whip fall away, Hélio dropped to his knees and assumed a position of prayer. Almost at once the little black cloud of angrily buzzing insects came swirling down.

Zzzzzzzzzeeeeeeeeuuuuuuuuuuuuuuuummmmmmmmm-mmm. A few whirled around his head, and several crawled up his arm. Even when one crawled across his face, Hélio remained as unmoving as a statue.

But de Onis let out a scream, his hoarse voice soon escalating into a series of screams as he rolled about, flailing his arms, slapping at the insects crawling over his body. Leaping to his feet, he began running with surprising vigor, still screaming, enveloped by the whirlwind of darting shadows furiously eager to deposit their fiery stings.

Hélio remained in his position of prayer, hearing the retreating sounds of agony that came as God meted out His punishment. Hélio had received not a single sting.

THIRTY-FOUR

It was three days later. Raul had flown with his brother's body to the family home at Granja do Sol. The funeral had been set for yesterday, and Raul was due back at the rubber plantation today.

Dr. Valentim Alves had arrived with federal police, who had removed the several dead and critically ill provincial police. Depositions were taken from all witnesses, and as a result, additional criminal charges were lodged against the missing Vinicius de Onis. The business tycoon had last been seen fleeing into the jungle, but an intensive search failed to turn up a trace of him. It was speculated that he may have been lost in one of the swamp areas and perhaps devoured by crocodiles. Alves, meanwhile, had accumulated enough solid evidence of bribery among cohorts of de Onis and certain bureaucratic officials to place them all under criminal indictment.

In her room at the plantation, Peggy was packing. Dejectedly, Matt Riordan watched her, his tall, lank frame leaning in the doorway. His wound had been relatively minor, the bullet having passed cleanly through a shoulder without hitting bone or arteries. Infection had been prevented by Peggy's prompt action of cleansing it with methanol and bandaging it tightly with strips torn from his shirt. She had also recovered the gun and remained protectively at his side throughout the ruckus outside.

"I wish you'd reconsider and stay a while longer, Peggy, at least until Hélio gets back with his bride to be, Generosa. He'd be hurt."

"I'll stay that long."

"I was hoping that perhaps our relationship had grown close enough so that—"

"That's exactly why I'm leaving, Matt. It's the wrong time for me. At the moment I feel too dirtied, too tainted by those beasts. I need to get away. I want to go back to the States and get my head together. I'll keep in touch, and if after a few months you still want me, I'll come back."

The radiotelephone in Raul's study was ringing. "I'll get it, Matt," she said.

She was gone for several minutes. On returning, she went over to her suitcase on the bed and began unpacking. Matt's eyebrows arched in surprise.

"That was Vivi," she said after a few moments. "Her father's funeral was yesterday. It seems that Raul has been in touch with her, and he insists that she come here to live."

"In sin?"

"Hardly. Vivi wants me to stay as her chaperone until the wedding, which will be as soon as possible. It will be a simple wedding—just family, except for you and me. You're to be best man and I the maid of honor."

Riordan grinned. "Maybe by that time you'll have your head together."

"Maybe." Peggy smiled. "We'll see."

EPILOGUE

The world's greatest and most fantastic highway was finished, and the first influx of tourists had begun to arrive.

A brand new Ford, its bright blue enamel glistening under the white brilliance of sun, hummed along at a sedate speed while its occupants—an elderly American couple—gawked avidly at everything in sight.

"Hey, whaddya know," said the driver, a portly silver-haired gentleman, "look at that great big building over there—a modern plant way out here in the jungle. Wonder what it is?"

"I'll check the travel brochure." The wife, a sweet-faced woman almost as portly as her husband, busied herself with the crinkled pamphlet in her lap. "It's the Carvalho Alcohol Refinery, it says here. That's where they make gasahol from all these trees."

"You have to give these Latin birds credit for having the smarts when it comes to making money. That's what I call progress."

Ahead they saw a straggling group of Indians standing along the highway, their hands outstretched, begging. They'd passed several such groups within the hour. Most of them were naked, or close to it.

"It's a shame the government doesn't make the poor buggers dress decently."

"Let's stop and give them a little money, Harold."

"Why give 'em money? If they weren't so lazy, they'd work for a living like everybody else."

"But these Indians are so different. Look how some of them have such pretty rose-colored skin. They must be a rare type. Stop for just a few moments."

"Okay, Clarice, but don't let any of 'em touch you."

361

The moment the car stopped, the Indians scurried up to the window, hands extended.

"My God, Clarice—that isn't the color of their skin —it's a disease! Those are pink scabs all over their bodies—"

The motor roared and the Ford raced away.

"I feel a little nauseated, Harold."

"I could use a drink. First liquor joint we come to, we'll stop."

Reaching the thriving little town of Inchaco, they stopped at a quaint little bar called the Casa Hospitalidade.

Just inside the door, Clarice gave a little gasp at the sight of a upright crocodile grinning at them, a red light bulb in its mouth. Harold chuckled. He was equally amused by the stuffed anaconda looping from the rafters.

But what tickled him most were the dried little human heads suspended over the bar. Four of them. No bigger than coconuts. It puzzled him that one of them was white.

"That really the head of a white man up there?" he asked the bartender.

"Yup."

"How much will you take for it?"

"Ain't for sale. They're illegal to sell, you understand, and damn hard to find. I was lucky to get that one from an old Indian who claimed he was a big chief, name of Xanqui. Indians ain't allowed to buy booze, you understand, so I traded him a bottle of whiskey for it."

"It really looks weird with that white stripe through the black hair."

"Yeah. That's why we nicknamed it 'the skunk.'"

ABOUT THE AUTHOR

ROY SPARKIA grew up with a love of the outdoors and nature. His birthplace in Owosso, Michigan, proved the perfect place to explore and get to know the woods and waterways. It is this understanding of nature that Sparkia brings to life in the Amazonian jungles of Brazil, where man wages a constant battle with nature.

Sparkia has also experienced a different jungle—that of New York City, where he studied at the Art Students League. Aspiring to be an artist and a writer, Sparkia later studied under Paul Gallico at Columbia, and with Saul Bellow at New York University. He gave up writing when the demands of his family dictated the need for fulltime employment. After various excursions into the business world, Sparkia found in his art a livelihood. His career as an artist flourished for many years, and, as evidence, eight illuminated panels that he designed adorn the lobby of the Empire State Building. Yet writing is his love, where he can "use the universal elements of life with high entertainment," and he is now devoting his full time to writing. Another novel is currently in the works.

Sparkia currently lives in Michigan with his wife Renée, a sculptress. They have a daughter, who recently graduated from law school.

SAHARA

The enormous, sun-glazed desert stretched all around him as Taim lay gasping for breath, trying to clear the whirling dark haze that seemed to fill his head. Around him the commotion of horses and men lessened. When he was able to push himself up to a sitting position, the robbers were gone. They had taken everything except a scattering of cheap cooking ware and other things too trivial to bother with. He stared around, disbelieving.

Only then did he seem to realize what had happened. All of them were dead. His dear mother, old Hafez who had been so kind to him, his father. His eyes swam, and for a moment he thought he was not seeing right. One of the bodies had moved.

"Taim...." The weak voice came from Najib. "Come...."

Taim crawled fearfully toward his father, whom he had thought was dead. Najib's burning eyes were staring at him with a wild intensity.

"I am dying—but too slowly," said Najib in barely more than a hoarse whisper. "The bullet was not aimed well, and missed my heart. To save me from the terrible pain, you must kill me quickly. Under my robe is a knife—"

"No, father, no!"

"I order you to do it! Take the knife and kill me quickly so that I may hasten to Allah."

As if hypnotized, Taim reached under his father's *jalabiya* and withdrew the knife. He had the feeling of being trapped in a horrible dream. Crazy thoughts and emotions tumbled through his head. Allah had failed to protect them, despite all their prayers. Soon he, too, would be dead or dying, shriveling up under the scorching sun while ugly black vultures swooped down to tear away at his flesh with their rapacious big beaks. Old Hafez had told him many tales of the desert and about how the terrible sun sucked up all moisture and brought death within hours to one without shelter or drink.

But he had to live! His whole being screamed with undying hatred and the need to live long enough to find and kill the one who had desecrated his mother.

And to live he must drink.

He stared long and hard into the fiery eyes of Najib. "Yes, my father, I will hasten you to meet Allah."

Nimbly he scampered a few steps to snatch up a large earthen bowl that the robbers had scorned. Setting it beside Najib, he readied the knife, and then with gritted teeth and a choking sensation drew the sharp edge across his father's throat in the manner that he had seen goats slaughtered.

As the bright red blood came spurting out, he positioned the bowl to catch it. By the time it was filled to overflowing, scarcely a dribble was still coming, and Najib's unseeing eyes were glazed over with death.

Carefully Taim lifted the bowl to his lips. Trembling, he took a tentative sip of the salty-sweet fluid; then a swallow. Now there was no turning back.

"Praise be to the devil," he murmured. "If you allow me to live until I have avenged my mother, I will serve you faithfully."

He drank more. . . .